About the Author

Luca Veste is the author of several police procedurals and standalone crime novels including *The Bone Keeper* and *The Six*. He is the host of the Two Crime Writers and a Microphone podcast and the co-founder of the Locked In festival. He plays bass guitar in the band The Fun Lovin' Crime Writers. He lives in Liverpool, with his wife and two daughters.

LUCA VESTE

YOU NEVER SAID GOODBYE

HODDER

First published in Great Britain in 2022 by Hodder & Stoughton
An Hachette UK company

This paperback edition published in 2022

1

A CIP catalogue record for this title is available from the British
Library

Paperback ISBN 978 1 529 35735 6
eBook ISBN 978 1 529 35736 3

Typeset in Plantin Light by Palimpsest Book Production Ltd,
Falkirk, Stirlingshire

Printed and bound in Great Britain by Clays Ltd, Elcograf S.p.A.

Hodder & Stoughton policy is to use papers that are natural,
renewable and recyclable products and made from wood grown in
sustainable forests. The logging and manufacturing processes are
expected to conform to the environmental regulations of the country
of origin.

Hodder & Stoughton Ltd
Carmelite House
50 Victoria Embankment
London EC4Y 0DZ

www.hodder.co.uk

For Phil Patterson – My agent, my biggest supporter, my war film expert, but most of all, my friend.

You don't always get to choose your final words.

Sometimes, you don't know it's the end. When it's all over and there's no chance for a last goodbye.

They hit the water and the force knocked Laurie forwards and into the dashboard. Her head spun, as water began pooling around her feet instantly. She looked over to the driver's side and saw David was out cold. Blood dripping down his face.

She tried to open the door, but it wouldn't move. The window was open, the river rushing in. Her vision blurred. She turned around slowly but couldn't see a thing. Only darkness. Shadows. Ghosts.

She couldn't see her children. Her two boys, sitting in the back.

She wanted to see them. One last time.

Her last thoughts, as unconsciousness took her, were of her family.

At least they were all together.

She couldn't even say sorry.

And as the water filled her lungs and she couldn't breathe any longer, she thought of nothing but the fact she had failed them all.

Anthony was up there somewhere, she knew. Watching them die.

He had won.

She had always been his.

TWENTY FIVE YEARS LATER

H e was a long way from what had once been home. *Wallace, Idaho.*

The centre of the universe.

Parker Rogers had been there, back in 2004, when the manhole cover over at the intersection between 6th Street and Bank had been unveiled. The mayor had decided that, because it couldn't be disproven, he could declare the town of Wallace the centre of the universe and that was that.

Probabilism. Greek philosophy. A thought experiment that Parker had tried to explain in the local bar a few times, to ever-decreasing interest from the other drinkers.

He was eating yet another TV dinner, sitting at the kitchen table with Elvis playing on the stereo. 'An American Trilogy', the live version. Where you could hear all the emotion pouring from him.

It was a recording of the 1973 Honolulu concert – *Aloha from Hawaii* indeed. He could close his eyes and see the man himself performing. Sweat dripping from his face, like tears cascading down his cheeks. The leis around his white, rhinestone-dappled suit.

He preferred the later years – the Vegas period, when the jumpsuits began to look a little tighter and the King's face was red and mottled. In the Eighties, Parker could probably have passed for Fifties-era Elvis. Now, forty years later, he was almost sixty, and closing in on the three hundred and fifty pounds that the King apparently weighed at his death.

There was always talk that he had faked it – Parker had even seen a video recently, of some pastor out in Arkansas, singing in a bar. Older guy, white hair and white beard. The voice had been similar enough for him to pause. Wonder for a few brief moments if all those conspiracy theories had been right.

Wallace was a small town. An old mining community. Good, stubborn people. Friendly, even accepting of a fool like him. It had taken a couple of decades, but they had finally stopped calling him the new boy in town a few years back.

Back in the Seventies, they tried to build the I-90 through the town, but the villagers fought back. Had the downtown area listed on the National Register of Historic Places. It meant that every building is now on that list, so they can't be touched. The freeway ended up skirting around the town.

That's the type of people they were in Wallace, Idaho. Tough. Uncompromising.

Loyal.

Parker sat down on the couch but didn't turn on the TV. Instead, he stared at a picture of himself on a local news website. A mugshot, to be precise.

Thought about how much time he had left.

Tom wouldn't get there in time.

Twenty-five years he'd managed to stay under the radar. Made something of a life for himself. Yeah, he'd never had kids, or a woman who stayed longer than the run of a failed sitcom, but that didn't matter much to Parker. He had a good job working at an auto repair shop in town, a roof over his head, and all the TV dinners he could eat.

Oh, and a regular seat at Alby's bar, which had landed his mugshot in the local news.

Tom would be too late to help him.

It didn't matter. At least Laurie wasn't around to see him now.

He just wished he had been there for her when it mattered most. Then, this whole mess might not have happened.

He hadn't seen her in twenty-five years. And wouldn't see her again.

He remembered how scared Laurie had been when she'd come back in '95. She'd tried to hide it, but Parker had known she was thinking about him.

The bogeyman.

And he had caught her.

Elvis's backing singers were harmonising away, as lights flashed across the front of the house. A car pulled up onto the driveway and shut off its engine.

Parker reached slowly to his waistband and made his way over to the door.

He could see a shadow fall across the stoop.

They had come for him.

If it had been ten, twenty years earlier, he might have had a better chance. It didn't mean he wasn't going to do everything he could to save his own life.

As the King built to a crescendo, his voice filling the kitchen-diner and escaping into the hallway, Parker Rogers took out his gun, flicked off the safety, and levelled it at the front door. Placed his back to the wall and kept his focus straight ahead. Two hands on his gun, waiting for a clear shot.

There was a soft knock at the door. Parker didn't move.

'Parker?'

He didn't recognise the voice, but he knew who had sent them.

He stepped to the side and crouched down. The shadow moved and another knock on the door came.

'Open up, Parker, we need to talk.'

Parker was a breath away from squeezing the trigger when he felt something hard and metallic at the back of his head.

'Don't move,' a man said from behind him. 'Drop it, or they'll be scraping your brains out of the wood panelling for the next thirty years.'

The music grew louder. Filling Parker's ears, until they felt they would burst. Fear crawled up inside him and consumed his body.

He knew in that moment that he would do anything not to die that night.

Joe Carson felt the bone snap beneath his grip and smiled.

Hunter was standing close by, keeping his gaze on the way Carson was manipulating the wrist under his grip. He was younger than Carson – thirty years at least. Still, he seemed eager to learn. They hadn't worked together all that long, but the way his young eyes darted over the skin and bones of the poor guy in the chair told Carson he might stick around a while.

Carson moved to the other side of the chair, giving the older man a brief moment of respite. He shook with pain, tears turning red as they rolled down his cheeks. Blood seeped slowly from his nose, his body jerking with shock waves. Carson took hold of his right wrist, feeling his way to his target.

Hunter shook his head slowly, as fire danced in his eyes, watching Carson move carefully along the man's hand and arm. Stared in fascination, delicate thunder emanating from his body. Carson wondered if the younger man would be able to learn this graceful sort of technique. He didn't look the type – all muscle-bound, with biceps bigger than some people's waistlines. Hands built for power rather than precision. He was an overbearing presence in the room. Even at full height, Carson was still a fair few inches below Hunter. Less stocky too. It mattered little to him. He never compared himself to other men. It was a waste of his time.

'Nice place to settle down, Parker.'

He flicked his own wrist and another bone snapped. The gag across Parker's mouth muffled the scream that followed.

'Now, Parker,' said Carson politely, letting go of his arm and squatting down in front of the older man. His eyes screamed in agony; reddened, filmy. 'We've been here before. Over twenty years ago, would you believe it? Time goes by so quick. You gained a hundred pounds and I lost half my hair. Ain't life a bitch. Last time we spoke, I let you live. This time, unless you tell me what I need to know, that ain't going to happen.'

Parker stared back at him, pleading soundlessly. He neither nodded nor shook his head.

Hunter was standing directly behind the chair now. He loomed over them, blocking out the soft shards of light escaping into the room from the hallway beyond him.

'Parker, I'm going to remove the gag now,' Carson said, standing up slowly. 'You're going to tell me what I need to know and then this will be over. Do you understand?'

Parker's arms and legs were tied to the chair. He couldn't move far, even if he wanted to. He could move his head but seemed to have frozen. Whether out of fear or something else, Carson wasn't sure.

Carson reached down and tore away the tape covering Parker's mouth. 'Where is she?'

Parker gasped for air for a few seconds, before looking up at his captor. 'Like I said twenty-five years ago, I don't know where she is.'

Carson thought he saw the ghost of a smile play across his lips. He looked past Parker at Hunter and shrugged.

Sometimes, you can't make them do the right thing.

He pulled out his gun – a black STI 2011, single-action, low recoil – and gripped it firmly. Levelled it between Parker Rogers's eyes and waited.

'Last chance,' Carson said. 'Tell us, or your brains will be splattered across your nice tiled floor.'

'She's dead.'

'We both know that's not true.'

'Of course it is,' Parker replied, red spittle flying from his mouth. His gums were bleeding, mouth filled with blood. 'Your boss needs to accept it and give up.'

Carson shook his head. 'You're going to die for nothing. We know she's alive.'

'She's not,' Parker said, his pleas falling on deaf ears. 'It's over. There's no one left. You have to believe me.'

Carson didn't believe him. That was the problem. He placed his gun against Parker's forehead and pushed a little. Let him see how close he was to squeezing that trigger. 'Five . . . four . . . three . . . two . . .'

'Wait, please,' Parker said, his voice strained. It seemed to take every last ounce of effort not to betray her. 'You should see David.'

Carson cocked his head. 'Who?'

'David Cooper.'

'What about him?'

'I know where he is. Maybe you can see for yourself that she's not alive. Because if she was, she'd be with him, wouldn't she? If you're going to kill me, then it'll be for nothing. Because that's it. That's all there is. Just listen to me . . .'

Parker continued talking, but Carson waved away his gabbling. 'Where?'

'He's back in England,' Parker said, his voice suddenly quiet. Almost a whisper. 'A village called Firwood.'

'And that's all you know? Really? That David Cooper lives alone in a village called Firwood?'

Parker agreed and dropped his head. Carson thought it over and decided he was telling the truth. It was all they were going to get.

'See. That wasn't all that hard, was it?' Carson said. He smiled, then squeezed the trigger.

Parker Rogers jerked back violently, but he was dead before the chair righted itself.

CHAPTER 1

Sometimes, you just know. Sitting in that bar in the centre of London, I could feel that certainty. This was the beginning of something.

Outside, the usual bustle of activity lived on, but inside, it was calmer, filled with the clink of glasses and hushed conversation.

I looked across the table as Rachel placed an elaborate glass of gin and tonic in front of her.

It was our third date. I already knew it was going somewhere – and this time I wanted it to.

'How's work then?' she asked, catching my eye and not letting go.

Rachel. Thirty-three years old – only a year younger than me. No children and lived alone. Dark brown hair and worked in the city.

That was all I'd known about her before we'd met for the first time a few weeks earlier. Now, I knew she worked in finance – whatever that might mean – and was an Arsenal supporter. The game was playing silently on a television above the bar, but she didn't glance at it more than a couple of times.

'Work is work, you know,' I replied, my hand resting against my glass of IPA. 'It's really not as intriguing as I made it sound. Yeah, it's a charity thing, but I'm at head office, reporting statistics, press releases, that sort of thing. That's my day, basically. Glorified admin.'

'Still sounds more interesting than finance to me, Sam,' Rachel said, giving me a smile that seemed to flash with electricity. 'Worthy, at least.'

Rachel glanced up at the screen for a second or two, before turning back to her drink. I felt the back of my neck, the heat from where the barber had razored it clean earlier that day warming my hand. I could smell the aftershave I'd squirted onto my wrist before leaving work an hour or so earlier.

'Let me ask you this – Arsenal. Why?'

She laughed and the sound of it cut through the air between us like it was silk. 'Well, they used to be good, you know? And you don't even follow football.'

I held my hands up in defeat. 'You've got me there. I just don't get it. It's, like, never finished. There's no end to football, right? It just goes on and on, every year.'

She laughed again and I swigged down some of my drink.

I'd been on a fair few dates where silence seemed to be the only thing we had in common. This was easier.

This was something.

Sometimes you just know.

Or hope you do, anyway.

My phone buzzed quietly against my leg, but I ignored it. Whatever it was could wait. Instead, we continued talking – no awkward silences, or breaks in the conversation. It was easy. Swapping stories, well-worn tales of our childhoods.

We made each other laugh.

I was in the middle of another story when my phone buzzed again. I stopped mid-sentence, but then continued. 'So, I'm reading the instructions on the packet.'

'You're how old?'

'About eleven or twelve,' I said, taking a sip of my drink. 'I'm reading the instructions, right, and it says boil milk.'

'You wanted to eat just custard?'

'*Yeah*,' I said, like it was obvious. 'I wanted custard and the packet was right there in the cupboard. I read the instructions, and they said to boil milk and add the contents of the packet. So, I thought logically about it.'

'*Logically?*' Rachel asked, raising her eyebrows.

'Yes. And where do you boil things? In a kettle. So, I measured out the milk, poured it into the kettle, and switched it on. Waited for it to boil and then poured it into a bowl and added the packet contents.'

'Oh my God . . .'

'I looked inside the kettle and realised I'd made a mistake.'

'Logic has left the building at this point.'

'It didn't even taste that nice,' I said, smiling as Rachel burst out laughing. 'I was disappointed beyond belief. Anyway, I learned my lesson about reading instructions after that; I swear.'

'Well, I hope you cook better now.'

I caught her eye and we both knew.

'What did your mum say? I bet she went mad?'

I shook my head, a split second of guilt coming and going in an instant. 'No, no, it was just me and my dad by then.'

She flung a hand to her mouth. 'Oh God, I'm sorry. I didn't remember how old you were.'

I waved away the apology. 'It's fine, honestly.'

'Your dad then?'

I remembered my dad's face. The blank look he'd given me, that said everything that was needed. 'He wasn't too happy, but it was easier to just buy a new one rather than talk to me.'

'You didn't get on?'

I shook my head. Thought about explaining the situation and then decided against it. 'Something like that.'

We continued exchanging stories about our childhoods. She came from a large family, who all seemed to have individual quirks. She finished another story and then asked, 'What about other family? Aunts, uncles, cousins?'

I shook my head. 'No, no other family. It was just me and my dad after Mum died. And where I grew up, Firwood – let's just say, I didn't fit in. I have a good group of friends now. They're as good as family.'

'And even better, you get to choose this one, rather than be lumbered with them by accident of birth.'

I chuckled softly. 'You're right.'

Other dates had zeroed in about that, wanting to know how I couldn't have any kind of family at all, but Rachel seemed to just accept it. Not push back and want to know details. It was better. Maybe, at some point, we'd talk about it, but there was no pressure.

I felt my phone vibrate again in my pocket. I continued to ignore the interruption, as I listened to Rachel talk.

An hour passed in the blink of an eye. The sky outside changed from an almost indigo-tinged blue to black. The bar filled around us, but I barely noticed until Rachel excused herself to use the bathroom. As I waited for her, I pulled out my phone.

Five missed calls and a voicemail. I checked the number and felt my heart slow. A hollow feeling in the pit of my stomach suddenly appeared like a chasm of darkness. I recognised the area code instantly.

It was from home.

Two hundred miles away. It should have been far enough.

I gritted my teeth at the thought of thinking of somewhere as 'home' even though it was two hundred miles away and almost two decades into my past and I spoke to no one connected to the place. It had been over sixteen years since I'd left the village where I'd grown up – or been dragged up, as I'd like to imagine. Sixteen years since I'd left and never returned.

The walls seemed to close in around me, as I felt beads of sweat form on my forehead.

I locked my phone again and shoved it into my pocket, as if

it were about to burn its imprint into the palm of my hand. Tried to ignore the feeling inside me, as my stomach churned.

When Rachel returned, I gave her a tight smile and said, 'I'll be back in a minute.'

In an empty corridor by the toilets, I pulled my phone out and tried to catch my breath as my finger hovered over the redial button.

Suddenly, it vibrated and I almost dropped it to the floor in surprise. I swiped a shaking finger across the screen.

'Hello?' I said, expecting to hear *his* voice for the first time in almost twenty years.

'Hello? Is that Sam Cooper?'

It was a woman's voice. Someone official, I guessed. I wondered if I should simply lie and end the call. Only, I recognised the tone of someone with bad news. 'Yes, it is.'

'This is Isabelle Levy, I'm calling from Firwood Community Hospital.'

'Okay. How can I help you?'

'Your father, David Cooper . . .'

As Isabelle spoke, I thought about how long I'd been waiting for this phone call. As if I'd known at some point it would come. Isabelle continued to talk, as my thoughts and memories ran into each other.

'You should come as soon as you're able to,' I heard Isabelle say and I realised I was holding the phone too tightly in my hand. I breathed deeply and massaged my temple with my free hand.

'Is he . . .'

A cough and shuffle from the other end of the phone. I didn't hear her answer. Instead, I screwed my eyes shut and imagined going back. Travelling those two hundred miles and returning to that place. Seeing those buildings, those people again.

There was only a black hole, dragging me into somewhere I didn't want to go.

CHAPTER 2

I walked to the nearest tube station with Rachel, apologising the whole time. She was understanding, which only made it more difficult to leave her.

'Look,' I said, as we reached the station and I pulled her aside from the people almost running inside. 'I didn't want tonight to end this way.'

'It's not your fault,' she said, tucking a strand of hair behind her ear. 'Look, are you sure you want to go alone?'

I nodded. 'I'll be fine. I'll call you, okay?'

She took a second and then smiled at me. Made as if to leave, then hesitated. By the time she had turned around, I was already kissing her.

Moment saved.

'You best had,' she said into my ear, once it was over. Then, she was gone. A blur amongst the crowd of people pushing their way through barriers.

I was on the train in minutes and not long afterwards I was making my way out of Coulsden Town station, walking the short journey back to my flat to pick up my car.

A two-and-a-half-hour journey down the M3 and A303. Past Basingstoke, past Salisbury. Across the bottom of the country and through the countryside. Straight into old England and the villages people in London always talked about wanting to retire to. Or the concept of them, anyway. A few days without a restaurant that opened past eight p.m. and a coffee place on every corner, and they would come running home.

I wouldn't remember any of the journey a few hours later.

A calmness began to wash over me as I saw signs for places I knew – *Ilchester, Martock, Tintinhull* – and the road became the only thing I could see, the dream gradually turning into reality.

In the light of day, I would have seen fields of green, broken only by the grey of the A-road. The occasional village encroaching on the space. At this time of night, there were only walls of black, surrounding me.

I'd left the looming buildings and endless faces in the streets behind me. Replaced by manicured shrubbery on small round-abouts. Small cottage-style houses, desperately trying to hang on-to their past.

It was getting on for midnight when I arrived in Firwood. The roads were deathly quiet – not that they would have been much busier earlier in the day. The village was small, built around the large church in the middle. Narrow streets running off the roundabout that bordered it. Community noticeboards, phone boxes turned into libraries by locals. Clean, conservative, contained.

Claustrophobic.

In a fading streetlight, I saw an older man stagger towards home from the local pub. Red-nosed and smiling to himself. He barely looked towards my car, as I drove past slowly.

The quintessential little England village. With all the dreariness and mundanity that went along with it. Manicured lawns, muted colours, anything but multicultural.

It was much as I remembered it, often in dreams that ended in nightmarish childhood memories.

My phone continued to bark instructions at me. I reached over and switched it off.

I didn't need it any more.

The hospital came into view and I turned off the road. I parked up and made my way to the main entrance and stopped outside. Smelled the sickly aroma of cigarettes and anxiety as I moved towards the automatic doors.

Inside, I could have been in any hospital in the country. The same smells, the same faces, the same workers. It was quiet though – not the late-night carnage of a Friday night in a big city A&E. This was a place of hushed voices and perfected caring looks.

I approached the front desk and the woman sitting behind it looked up at me, tilting her head to one side as if she recognised me. It was possible, but she was a stranger to me.

'I'm here to see David Cooper. Someone called me.'

'Okay and you are . . . ?'

'I'm his son. Sam Cooper. I've just come from London.'

'Ah, that's why you're here so late,' she replied, tapping away at the computer in front of her and then rifling through folders in a tray to her side. I was taken aback by her tone for a second, then remembered that was normal for this place. Forthright was part of the local motto, it had always seemed to me.

'If you take a seat, someone will come and see you as soon as possible.'

I thanked her and moved to the small seating area. I looked at the walls and read the posters. They listed various diseases, cancers, disorders, that I possibly had or could have soon. I took my phone out and scrolled through social media for a few minutes, before all I was seeing was a blur.

'Sam Cooper?'

I looked up and saw a nurse waiting for me. At first, I didn't think I could stand up; my legs felt like jelly. But suddenly I was on my feet and following her as she spoke to me. I didn't hear a word of it. I don't think I breathed during the short walk.

The nurse stood to one side and allowed me to enter the room alone.

Then, he was there, in front of me, lying on a bed. Not moving. His face was much older since I'd last seen him. His hair had thinned and greyed. The skin on his hands was pale and loose.

I ignored the parts of him that didn't fit. The flashes of colour on his skin. The white patches covering open wounds beneath.

'I'll come back to you shortly.'

I nodded towards the voice but kept my eyes on the man in the bed.

My father.

I felt my hands clench into fists, nails digging into my palms.

The machine next to him wheezed and released.

'Hello, Dad,' I said finally, and waited for him to open his eyes. Nothing happened.

I moved closer until my face was only a few inches from his. Anyone glancing our way would think I was embracing him.

I swallowed and felt suddenly calm. As if I had been waiting for this moment without knowing.

'I'm here, Dad. I've come to watch you die.'

Jackson was drinking coffee. He was sitting in what the Brits called a 'canteen' but was pretty much a diner that had maybe seen some bad times. In the middle of a hospital, of all places. There was grease hanging in the atmosphere and an air of disappointment that seemed to settle over every patron.

He was trying not to think of the old man lying at the bottom of the stairs. The sound of police sirens. The quickening of his heartbeat, as he realised what had happened.

Jackson knew the old man was going to die. Maybe not at that moment, but soon.

He was broken. Beyond repair. Somewhere above him, in a hospital bed, waiting for the doctors to finally give up on him.

Jackson missed the gun he would normally carry back home. If things went wrong, it was comforting to know you had an equaliser. A Glock in your hand always went some way to making a situation better.

David Cooper had looked older than Jackson had been expecting. Life had really done a number on him. But then, he had watched the old man being asked to leave the local bar on two separate occasions in the few days he'd spent watching him.

Jackson sat and drank his vending-machine coffee and hoped he wasn't being too conspicuous.

Not that it mattered. He wouldn't be there much longer.

That was now the plan.

He could almost hear God laughing.

There was a sense of failure. As if he had messed up and this was only the beginning.

David Cooper was going to die.

And it was his fault that it was for nothing.

He took out his cell phone – a burner he had picked up at the nearest store that sold them when he'd arrived. Followed the instructions and called the number. Cleared his throat, hoping that the anger that was burning inside him could be contained.

'You didn't tell me he had a son . . . Sam Cooper . . . He arrived an hour ago . . . The old guy probably won't make it . . . I want the whole story, now, or I walk away.'

Jackson listened to the end of the call and then pocketed the cell before the anger swelled again.

Sam Cooper.

Jackson drained the last of the dishwater coffee and thought about what little he knew. And how it changed everything.

CHAPTER 3

Anthony Sullivan was standing on the balcony outside his home office, staring out across the grounds that surrounded his estate. Six acres, wrapping around the white monolith he called home.

The sweetgum and ginkgo trees stood at the perimeter of all he could see. Their yellow and red leaves wouldn't return for a few months yet, but he always looked forward to the fall, when they would explode with colour.

It wasn't the most expensive piece of real estate in Greenwich, Connecticut, but it was close. *An architectural delight*, was what the agent had said when he'd bought it decades earlier. He cared little for that. To him, it was a stamp on the world. A marker for what he had achieved.

Standing there, drinking coffee, he should have been happy. Relaxed.

His hair may have been thinning a little now. His waistline expanding every year. It didn't seem to matter how often he spent time in his squash court, or the home gym, age was beginning to take over. Still, he knew other men in their late fifties would kill for his physique. His dark hair, greying only a little at the temples. His ability to still move with grace and speed, even with his frame being a few inches over six foot.

It didn't change the fact that Anthony Sullivan was tired.

Not from working. The business mostly took care of itself these days. It was an aching tired, that you feel in your bones every minute of the day. A headache that never really passes. A weak feeling in your muscles, that can never be stretched out.

Anthony placed the coffee down and felt the silver of the pendant that hung around his neck. Ran his fingers over the words that were engraved there. The split in the metal heart, the other half of it still missing.

His cell phone rang, and he let go of the necklace.

'Go ahead,' he said, taking another sip of coffee. It tasted bitter and rich. 'What have you got for me?'

'A dead end.'

Anthony sighed and resisted the urge to throw his cup into the courtyard below him. 'Anything else we can do to crank up the pressure a little, perhaps? I want this deal over the line within the month.'

'Possibly. We have footage of him with a young woman. I'm talking Epstein-young. He'll crack quickly, but we'd be showing our hand.'

'Okay, I'll think it over,' Anthony said, feeling his jaw tense, his teeth scraping against each other. 'We'll discuss it further in person.'

Anthony ended the call, pocketed the cell phone and gripped the balcony stone with both hands. Saw the scars on his knuckles from his younger years and wished he could be back there. Then. When his bulky frame was enough to quieten even the loudest room. When a look was enough to suggest he should get what he wanted. When a word was enough for him to win every time.

He took a cigarette from a box he kept in his jacket pocket. Considered it in the low sun. He had once liked a cigarette after a successful business meeting. Once a deal had been done.

Now, he only ever associated smoking with death.

He was getting older and more aware of the passage of time than ever. And the passage of smoke into his lungs, that would inevitably end with him coughing his guts up into a gutter.

It had been a long time since he'd had to perform his own violence, but it still gave him a certain sense of satisfaction that it had been carried out.

After Parker Rogers had been killed, he'd lit a cigarette and watched it burn in an ashtray.

That was a week ago, and now, he was waiting for a call from England.

He stuck a cigarette into the corner of his mouth and didn't light it. Let it dangle there like he was Sammy Farha.

The air turned colder, the sky seeming to darken around him. As if it sensed his mood.

He felt he had been one step closer to finding her. For the first time in decades, he really believed he could.

Anthony tore the unlit cigarette from his lips and let it fall into the empty ashtray on the table at his side.

'Zoran,' Anthony said, knowing the man would be close by. He appeared in the doorway leading back inside. He was taller than Anthony – taller than most people. A little under seven feet, he guessed, and as pale as the moon on a cloudless night. He had a quiet sense of death that seemed to seep from his soul. 'Cancel whoever I'm supposed to see this afternoon.'

Zoran left with an almost imperceptible nod. Anthony checked the time on his Breitling watch and calculated five hours ahead. It would be late in the UK.

He took out a separate cell phone. One that couldn't be connected to him in any way, and dialled the only number that was stored on it.

It was answered on the second ring.

'It's me,' Anthony said, waiting for a code to be recited back to him. He was nothing if not security conscious.

'He's still alive, barely. Cops showed up. We had to leave him.'

'No sign of her?'

'I wish I had better news.'

'What else can you tell me?'

'His son is here,' Joe Carson said, his tone steady and unfazed. He hadn't blinked when Anthony had sent him to the UK. Simply did as he was instructed. 'I thought he was dead?'

Anthony felt his heart slow. 'What's his name?'

'Sam Cooper.'

'Sam . . .' Anthony said, quietly to himself. 'That was the oldest. They survived that crash.'

'I guess so.'

'How did they get away?'

'I wish I could tell you,' Carson said. 'We talked to all of them, back in '95. The mom, the brother . . . they all told us the same thing. There was a funeral. The local press did a story. There was nothing more we could have done.'

Anthony sighed and tried to quell the anger rising inside him. 'They all lied to us. They were all supposed to be dead. Instead, David manages to escape with at least one of his sons without us knowing. How does this happen?'

'I don't know, boss.'

'Someone didn't do their job properly. Find out who.'

'I will,' Carson said. 'What about this Sam? Should he be dealt with?'

Anthony closed his eyes. His heart rate returned to normal. 'I guess he needs to be questioned just like his old man. Only this time, make sure he ends up like his uncle. Not in some hospital.'

When Laurie's brother, Parker, had told them David was alive, Anthony hadn't believed it. Now, there was at least one son on the scene.

It was all stacking up. He was closer to finding Laurie than ever before.

'I'll talk to him,' Carson said, calm, cool. As if this was nothing. 'I'll make sure to find out what he knows.'

'Yes, you should.'

And that's how easy it was for Anthony to kill someone from four thousand miles away.

'Make sure he can't answer anyone else's questions. I want you to get every detail from him and end it. And see if you can find the other kid. If all three are around, she'll be close by. You understand?'

'I understand. I'll make sure the job is finished.'

Anthony ended the call and looked out across the courtyard below. Past the swimming pool, the trees. Until the ground faded in the distance and he could imagine her somewhere out there. Staring back towards him.

He had waited a long time. The trail had been cold for almost twenty-five years.

Now, as he closed his eyes and lifted his head towards the sky, he could feel the heat.

1982

He was waiting for her at midnight. Leaning against the hood of his Ford Mustang, arms crossed over his chest. Anthony kept the car looking pristine, despite it being over twenty years old. With every mile he covered, the engine died a little more, but Laurie thought he would keep driving it until it fell to pieces. It was a part of him.

He was never late.

He was smirking her way, as she climbed out of the bedroom window and dropped down to the ground with a soft thump. Even from a distance, she could see the fire in his eyes. Lust, love, anger; bleeding from his stare, as he drank her in.

She'd let her hair hang loose the way he liked it, and her dress, which matched the electric blue of his car, was one she knew he approved of as well. It clung to her body as if it were a second skin. Her feet were bare, her white pumps hanging in her hand.

Even now, after dating for over two years, he could scare her with his intensity.

It had always been the same. The fearful excitement that would drive through her eighteen-year-old body was something she couldn't explain. She felt the frisson of apprehension and desire coursing through her veins, as she counted down the minutes before he would arrive.

They met at this time a few times a week. Usually, they would spend an hour or so together. They would drive over to Riverfront

Park, make out a little, fool around some, then he would drive her home.

That night, it was different. She would be out longer.

Thursday night, late October. She had lain in her bed, listening to Dad laugh along to *Cheers*, before the volume was turned down so he could watch *Hill Street Blues* as her mom read.

It didn't matter that she was a senior now and that she would be off to college in a matter of months. She still had to sneak out of the house at midnight to see him.

She could almost feel a curtain twitching. Only it wouldn't be her parents watching her. It would be Tom Miller looking down at them.

'*Sappy*,' Tom had said, a year or so earlier. His nickname for her, making her smile. '*I don't trust him. He's no good.*'

She hadn't listened then and he'd never brought the subject up again, even though she knew he wanted to.

Anthony saw her coming and his smirk fell a little. There was a ferocity of longing in his eyes that threatened to bring the fear more to the fore than the desire. Then he was opening the door for her and that feeling dissipated some.

Anthony climbed in, lit a cigarette and pulled away from the curb. They sat in silence as they drove west towards the coast. She stole glances, seeing his features in the darkness beside her. Her friends all talked about him. How lucky she was to be with someone as attractive as him. As if that was all that mattered. If she squinted a little, he looked like John Travolta. If she tried harder, he looked like the devil. They didn't see that – they concentrated on his looks, without seeing the coldness behind them.

When they had first met, he had taken her breath away. Movie star looks, only with the ability to make you feel as if you were the only person that mattered to him. She had known from the start that she was in trouble.

'You sure you're not going to get caught?' Anthony said, as they were leaving Middletown. Merging onto the I-91, the roads almost empty in the moonlight. 'We've never been gone this long before.'

'They won't notice me gone,' Laurie replied, her hands clasped together in her lap. Her stomach fluttered with a million butterflies taking flight inside. 'Easier to wake the dead than my parents. I'm more worried about falling asleep in school tomorrow. Math class is going to be a bitch.'

Anthony snickered at that. He was a few years older than her; high school a fading memory for him. He had bigger plans than a good education. He was always going to follow in his father's footsteps. She couldn't imagine him in a classroom anyway. The image didn't fit in her mind.

'We'll be there before one thirty, I bet. Maybe sooner. Once we get away towards the coast, there'll be nothing on the roads.'

That meant he would be driving fast, Laurie thought. Even this old car still had some go about it.

'I didn't bring a jacket,' she said, hands reaching up and holding herself. 'The heater still not working?'

He sighed to himself and reached back past her. It took everything she had not to jump in fright from his sudden movement.

He didn't like it when she showed the fear.

'Here,' he said, dropping a blanket in her lap. 'I took this from Maria's closet. She won't mind.'

Laurie pulled it around her. She knew if Maria could see her wrapped in it, she wouldn't be happy. Something inside her liked that idea, that small act of defiance. The material scratched at her, but at least she didn't feel as cold any more.

They drove on, the radio playing quietly as they went. Anthony cracked a few gags – she laughed and tried to mean it. Sometimes she did.

'I set him straight,' Anthony said, finishing yet another story of problems at work. 'Soon, they'll not even need me to do that. They'll just do what I say first time. It's taking them a little too long to get used to the fact that I'm the boss now. And that I'm going to be making them a lot of money for a long time.'

Laurie murmured agreement. She knew he didn't need her to say anything. She was there to listen and be impressed. And she was. Anthony was so different to every boy she knew – none of them knew what they wanted to do in life. Vague ideas of college, of frat parties and spring breaks. They couldn't afford more than a few dollars for a date, while Anthony was already making more money than she could imagine.

'I'm twenty-one years old and already rich. I'm only going to get richer. The business was fine when Dad was running it, but I've made it bigger. I'm willing to do what he couldn't.'

His parents had died almost a year ago. He took over his father's construction business and had excelled instantly, he'd told her. He knew how to make things happen. Seemed to be good at it.

Anthony knew what he wanted, how he was going to get it, and that was why Laurie was sitting in the passenger seat of his car.

She wanted to be along for the ride.

She smiled as the coastline came into view, the breaks in the trees giving her sights of the dark water and the moonlight shining on its dull surface. There was beauty there, if you looked hard enough for it.

They passed Bridgeport, Fairfield, and Stamford in a blur. Anthony drove faster, the car rumbling in protest. She grasped hold of the door at one point, Anthony turning towards her and sniggering.

'You're not going anywhere,' he said, patting her on the elbow, as he lifted his foot a little. 'You're safe with me.'

Then, he floored it again, as the radio played on.

The light dimmed further as they left the freeway, onto the smaller streets of Greenwich. Trees lined the roads – their yellowed leaves drifting from the branches, landing on the ground in front of them. They were shadows in the night, floating to their death.

'Not far now.'

Anthony's voice had become softer, quieter. He took an exit, and the woods became thicker around them. The Mustang protested on the soft ground beneath them, but he coaxed it along. The headlights cut a path through the forest, disturbing the darkness as it went on.

They came to a stop a few minutes later. Laurie shivered, bringing the blanket tighter around herself.

'Are you ready?' Anthony said, turning to her. He was nothing but a silhouette in the black sky now. He smiled, but his teeth didn't shine in the moonlight. They merged in the darkness and became nothing.

He got out of the car to open her door. For a second, she wished he would stay out in the woods and never emerge. He reached out, opened the door wide and stepped back.

Laurie hesitated, then stepped out. She could feel the wind swirling around them and the sound of cicadas. The smell of earth. It surrounded her and crept over her skin.

A fleeting thought came to her then. If he killed her here, she would never be found. She would become nothing but a memory. Her parents wouldn't even know where to begin looking for her. She dismissed it quickly.

He wouldn't hurt her like that.

'Come on,' Anthony said, taking hold of her arm. She could hear the excitement in his voice, almost a whisper.

She felt the weight of his arm, the power in his shoulders, as he draped himself around her. The air was thick with ice. She shivered against the cold and he held onto her tighter.

'Here,' Anthony said, moving a few branches aside and bringing them to a stop. 'Can you see it?'

Laurie peered into the distance. There was a pinprick of light a few hundred yards away. The outline of a building, she thought. 'What is it?'

'That's where I'm going to live one day,' Anthony said, as if it could become true simply by saying it aloud. 'Where *we* will live someday. We've been going steady for almost three years now. That means we're in it for life, you understand?

'We'll have kids and grandchildren in this place. We'll grow old here.'

Laurie looked into the distance and saw the size of the house. The way it jutted from the ground as a white monolith. The grandeur of it made her feel something inside that she didn't expect.

Desire. Want. Need.

A longing for the life she knew Anthony could provide her. That he *would* provide.

'A Christmas tree during the holidays, bigger than you've ever seen, Laurie,' Anthony said, excitement dripping from his tone. 'Gold bathroom, a bed that you can get lost in. The parties we'll hold, with all important people. We'll be one of them. We'll have everything.'

She would never have to leave. Everything would be there for her.

It was both heaven and hell. A prison she wouldn't want to escape from.

'We belong together. You know that, right? I'm going to take care of you. You'll be mine forever.'

In the moonlight, with his arms around her, he looked like everything she had ever wanted. She was his.

She gave herself to him under the stars.

And for a moment, she wasn't afraid of him any more.

She was afraid of herself. Of what she was going to do, of what she was going to let happen.

She saw the pendant around his neck, his bare chest, the goosebumps on his flesh. The silver broken heart on its chain, swinging.

Glinting in the moonlight. She concentrated on that and tried not to think of what might happen if she made a different choice.

If she decided she didn't want this any more.

If she broke *his* heart.

CHAPTER 4

I pulled up a chair and sat down next to my father.

A machine was measuring his vitals constantly. Wires going in, going out. His skin broken. Dried blood on his wrist. Machinery that was the difference between life and death. Keeping breath in his wasted body. The sound grated at the back of my mind. A rattle and hum of parts that swished together into a cacophony of sound. It scratched its fingernails down the chalkboard of my consciousness and wouldn't stop.

He hadn't heard me when I'd told him why I was here.

I wished he had. I wished they were the last words he would ever hear.

I watched the slow rise and fall of his chest. He looked diminished somehow. By time, distance.

By life.

A memory came to me of sitting on the arm of Dad's chair. In the house we lived in before the move to Firwood. Before my mum died. Me, sitting in the crook of his arm, my head on his chest. Feeling him breathe slowly, my head rising with each inhalation. Watching his favourite sitcoms – *Fawlty Towers, Only Fools and Horses, Blackadder*. The feeling of the vibrations running through his body as he laughed uncontrollably.

I remembered feeling safe.

The swell of happiness inside me dissipated as the memory faded.

I stood up and left the room. Outside, the air felt cleaner.

Easier to breathe. I glanced up the corridor and saw the nurse who had shown me into the room where my father was. She spotted me and came over.

'I wanted to give you a chance to see him first,' she said. 'Are you okay? Do you need anything?'

I shook my head. 'What happened to him?'

She looked at me with the tired eyes of someone at the end of her shift but reached out and touched my shoulder. 'It must have been a shock to be told over the phone. We didn't have anyone else to contact.'

'How bad is it?'

'He's not in any pain at the moment. We're keeping him under sedation to help him rest. He's comfortable. There's a risk he may have a bleed on the brain, so we're waiting for scan results. He may need surgery, if he makes it through the night.'

I tried to understand. 'A bleed on the brain?'

She nodded. 'It can happen in situations like this. There's a constable on the way to have a chat with you about what happened.'

I shook my head in a daze. 'This isn't some kind of illness then?'

'Not quite, no, but you should speak to the constable when he gets here.' She looked back towards the room. 'Poor man. I tell you, these kinds of attacks never used to happen in Firwood. Things are changing so quickly. On top of this, any infection right now is tough for him to deal with, especially at this stage of his cancer.'

'Cancer?'

'You know about his diagnosis?'

'Yes,' I lied, 'although I didn't know to what extent it had got.'

'Parents sometimes don't want to tell their children the whole truth,' she said kindly, giving me another pat on my arm. 'No matter how old they are. To protect them.'

I bit on my lower lip to stop myself from saying the first thought that came to mind.

'Bladder cancer is treatable if caught early enough, but sadly your father ignored the symptoms until it became a little late. After the surgery to remove it, he's had some issues with his stoma. This time, his infection has been left untreated longer than we would have liked.'

'Is he . . . is he going to recover?'

'We'll know more in a few hours,' the nurse said finally, another reassuring pat on the shoulder. 'You just spend some time with him.'

I made my way back to my father's room, processing what I'd just learned.

Cancer.

I'd always thought that's how I would see him finally. In some hospice, receiving palliative care. I hadn't imagined those last moments too much. Whether there would be any meaningful reunion. I'd always seen it in the distance as one last task to take care of, before I could close the chapter on that part of my life.

I re-entered his room and stood watching over him for a few moments before someone cleared their throat behind me.

'Mind if I come in?'

I turned to see a police officer in uniform standing in the doorway and instantly felt my heart start beating guiltily. I hadn't done anything wrong, but I still felt like one errant word would have me in handcuffs before I could correct it.

The plight of the innocent man.

'I'm PC Hale,' he said, extending a hand. He had a firm grip that he released quickly. 'Have you been here long?'

'An hour or so,' I replied, yet it already felt a lot longer. I wasn't sure if it was his uniform making him look sturdier, but it looked like it would take a lot to push him down. His hair was cropped short and I could see the red of a shaving rash on his neck, poking above his collar.

'And you're his son?'

I nodded. 'Sam Cooper. I drove over from London as soon as I was called.'

He thought for a second, then took out a notepad and wrote something down.

'What happened?' I said, folding my arms across my chest. 'The nurse said it was some kind of attack, maybe?'

'It looks as if he may have disturbed someone burgling his house.'

'During the day?'

PC Hale shrugged, unfazed. 'A neighbour heard the commotion and called us. We arrived and it seems as though we just missed whoever it was. The house is in a right state. We found your father in the hallway. It looks as though he took a fall down the stairs, probably in the struggle.'

'Was anything taken?'

'We were hoping you would be able to help with that.'

I shook my head. 'I haven't been in the house for almost twenty years. I wouldn't know what he had and didn't have.'

He eyed me for a second, then made another note. I felt like I should explain myself, then closed my mouth before I said something I couldn't take back.

'Do you have any reason to think this may not have been a random attack?'

I thought about all the people my father may have upset over the years, especially since I hadn't been around. The drunken fights he may have had, late-night gambling sessions that could have prompted debts he couldn't pay.

'Not that I'm aware of, sorry,' I said finally. 'We haven't really been in touch lately.'

'I see.'

'I could head over there,' I said, hoping he would tell me I couldn't. 'Just to check things over.'

'I'll take you when you're ready,' Hale replied, then snapped his notepad shut. 'I'll be at the front desk.'

He turned and left me alone in the room. I looked back at my father, staring at his covered stomach. I imagined the scars of surgery underneath. I couldn't imagine how he might have felt living without his bladder. He would have hated it. The powerlessness of it.

The anger began to leave me, as I thought of the man he'd once been. I'd worshipped him at one point. Loved him unconditionally. Before everything changed. Before he pushed me away.

Before I became the focus for his pain. His grief.

I felt an uncomfortable mix of loss and pity.

'I'll come back,' I whispered, reaching a hand out towards his. I let it hang in the air and then took it back.

CHAPTER 5

The house looked smaller. The street the same.

My knuckles were white in the dimness, tight around the steering wheel. The clock on the dashboard ticked past one a.m. and I wondered where I would sleep that night.

When I thought about the place – in those brief moments I allowed myself to – my memory was of it being large and imposing. In reality, it couldn't have been more different. It was amongst the first few houses in the street, which ran to a dead end at the bottom. On one side of the street, there were smaller cottage-style houses. Our house was part of a terrace that had been built later. It didn't fit in well now – shabbiness overtaking. The houses surrounding it were still being cared for, while my father had grown even less house-proud, it seemed.

I remembered names, flitting into my mind without warning. Mr and Mrs Woodson lived in the one directly opposite. The McCaws, the Smiths. Names I hadn't thought about for years, suddenly coming to mind so easily. Everyone knew everyone else. And they had never really welcomed us to the party.

I took a deep breath, stepped out and met PC Hale at the end of the path that led to my childhood home.

'I'll let you have a quick look around,' he said, handing me a pair of foot coverings and gloves. I snapped them on silently in the darkness.

'Just in case,' he said, as I finished. 'Forensics were here for a few hours and seem to have wrapped up. If something happens and they need to come back . . .'

He left the thought there. I knew what he was alluding to. An assault was different to a murder.

There was crime scene tape, hastily affixed to the door. The door was still red but had faded since I'd last been there. The plants that had once grown in the front garden were now replaced with weeds.

It's just a house. It's just a house.

I listened to the voice in my head and followed PC Hale as we stepped inside.

I could almost feel the years slipping away. The sound the door made as it opened inwards. The scrape of it against the carpet in the hallway.

It had been home.

No.

This had *never* been home. It was somewhere we had come after my mother died. The moment I'd found out that there was no light at the end of tunnel. That she was gone. Forever.

I felt the anger rise within me again and tried to ignore it. Instead, I flicked the switch for the hallway light on impulse and heard the door close softly behind me.

The wallpaper was the same as it always had been, although it was chipped in places now and a little yellowed. I looked up and recognised the lampshade above me, with the same crack in it that had always been there.

The place reeked of damp and cigarettes. Dad had been a secret smoker before Mum died. One or two in the backyard, when he thought she was asleep. A few more down the pub when he popped in for a few beers after work.

I had been there, nine years old, when Mum had finally got him to admit his secret.

'*What do you have to say for yourself, Mr Cooper?*'

'*I . . . I'm sorry,*' Dad replied, his hands clasped together in a prayer of contrition. '*I only have one or two, here and there.*'

'*Not good enough. I'll have to think of a proper punishment for this outrageous behaviour.*'

'*Wait . . . you're having me on, aren't you?*'

She had laughed then, as Dad realised she hadn't cared all that much really.

'I'm going to give you what you deserve,' Dad had said, and then chased her round the dining room table. I remembered her laughter, echoing around the old house. Her breathlessness as he finally caught her and tickled her sides. His arm beckoning me to join him and ending up in a pile on the floor.

The house was still, but I could feel its secrets in the walls. Pulsing, wanting to break out. A silent scream, desperate to be heard. It was a dead weight that hung in the air, threatening to suck all the life from you.

This place held no happy memories for me. Nor for my dad, I guessed. Which is why I didn't understand why he had stayed once I'd left.

I moved through the hallway and felt around the corner into the living room, finding the light switch and flicking it on. Then, took a breath and stepped into the doorway.

It was as if I had never gone.

The television was the only difference. It was a small flat screen, black and lifeless. And on the floor, dropped from its stand in the corner.

The furniture was all still the same. The pictures on the wall, all still there, for the most part, although some had been thrown to the floor too. Ornaments swiped off the mantelpiece.

I walked slowly into the room, feeling the hard floor through the holes in the carpet. I looked down and saw underlay poking its way through. I smoothed a hand over the arm of the sofa. It was worn with age, rough and damp. Opposite it sat Dad's chair. I looked at it and pictured him sitting there, a cigarette in one hand, a glass of whisky in the other, staring into space for hours on end.

The photograph was on the floor, torn from the wall where it had been hanging since we'd moved to the village twenty-five years earlier.

My family. I picked it up and ran a finger over the glass. Wiped the dust on my trousers.

I had been around four or five years old. My whole family sitting on the sofa, back in the old house. The one that had been home. I slid the photograph from its shattered frame and pocketed it.

It felt as if the walls held my thoughts. The building shifted, as if threatening to release more than I could handle.

I would be the only one of us left soon.

The curtains were still open, so I moved towards the window to look out. Thin material, that looked like a strong breeze would tear them apart.

I placed a hand on the sill and disturbed the dust settled there. Picked at the paint flaking away and looked out the window.

How many times had I looked out here, expecting her to walk up the path?

The street outside was calm and still. Only, I could have sworn there had been four cars on the road ahead of where I'd parked. Now, I could see five. I shook the thought away. I could still feel the pain in the pit of my stomach. The same feeling of loss when we had arrived one day. A few weeks after the accident. Just the two of us – lifeless and dull. Not speaking to each other. As soon as we'd got inside, I'd gone up to my new room and sat on the bare floor, my back against the wall. I had cried silently, until I'd fallen asleep.

I moved away from the window and out of the living room. PC Hale was leaning against the wall in the hallway, his face illuminated by the mobile phone in his hand.

'Definitely not just an accident then,' I said, pointing to the living room behind me.

'No, certainly signs of a disturbance.'

He went back to the phone in his hand and I kept moving. Another door from the hallway led into the dining room and kitchen. I turned on the light.

The table had been upended; one leg snapped off. A couple of wooden chairs, resting against the far wall. There was an old mahogany bureau, in one of the alcoves. The door had been taken off its hinges and its contents spilled to the floor. The kitchen drawers had been thrown to the ground.

I walked carefully over the floor, picking my way through the carnage, to check the back door.

I'd expected to find a window smashed, or a broken lock, but there was nothing except some black smudges on the door left by the forensics team.

I went back into the living room and looked for anything missing. I couldn't be sure, of course, but it didn't look that way. The TV was still there, a DVD player. An old stereo that looked like it was being held together by dust and hope alone.

Was this really a robbery, as the police seemed to think? To me, it felt like someone had come looking for something. But for what, I didn't know.

The sofa kicked up a little dust as I dropped down onto it.

It was almost as if I was waiting for someone to return. To come back and finish off what they started. Or to find what they were looking for, perhaps.

The worrying thought was that they had already found what they were looking for and I had no idea what that might be. It had been almost twenty years since I'd last spoken to my father.

I had no real idea what he had been up to in all that time.

What enemies he may have made.

I made my way out to the hallway and waited for PC Hale to lift his head and look my way.

I shrugged. 'I can't see anything missing down here,' I said, shoving my hands in my pockets. 'But like I said, I've not been here for so long, I'm not sure I would know anyway.'

'You want to take a look upstairs?'

I shook my head. 'That's okay, I don't even know what I'd be looking for. I'm just going to head out and see if I can find a hotel or something.'

'There's a Premier Inn, a few miles up the road. I'm sure they'll have a bed.'

I thanked him, then tore off the gloves and shoe coverings as soon as I was outside. Shoved them on the passenger seat, once I was inside the car, then drove away.

Tried to ignore the feeling that someone was watching my every move.

1985

Whenever Anthony had to visit a site, she would go along with him. Anything to get out of that house in Greenwich. It was too big – she'd known that from the moment she'd moved in. Every room seemed cavernous, so when he asked if she wanted to go with him, she always said yes.

Anthony had told her that after the wedding, they would start having children right away. That would fill some of the rooms, she guessed.

She waited in the on-site office for him. The boredom was the hardest part. Nothing to do but just sit there and kill time counting the different cars that pulled up on the construction site. She had a narrow view to the outside world – a small window, covered in mesh, that looked out onto the yard. The sounds of work seeping through into the small cabin.

She looked over the mess on his desk. Boxes of paper, order forms and the like, she guessed. The corkboard above what amounted to a desk was filled with various notes.

She sighed and leaned back in the chair. Her feet were hurting her, but she didn't dare kick off her heels. She was cold from the chill in the air, her legs bare and exposed to the elements. She had tried to wear pants one time and Anthony had made his feelings clear on that.

'You have to remember, what you look like is a reflection on me. I wear a suit. You wear a dress. We look a certain way, we're treated a certain way, understand?'

There wasn't even a newspaper to read. She would have even taken the *TV Guide* at that point. Anything to stop her mind wandering to places she didn't want it to go.

Outside, she heard shouting. Male voices, deep and angry. She turned towards the window and looked out.

Anthony was flanked by two men, as someone hopped out of the cab of a truck and moved closer to him. She held her breath, as he pointed a finger in Anthony's face.

She watched as he smirked back at the finger-pointer and then glanced to one of the men standing beside him. Nodded towards him.

She looked away before she could see what happened next.

She had spoken to Tom about Anthony's quick temper once – but he didn't have any solutions for her. He would only make puppy-dog eyes at her and ask if she was *really* happy.

There were footsteps outside and she straightened herself up, plastering a smile on her face that made her skin feel tight and fake.

The door opened slowly and a head popped round it. Laurie's smile slipped away.

'Sorry,' a voice mumbled. 'I didn't know anyone was in here.'

'It's fine,' Laurie replied, as the guy entered. 'Pretend I'm not here.'

'That would be a little difficult,' the man said, then breathed in as if he could take the words back. His face turned red. 'I'm sorry, I didn't mean to say . . . I wasn't suggesting . . .'

'It's okay,' Laurie cut in, waving away his apologies. 'Don't worry about it. I'm not offended.'

'I just meant that you're difficult to ignore,' he said, then closed his eyes, shaking his head. 'Let me start again.'

'Are you sure you can?' Laurie replied, enjoying his growing discomfort. It was silly, but he seemed to be getting more flustered by the second.

'I was sent over for an . . . erm . . . an order form, that's all.'

'I'm Laurie,' she said, standing up and extending a hand his way. He removed a glove and took it in his quickly. 'Nice to meet you.'

'David,' he replied, holding onto her hand for a few seconds too long. 'That's my name, I should say.'

'You're working on site?'

'Yeah, not that much is getting done right now. There's an issue with a delivery and it's getting pretty heated out there. Hopefully it'll all be straightened out before anyone loses their cool.'

Laurie cocked her head. 'Where you from? Your accent doesn't exactly sound local . . .'

'Not local,' David said, a boyish grin appearing on his face. 'Guess that was obvious. I'm from England. Place called Chester.'

'Oh right. Is that by London?'

David shook his head, laughing. 'Not quite. Bit further north. By Liverpool? You heard of that?'

'Of course, the Beatles.'

'I should have just said that,' David said, shaking his head. 'Everyone over here knows them at least. Chester is a couple of miles away from there.'

'Why are you here then?'

'Work, basically. Dried up a fair bit over there. Not much need for labourers at the moment. Not in the north anyway. Someone told me there was work over here and I was on the next boat out. Or plane, I should say. I thought it'd be closer to New York, but I guess here is better than nowhere.'

'How are you finding it?'

He took a while to answer, glancing over his shoulder as the voices got louder in the distance.

'It has its moments,' he said eventually. 'What about you? Are you working in the office now?'

Laurie opened her mouth to answer, then closed it again. She wasn't sure what she was doing any more. Why she was there. She just *was*. 'I'm with Anthony.'

David nodded quickly as if he understood, before realising who she meant.

'You mean, Mr Sullivan?'

She chuckled, as he lowered his voice a little. Deferential was the word she would have used, if anyone asked her questions any more.

'I guess I do,' Laurie said, leaning against the desk. He still had his safety helmet dangling in one hand. His hands were grey with dust and dirt, but his face was unlined and smooth. 'Is it bad out there?'

'Oh, nothing that won't sort itself out. Mr Sullivan is just in a little disagreement with a supplier. They've probably forgotten I came over here.'

As the voices continued arguing outside, they talked. He told her about the journey he had made over to her country. What he liked about the US. What was different.

It was comfortable.

'So, I never knew my dad, and my mum died of cancer when I was seventeen.'

'I'm sorry,' Laurie said, tilting her head in sympathy. 'That must have been hard.'

'My grandparents took me in, but they're almost in their seventies. Didn't really know what to do with a teenage tearaway like me. My mum was their only child too, like I am. A really small family.'

'I have one brother. Parker. Mom and Dad are still around, but we're not all that close now.'

'When's the wedding?'

Laurie looked down at where he was pointing to her hand. She wanted to hide the ring that he had spotted and didn't know why.

It was ostentatious. Something she would never have chosen. It weighed heavy on her, dragging her down.

She was never allowed to take it off.

Laurie smiled, the first time she faked one since David walked into the office. 'Next year. We're thinking spring.'

'A year to plan then,' David said, raising his eyebrows. 'I bet it'll be something to remember.'

She had no doubts about that. It was going to be at the house in Greenwich. The white monolith that was supposed to be a home, but felt like anything but.

Laurie spent most of her time there now, even if Maria didn't like the idea of her and Anthony living in 'sin'.

'Are you working here at the moment then?' David said, looking around. 'I mean, in the office?'

Laurie shook her head. 'I'm not working anywhere at the moment.'

'Right, right,' David replied, casting his eyes to the floor. 'I guess you probably don't need to.'

Laurie pursed her lips at that. 'I'm working out what I want to do. Anthony gives me the safety to do that.'

What she didn't say was that she wanted to work but couldn't. She had wanted to finish college too, but that hadn't worked out either. It had been hard back at home after she'd dropped out. Her parents had done the whole *we're not angry, just disappointed*. As if that wasn't worse.

She loved them and knew they loved her. That was all. It didn't make things any easier though. She could tell they weren't as enamoured with Anthony as everyone else seemed to be around him.

She knew that the neighbours talked about him and the way he was making money now. *How* he was doing it.

Everyone talked.

'In the meantime, I'm still looking for something I want to do,'

Laurie said, shaking away the bad thoughts that had come into her head. 'I guess I just haven't found what I want to do for the rest of my life.'

'I'm sure you'll work it out,' David replied, his eyes finding hers. 'You just need a plan. Or not. You probably shouldn't take the advice of some Brit who moved halfway across the world on a whim. Who didn't know just how far away Connecticut was from the bright lights of New York.'

She laughed and realised she was feeling something that she hadn't in a long time. Listened to.

It was an odd feeling. One she couldn't remember.

Laurie was still laughing as the door to the cabin flew open and Anthony appeared. His focus was on David in front of him, but then turned to her just as she stopped laughing and sat back down in the chair. She stared at the floor, feeling his gaze fixing on her.

'What's going on?'

'Found it,' David said, holding a piece of paper in his hand. 'You were right, as we all knew. They were supposed to deliver a hundred, not ten.'

Laurie glanced up, seeing David handing over the order form to Anthony, his hands steady and unfazed. Anthony tore his eyes away from her and back down to David. He snatched the form from his outstretched hand and gave it a cursory look.

'Good. Take that over to them and tell them if they're not back by three o'clock with my order, we're going to have a problem. Then, get back to work. I'm not paying you to hang around talking to people you shouldn't.'

David nodded, stealing a glance at Laurie as he left the cabin. She tried not to return it, but she felt Anthony's presence looming over her as she looked his way.

Anthony closed the door and walked slowly over to her. Lifted her chin up with one hand, so she had no choice but to look up at him. She could see the blank expression on his face. Inscrutable, impenetrable.

'Now,' Anthony said, his tone light, but the pressure on her face increasing by the second. 'Do you want to tell me what was going on in here?'

It didn't matter how fervent her denials would be. How strongly she pleaded her case.

'Have you forgotten why you have a ring on your finger?'

'Anthony . . .' Laurie began, but he shushed her with a thin smile. A finger brought to her lips.

'I don't like having to do this, Laurie,' Anthony said, shaking his head. 'But you make me.'

She tried to remember David's smile as the first blow landed.

CHAPTER 6

I managed to book a room in the Premier Inn and caught a few hours' rest before my phone trilled as dawn broke outside.

There was a sense of inevitability as I answered. 'It's Firwood Hospital here,' a voice said. 'Your father's awake. He's asking for you.'

I was dressed and driving in minutes. I made it to the hospital within half an hour. It was quiet, in the blur of the early morning. A chill in the air that seemed to bite me as I got out of the car. I pulled my jacket tighter around me, but I was still shivering as I walked into the building. A different nurse greeted me when I reached my father's ward.

'Things have changed since you were last here,' she said, smoothing a crease out of her blue tunic. She didn't meet my eye as she spoke, and I could see from the look on her face that it wasn't good news.

'The consultant will be doing rounds later,' she continued, closing the notes on the stand beneath her. 'He'll be able to speak to you properly, but I thought it best I prepare you. Your dad woke for a short period earlier, asking for you. He wasn't awake long, but I thought it best you come in now.'

I found my voice. 'What's happening?'

'His liver and kidneys are shutting down,' she said, and it was as if the air was sucked out of the room. I felt my legs go soft.

'I don't . . . I can't . . .'

'You're here for him,' she said gently. 'That's the main thing.'

I knew then, in that moment, that all the thoughts about wanting to watch my father die – of wanting to see his final moments and hoping they were painful – were all bravado. It wasn't what I wanted at all.

I wanted normal. I wanted what everyone else had.

I didn't want to be there.

I was standing in a hospital corridor at six in the morning, wishing I'd never answered my phone.

Wishing I'd never come.

'What's the . . . how long has he got?'

She shook her head. 'That's not for me to answer.'

'What do I do?'

'You go and sit with him,' the nurse said, her hand on my shoulder, squeezing gently. 'Talk to him.'

So this was how it ended for us.

He somehow looked worse than before.

I fell into the chair next to my father and thought about what she'd said. Knew what the words meant.

Organs failing.

Body giving up.

And then, I'd be the only one left of our little family.

There was a new machine next to his bed, a tube running underneath the bedclothes and out. He was a different colour now. More yellow than grey. His skin had seemed to sink even further, highlighting how small and weak he'd become.

His eyes were closed, but I could see there was someone behind them this time. I placed my hand over his. The skin sagged from the bones, his fingernails almost translucent, a ghost of an extremity. There was no life there. No tremble, no movement. He felt cold to the touch, as if no blood were running through the veins.

I moved my hand slowly and felt the ring on his finger. Lifted it away fully and saw it for the first time. Yellow gold, softened with age. It was hanging on by a thread – too big for him now.

'You still wear it then,' I whispered, my voice shaking as it was released between us.

I let go of his hand and dragged the chair nearer, the noise stark and loud in the quiet room. His eyelids flickered and opened slowly. He turned his head towards me.

'You got older.'

His voice was nails on a chalkboard. Rasping, drowning with effort.

'We both did,' I replied flatly. My head swam with everything I'd wanted to say to this man for so long, but never had the chance to. All the conversations I'd had with myself late at night, as I stared at the ceiling in my flat unable to sleep. This was clearly my last chance to say them, and yet the words didn't come.

I wanted to tell him how it felt to live in silence. To have someone there but not present. The missed parents' evenings, the nights I had to clean up after his drunken blackouts.

All the times he made me feel like it was all my fault.

I didn't tell him. It wasn't like he could take any of it back.

'I'm on my way, aren't I?'

'It's okay, you're going to be fine,' I lied. I could see instantly that he knew.

'I won't even know when it ends anyway. It'll just be . . . black.'

'What happened?'

He shook his head. 'I don't know. Someone was there.'

'Who was?'

He didn't answer. His eyes closing for a few seconds, before they opened again, seeming to see me for the first time.

'Have . . . have you seen the house?'

I nodded in response. 'Someone was looking for something.'

'They didn't find anything,' he said, trying to lift his hand to his mouth, but failing to get it more than a few inches off the bed. 'Nothing to find.'

I looked over at the cabinet next to his bed and watched his eyes track mine. He nodded silently and I poured him a cup of water. Lifted it to his cracked lips and watched him sip. It seemed painful for him to swallow.

'I remember when you left,' he said, his voice a whispered effort. 'I thought you would have come back sooner.'

'What for?'

He closed his eyes slowly. 'I never meant for this, Sam.'

'Who was it, Dad?' I asked again. 'Who was in the house?'

His hands began to shake.

'You can't be here,' he said, moving his hand to my wrist, where it was resting on the bed. 'It's not safe.'

'It's fine,' I said gently. 'It's over now. They couldn't find anything. Money, I'm guessing?'

'No. Listen to me. They'll come back.'

'How much do you owe?'

I thought about the last time we'd seen each other. When I told him I was leaving. He had looked at me with nothing in his eyes. A quiet acceptance. As if he had been waiting for me to leave and was relieved it was over.

'You never fought to keep me around. And now look at where that's got you.'

'Sam . . .'

'No, Dad. It was only the two of us left. We should have been closer than ever, but you pushed me away. I was barely ten years old and I didn't know what I'd done wrong.'

'He's back, Sam.'

I was confused for a second. 'Who is back?'

'I never knew, Sam. You have to believe me. I didn't know.'

'What, Dad? Knew what?'

He coughed and his body shook. I felt pity for him then. Mixed in with the anger. I could see the fear in his eyes.

'Sam, he's come back. He came back to find her. Tom can't help us. They told me . . .'

The machine next to him began to beep a little more insistently. I looked across at it, trying to make sense of what it was trying to say. His heart rate had dropped. His blood pressure was even lower than when I'd entered the room.

'Dad?'

His hand felt cold in my grasp and I realised I was holding on too tight. I released him, but he held on.

'She's alive, Sam,' he said, opening his eyes wide and fixing on mine. 'Your mum's alive.'

Then, his eyes closed and the machine next to him began to sound an alarm.

1985

She was in love with him.

It was real. Visceral. Not like anything she had felt before. An almost overwhelming feeling, that seemed to consume her.

Only it was accompanied by a knowing, lodged deep inside her, that it could never be. There was a danger that loomed over them endlessly.

Anthony finding out.

From the moment they had met, the danger had been there, like a dark passenger along for the ride. Waiting for her to make a mistake and have it all come crashing down on them both.

After that day in Anthony's office, David began dropping by more and more often, until it was every time she was there. They would chat about everything and nothing.

She hadn't been expecting him to make a move.

She had hoped for a long time that he would.

The first kiss had been quick and almost accidental. The second one had been longer and more heated than any she had experienced in her life.

He shifted in his sleep and seemed to hold her tighter. As if he could sense her thoughts and wanted to protect her in some way.

For a moment she pretended that everything was going to be okay. That they would live forever in safety and security. They would get married, start a family, be happy. She scrunched her eyes shut and tried to picture it. The future for them both.

All she saw was fire.

Lying in his arms, his breathing a constant hum of comfort, it was as if the outside world didn't exist. Only, she couldn't completely switch off from it.

It was always waiting to drag her back down.

His apartment was barely big enough for the both of them. There was an almost imperceptible smell of decay that seemed to seep out of the walls. The floorboards creaked with the slightest movement and the faucets dripped constantly.

It was a world away from Anthony's home.

'Was I snoring?'

Laurie peeled her head away from David's chest and tried to find his eyes in the darkness. 'No, you never do.'

'I dropped off for a while there,' David said, his voice almost a whisper. 'You knackered me out, it's not my fault.'

'Knackered?'

'Yeah, knackered. As in tired?' He laughed. 'I swear, it's almost like we're speaking a different language. You've never heard that word before?'

Laurie shook her head. 'This is like when you called that guy a prat.'

David chuckled softly and the sound of it made Laurie melt a little. 'Well, he was a prat, at least. Cut me off, right? No one knows how to drive properly over here.'

'I'll take your word for it.'

'What time is it?'

Laurie shifted and turned over to check the clock. 'Twelve thirty.'

Anthony was away on business for a week and David had wanted her to stay over.

'Yeah, I should be going soon.'

'He wouldn't know if you stayed. It would be nice to wake up with you one morning.'

Laurie sighed, sitting up in bed, the bedsheet wrapped around her body. 'I can't . . .'

'This can't go on forever, Laurie. I want more than this. Meeting up for an hour here and there. It's not enough. And I know you want that too.'

'If he found out about us . . .'

'I know, I know,' David said, a trace of fear in his voice. 'Maybe we could just run away.'

'He'd find us.'

'He doesn't own you,' David said, sitting up and looking towards her. 'He doesn't suspect us. He's too busy to notice what's going on.'

'It's not that easy,' Laurie replied, searching the floor for her clothes. She slipped her underwear on and then her sweatpants. It never mattered what she was wearing when she turned up at David's apartment – he always called her beautiful and took her in his arms. She tied her hair back and continued to dress.

David knew, she was sure, who Anthony was. What he did. He had been working for the man for almost a year. She guessed he must have some knowledge of what he was capable of.

It didn't seem to have stopped him pursuing her. Or falling in love with her.

'It won't always be this way. I just need time.'

'You want to be with me, right?'

Laurie thought for a moment. A life without David flashed through her mind and it hurt her heart. 'I do.'

'Then, it should be easy.'

Laurie shook her head. 'I'll work it out.'

'I will have to go back at some point,' David said, his voice low, serious. 'Then, what will you do?'

She didn't answer him, but instead kissed him and then turned to the door before she made a decision she couldn't take back.

Hurried down to the building exit and stepped out onto the street. Got into her car and drove off without looking back.

Anthony would kill David. She had no doubt about that. She was only a little sure that he would spare her. She remembered what Tom had said to her.

'I'll do anything for you, Sappy. If you need help, just say the word.'

Tom would do whatever she asked for, she knew. He would keep her family safe. Only, she was too scared of what would happen if he tried.

Laurie pulled onto Anthony's driveway – she still couldn't think of it as both of theirs – and silenced the car. The house loomed over her in the darkness, a monstrosity that could never feel like home. When she had first moved in, it had seemed as if she had everything. Seeing it from a distance was nothing compared to actually being there. Walking through its grand entrance, feeling its richness ooze from every surface. She had looked up and up at the tall ceiling and knew it wasn't what she actually wanted.

It could never be comfortable.

It was *his*. Nothing of her life, her likes, her wants, had touched the place.

She went inside and the silence was almost claustrophobic. Only her own thoughts could be heard and they were tossing and turning in her head, making her feel dizzy.

The marbled floor echoed as she walked across it. She slipped off her sneakers and then tiptoed silently towards the stairs.

At that moment, a light came on above her and her heart stopped beating.

Then, she saw the black eyes staring down at her.

'Oh, did I scare you?' asked Maria, a sick smile playing across her lips. 'Did Anthony not say that I'd be popping by? I decided to stay over when you didn't come home.'

Laurie shook her head. 'I . . . I . . . didn't know.'

'Where have you been?' Maria said, arms folded across her chest. 'It's late. Anthony wouldn't want you out at this time. Anything could happen to you.'

Laurie opened her mouth to answer but her mind was a blank space. A thought began to roll around her mind over and over.

I've got to get out of here before she tells him.

CHAPTER 7

I wasn't with my dad when it ended.

He died alone, save for the nurses and doctors who worked on him. Little substitute for those he knew. I didn't get to speak to him again. I had to wait outside, for what felt like hours.

They let me in to see him, but I could only stay a few seconds. It wasn't him any more. I couldn't ask him what he'd meant by his last words to me.

I left the hospital quickly, driving back to the house and parking up outside. Returning to the hotel seemed too final, back home to London a journey I couldn't face, and I suspected I'd be turning around and coming back before I'd opened the door to my flat.

So, there was only really one place I could go.

I leaned my head forwards onto the steering wheel, my eyes stinging with exhaustion.

His last words to me had to have been confusion or a lie.

Only, that's all I had been left with. And it was impossible to let the idea go.

I sat back up and got out of the car. I checked the time and saw it was already eight in the morning.

Over the road, I saw a curtain flicker and move.

The Woodsons.

I decided they would want to know.

I walked over and knocked. She answered almost the second my knuckles left the wood.

'Sam?'

Valerie Woodson was older than I'd been expecting, but I recognised her instantly. Her face was more lined, more weathered by age, but she still had the same kind eyes.

I grimaced and shook my head. 'He's gone.'

Her glasses were perched precariously on her head, as if they could topple at any point. Her hair was silver, tied back from her face in a tight bun. Lines in the skin above her upper lip. She looked like everyone's grandmother, and when I was a child, that's who she had tried to be.

'I am sorry,' she said, moving to one side. 'Why don't you come in?'

'It's okay, really. I don't want to impose. I just wanted you both to know.'

'Sam, you should come inside.'

I hesitated, then relented. Within a few minutes, I was sitting at her dining table, with a cup of tea.

'Where's Mr Woodson?' I asked, cradling the cup with both hands, enjoying the warmth.

She winced as she lowered herself into a chair on the other side of the table. Released a sigh as she settled into it. 'I lost him three years ago. Lung cancer.'

'I'm sorry,' I said, knowing it wasn't enough. Wishing I'd been there and also glad I hadn't been. 'I didn't know.'

'That's okay,' Val said, waving away my apology. 'You left in such a hurry and whenever I asked your father about you . . . well, he didn't know.'

'I always felt guilty about not saying goodbye properly. You did a lot for me when I was younger.'

'You were a good lad. Quiet, mostly. You used to like the lemon drizzle I made, do you remember?'

'Of course,' I said, with a smile. 'I'd have to do a few jobs to earn it, but it was always worth it.'

Her face deepened into a frown, as she looked me over. 'Now look at you. All grown up.'

'It *has* been almost twenty years,' I replied, as she continued to look over me. I shifted in my seat, feeling like a fish in an aquarium. I was waiting for her to bang on the glass. I cleared my throat and leaned back in my chair. Held her stare. 'A few years and it will be the big four-oh.'

'Did you marry, Sam? Kiddies?'

I shook my head. Rachel flashed through my mind for an instant. 'Not yet.'

'All you young people wait too long these days.'

'Were you the one to call the police?'

'Of course,' she said. Then, she lowered her voice to a whisper, as if she were telling me a secret. 'I heard him scream.'

'Do you know what happened?' I said, lifting the cup to my lips and wishing I'd asked for sugar after the first bitter taste.

'I don't know. He's had some health issues lately, but I'm sure you know all about that.'

'I didn't really,' I replied, remembering the way my father had looked in that hospital bed. The thinness of his body, the bones trying to poke their way through the skin on his arms. The yellow tinge to it. The faded bruises, the new ones being covered up. I blinked the images away. 'We haven't really been in touch since I left.'

'I always wondered about you both. It was as if you were strangers.'

'Too much water under a bridge the size of the Golden Gate. After I left home, I guess we both decided it was easier for us if we didn't keep trying. Every now and again, I would type his name into Google and see what popped up. I thought that would be how I'd learn he'd died.'

'I always thought it was a shame. A crisis usually brings people together.'

I looked up and saw the kindness and obliviousness in her

eyes. I thought of what had passed between me and my father and wished I could make her realise that there were some things that even a crisis can't fix.

As if *crisis* was enough of a word to describe what we had been through before arriving in Firwood.

'Well, now, he's gone,' I said, as if that was enough. As if that summed up my father's life in two words.

'You were a good boy, Sam,' Valerie replied, her tone quieter and sadder. A great weight sitting on her words and struggling against her speaking them. 'Grew up to be a good man as well.'

'I don't know about that.'

'You're here, aren't you? He wasn't on his own at the end. Someone who wasn't a good man wouldn't have come back.'

I looked around the room again, looking for parts that didn't belong from my childhood version of it. I couldn't see anything. The porcelain frog was in the same place, on the dark wood display cabinet holding the Wedgwood plates that would never increase in value. The pictures in frames that hadn't been changed in decades. The carriage clock on the tiny TV stand in the corner.

The television had been replaced with a modern one at least, but everything else was the same.

I turned back to her and studied her expression, before I spoke. 'He was pretty confused at the end. Even tried to tell me that my mum was still alive.'

Valerie Woodson stared back at me, then averted her eyes after a few seconds. 'I don't go looking to get involved in things that don't concern me, Sam. I'll just say this – your dad has lived in that house for twenty-five years and never had a problem. Until, a couple of days ago, he comes over here looking scared.'

'The police seem to think it was a burglary gone wrong, that's all.'

She laughed at that. 'We have problems round here, Sam, but that sort of thing doesn't usually happen in this street. Up the road, towards the more expensive houses, maybe. I bet they have problems all the time, with their posh cars and such, up north in Nimmer and Hornsbury, but not here. There's nothing for them round these streets. He had nothing, your dad. Nothing of value. Anyone could tell that.'

I shook my head, knowing that just because it didn't make sense to Mrs Woodson, it didn't mean someone hadn't thought it made perfect sense to rob my dad's house. Get desperate enough and everywhere looks like a good place to try and steal from. 'Well, maybe he just owed someone money. I know he's been drinking, probably gambling more, as well. Not like he works that much, right? It could be anything.'

The look she gave me was definitely pity this time. As if I were a small child again, who needed to be taught something fundamental.

'The way he looked the last time I saw him,' Valerie said finally, reaching across the table and holding onto my wrist, 'like he knew something, or *someone*, was coming for him. I've never seen him like that.'

I swallowed back a response and tried to clear my mind.

I couldn't get his last words out of my head.

'He told me that if anything happened to him,' she continued, placing her cup back down in front of her and fixing me with a stare that was hard to hold, 'that you need to speak to someone called Tom. Said he'll tell you what to do.'

'He's gone.'

Carson didn't wait for Anthony to respond. Instead, he took a breath and continued talking, choosing his words carefully. 'Happened some time this morning, before we had a chance to speak to him again. It's just the one son here. No sign of the other. He's spoken to the police and stayed in a motel last night. He's back on the street now, but he's speaking to a neighbour. It's your call.'

Carson listened and then ended the call. Turned to Hunter in the driver's seat and shrugged.

'The plan stays the same. He wants him questioned and then terminated.'

Hunter smirked in response and then they watched as Sam Cooper left the neighbour's house. Saw him standing by the car, seemingly lost in thought.

'He's going to go in the house,' Carson said, quietly, almost to himself. 'Just you watch.'

They waited for a few minutes and then Hunter pulled the car from the curb. Turned out of the street and parked out of sight.

CHAPTER 8

Could she really be alive?

I shook the thought away, but it didn't leave easily.

I was standing on the street, looking back towards my old house. The crime scene tape was still stretched across the front door and now that it was a murder investigation, it was unlikely that it would be removed any time soon. I could wait for the police to contact me. To tell me what would happen next.

I should have waited, but the gnawing at the back of my mind was too insistent. I needed to know the truth. My father had been scared, according to Mrs Woodson. An emotion that I would never have associated with the man I'd known. I wasn't going to walk away now.

Speak to someone called Tom. He'll tell you what to do.

There was only one person I could think it could be. I remembered that trip to America. Back to my mother's home state. There was a man – a friend of my mother's.

He had been the one to pull us out of the river.

I didn't remember his name. I tried as hard as I could to remember, but there was only the river. The water.

I almost felt the pain as something real in my chest. I could feel my breathing increasing as I felt the crush of water around me. I breathed in and out slowly and counted to ten. By seven, I was breathing normally.

There was only one place that could give me the answer.

I knew the layout of the house better than anyone and from

my visit the night before, I didn't think much had changed in the years since I'd left. Maybe my father had left something behind for me to find. I couldn't walk up the path and open the door, though. That would be too conspicuous. Instead, I left my car parked up outside and walked to the top of the street. Found the alleyway that ran behind the house and ducked down it.

The back wall was low enough to jump up and clamber over. I dropped down into the backyard and dodged a broken-down washing machine that had been left in the middle of the weed-covered paving stones. Jagged and untreated. The shed in the corner was barely standing – leaning to one side like the Tower of Pisa, looking like a strong wind would put it out of its misery. The back door was wood, with a single pane of mottled glass that had a crack running down its length. There were various bits of broken brick on the ground that would make short work of breaking through.

I shoved my hand in my jacket pocket and took out the keys that I hoped would forgo the need to smash my way inside.

I slipped a key into the lock and said a silent prayer. It turned stiffly, but the door swung open.

The smell hit me again. Rotting rubbish and damp. I expected to have to swat aside flies and watch my step for maggots on the floor, but it was simply my senses adjusting.

Once inside, I made my way carefully through the detritus in the back room. Stepped over broken pieces of furniture and the mess that had been left behind. I paused in the hallway, staring at the front door, waiting for any movement from outside.

I turned around and looked at the floor where my father's body had been found. Wondering what he was thinking as he lay there. Alone, afraid.

I moved up the staircase, not touching the banister. Trying not to touch anything. The air felt closer upstairs, staler, as if it hadn't been breathed in years. All the doors to the bedrooms were closed, leaving the landing in almost darkness. Some light permeated from downstairs, allowing me to see each door in turn. The middle room, which had been mine for almost ten years. The one at the far end, the box room. The front, where my dad's room was.

Dad, alone, for all the years I'd lived there. Sharing a house, a life, but not in any meaningful way. We would pass each other, like ships keeping a wide berth.

I had the urge to knock before entering, but it didn't last long. I pushed the door open, feeling it resist as I did so.

I felt for the light switch and flicked it on. Dust motes danced in the air, disturbed by my presence. The walls were bare. Not only of photographs, but wallpaper also. Crumbling plasterwork was all that remained. The curtains had been pulled down and replaced by a black sheet of some sort. The bed was a mess. A stained sheet, that was barely hanging onto the mattress. The duvet thin and balled up at the bottom.

The smell of stale alcohol and sweat assailed me as I crossed the threshold and made my way further into the room. I could see empty cider bottles, lined up against what used to be a wardrobe, but now looked like two planks of wood being held together by hope alone. An overfilled ashtray, shadowed by a similarly full saucer next to it. I looked up at the nicotine-stained ceiling and wondered how anyone could live like this.

I crossed the floor, out of need rather than desire, and saw the chest of drawers, the drawer front missing in the middle of the three. The corners all pulled apart and scuffed.

There wasn't an exact plan in mind, but I thought if there was something to be found, it would be here. In his room. I remembered years earlier, my dad scoffing at leaving anything important in a kitchen drawer or the like. That's not where those things should be kept, he'd told me.

*They should be right next to you, where you sleep. That way, if
someone tries to break in, they'll have to get close enough to breathe
on you to take anything you might really need.*

I opened the top drawer and released a waft of damp air and
almost gagged on it. It stuck open halfway and wouldn't budge
any further. I skipped the middle one, after I'd confirmed it
was empty behind the broken-off drawer front, and opened the
bottom one.

It was filled to the brink with papers. Letters and envelopes
shoved in, without any sense of order.

I grabbed a bundle and began leafing through them. Various
utility bills, stretching back over years. Entitlements, pensions. I
found my birth certificate, fraying and sellotaped together in the
middle. The mortgage papers for the house, paid off more
than ten years earlier. An old passport, cut and disused. I looked
at the picture of my father, almost forty years younger. If I hadn't
checked the name first, I wouldn't have believed it was the same
man. It wasn't only him being younger than I was now, it was
the life that was dancing in his eyes. Staring back, a glorious
future twinkling there.

Nothing suggested any truth to his dying words. No long
explanation of the lies that had been told until this point.

Crumpled bits of paper, filled with disorder.

End of year tax statements. Wage slips, receipts for long forgotten
household appliances. The collected paperwork of a life now over.

Then, I tested the bottom of the drawer. It didn't look right.
I laid my palm against it and felt it move slightly. I slid my
fingertips into one end and, with a bit of work, pulled it up.

Underneath, there was a shelf of sorts. Only small, but enough
to hold a few items. I put the stack of papers to one side and
pulled out the only thing in there.

A phone. An old brick of a Nokia, a model that I didn't think
I'd seen for well over a decade. I remembered my dad using a

phone exactly the same as this one. The calls coming late at night and him sending me out of the room when he answered it.

I turned it over in my hand and was about to turn it on when I heard a noise from downstairs.

Only a creak. A floorboard groaning under new weight. I waited for another noise, but nothing came. I stood up, pushing the phone into my pocket as I did so, and walked over to the window. Shook the black sheet to one side and looked out, expecting to see a police car idling outside. Running through the excuses for my being there in my head.

The street outside was empty, save for the few cars that had been there when I'd first pulled up.

There was another sound and I could feel my pulse increase rapidly. My heartbeat seemed to echo around me. I turned slowly and stared at the bedroom door. My legs turned to jelly and something turned and churned inside my stomach.

They were back.

That's all I could think. I couldn't move, couldn't make a sound.

I was stuck there, with no escape.

There was another creak of a floorboard, this time closer, coming up the staircase. I was transfixed on the door, waiting for it to open up, and for the same fate that had befallen my father to happen to me.

I was trapped.

1985

Maria came closer and the smell of the cloying flowery perfume she wore washed over Laurie.

'Where have you been?' Maria repeated, in her sing-song voice that cut through your skin like a knife. Her face glimmered in the light – the lotion she'd applied before bed had soaked into her pores, leaving behind a sheen. She was a year younger than Laurie, but she was already worried about the future and the way she would look. 'You know what time it is?'

The Christmas tree was still twinkling away in the grand entrance hall. 'Did I wake you? I'm sorry,' Laurie said, surprised to hear that there wasn't a waver in her voice. That she didn't sound terrified, nervous. 'I didn't know you would be here.'

Maria came to a stop a few feet away and seemed to study Laurie. Up and down. 'You're taking advantage of my Anthony while he's away, that right? Going behind his back as soon as it's turned? I always knew you didn't appreciate him. He won't like this. He won't like this at all. You'll have some explaining to do. In fact, I'd bet that he'd like to hear about it right away . . .'

'No!' Laurie shouted back, as Maria turned to walk away. She grabbed her shoulder and made her stop. 'It's not like that.'

'Oh, I'm sure it's not,' Maria replied, shrugging away Laurie's hand on her arm. 'That's what all your types say. I told him you had the makings of a whore.'

Laurie saw fire flash across her eyes and for a second, she imagined reaching out and slapping Maria's face. Imagined the echo her hand meeting skin would make. The red mark it would leave. She closed her eyes and breathed in deeply. When she opened them, Maria was staring back at her, a wide smirk on her face.

'Just try it,' Maria said. 'I bet Anthony would react real well to his only family being hurt.'

'My dad is ill,' Laurie said, and enjoyed the flicker of doubt that ran across Maria's face. 'I had to rush over to help my mom. She panics when he gets ill, as he almost never does. He has the flu or something, but he's going to be okay. We almost had to call 911, it was that bad. His breathing isn't too good. He's settled now, but he gave us quite a scare. His health hasn't been good this winter. I didn't know you'd be here, so I didn't think I'd have to explain myself.'

'Well, you could have left a note. You know I come over here and you wouldn't want me to be worried.'

'It was all a bit of a rush,' Laurie replied, moving past Maria and towards the staircase. As she reached the top, she breathed a little easier.

'I hope he feels better,' Maria said from behind her, but Laurie didn't turn around. She moved quickly towards the bedroom and closed the door behind her.

There was too much fluster for Maria to believe her. It was only a matter of time before she said something to Anthony and then that would just open her up to more questions. Now, she'd dragged her parents into her lies.

She didn't have much time.

She had to make a plan to get out of there.

Anthony came home on New Year's Eve.

Just in time for the party.

Over a hundred people, all dressed in the most opulent way possible. Men in tuxedos, women in ballgowns. The glamour of money and power.

Laurie couldn't help but stare at the women. Hanging onto the arms of their dates. Their husbands.

They all looked dead behind the eyes.

She would be next if she didn't do something about it.

'*This isn't just some party,*' Anthony had said, before the guests had started to arrive, as he fixed his tie and considered himself in the mirror. '*It's an opportunity. We're mixing with a higher class of people now. Some of them don't like that I'm young. Twenty-five years old and already richer and more powerful than them.*'

Laurie looked around at the grey-haired men, the lined faces and faux merriment. Middle age was turning to memory for so many of them. They all had that look of envy and fear in their eyes as they watched Anthony.

Anthony had crossed the bedroom, as she chose her earrings. Wrapped his arms around her, pulling her head into his chest.

'*They're all marks, that's the truth. They're only here because they can be useful to me in some way in the future. Maybe not soon, maybe not ever, but they'll be willing to listen and that's what's important. I'm going to own this city. This state. My name will be everywhere. People will look at me and see nothing but power. And you'll be at my side. We'll be married in a few months. You'll have children to look after. We'll be a family. And nothing is going to get in the way of that.*'

Music played – a string quartet, playing songs that Anthony wouldn't have known given a year to learn. It was all for show. He was a twenty-five-year-old trying to mix in with those thirty, forty years older than him. Trying to show he was someone. The champagne glasses clinked and Laurie smiled in all the right places.

She didn't belong with these people.

All she could think about was David.

Every few seconds, she heard Maria's laughter cut through the air and it made her teeth clench.

Laurie was sure she had told Anthony. Yes, he smiled at her in the same way – with his mouth alone. Never reaching his eyes. Yet, she could feel something coming. She couldn't help but see how he commanded the room – walking between groups and making jokes that people laughed at uproariously. Pretending to enjoy himself. Pretending he was one of them.

She could see right through him.

As midnight approached, Laurie extricated herself out of a conversation with a state senator and his second wife. The age difference between the two had been more than her own age.

She walked away and stood on the edge of the crowd, as the countdown began. The cacophony of voices grew louder, and as the countdown reached its end, she felt his hands on her bare shoulders.

Anthony turned her around and leaned down to kiss her. She almost recoiled, before giving in.

He tasted of cigarettes and alcohol.

He pulled away from her, his eyes narrowing. She tried to move away, but he had a firm grip on her.

'What's wrong?' he asked her, the sound of everyone else celebrating the new year dimming. It was as if they were the only two people in the room.

'I'm just feeling a little out of it,' Laurie replied, unable to look him in the eye. She felt the pressure increase on her skin and did her best not to wince. 'Probably too much champagne.'

'You've barely had one glass.'

'Oh, I've had more than that, you just haven't noticed.'

He stared back at her, a thin smirk appearing on his face. 'I know you've been lying to me.'

'You're hurting me,' Laurie said, as his grip grew tighter and his fingers dug into her shoulders. She tried to release herself, but it only made him hold on more. She could feel people around them, but no one was taking any notice. 'Please . . .'

'Maria told me you were out late while I was away. Told me you said your dad was ill. Strange that you didn't mention it.'

'I didn't . . .'

'Shush, now, I don't want to hear any lies,' Anthony said, his voice barely above a whisper. 'From now on, you go wherever I go. Is that understood? You see those men over there?'

Laurie followed his gaze and saw two men, leaning against the wall, staring back. One in his late fifties, looking uncomfortable in his suit, as if it was the last thing he would usually wear. The other, younger than her.

They both looked as if they would be more comfortable in a bar fight than a dinner party.

'That's Henry Carson and his son Joe. They'll be watching every move you make. You so much as breathe, I'll know about it.'

He released her finally and then placed a finger under her chin. Lifted it up so she had to look him dead in the eyes.

'We're together forever, Laurie. Nothing can tear us apart.'

Laurie felt a tear escape, but she couldn't wipe it away.

'I love you, Laurie,' Anthony said, then tenderly kissed her forehead. A man in an expensive suit clapped Anthony on the shoulder and handed him a cigar, and Laurie took this moment to rush away to the bathroom.

Perched on the side of the bath, she wanted to scream.

Instead, she wrapped her arms around her body and cried.

For herself, for David.

But mostly for their growing child inside her, that didn't deserve any of the pain she was bringing into its life.

CHAPTER 9

I could hear a low voice coming up through the floorboards.
Someone was making their way through my father's house.

My chest tightened and my vision went blurry. I felt sick, nauseated, a million butterflies taking flight inside my stomach.

I closed my eyes and felt my insides spinning out of control.

Thoughts flew in my head, before suddenly, there was one voice rising amidst them all.

'Calm down. It's going to be okay.'

Over and over. Until it began to sound like my dad's voice and I stopped. I breathed in and out once more and opened my eyes.

I could hear the sound coming closer now. Reaching the top of the stairs.

It wasn't the police. They would have announced their presence.

Only one other option made sense.

They had come back.

Fight or flight.

I stepped back from the window and thought about escape. I thought about rushing past whoever it was out there, down the stairs and out the door. But if there was more than one person out there, which I thought likely, I wouldn't get further than the landing.

Minutes were rushing past like seconds.

I had to hide.

Fight or flight?

Neither.

My heart suddenly seemed to kick into life, crashing wildly against my chest.

I scanned the room for options, and then quietly, I dropped to the floor and slid under the bed, almost swallowing a mouthful of dust in the process. I clamped a hand over my face to not spit it out.

Footsteps on the landing. I couldn't do anything but listen, as they searched the rooms on the same floor. I heard a whispered voice, but not the words being spoken.

I was trapped, under a bed that seemed to have last been cleaned around the turn of the century, and without a single thing to defend myself with.

I heard another whispered conversation, both voices low and indistinctive.

Heavy footsteps on the floor outside made the hairs on the back of my neck stand to attention. The floorboards creaked in protest. I heard another movement from the room that shared a wall with this one and realised they had split up.

I held my breath as footsteps came back out of the room and onto the landing. I could see a small sliver of the bottom of the bedroom door. The better option may have been running at the bedroom window and crashing out of it. Landing on the ground outside and hoping for the best. But I was stuck with the decision I'd made.

I heard the door catch on the carpet and saw his boot come into view. First one, then the other. Standing less than a metre away from my head. If I'd reached out, I could have touched his leg.

I resisted the urge.

The boots seemed to pivot on the spot. They moved out of sight, but I could hear them crossing the room. Pulling open the curtain and looking out onto the street.

Another set of footsteps entered the room and I saw black trainers come into view, the cuff of black cargo pants nestling at the top.

'Any windows open?'

The voice came from the first man. It was low, gruff. Almost a growl.

American.

I tried to ignore the gnawing need to move my body in some way.

'No, not a single one.'

The second voice was lighter, younger. There were two Americans in my father's room.

'Do you think he'll even know anything? He was what, nine or ten when it happened?'

'Yeah, but if she's here, he'll know. No reason to keep yourself from your own son, right?'

'I guess. It's some place to hide – long way from Connecticut.'

'Go check downstairs again.'

The first man was obviously in charge.

They were talking about my mother.

They weren't there to finish the job on my father. He was already dead.

They were there for me.

I could only think of two possibilities. Either they wouldn't find me. Or . . .

I was thinking of the second possibility when a hand gripped the edge of the bed and mattress and tossed them aside with ease.

And I was suddenly staring into the eyes of a stranger.

CHAPTER 10

The office was silent as Anthony looked over the plans. Yet another project to distract him. Yet another set of problems that would steer him away from thinking about what was happening elsewhere.

He glanced up and saw the back of Zoran's head, standing outside the door. A breezeblock of a man. His hands would be loosely linked in front of him, Anthony knew. He never moved. Blending into the background, until he was needed.

The early morning sun broke through the clouds outside and brightened the room. The windows stretched across one wall – floor to ceiling – giving a view of the entire city.

Sometimes, he would bring people in and point out all the buildings he either owned or had built from scratch.

This office was different from the one he had at home. More activity, more connection to other people. At home, it was him and the walls, cocooned from the outside world. Here, he would hold meetings; he would turn the decisions he had made alone into reality.

Here, there was nothing personal. Back home, he had two photographs on his desk. His family.

A reminder.

He tried to concentrate on the architect's hard work, splayed out in front of him, but it was difficult to keep focus.

He was thinking about her.

Where she might be, what she might be doing. The idea that she had been out there, all this time.

The drawings blurred in front of him, as red and black flashed in his vision.

Parker Rogers had given them information Anthony should've had years ago. David Cooper and his sons, alive and well, back in England.

Now, David Cooper was dead. Joe Carson had informed him of this a few hours earlier. The news hadn't affected him any – he had expected it to be the case. The only reason for the all too familiar feeling of anger inside him was that he was no closer to finding her. David had crumbled too quickly.

And there had been no sign of her.

Now, the son was the next target. Sam. Nine or ten years old when she had supposedly died.

Anthony still struggled to think of her with another man's child. The idea of her being with David Cooper for all those years was hard enough. The fact she had borne his child was another level of betrayal altogether.

They weren't her family.

He was her family.

He focused on the project in front of him – a multi-million-dollar development, over in Danbury. Hundreds of apartments to be built, office and retail space, yada yada yada. The same old, same old. It had taken some intervention to make it a reality. A few words here and there. Polite requests from those politicians and their fake power.

He would get the go-ahead soon and would add a couple more million to his bank account. And wasn't that all he really wanted?

No.

That was the answer.

If she were alive, that would – and *should* – be his only focus.

There was a knock at the door, snapping Anthony from his thoughts. He looked up and beckoned the visitor inside.

Len Brown was wearing a suit that seemed to be struggling for breath. Straining at the seams, every movement he made a test of the fabric's strength. He dropped into the chair opposite Anthony and the ground shook a little. He looked over his shoulder at Zoran who had followed him inside, and then turned back to Anthony.

'Good morning, senator,' Anthony said, leaning back in his chair and linking his hands across his chest. 'Nice of you to finally join me.'

'You flatter me, as always, Mr Sullivan. It's *state* senator.'

'Of course,' Anthony replied, a smile crawling across his face. He watched a bead of sweat bubble up on Len's forehead and begin its descent. He waited for the *state* senator to take out a handkerchief and wipe it away. The chair creaked as he leaned over to one side to place it back in his pocket. 'Thank you for coming at such short notice.'

'I just wish I came with better news.'

Anthony's expression didn't change. He had been expecting this. Len Brown was a new player on the scene. He'd been elected recently on the back of an aggressive campaign against a long-held incumbency from the opposite party. Anthony had run into issues with his predecessor, which he hoped would be smoothed over with someone more malleable.

'I'm afraid we were unable to approve your plans as they stand,' Len continued, holding his hands up apologetically. 'Couldn't get it through, unfortunately. We'll be happy to look again at any proposals . . .'

Anthony allowed him to go on, smiling back at him the whole time.

He didn't know.

That was a good thing, Anthony decided.

When he was finished, Anthony stood slowly and walked around his desk. Leaned against its edge, looking down at Len Brown. He could smell the sweat that followed Len around like a cloud. Fish – possibly tuna – on his breath.

Anthony looked up at Zoran and gave him a nod. He didn't say anything in return but moved to the windows that faced out onto the corridor and lowered the shades over them. The room grew a little darker.

'How is your wife? Fiona, isn't it?' Anthony said, as Len switched between him and Zoran's movements to his side. He didn't look nervous yet, but he was getting a little twitchy. 'And is it Lisa and Rebecca, your daughters? One already married, one about to do the deed. One grandchild, one on the way. And your sister, she lives over on Long Island, right?'

Len shifted in his chair. 'Now, look . . .'

'Your sister has children, and they have children too,' Anthony said, as if Len hadn't interrupted him. 'Both your parents are no longer with us, but you have aunts and uncles. Cousins. One big, extended family, right?'

'I guess, but what does that have to do . . . what's going on here? I won't be threatened.'

Anthony held his hands up in mock surrender. 'I'm not suggesting anything. Just a friendly chat between acquaintances. You're a family man, right? That's why people voted for you. They saw you as a return to simple family values.'

Len shifted uneasily in the chair, seemingly torn between wanting to storm out of the office and his need to know what Anthony was going to say next.

Zoran was standing behind Len now. Anthony leaned closer to the state senator and could smell the sweat and hypocrisy emanating from him in waves. 'It would be a terrible shame if, say, someone had evidence of you not acting as a *family man*, wouldn't it? Like, I don't know, banging two *very* young females in a hotel room, snorting coke from their naked bodies, and throwing wads of cash around . . . now, that wouldn't be good for you, would it?'

Len was really sweating now, hands gripping the sides of his chair, a second away from getting up and running out the door. 'This is the most ridiculous thing I've ever heard.'

'I'm talking hypothetically here, Len.'

Anthony fixed him with a stare. He could see it dawning on Len now. The position he was in.

'Look, there's nothing I can do . . .'

Anthony gave Zoran another nod and he moved so quickly, Len didn't have a chance to suck in a last breath of air. His hands flapped pathetically against his neck, as Zoran curled his forearm around it.

Len's face turned red, then purple, sweat flying as he thrashed about. Zoran put his weight down and kept him sitting in the chair.

Anthony didn't blink.

'Now, Len, you're going to go away and come back with a different answer. Or Zoran here will pay a visit to your family and show them a movie starring you. Then . . . well, Zoran can be a little unpredictable. You don't have many options here, understand?'

Len couldn't move, but Anthony stared into his watery eyes, as they flickered dully.

'Make a decision, Len,' Anthony continued, pulling at a loose thread on the cuff of his white shirt. 'Your lungs won't take much more.'

He looked back at Len and thought he saw something change in his expression. It was enough for him to glance up at Zoran, who released him immediately. He moved back a few steps and it was as if he hadn't moved.

Len breathed hard and fast, taking in oxygen as if it were the first time he'd experienced it. His colour slowly returned to normal. His tie was halfway round his neck and he flinched as Anthony moved closer and turned it straight for him.

'Good man,' Anthony said, giving him a smack on his shoulder that would leave a red mark Len wouldn't remember getting later that night. 'You'll be in touch?'

Len nodded slowly, then looked behind him. He cowered as Zoran stared back at him.

'One more thing,' Anthony said, smirking as Len flinched at the sound of his voice. 'You have access to information I require. The current whereabouts of a person. Now, I haven't been able to locate them myself, but you should have no issue.'

'I can't do anything illegal—'

'You'll do whatever I ask you to,' Anthony cut in, as Zoran leaned closer to Len. 'You're not going to question me further. I'm going to give you a name and a previous address.'

Anthony passed him a card lying on his desk and Len stared at it as if it held the answers to the universe.

'She lived here years ago, in this state. Moved away in 1996, but I have a suspicion she might be living somewhere close by. Go away and find out what you can. That sound good to you?'

Len's shoulders sagged a little, as the weight of what he had got himself involved in began to filter through to him. He had no idea, Anthony thought. This was just the beginning.

'Now, go on, it's fine,' Anthony said, moving back around his desk. 'We're done.'

A minute later, Anthony was alone again, the high from Len's visit slowly wearing off. It didn't last as long any more.

He thought about her again.

Thought about being in a room with her, alone. What he would say, what he would do.

That was enough for him to keep the high going for a little while longer.

CHAPTER 11

I moved quickly, sliding from my hiding place and clambering up from the bedroom floor. Only, he was on his feet and grabbing my shoulder as I tried to get myself upright. I felt his hands on me and then suddenly I was airborne.

I landed with a crash, a few feet from where I'd emerged from underneath the bed, and for a second I wasn't sure what had happened. I felt a sharp pain in my back, managed to turn over and get back up onto my feet. I grabbed the first thing I could find, threw it in his direction and tried to run.

I was at the doorway when I felt his hands wrapping around my arms. I threw an elbow behind me, but I didn't get much weight behind it and it landed with a soft thump. I felt his grip relax a little and I turned instantly.

My foot connected with his knee and I heard a small sigh of pain escape him, before I threw a punch that landed on the side of his neck. I threw my hands up towards my face, expecting him to hit me, but instead I was dragged up underneath my arms and I was off my feet for a second.

Only a second.

As I slipped to the floor, I realised he had hit me in the stomach. It was as if there had been an explosion in the room and my ears were ringing and there was nothing but confusion and fire all around me. I opened and closed my mouth, trying to breathe.

At my periphery, I was aware the other man had come back in the room.

'You got him?' he said.

'I'm good.'

I looked towards the man who had walked in, and it took a second, as I continued to gasp for air, to realise that the monstrous entity blocking the doorway was an actual human being.

He ducked into the room and stood over me, considering for a moment, before shaking his head.

I felt my insides turn to mush.

'Get him up,' the first man said, and before I had a chance to react, the second man had sat me upright. I shuffled back against the wall, the coarseness of the plaster scratching at the nape of my neck.

'Sam?'

I shook my head, trying to clear my mind. 'What are you doing? Why are you here?'

'We know who you are,' he said, coming to a stop opposite me. He squatted down and I could see his eyes. They were almost black.

'What do you want?'

'You know why we're here.'

It wasn't phrased as a question, but I felt the need to answer it anyway. 'You killed my dad.'

He held a hand up to stop me in my tracks, raising up from his squat position and standing over me. 'Let's not get side-tracked here. You know what we want.'

'Side-tracked? You think you can get away with this . . .'

I felt the blow land and my ears ring, but I didn't see it coming. My hand went to the side of my head instinctively, as he drew his open hand back.

'You need to think clearly, Sam. You know what happened to your dad. You know what we're capable of.'

I looked up and tried to hold his gaze. I wanted to look into the eyes of the man who had killed my father. I wanted to do something, say something, that would matter. I couldn't find the words.

This man had killed my dad and it didn't seem to faze him in any way. I stared into his eyes and my teeth ground together as my jaw tensed with anger.

He looked back at me with an air of indifference. As if I were simply an insect to be dealt with as and when he decided. I turned and looked at the younger man, who was again blocking the doorway.

'What did he owe you?' I said, trying to keep calm enough to make it out of the room alive. 'I don't have much money, but maybe we can come to some sort of arrangement, yeah?'

The two men shared a glance, before the older one turned back to me shaking his head. 'It's not about money. We're here to find out where she is.'

I propped myself up further, sitting more comfortably as my breathing began to return normal. I looked between both men and shrugged. 'Who? I don't know what you're talking about.'

The younger man shifted from the doorway and I was lifted off my feet in half a second. I braced myself for another punch to the gut, but it didn't come. The older man reached forwards and put a hand on the other's shoulder.

'Wait.'

The younger one relaxed his grip slightly, as my feet sought purchase on the floor. I looked down and his hand seemed bigger than my entire upper arm.

The older one stepped to the side and leaned against the wall next to me. The younger, much larger one, kept his grip on me. 'He ain't gonna talk, Carson.'

Carson. Now I knew his name. I didn't think that was a good sign.

'You know exactly who I mean,' he said, as if we were having a casual conversation. 'Your dad knew. Only, he didn't think we were serious. Now, you know what'll happen if you don't tell us everything. Have I got that right? Thing is, my friend here doesn't have the patience I do.'

'I don't know anything . . .'

'Let's not get ahead of ourselves,' Carson said, waving away the younger one and taking up the space he'd vacated. 'Laurie Cooper. Your mom. That's who we've come for, no one else. Now, if you just help us out here, we can all move on without any more unpleasantness, that sound fair?'

'She's dead.'

He raised an eyebrow to that. 'She's alive and we'll find her. You can either help us do that or not.'

I looked back at him, knowing there was no way I would leave that house alive, no matter what I said.

'There's been some kind of mistake,' I said finally, as the younger man crossed the room and made his way to the window. 'My mum died twenty-five years ago. Back where I think you've come from. She's gone. There's no one to find.'

'I see. That's your story, is it?'

'Honestly, I can't tell you anything, because there's nothing to tell. She's gone.'

'Twenty-five years ago, there was an accident. In a river, some-where in Connecticut, right?'

I tried not to think of the water. Scrunched my eyes tight, so all I could see was black.

'Your mom died supposedly. Your dad brings you back all the way to England. Only, we know she didn't die that night. And we think she's been here the whole time.'

I shook my head. Started talking quickly. 'That's not true. I haven't seen my mum since 1995, the night she died. She's gone. She's never been back here – look at this room, this house. Can't you see he's lived here alone? Don't you think she'd be here now, after you killed her husband? She's dead. You killed him for nothing.'

Carson hesitated, glancing around the room for a second.
The younger man peeled back the black sheet covering the
window and looked out onto the street. I shifted a little, but
the older one was too close to do anything more than move a
couple of inches.

I needed to get out of there.

Finally, Carson shook his head. 'Kid, this is serious. We *know*
she's alive. And we're going to find her, with or without you.
Think about it.'

'How can you say that? She was my mother. I *know* she's gone.
I've had to live with that fact for most of my life. You don't know
anything.'

I braced myself for another blow, but the older man only came
closer to me.

'She's alive. Stop playing games.'

'I'm not playing anything.'

He stared at me for a few seconds, suddenly uncertain. Then,
he tensed and kept on. 'I understand you want to protect your
mom, but this is really the end of the line. When did you last see
her?'

'When she was drowning in Mystic River. That was the last
time I saw her. The last time any of us saw her. Because you're
searching for a ghost.'

I thought about crashing into that river. The silence that
followed. I had only been young, but it was one of the memories
that I couldn't shift. No matter how hard I tried.

He opened his mouth to say something else, but his partner
spoke before he had a chance.

'Someone's out there,' the younger one said, his voice flat,
emotionless. 'About to walk up.'

The older man glanced his way. 'Cops?'

I didn't wait to hear the answer. I took my shot.

I drew my foot back and this time I concentrated hard on Carson's knee. All my weight went into the boot. I turned my foot sideways and almost stamped down onto it. I heard him shout in pain, as I started running as fast as I could. Out of the room, over the banister and landing on the stairs. I could see the front door ahead of me and tried to ignore the sound of two men following closely behind.

I reached the door and pulled it towards me, the outside air suddenly hitting me like the backdraft of an explosion. I almost collided with someone on the front step, losing my balance and staggering to the ground. I pushed them with force, out of my way. I heard a cry of alarm and a red satchel fell to the side.

The postman.

I barged past him, thrusting my hand into my pocket and taking out my car keys. I was on the road and around the bonnet of my car, reaching to unlock the driver's door.

I pulled it open and jumped inside, just as the poor postman went flying into the road ahead of me. The two men were outside now, coming towards me. I grabbed the door handle and pulled it shut. Pressed the lock button and tried to steady my hand enough to get the key in the ignition.

The younger one stood in the road, blocking my way. The older one was at the side of me in a flash.

Glass shattered as he punched through the window to grab me by the throat.

The car started up, and I shoved it into reverse. The man's hand still around my throat, I put my foot down, released the clutch and shot backwards.

I braked hard, after going back a few yards or so and he jerked forwards, releasing his grip on me. He swore loudly in pain.

I didn't wait for him to recover. I spun the wheel and reversed again, threw the car in gear and put my foot down hard.

Glancing up at the rear-view mirror, I could see the postman running off into the distance. Then, the two Americans, staring at me as I drove away.

CHAPTER 12

I waited until I was on a busier road back towards London before I called the police. After I'd explained who I needed to speak to, I was connected to a confused-sounding constable.

'Two Americans?'

'Yes,' I replied, checking in the rear-view mirror for them in a car behind me. I couldn't tell. 'They were in the house. They . . . they're the ones who killed my father.'

'Description?'

I gave them as much as I could. Apart from the size of the younger one and the fact the older one was called Carson, it wasn't much.

'Where are you now?'

'Just look for them,' I said, then disconnected. I kept driving, until I made it back to my flat a couple of hours later.

Finally, I let myself inside and closed the front door behind me. My body was shaking as the panic and despair that had been staved off by adrenaline finally hit home. I made my way through to the kitchen and poured myself a generous measure of brandy. Took a large mouthful and then forced myself to swallow. It burned my throat all the way down and I took another drink.

I leaned against the kitchen worktop and steadied myself.

I hadn't told the police about my father's last words. Or that the two men were supposedly looking for my mother.

The phone I had taken from my dad's bedroom was still in my pocket and I pulled it out. I knew it was the same one he had used from around the year 2000. It was still in good condition – barely used, I guessed.

This was something he kept special. I powered it up and wasn't surprised to find it had enough battery left on it. 'They don't make them like they used to,' I whispered to myself, the sound stark in the quiet flat.

It took me a minute or so to familiarise myself with what each button actually did, but before long I was looking at the last calls made and received.

And the text message.

There were only two recent calls, to and from the phone, both the same number. A quick search on my own device told me where it came from.

American in origin.

One text message.

I wish things were different. They're coming. I'm sorry.

The number hadn't been saved, so I didn't have a name, but I guessed what it might be. I checked the time and thought about the eastern United States. Five hours behind. West coast a few hours more.

Early morning, midday-ish, I thought. Whoever was behind the number would be awake at least.

+1 602 348 2503

I googled the number, but didn't get a result that made any sense.

The area code was Arizona.

I knew my mum was from the US, but it was Connecticut, not Arizona. I checked: there were about two and a half thousand miles between the two states.

My father had said to contact Tom. Maybe this was the way

to do that. There were only two members of my mother's family left back in 1995 – my grandmother and my uncle.

I didn't think the number was likely to be either of them. My dad hadn't seemed to want anything to do with them, after my mum died. He'd never mentioned them once. I'd tried to ask over the years, before I left for good, but had been met with barely a response. A mumbled reply, that they didn't matter any more. That we were the only family left. The message was from Tom, I decided.

And he was contacting my father to warn him.

I took a breath, typed in the number on my own phone and waited for an answer.

Carson cursed and struck the steering wheel again. They had been driving round for the past couple of hours trying to find Sam Cooper but had come up empty. When they'd returned to David Cooper's house in Firwood, a cop car had made sure they kept driving on.

Now, they were pulled up in the parking lot of the hotel where Sam had spent the night before, but there was no sign of him.

'We'll find him again,' Hunter said from the passenger seat, his voice far too calm for Carson's liking. 'He'll have to come back at some point.'

'Yeah, and you don't think the cops are going to be all over us like a rash if he does?'

Hunter didn't seem to have an answer for that.

Carson still couldn't believe they had been so careless. Two against one, with the experience they had – how Sam Cooper had escaped from that house was beyond him.

'Are you going to tell the boss?'

Carson grunted a response, trying to ignore the question. It had been grating on his mind since the moment they had watched Sam's car drive off into the distance. Carson had worked for

Anthony Sullivan long enough that he could almost map out what would happen next if they didn't track Sam down and finish what had been started.

'Maybe he really didn't know what's going on,' Hunter said, oblivious to Carson's unwillingness to talk. 'It's not like we got anything from the father. Maybe both of them had no idea she was alive?'

'I could care less. We have a job to do and so far, we've got nothing. The son has disappeared, and the father is dead. It ain't the best of jobs we've done.'

'I guess not.'

'And now I've got to let the boss know we failed. So, excuse me if I don't want to speculate about who knows what around here. It don't matter much, when he's waiting for us to tell him what he needs to know, you hear?'

'I get it.'

'Good,' Carson said, then stared down at the number saved on his cell phone. He wondered where Anthony Sullivan would be when he made the call. How close he might be to being done with both him and Hunter.

'We can't stick around here,' Hunter said. 'We hardly blend in with the local crowd.'

'You're right,' Carson replied and pocketed his cell phone. Anthony Sullivan could wait for the bad news.

He shifted into drive and pulled away.

Jackson arrived at the same time as the local cops did. He watched them enter David Cooper's house and then cursed under his breath as a uniformed officer stood outside, showing no sign of moving on.

Sam Cooper was nowhere to be found.

Jackson hadn't pegged the two other Americans as amateurs, but now he wasn't so sure.

The plain-clothed detectives left the scene, but the uniformed officer stayed behind, confirming his suspicion. There would be no way of getting into the house now.

Which only left Sam Cooper as the main lead. Jackson had thought he would return soon enough, since his father had only been dead a few hours. But if there had been some sort of encounter with the two Americans, then he doubted Sam would stick around all that long.

He had to make a phone call. One he didn't want to make.

'It's Jackson.'

A pause. 'Where are you?'

Jackson explained as best he could. He'd braced himself for shock on the other end of the line, but to his surprise, he was met instead with a quiet acceptance.

'You didn't know.' It wasn't a question. 'What should I do?'

It was a short response. 'Take care of Sam. Now.'

Jackson ended the call and thought hard. Without a gun, it would be tricky. He had been training for moments like this for a long time, but he still had to think. He was on the back foot – had been since he'd stepped off the plane a few days earlier.

He placed another call and within an hour, having provided Sam's licence plate details, he had something he didn't think the other two tourists to Firwood had yet.

Sam Cooper's address in London.

He entered it into his GPS. Less than a few hours away. He made a quick calculation and decision.

He would be there in a couple of hours.

Waiting.

CHAPTER 13

The phone rang a few times, then someone answered.

No one spoke, but I could hear breathing on the line.

'Hello?' I said. 'Is someone there?'

'Who is this?'

The voice was deep, gruff. The kind of voice you wouldn't want to hear in your ear in a dark alley. I swallowed and found my own voice.

'It's Sam Cooper. My dad is David Cooper—'

'I don't know no Coopers,' the voice said, talking over me. 'You got the wrong number.'

'Wait,' I shouted, my voice echoing around my small flat. 'You sent my father a message. You told him that someone was coming. That you were sorry.'

There was a pause, but he didn't hang up the phone. 'What's your mom's name?'

'Laurie,' I replied, slowly, knocked off course for a second.

'Your dad's middle name?'

'Edward.'

'How did you get the scar on your elbow?'

I opened my mouth to reply and then checked myself. 'Wait, how would you know that?'

'Answer the question if you're Sam.'

I absent-mindedly touched the small, thin scar that ran along my elbow. It was barely noticeable now, a line of white against pink. 'I ran out of the house too quick and scraped it against the lock on the door.'

A long exhale. 'Okay, Sam. Why are you calling me?'

'Wait a minute. Who are you?' I asked, trying to keep control of the conversation. 'Do I know you?'

'You did once, kid,' he replied with a humourless laugh. 'It's Tom.'

'Were you my mum's friend?'

'You remember me?'

I thought back to the last time when we were in the US. All of us together. My grandfather had died, but I could sense something else going on. Both of them had been on edge the entire time. Even at that young age, I knew I wasn't being told the whole story.

Hearing Tom's voice, more memories came to me. Of him ruffling my hair, as if he'd known me for longer than a few minutes. Of him hugging my mum and whispering something to her. Of him shaking my dad's hand and giving him a friendly pat on the shoulder.

A *reassuring* pat, maybe?

'This is Tom. My oldest friend, Sam.'

It was difficult to remember my mum's voice. Every time I thought of her, I remembered the river.

'I think I do.'

'How did you get my number?'

'I have his phone,' I said, holding the old Nokia in my hand. 'He had it hidden.'

'Yeah, we didn't exactly keep up to date with new numbers. That's the cell he gave me for contact about twenty years ago. Why do you have it?'

'He's dead . . .'

There was a pause. Then, Tom cleared his throat. 'I'm sorry to hear that, buddy.'

'And there's calls between you and him, and a text message saying someone was coming for him. And that you were sorry.'

'Sam . . .'

'Who was it? Did you send them?'

There was a sharp intake of breath over the line and then a voice in the background. 'Look, Sam, it isn't safe to talk like this.'

'I don't care that it isn't safe. I need to know what you had to do with my father being killed.'

'Tell me, what happened to him?'

'The police think he disturbed a burglary. Only, we both know that's not what happened. Two Americans almost killed me too, earlier today. They were the ones who got my dad. So, now, I'm talking to another American, who is the last person to contact my dad, on a hidden phone. Explain to me why I shouldn't be piecing things together in the way that would make life difficult for you.'

'I would never do anything that ended with your dad being hurt.'

'Then start talking.'

'I was trying to warn him. I was worried that they might come after him next. Did he never say anything to you?'

I ignored the question. 'They would have killed me, if I hadn't got away.'

I could hear the fear in Tom's voice. 'You need to get out . . . give me a sec.'

In the background, I heard a muffled conversation. Words drifted through, but I could only make out a few here and there. '*When . . . how long . . . why . . . you don't think he's . . .*'

'It's not safe,' Tom said, again, as if it were the answer to everything.

'Listen to me,' I cut in. 'I don't know what's going on, but I want answers. Now. The last thing my dad said to me was that my mum was alive.'

'I can't talk about this over the phone,' Tom said, and I could sense a sadness in his voice. 'There's things that need to be sorted out first, so it's all safe. A long time ago I promised her I would look after you and make sure nothing happened.'

'It's true? She's alive?'

My voice was higher than it had been and I realised I hadn't really believed it until this point. Even after my father's words, after the two men in his house attacking me.

I hadn't thought about the reality of my mother being alive.

'Are you somewhere safe now? Where are you?'

I didn't want to tell him too much. 'I'm not in Firwood.'

'Good, good,' Tom said, beginning to regain some of his composure. 'Listen, it's going to be okay. Just keep safe and keep your head down and it'll all be fine.'

'You didn't answer my question.'

'These two men, did they say anything to you? Did they tell you who they were or what they were looking for?'

I ignored his questions. 'If they know who I am, then I'm sure they won't take long to find me, and then what? I need to know what's going on.'

I could almost hear Tom thinking. I peered out of my front window onto the street below, expecting two men to appear. When my hand let go of the curtain, it was shaking.

There was a pain behind my eyes. Tiredness, stress – either way, it was adding up to a pounding headache.

I flopped down on my sofa and wished I'd never left London in the first place.

'Sam, I know this is a lot to take in, but you've got to trust me. I can work all of this out.'

'What's happening? At least answer me that.'

'It's best you don't know.'

'Is she alive?'

There was another long exhale of breath. 'Sam . . .'

'Just answer me. Is she alive?'

A long pause, then a stuttered reply. 'Sam, I promise I'll be in touch. I'll give you all the answers you need, but for now, you need to just get somewhere no one knows where you are. We can talk about all of this then.'

'Tom—'

The phone went dead. I watched the screen turn to black and saw my dull reflection in the glass.

I stared at it for a while and thought about the idea of her being alive. The impossibility of it.

I wanted it to be true. So much, in that moment, that I ignored what it would mean.

That for twenty-five years, my life had been a lie.

Tom Miller put the phone down and looked at the woman sitting across from him.

'He's safe for now.'

Quinn stared back at him. She opened her mouth to speak, then hesitated.

'It's for the best,' Tom continued, wondering if he was trying to convince her or himself. 'If he knew everything, then he wouldn't stop. He would come here and that would just make things more complicated.'

He waited for a reaction that didn't come.

'You think this is connected to Laurie?'

Tom thought for less than a second, then nodded. 'Anthony found Parker Rogers. Parker was the only other person in the world who knew David Cooper was living there. It's no coincidence that a week or so later he ends up dead too.'

'Maybe it would be safer for his son to come here. At least there would be protection.'

'Maybe, but I'm not going to take that chance.'

Quinn seemed to accept it, on the surface anyway. He could see the cogs turning in her mind.

She had been at his side a day or two now. Almost as soon as he'd arrived back in Connecticut. He had landed at JFK from Phoenix and made his way back to his home state. Then, he'd gone straight to the one person he knew wouldn't turn him away. Quinn's father, Robert Walker.

They had served together in the military for a number of years. Had met in basic training, back in the early Eighties. They hadn't spoken in almost a quarter of a century, so when he'd turned up on his doorstep, he'd been shocked to find Robert wasn't what he'd once been.

A car accident ten years earlier had left him confined to a wheelchair.

Tom had accepted it quickly. That he was going to have to do this on his own. Then, Robert had introduced him to Quinn.

Now, he was worried what he'd got her involved with.

'When I asked for your help, it was because your father said you were stubborn. That you didn't let things go.'

She seemed to take it as the compliment he'd intended it to be. Robert had told him that she worked freelance for a number of law firms. A PI, of sorts.

'In my line of work, you can't be anything but that,' Quinn said, leaning back in the chair, choosing her words carefully. 'But, so far, I've found nothing to suggest that she's . . . that she's *here*.'

Tom knew what she meant. *Here* meant alive.

'That's not important right now,' Tom said, resolute, confident. Trying to project that, anyway. 'I hired you because I needed help on the ground. You have to trust me a little, but not as much as I'm trusting you. We have to deal with Anthony Sullivan before anything else, because he's only got one thing on his mind. Finding her. And he'll kill anyone who stands in his way.'

CHAPTER 14

M y phone was buzzing away in my hand.
Rachel calling.

I swiped answer without thinking.

'Hey . . . how are you doing?'

I hesitated, thinking about how much I wanted to say. 'He died this morning.'

'Oh Sam, I'm so sorry.'

'I'm back at my flat,' I said, thinking back to those final words I'd shared with him. It felt like it had been days since, but I looked at the clock and realised it had been less than twelve hours. 'It's been a long day.'

'Are you on your own?'

I looked around the flat. 'I hope so.'

'Shall I come over?'

'It's fine . . .'

'Sam, you shouldn't be alone.'

I opened my mouth to argue, but realised I didn't want to be alone. And it was safe here for the time being, I thought. They hadn't followed me.

'That would be nice.'

Within thirty minutes, there was a knock at the door.

She wrapped her arms around me as soon as I opened it. I closed my eyes, feeling calmed in an instant. I held on until she let go of me and led me into the living room. She sat down next to me on the sofa, but didn't let go of my hand.

'I'm sorry,' she said, stroking the back of my hand. 'Was it sudden?'

'You could say that.'

I told Rachel everything that had happened. She listened, not giving any reaction until I told her about the two men who had attacked me earlier that morning.

'What did the police say?'

'Not much,' I said, wondering if I'd made the right decision leaving Firwood. 'I'm not sure they took me seriously. It's a small place. I doubt they have many murder investigations.'

'And they were American?'

I nodded. 'They were looking for my mum.'

'Is there . . . is there any chance she might be alive?'

'I didn't think so. I mean, my dad and I barely survived the accident. We were lucky. There was a funeral, but I wasn't allowed to go. We didn't stay much longer. Dad brought me back and we moved to Firwood that week. And . . . well, you can't fake the kind of grief he felt.'

'But your dad also said she was alive.'

I shook my head. 'None of it makes sense. Maybe he was confused.'

Rachel stared at me for a few seconds. 'You don't believe that.'

'No. Those two men – they seemed professional. Hired, if that makes sense? They were adamant she was alive.'

'What do you know about her life in America?'

I sighed. 'Not much. When we went over in 1995, it was because my grandfather had died. The accident happened after his funeral. I didn't know anyone though. Mum seemed to have a really small family. A brother, her mother. My dad told me they were gone when I asked him once. It wasn't like I knew them.'

'Do you know their names?'

'I think my uncle was called Parker or something,' I replied, trying to think. 'Not sure about my grandmother. They didn't say her name. Mum and Dad never talked about them. It was a surprise when we were suddenly travelling over there. Then, after what happened, my dad refused to talk about them and over the years I tried not to think about them, but they were my only connection to my mother. I've tried finding them online but had no luck.'

Rachel leaned back on the sofa, her head close to mine. 'You had it tough.'

'You could say that.'

'Over the years, did he really not say anything about your mum?'

I shook my head slowly. 'It was just silence. Like we were existing together, in the same space, but if I wasn't there, nothing would be different. I felt like a constant reminder of everything he had lost. He didn't know what to do. But, I was a child. He should have looked after me.'

I swallowed and bit down on my lower lip, before I continued. 'It wasn't abuse, as such. We were just lost.'

'He was the adult . . .'

'I know, I know,' I said, placating quickly. 'I blamed myself most of the time. Like it was something I'd done wrong. I'd do things to get a reaction from him. Just anything to make him notice me. It never worked though.'

'I can't even imagine.'

'Try not to,' I said, exhaling loudly. 'Look, it could have been so much worse. He never laid a finger on me. He didn't scream at me, or push me around. He just didn't care if I was there or not. Sometimes, I just wanted him to do something to acknowledge me at all. To show he cared. That he actually loved me. When I left, he didn't even ask me where I was going. Never said goodbye.'

Rachel didn't react. I kept talking.

'I had a brother. His name was Michael. He was in the car too that night. He didn't get out in time.'

'Oh God . . .'

I pulled out the photograph I'd taken from my old living room and handed it to her. She stared at it for a few seconds, then handed it back. I kept hold of it.

'He was five years old. Only just. It had been his birthday the week before. I got him a *Shoot* annual, that had Gazza on the front. I have no idea why he was Michael's favourite player. It wasn't like he played for our team. And he was only a few months old when Italia '90 happened, so it wasn't that.'

'I'm . . . I don't know what to say. I didn't know, sorry.'

I waved away her apology. 'This is my fault. I never tell anyone. Anyway, Mum and Dad had said they would take him to an England match that summer. We'd all go, even if Mum sometimes called it soccer and we had to correct her.

'He couldn't get his seat belt off after the car went into the river. I usually helped him, because he couldn't do it himself.'

I didn't tell her that I still saw him in my nightmares – disappearing into the black of the river, as I floated up to the surface. I screamed out to him in my sleep, but the water always stole my words.

I put the photograph back in my pocket. Out of sight.

'Years after, I tried to talk to my dad about it. I told him that I was having nightmares about what happened and I'll never forget the look he gave me. It was just pure disappointment. As if I had let him down in some way. Anyway, when they found Michael's body, he was still safely buckled up in the back seat of the car. They had divers find the wreckage. There was a joint funeral. Mum and son. They didn't let me go. I remember sitting in this house, with people coming up and saying how sorry they were, as if it were their fault.'

I remember the way they'd all looked at me – the pity in their eyes and how it stained my mind.

I didn't deserve it. It was my fault.

I couldn't save him.

Rachel shifted and wrapped an arm around me. Cuddling into me. 'You've done well to come out of your childhood.'

'This is probably the last thing you want to hear from someone you only met a few weeks ago.'

'I'd rather this than something weird, like you're into puppets, or *Love Island.*'

I laughed softly, enjoying the weight of her on me. 'Still, it's probably why I'm still single in my mid-thirties. Lot of baggage.'

'We all have our own.'

'I guess so. I'm regretting going back there, put it that way.'

'I know you didn't have the best relationship with him, but I think it was important that you were there for your father at the end. What happened to him, those men were looking for your mum. They must have thought he knew where she was.'

'No, if it's true, he didn't know for a long time. The way he was, the way he let our relationship break down . . . he wouldn't have done that if he'd believed there was any possibility she could come back.'

'But in that case, what would possess two men to travel all this way?'

'That's what I have to find out, and it seems to me I have two options. I either let the police do their job and find out what happened to my dad. The problem with that option is that I'd be looking over my shoulder for a while. These men, they don't seem the type to wait around to be caught. They'll be looking for me.'

'And what's the other option?'

I felt something akin to excitement. As if I had been waiting for this my whole life.

'I can't sit around waiting. Pretending none of this has happened.'

'And the guy you spoke to in America . . .'

'Tom,' I said, thinking about the way he'd sounded on the phone. 'He wouldn't give me a straight answer. He didn't want me to get involved, but if there's even a minute chance she's still out there, I can't give up on that.'

I sounded sure of myself, I thought. Even if that wasn't what I was feeling.

'You're going to go over there, aren't you?'

'There's no other choice to make. I have to face the past at some point.'

'Face the past?'

I caught her holding back a giggle.

'I'm sorry,' Rachel said, a hand over her mouth. 'I just felt like I was in one of those *Based on a True Story* movies you see on Channel Five for a second.'

I smiled. 'Okay, I'm not the best with my words, I know.'

'No, it's just all a bit crazy. I mean . . . you've got to agree that this isn't usually the type of thing you'd tell a woman you've only seen a few times.'

'Definitely not.'

'Still, I think you need to be careful,' Rachel said, her tone turning more serious in a heartbeat. 'I don't think you should do this, but who am I to say anything? You don't have to listen to me, but you could just wait for the police to investigate and find whoever killed your dad.'

I closed my eyes for a second and I was watching my father die again. Lying in the hospital bed, using his last breaths to tell me my mother was alive. The man I had known all my life, before leaving that village. That place. The man who I had looked up to without knowing why. Even after he shut down and seemed like he didn't want anything to do with me at all.

The grief came over me slowly, but I didn't cry. I almost felt myself turning to stone. I could deal with the emotion more easily that way. It was still there, like a knot in my stomach, but I could compact it, over and over.

I scrunched my eyes tight shut and forced myself to forget about it.

'It comes down to this,' I said, turning on the sofa so I was almost facing away from Rachel. 'Do I believe there's a chance my mum is alive? I was in hospital after the accident, so was my dad. I remember my uncle and grandmother visiting once. Dad was sitting in a brown chair next to the bed and he went outside the room with them. I have a vague memory of him shouting in the corridor, but I'm not sure. Then, I never saw them again.'

I paused for a second. 'I never saw her body. If my dad did, he never said anything. And I wasn't about to ask. I've tried over the years to find the story online, but I've never found anything. So, is it possible?'

There had been a hole inside me for so long, that I didn't recognise what was beginning to fill it.

Hope.

And it wasn't just for me. It was for the family that had been torn away from me. It was for my father. My mother.

My brother.

'What about your mum? Did they find her in the car as well?'

I hesitated and tried hard not to look at her. I shook my head instead.

'I don't know,' I said, because in that moment I knew what I was going to do next. 'I never asked.'

I opened my phone and began searching.

Flights to Connecticut.

Rachel stood up from the sofa and looked out of the window onto the street below. I found a flight that left in a couple of days and booked it before I had a chance to change my mind.

'We should order some food,' Rachel said, turning towards me and leaning against the sill. 'I'm guessing you haven't eaten much.'

'If you have somewhere to be, I don't mind—'

'No,' she said, cutting me off. 'But you shouldn't stay here. Pack your bags and we'll leave tonight. You can stay at mine.'

I hesitated, then caught her eye. 'That's probably a good idea.'

She was by my side for the next two days.

1986

The only time Laurie was alone was when she went back to visit her mom and dad. Even then, two men waited outside in a car.

That's where they were now. She let the drapes fall back, as she stepped back from the window of her childhood bedroom. It was still as she'd left it, a few years earlier – her parents hadn't changed a thing yet. Probably waiting for her to see sense and come home.

She wished it were as easy as that.

She leaned against the sill and closed her eyes. Felt something flutter inside her and a tear roll down her cheek.

'Hey, Sappy.'

Laurie jumped in fright, her heart beating hard in an instant. She turned around and saw Tom standing in the doorway.

'Sorry, I didn't mean to scare you,' he said, stepping into the room and coming over to her. He hesitated for a second and then wrapped her in an embrace.

His body had changed since he'd joined the military. His muscles were more defined, his skin darker, his eyes a little more aged. She remembered how skinny he had been when they were younger. Until junior high, he had been around the same height as her, but then had grown a foot taller overnight, it had seemed. None of the changes had affected his personality though. He was still the same old Tom she'd always known.

She felt safe for a few seconds, then she pulled away suddenly. 'Did anyone see you come in? They're out there watching me. If they saw you, they'll tell him . . .'

'Don't worry,' Tom said, holding her by her shoulders and looking down at her. 'I was here before you arrived. Your mom let me in. She understands.'

'Understands what?'

He let out a long exhale and stared back at her, until she couldn't stand it any more.

'It can't go on like this, Laurie.'

She tore herself away from him and flopped down on the bed. 'It's fine . . .'

'We both know that's not the case,' Tom said, leaning against the wall opposite her. He folded his arms across his chest. 'Your mom was telling me you have to see her at the same time every week. That's all you're allowed? That ain't right.'

'It's not like that.'

'Stop pretending everything is okay. I'm not some stranger you can fool into thinking things are fine. We both know what's happening. Tell me. Everything. I can help you.'

Laurie hesitated and was about to lie to him again. Just like she had for the past five or six years. That everything was fine. That nothing was wrong with the way he was treating her. That she loved Anthony and she was going to be married and they were going to grow old together, happy and rich.

All those things she tried to tell herself late at night, as he slept beside her and she talked herself out of sticking a pair of scissors into his neck.

Instead, she looked up at her oldest friend and realised she couldn't lie to him any more. It wasn't just herself she had to consider now.

'I'm scared, Tom.'

He came over and sat down beside her on the bed. Wrapped an arm around her, as she told him everything.

When she was done, his arm was no longer around her and he was pacing the room.

'I'll kill him.'

Laurie shook her head. 'You can't do that, Tom . . .'

'Are you serious? Of course I can. It'll be nothing. I can do it now. Tell me where he is.'

'Things have changed since we were younger. He isn't some local, James Dean, rebel without a cause now. He's powerful.'

'Ain't nothing more powerful than a bullet in his head.'

'Tom . . .'

'I'm serious, Laurie,' Tom said, coming to a stop in front of her. She could see beads of sweat appearing on his forehead. 'I'd do that for you. You know that. I'd do anything for you.'

She tried to smile, but she knew he meant it more than he should. More than she wanted him to.

'We've always had each other's backs, Sappy,' Tom said, dropping down to his haunches in front of her. He took hold of her hands and lifted her chin to look her in the eyes. 'It doesn't matter what it is, I can fix it. For you. I'll find a way.'

Laurie wanted to believe him, but she knew what she would be doing if she sent him off to take care of Anthony. 'It would be suicide.'

'Remember when you got drunk at a party when we were fifteen and I took the blame when your parents found out? Or that time Chaz Gilmour kept following you home and wouldn't leave you alone? Who took care of him? I didn't care that he was a senior and his dad was a cop – I went and found him and dealt with the situation properly. He never bothered you again, right?'

'No . . . but this is different. This isn't some kid, Tom.'

'He's what, twenty-five, twenty-six?'

'And already one of the most powerful men in the state,' she said, pulling her hands away and moving further up the bed. She drew her knees up to her chest and wrapped her arms around them. 'You should see the type of people who are around him. They're bad news, Tom.'

'We have to get you out of there.'

Laurie sighed. Thought about the only thing that mattered to her – the life growing inside her. 'I haven't seen David for two weeks. I don't know what to do.'

Tom sat at the end of the bed, quiet for a moment or two. Seemingly deciding what to say, what to do. She waited for him to speak. When he turned back to her, she could see the pain in his eyes. The wrench it was to say it.

'I'm going to get you out of this. Both of you. You love him, right?'

Laurie stared back at him and nodded. 'More than anything.'

'Then you should be together,' Tom replied, seeming to struggle to get the words out. She had always known about his feelings for her. A childhood crush, that had never really gone away. She wanted a friend and that was what Tom got. And he never asked for more.

'I said I would take care of you, no matter what. I made a promise when we were kids, remember? And it doesn't matter what that means for me.'

He began to tell her what he was planning and with each passing moment, she started to believe.

CHAPTER 15

Before I left for the US, I went to see my father for the last time.

I went late, hiring a car for the journey, knowing they were probably looking out for mine. I scanned the car park before I got out, looking for anyone watching.

I'd told the police I was coming and they said they'd have someone patrol nearby in case, but I wasn't about to trust that alone. They had no update for me. No one else had seen the two men and I was starting to wonder if they believed my story at all.

The car park was quiet this time of evening, visitors all gone home and fewer staff on duty. It was a short walk, then I was inside, the corridors empty as I made my way down into the basement of the hospital. The funeral directors would be picking up my father the following day. The funeral could be arranged over the phone, I'd been told. And it'd be a couple of weeks at least until I could bury him.

The nurse on duty let me sit with him in a private room. Unlike upstairs, it was cold – intentionally so, I guessed. He was lying on a trolley, his body covered, leaving only his arms and head free.

It was a strange thing to see. I had never been this close to a dead body before and for some reason, I'd expected to still feel something of him there. A presence at least. However, he was so overwhelmingly still that it was obvious he wasn't there any more.

'Remember what Mum used to say,' I said, the room growing colder the longer I sat there. I leaned in closer to my dad. '*That I did always love.* It was some poem she loved. It's one of the few memories I have of her that doesn't hurt. It makes me smile, because it tells me that there is an *always . . .*'

The air felt thicker. A chill of antiseptic, an anti-bacterial smell of hospital cloying at the back of my throat. 'I spoke to Tom,' I continued. 'He wouldn't tell me much, but I'm sure you knew that would be the case. This wasn't a burglary gone wrong, or a stupid drunken assault, although I imagine you've been in a few of them over the years. I think you chose your last words well. You knew what I'd do. I don't know for sure that you didn't know she was alive, but I want to believe you didn't. I only know that by shutting me out, you punished me for what happened. I know you didn't really blame me, but that didn't matter. I was a child. You should have thought about what *I* was going through. What I was feeling. I thought it was my fault. That you held me responsible for what happened. That he would have survived if I had just been able to help him.'

For a second, I imagined I saw a flutter of his eyelids. I held my breath, but nothing came after. No movement, no change.

'It wasn't an accident, what happened to us. I'm not going to rest until I find out who is trying to find her. Why you had to die. And it's not for me. Not for you. Not for her. But, for Michael—'

Saying my brother's name out loud caught in the back of my throat. I swallowed back something. A cry, or worse. I shook my head, trying to get rid of the feeling, but it wouldn't go.

'He died and we lived. Only, it wasn't really living, it was *surviving.* I ran away as soon as I could and left you behind. Everything that we had gone through, I ran away from it all. I'm tired of running. I'm not going to hide away from that part of me any more. Michael's memory deserves more than . . .'

I thought of him, the last time I saw his face. The look of horror on it. His eyes locking with mine.

The pain it caused me to remember, still as raw now as it always had been. All these years later. The memory was easy to recall. It was always there. I carried that image with me, wherever I went.

'Michael died and you made it my fault. I'll never forget that. You have no idea what you've done to me. Well, no more. Finally, I'm going to do something about it. It has to end.'

I took hold of his hand and squeezed it softly. It was cold to the touch. 'I'm going over there. I need to know why this has happened to you, now, after all these years. Why people are looking for her. And if Tom won't tell me over the phone, let me see if he can do the same face to face.'

I held onto his hand until the skin under my fingertips turned white.

There was nothing.

'It comes down to this, Dad. I hope she's alive. Only, if she is, where has she been? Why has she never come back? And why would she let me believe she was gone forever?'

I stood up and let go of my father's hand. I looked down at the man on the bed, wondering when he became a stranger. I gripped the side of the trolley and stood over him.

'I loved you, Dad. But I hated you as well. I didn't realise that was possible.'

Then, I was gone. Leaving him behind again. And as I walked out of the hospital, I felt like I was finally free.

I wasn't running away any more.

I was running *towards* something.

Jackson watched Sam Cooper cross back onto the sidewalk outside the hospital and disappear into his car. He had been tracking him for over a day now and was beginning to find it difficult not to announce his presence.

He was under strict instructions, but sometimes it was hard to see the reasons behind it.

Jackson pulled away from the curb and followed Sam's car at a distance.

He thought of the two other Americans that had been in town. While Jackson knew of their presence, he was pretty sure they didn't know of his.

When he'd asked about the two men, he hadn't received a satisfactory answer. That put him on edge. He'd always been taught that having a complete picture, all the information it was possible to have, was important.

Now, he was being asked to fly blind.

Sam Cooper was driving back to London, it became clear a few minutes later. He had been watching him since he'd gone back to London. Followed him to what he assumed was Sam's girlfriend's place and parked close by. He had walked past every few hours, catching sporadic moments of broken sleep.

He'd been trained for this type of surveillance.

The situation didn't sit well with him. These trips back and forth between London and Firwood. As if Sam Cooper was planning to do something.

All Jackson could do was wait, and watch.

And then take action if it was needed.

Or he was told to end it.

CHAPTER 16

A couple of days later, I was landing on US soil.

It was gone midday at Boston Logan International when the plane landed. I took my place in the line at passport control. I was tired from the journey – seven and a half hours, stuck in a seat that supposedly had thirty-one inches of legroom, but felt like six after a couple of hours. It was almost six p.m. at home, but here it was just past noon and a cold winter sun was shining above me.

I managed to make it through the border check and braced myself for the hustle and bustle of a major airport. Imagined it would be like everything else I envisaged about the US – bigger, brighter, busier. Heathrow on speed.

It wasn't that bad, but I still pulled my backpack across my shoulder. There were people moving constantly, it seemed. A river of faces. Everything seemed designed to be imposing. Glass fronts separated the inside from the bus stops outside. The sickly smell of the sugar-coated donuts from the Dunkin' Donuts stand a few yards away overwhelmed my senses. It was quickly replaced by that of coffee from the Starbucks opposite. I queued up, asked for a large, and received a cup bigger than my head. It was a much-needed caffeine hit. As I made my way outside, I passed a relieved smoker, who couldn't look more English if he'd tried. He sucked hungrily on his cigarette, looking upwards as he blew out a large plume of smoke.

The cold air slammed into me and I tried to pull my jacket tighter around myself. I shoved my free hand in my pocket and followed the signs for the bus that would take me to the train station.

I stared out the window as we made our way into the city. The buildings were silver monstrosities reaching towards the sky above. I leaned forwards to see the tops of them, the amount of traffic on the roads affording me ample opportunity to take everything in.

The closer we got to the station, the buildings began to change a little. Red-brick architecture, that looked like old cities in the south of England. My heart beat hard, as the bus came to a stop opposite the train station. I crossed over the road and spied four men, who I assumed were police officers, but could have simply been security. Guns strapped to their belts, standing around and laughing. I looked away before they could see me staring.

I wasn't on a stag weekend, or a city break in Europe. I was in Boston, USA, and everything seemed designed to remind me that it was the biggest trip I'd ever taken alone.

I could hear various accents flying around from the people walking past. The Boston accent I'd only heard from *Good Will Hunting*. Matt Damons and Ben Afflecks pushed past me, hollering to each other. Pronouncing the 'r' in the word 'car' in a way that no one had ever intended. I stared around in wonder for a few seconds, thinking about their lives. How different they seemed, but also so familiar.

I made my way into the station and found my platform. The smell of diesel scratched at the back of my throat – a design flaw, I felt, as the trains shuffled into the station, and the fumes had no place to escape. I couldn't help but stare wide-eyed at the trains passing by on each platform.

Double-decker trains, the size of buildings, thundering past me. The Amtrak arrived and I settled into my seat. I wondered if I was the only tourist there, given everyone else seemed so relaxed. Commuter-like. Then again, I was hardly a tourist.

I was there for a very different reason.

I stuck my earphones in and selected a random playlist. Music thumped in my ears, as I tried to keep my eyes open. Tiredness threatening to overwhelm me.

It was a long seventy-minute journey.

I pulled out my phone as we reached Rhode Island. Watched myself move across the map, through Providence and past Cranston. Down through the small state and along a winding track that seemed endless.

The sky outside dimmed and clouded over. The scenery kept changing, from deep countryside to wide open sea views in a few seconds. The train rocked and swung from side to side, speeding through the eastern seaboard.

I tensed as I saw my stop coming up. I stood up and made my way to the doors. It was almost five p.m. now and even at this early time of year, it was still bright outside.

On the platform, the smell of the sea hit me instantly – fish and salt that reminded me of seaside towns of my childhood. I shifted the weight of the bag on my shoulder and glanced around to see who else was leaving the train. A couple of people, hurrying away towards wherever they were going. I waited a few moments and the doors closed behind me, the conductor jumping on ahead of me and pulling the door shut.

I pulled my phone out, calculating the route to the motel I'd booked the day before. It was at least a thirty-minute walk, so I ordered an Uber.

I gazed out the window as we travelled to the motel. This was the suburbia I'd read about in books. Watched in unfunny sitcoms. No terraced houses – it seemed you never shared a wall with a neighbour in this town. Most of the houses were painted white, punctuated by the odd light blue. Yet, even with the green patches of land and white picket fences, I could feel something pulling at my sense of fear. As if this was a town I knew already.

There was a familiarity in the scenery, in the buildings, in the quiet.

We reached the motel and I thanked the driver, who gave me a salute then pulled away. It looked almost like a church hall – a wedding chapel at the front, masking the row of rooms behind. There was a large wooden rocking chair to the left of the entrance, the name of the motel emblazoned on its back. A thing for tourists to place children on for photos they would share on social media, I imagined. I couldn't work out how you'd climb on the thing.

I pushed through the door and entered a small lobby with a high desk. A few older men and women were sitting across from it, looking over brochures. A woman appeared from the back, with a high-wattage smile and almost hidden lines stretching from her eyes. She could have been anything between twenty and forty years old.

'Welcome to Howard Johnson, my name is Andrea. How may I help you this evening?'

I smiled back, releasing my bag to the floor and leaning against the desk with one hand. 'I have a booking. Sam Cooper.'

'Excellent, sir, let me find your room for you.'

The lobby looked okay, if a little dated. Patterns on the carpet that would have been gaudy forty years earlier. A vase with plastic flowers, arranged with some care. The desk itself was a barrier, cut into the lobby area with no access behind it, unless you came in another way. A coffee machine and empty snack plate on another table.

'Here we are, sir. You have four nights in a double room.'

I nodded and listened politely as she explained how it all

worked, as if I'd never stayed in a hotel before. She spoke smoothly, barely pausing for breath. A well-rehearsed spiel.

'You're from England, right?'

'That easy to guess?' I said, picking my bag up with a smile. 'Yeah, just flew into Boston and got the Amtrak down.'

'We don't get many Brits this way at this time of year,' she continued, tilting her head and considering me anew. 'Usually they head for New York or Boston. Not much for a tourist in small towns like this one. There's rumours that they're thinking of having the Amtrak miss this stop out – but there's always talk around here. You here on business or vacation?'

'A little of both,' I said, trying to keep my voice level. 'I may need to stay an extra couple of nights, if that's possible?'

'Shouldn't be a problem. We're not in our busy season at the moment. Just come down and let one of us know, so we don't rent out the room on you. You hungry? There's a diner right next door, open 'til late. There's the steakhouse opposite. Or the McDonald's on the other side. Lot of options . . .'

I said thanks as she handed over a key card and directed me to my room and gave me a polite 'good evening' on the way. I hesitated about tipping her, but then decided against it and gave her a 'have a nice evening' in response.

The room was much as I'd been expecting it to be – matching the glossy photographs I'd seen on the website before arriving. The flowery bedspread and curtains that almost matched. There was a balcony, but I couldn't get the sliding door to open, so I left it closed. I looked out onto the street outside and saw a car pull away slowly from the curb.

Across the way was another motel, then a busy road separating the two from a petrol station and another Dunkin' Donuts. I couldn't see the places the helpful receptionist had mentioned.

The sky was dimming finally, as evening came closer.

I drew the curtains closed and opened my bag. Found my

phone charger and travel adaptor. Plugged it into the socket by the bedside table and felt calmer almost instantly.

The bed was hard, but not enough to worry about not getting any sleep. I pulled back the covers and checked the sheets and didn't see any worrying marks. The room smelled of lavender and disinfectant.

I found the TV remote and turned it on. Began flicking through channels, as I waited for my phone to charge up a little. It seemed as if there were adverts running each time I clicked. Mostly health related. A few debt relief ones. I found a news channel and left it on, recognising Anderson Cooper from when I'd become a little obsessed with American politics a few years earlier. Once 2016 had happened, I'd quickly got over that particular interest.

It didn't look like much had changed. Above me the ceiling was slicked in white paint and I stared at the swirls of pattern there. Tried to work out what the hell I was doing.

She couldn't be alive.

She just couldn't be.

Yet, I had come all that way to find out for certain. I messaged Rachel to let her know I'd arrived safely. She responded instantly and I realised I missed her already.

Then I searched my recent calls for the number I had found on my father's phone, and dialled.

When the plane landed in Boston, Jackson was on his feet within seconds.

He followed Sam until he went inside the train station. He knew he was travelling towards Mystic by now.

He had a car parked over on Dartmouth Street. He walked the short distance to the parking lot.

The city was bustling with movement and verve. The sun was shining, but the cold was still lurking behind it. By the time he made it back inside the parking garage, he was thinking about the heater in his car. He had picked up a soda on the way, enjoying the hit of the sugar. He hadn't been able to get anything like it over in England. The syrup was a shock to the system, after days of cheap knock-offs. Same name, hugely different taste.

He pulled out his cell.

'I'm back.'

'Sam?'

'He's on his way to Mystic. He'll be on the next Amtrak. What do you want me to do?'

There was a sigh on the other end of the line. 'I can't believe he's come over.'

Jackson waited, knowing his instruction would come sooner rather than later.

'Keep following him.'

'I'll catch him when the Amtrak arrives,' Jackson said, looking over the piece of notepaper where he'd scrawled the address of the station. 'It'll take me less than a couple of hours to get there. I'll be there to meet him . . .'

'Okay, but don't let him see you. I still need time to work out what to do about him.'

The call was ended, leaving Jackson sitting in the car. He controlled his breathing, as he felt the anger return. He turned the engine over and backed out of his space. Swore a few times, as the traffic in the city backed him up. Cars, bumper to bumper.

It didn't matter if he was being used to clean up a mess he hadn't made. It was for good reason.

Before too long, he was on the I-93 heading west.

He had been sitting only a few rows away from Sam on the plane. Seven hours, spent wondering what he would do if he'd been made.

He needn't have worried.

Sam had no idea he'd been followed for days.

At Mystic, he waited at the station and saw Sam get off the train. His hands tensed against the wheel. There was no doubt in his mind – waiting wasn't the right call here. It would have been better to get the job done now, before anything else went wrong.

Still, that wasn't what he'd been asked to do. So, he followed the Uber to a motel further into town and then stopped in the parking lot.

He'd wait until he was told.

The good thing was that the Glock he'd missed so much over in the UK was now sitting flush against his body.

CHAPTER 17

Anthony looked down at his cell phone as it vibrated in his hand, as Zoran drove them back home from the office.

TM – Flew in from Idaho – Four days. SC – Landed a few hours ago in Boston.

'Tom Miller,' Anthony said, staring at the back of Zoran's head through the privacy gap. 'He's here. Came in from Idaho four days ago, so I guess he knows about Parker Rogers. And not a single person I employ knew he was around. That bothers me.'

There was no reaction from Zoran. Not even a slight nod of the head.

'When is Carson arriving?'

Anthony thought he saw some sort of reaction from Zoran, but it was so slight it was probably nothing.

'Soon.'

'That's good,' Anthony replied, nodding to himself. 'I want to see him as soon as he gets back.'

Again, Zoran responded with silence. Anthony guessed he wasn't paying for the conversational skills.

Finally, they came to a stop outside the house and Anthony waited for Zoran to open the door for him. He stepped out and pulled his overcoat tighter as the wind whipped around him. The iciness in the New England air could still surprise him.

The door opened as he reached it and he went inside. His

coat was removed and a glass placed in his hand. Some sort of wheatgrass concoction that some quack had told him was good for his bones or skin. He drank it quickly once he reached the office. Poured himself a whisky once it was done, just so he could chase the good away with the bad.

He was resting his eyes when Zoran knocked softly on the door.

'They are here,' Zoran said, as he came inside. 'Waiting down the stairs.'

Anthony motioned for him to let them come up. Sat up straight and ran a hand over his hair.

Carson and Hunter entered the office and stood awkwardly at the door. Anthony looked them over and then shook his head. 'You guys look like hell.'

'So would you after the week we've had,' Carson replied, a smirk on his face as he gestured towards one of the chairs before sitting down. 'It hasn't been the easiest of jobs you've sent us on.'

'It's not over yet.'

Carson raised an eyebrow. 'It'd help if you could maybe see your way into letting us know the whole story. We weren't prepared for the son to be around.'

Anthony stared back at him until he finally broke off and looked away. 'What did you learn about him?'

'Who?' Hunter replied, hovering next to Carson. 'The guy we killed?'

Anthony waited until Carson looked back at him and then shook his head.

'Go check the car over,' Carson said, dismissing Hunter with a wave of his hand. 'See if you can get the heat working properly.'

'But it seemed fine to me . . .' Hunter began to say, but then seemed to catch the meaning behind Carson's words and walked out of the room. Shoulders slumping as he did.

Carson turned back to Anthony and held his hands up. 'He's young. Still got a bit to learn, but he did a good job over there, I've got to say. Does what he's told.'

Anthony leaned forwards and locked his hands together. 'Sam Cooper.'

Carson nodded, the smile falling away and back to serious. 'Yeah, about that . . .'

'He's here,' Anthony said, seeing an almost imperceptible flinch in Carson's otherwise stoic features. 'Landed a few hours before you did. You missed him.'

'Listen, we tried to work that out, but we couldn't find him after that day—'

This time, as Anthony slammed his open palm against the desk and the report echoed around them, Carson couldn't hide the flinch. His body jerked a little, before he caught himself.

'We had him contained over there,' Anthony said, his teeth grinding together as he tried to control his voice and failed. 'Do you think he was lying to you? What about the other son?'

Carson shook his head. 'He's dead. That's for damn sure. It was just the two of them – David and Sam. He had no idea she was alive. Of that I'm sure.'

'Still, you two managed to let this schlub get on a plane and make his way over here. Sam Cooper is now a problem, you understand? He's spent twenty-five years thinking his mother was dead and now all these questions are going to be running through his mind. And someone asking questions is bad for us. That make sense to you?'

'How do you—'

Anthony didn't let him finish. 'Now, he's holed up somewhere, looking for those answers. How long before he comes knocking on my door? Maybe he talks to the cops, maybe they want to ask some questions as well. This is a problem.'

Carson straightened up, his face becoming blank. 'We'll take care of him. Do you know where he's staying? I can have it done in no time at all.'

'Not yet. In the meantime, there's another problem I need you to handle.'

'Who?'

Anthony felt his heart rate decrease, but the anger still bubbled away inside. 'Tom Miller. You remember him?'

Carson's jaw tensed. 'How could I forget?'

'Yeah, well, it seems he's resurfaced. He's already been to Idaho. Obviously he knows we tracked Parker down. Now, he's come back here.'

'Do we know where he's been? That might give us a clue as to her whereabouts.'

Anthony shook his head. 'If I knew that, we would be having a very different conversation. What matters is that he's here now. I guess he's come to me, which can only mean one of two things. Either he wants to stop me looking, or he doesn't know where she is. Whatever it is, we can use him to draw her out.'

'Will you let me kill him this time?'

'I think you've waited long enough,' Anthony said, a knowing smirk on his face. 'If he had stuck around back in '95, you wouldn't have had to wait this long, I promise.'

'You really think she's still alive?'

'I'm counting on it,' Anthony replied, then waved Carson from his office. He leaned back in his chair, swivelling it round so he could stare out towards the woodland that surrounded the property. Imagined her out there, in the shadows, watching him right back.

Imagined being close to her again.

He smiled at the thought.

★　★　★

Tom Miller was sitting in the rental car, his eyes stinging from tiredness, as he waited for Anthony to return home.

'It's spooky out here.'

Tom grunted a response towards Quinn in the passenger seat. He was concentrating, waiting for the car to arrive. He couldn't disagree with her though. The road was narrow, winding its way through the thick forestland and open spaces of that part of the state. If you looked closely, you could see the mansions hiding from view, all with acres and acres of land surrounding them.

'I guess that's Greenwich for you,' Quinn said, shifting in her seat. 'Not had cause to be around here all that much. Bit too rich for my taste.'

'Well, we're not here to admire the scenery.'

They were parked off the road, nestled into a dirt track that gave them cover from passing vehicles, but also the ability to see anything approaching the entrance to the house.

The house wasn't visible from the road, hidden behind wrought-iron gates and high walls. Anthony had built his fortress bigger in the years since Tom had been there last.

If you didn't know what to look for, you could drive past the place without ever knowing it existed.

'How much do you think a place like his costs?'

'More than we'll ever know,' Tom replied, seeing headlights in the distance. 'This could be him.'

'Good, we've been here for hours.'

Quinn went silent as the lights came closer, until they were only yards away. They had parked up out of sight, but what they were doing was still dangerous.

Tom had decided it was the only way. To be sure, if nothing else.

He remembered being there a long time before. On a vastly different night.

The black limousine got closer and then turned into the drive that led up to Anthony Sullivan's house. Paused at the gates that guarded the compound, before they opened up and it disappeared.

'He'll be in the back,' Quinn said, turning to Tom. 'Although, it's not like we'd see much through those windows.'

Tom opened his mouth to answer, but was stopped by the ringing of his cell phone. He paused, looked down at the number calling, and felt his heart sink.

He lifted it up and answered.

'Hello, Sam.'

1986

L aurie was comfortable with the idea of being on the run.
It seemed like her whole life had been the opposite.
Always doing something someone else wanted her to do. This
way, she was taking control at last. Making her own choices, her
own decisions.

She had been looking for an escape for a long time. When she
was younger, it had been from home, from school, from the
drudgery of normal life.

That was how she had ended up with Anthony in the first
place.

Now, it was him she needed to escape.

Tom was waiting for her at her parents' house.

'It's time,' he said, and she could see the wrench in his
expression. The battle he was having. 'You can't take anything
with you that won't fit in a rucksack. It's got to be quick and it
has to be now.'

'I don't—'

'Laurie,' he said, the bark of his voice snapping her into silence.
'You want to leave, then you have to do exactly as I say. I've got
two tickets booked from JFK to London. It leaves later today.
Anthony isn't around, right? So we have a few hours.'

'What about my mom and dad? I can't leave without saying
goodbye.'

'Mom, Dad?'

'I sent them away.'

'You'll call them when you land,' Tom said, shaking his head. 'They don't need to see you like this. If you stop now, you'll run out of time. And do you think it'll be easy to leave after seeing them again? Trust me, this is the best way.'

'I can't . . . Anthony's men are right outside.'

'Don't worry about them,' Tom said, resting his hands on her shoulders. 'I'll take care of that.'

Laurie could feel her heart racing, beads of sweat breaking out on her head, as she thought about what she was about to do.

'David?'

Tom grimaced, but straightened his face in an instant. 'He's going to meet you in a car. He'll drive you both to Bronx Zoo, where you'll swap that car for a cab. I've gone through all of this with him.'

'He'll find out,' Laurie said, her voice shaking, tears springing to her eyes. 'How can we do this?'

Tom pulled her close. 'This is going to work. I promise.'

'What are you going to do to them outside?'

He didn't answer. Just held her close and then pulled her away. 'Out the back. Now. Hop the fence and sprint towards the parking lot of the church on East Street. He'll be waiting for you.'

Laurie tried to talk, but no words would come. Part of her wanted to do nothing. To carry on as she had been.

A stronger part of her knew this was her chance.

'They never watch the back,' Tom said, peering over her shoulder, down onto the street below. Two men were sitting in the front seats of the car. Father and son.

Her watchers.

'Don't look back. Just keep running.'

Laurie turned to leave, then came back around and pulled Tom to her. 'Thank you.'

'I told you, I'd take care of you. Now go.'

She didn't look back. She was out the back, over the fence, and running towards the church before her mind caught up to her body.

She didn't stop. She didn't turn around.

Even when she heard a gunshot in the distance.

David had been waiting for her. Just as Tom had promised.

She wanted to call Tom so badly. To make sure he was okay. Only there was no time.

They passed a movie theater, *The Color Purple* emblazoned on the outside. David had talked about taking her after the holidays, but instead they were in a cab to the airport.

The cab slowed as traffic built up on the busy streets. People crowded on the sidewalk, outside an electronics store, watching televisions.

'Space shuttle blew up,' the cab driver said, almost to himself. 'That teacher won't be coming home.'

Laurie caressed her stomach and reminded herself why she was doing this.

Beside her, a hand moved across and joined her own. She glanced towards him and smiled.

'It's going to be okay,' David said, and for a brief moment she believed him. 'He won't find us.'

Laurie tore her gaze away from his and looked over her shoulder. Imagined a car – dark, monstrous – crawling through the traffic behind them. Shadowing them, as they escaped.

David seemed to sense her thoughts and held on tighter to her hand.

She forced herself to look forwards again, concentrating on the road ahead. What she was going towards, rather than what lay behind her.

A new beginning.

The cab finally weaved its way out of the traffic and onto the open roads. The signs at the side of the road changed and JFK airport appeared as an oasis of freedom on the horizon – Idlewild, as her mom still called it.

Laurie felt a growing lump at the back of her throat as she thought about her mom. Her dad. The family she might never see again. Of not being able to visit whenever she wanted to, eat dinner, talk and laugh. Tell stories.

They couldn't be grandparents from thousands of miles away.

'We're here.'

She wiped away the tears that had crawled down her cheek. As David made his way towards the terminal, she followed him close, checking her surroundings over her shoulder.

'It's okay,' David said, placing an arm around her. 'We're already miles away from Connecticut. He doesn't know we're here.'

She smiled back at him shakily. 'I'll feel better when there's an ocean between us. He won't stop trying to find me.'

'We have a new life to look forward to now. You'll like England, I promise. It's all going to be okay.'

'What if I never see them again?'

David held her. 'You will. We just need to give it some time. I'm sure once you're out of his life, he'll move on. He'll realise that you don't belong to him.'

She was almost there.

Almost free.

Only, she knew this wasn't the end.

It wasn't even a beginning. There was a crushing sense of inevitability. Of certainty. That it didn't matter how much or how far she ran. She could put thousands of miles between herself and the danger, but it would always find her. As it always had. She could run for the rest of her life, but it would always be at her shoulder.

No matter what she did, there was no way out.

No hope.

No future. Laurie breathed in the recycled airport air and made a decision.

She was going to try.

CHAPTER 18

I didn't know what to say for a second. The news played on in the background, so I muted the television. 'Hello, Tom.'

'You're here,' Tom replied, not a question. I guessed he could tell from the number of my mobile phone. 'I told you to stay where you were.'

'Yeah, well, forgive me for not listening to a stranger.'

'You should have. It's too dangerous here.'

'I want to know the truth.'

'Sam . . .'

'I know you've been lying to me. I'm going to find out for myself.'

'Where are you now?'

'I don't think you need to know that. Listen, if you feel like talking to me and explaining yourself, call me. If not, then just be prepared. I'm not going anywhere.'

I woke early around six a.m. and felt as if I was emerging from a nightmare. One that involved a river. The water dragging me down. Stippled sunlight crept through the thin curtains, casting a muted glow across the room. The TV was still on from the night before – morning headlines on CNN. I pulled the curtains back from the balcony window and looked out onto the car park outside. There were a few cars on the road that led to it, but it was still quiet. The place looked more downtrodden in the morning light. A little dirtier, a little murkier.

Refreshed and re-energised somewhat after I took a shower, I grabbed my phone and wallet, stuffed them in pockets of clean jeans, and headed out.

Outside, the air wasn't as thick with the smell from the sea. Still a little salt in the air, if you went looking for it.

I checked my watch – seven a.m. I made my way towards the diner next door – the place had been open an hour already. From the outside, it looked every inch what I'd been expecting – peak Americana. White building, festooned with red and blue stripes.

To match the flag, I guessed.

Large windows, allowing a peek inside. A large sign on the building's brim proclaiming *Breakfast Served All Day*.

I pushed my way inside and was greeted by a cheerful waitress, who showed me over to a booth by a window. The place was cavernous inside – it could easily sit a couple of hundred people or more. At that time of the morning though, there was barely a dozen of us. A couple of young families, but mostly older people sitting alone.

The menu – or menus, as it turned out – was as thick as a Stephen King novel. Page upon page. The woman who had plonked it down in front of me continued to smile and told me someone would be over in just a short minute.

I was four thousand miles from home, in a place I couldn't point to on a map. A country where guns were legal, and anyone could be carrying one.

I turned around, expecting someone to walk in with an AR-15 slung across their shoulder. Instead, another waitress came over, just as I was about to stand up and find the next train out of there.

'Coffee?'

'Erm, yeah, thanks,' I replied, a mug appearing in front of me. She filled it almost to the brim, and as I opened my mouth to ask for milk, a basket filled with tiny plastic pots, along with various jams and syrups was placed down next to it.

'You ready to order food, hun?'

'Can I just have another minute?' I said, pointing to the menu with a smile. 'Haven't had a chance to go through it yet.'

'Of course, I'll be right over there.'

The menu seemed to cover every meal possible. I caught the eye of the waitress and she came back over. 'Bacon and eggs on toast, please.'

'How do you want your eggs?'

I wanted to say 'cooked', but she was already running through what felt like far too many options. I settled on over easy and stirred some sugar into my coffee.

There were a dozen or so televisions mounted to walls around the place, all playing the morning news from the local Fox station. Subtitles ran along the screen, as a variety of the whitest people I'd ever seen talked soundlessly. All incredibly animated and frenetic about something or other. There was a myriad of information bouncing around their heads, running news tickers, latest weather reports, sports scores – I was surprised anyone could stare at it for more than a few seconds without getting a headache.

The food arrived quicker than I was expecting. Strips of rock-hard crisped bacon and runny eggs. I tried a bite of the bacon and crunched through the mouthful. I wondered at what point Americans had decided that this was a better way of cooking bacon and couldn't come up with an answer. Still, it was the first proper meal I'd had since the day before, so I wolfed it down.

Once I'd finished, I pulled my phone out and googled a local car hire and found a place near the train station.

I left what was either a hefty tip or an insult on the table and grabbed my jacket. Zipped it up tight and braved the cold again.

The food and coffee settled well in my stomach. I'd eyed someone eating pancakes as I was leaving and thought about sitting back down. I shook the thought away easily – I needed to keep moving.

The first place to go was easy. The only choice.

From the motel, it was only a fifteen-minute walk. A blue metal sign welcoming me to Historic Mystic was the first marker. I passed a large cemetery on my right, on the long road towards the centre of town. Traffic was building – the highway was the end point. The river was hidden behind the tree line past the cemetery, making it easy to ignore.

It was almost peaceful, save the various cars and trucks passing on the road. Almost all of them much larger than cars back home. The pavement was narrow and I didn't pass a single other person making the same journey on foot. I waited for a break in the traffic and then crossed over. Passed a museum that had a large anchor outside.

I had my phone barking instructions in my ears as I walked. *Turn left. Turn right. Your destination is on your left.*

As the main road faded behind me, I was amongst the houses that were near the centre of town.

There was a church and a CVS pharmacy at the bottom of the road. A quiet street, not quite the abundance of homes, but a white picket fence still bordered the property. It had a homely, if slightly run-down, feel to it. It was tall, A-framed, and not like I remembered in the slightest.

The part of the river we had crashed into was only a few minutes away. I shook the thought from my mind and concentrated on the task ahead.

The last known address of the family of Laurie Cooper. Or Laurie Rogers, as she had once been.

I'd been here before. Once. When I was nine years old. My memory of it was a little faded, given what happened only a day or two after we arrived. I remembered Mum explaining how my grandparents had ended up here.

'*They moved down here after I left with your dad. They always wanted to be closer to the water.*'

Just being here was enough to unlock more memories. My mum excitedly talking about her home state. The place she had grown up, a fair distance from Mystic. I tried to remember the name, but couldn't quite grasp hold of it. Midtown, or something similar.

After the accident, we hadn't stayed long.

There were steps that led up to the porch and I made my way up them slowly. Took a deep breath and rapped on the door. I turned back to the street, saw a black Subaru parked up on the grass verge, and thought I saw someone in the driving seat for a second. When I blinked, it was empty.

The inside door opened and a woman in her forties looked back at me.

For a moment in time, I saw my mother.

Tall, dark blonde hair. Bronze skin, as if she had just stepped off a cruise ship in the Mediterranean. All striped sweaters and sandals.

'Yes?'

And, then she was gone. Again. I could see instantly that it wasn't her. That she was too young, and also didn't look anything like her now I was looking more clearly.

I cleared my throat and attempted a smile. 'I'm sorry to bother you, but I'm looking for a relative of mine.'

She narrowed her eyes, suspicion taking over as soon as she heard my accent. It didn't matter that we shared a language, I could already hear the thought in her mind: I wasn't from round there.

'Oh yeah?'

'Yes, my grandmother lived here, a while ago now. I was hoping she'd still be here.'

'How long ago are we talking?'

I shook my head. 'Sorry, it would be mid-nineties. The Rogers?'

There was a look of recognition that flashed across her face for a second, then she corrected herself. 'I'm not sure I should be giving that kind of information out to a stranger.'

'Just tell me, is there anyone here of that name?'

She shook her head. 'We bought the place over twenty years ago now. That name is familiar though.'

I nodded, knowing that had always been the most likely outcome. 'So, you have no idea where they are now?'

'I'm sorry.'

I stepped forwards as she began to close the door, held my hands up in mock surrender. 'Please, if you know anything, I'd really appreciate it.'

She paused, looking me over once again, then seemed to make a decision. 'Look, all I know is that whoever we were buying from wanted to get out quick. They didn't leave a forwarding address and it was a cash sale. A steal.'

'Has anyone else come looking for them in the past?'

She thought about it. 'Now you mention it, a long time ago, just after we moved in, a couple of men showed up. They were looking for someone. They wouldn't leave until we showed them ID. They said they were police, but after they were gone, both me and my husband didn't remember them showing us a badge.'

'Did they say who they were looking for? A name?'

She shook her head. 'I don't remember . . .'

'Please,' I said, stepping closer. She moved backwards instinctively. 'Anything you can tell me is helpful.'

'Laurie,' she said. 'That's who they were looking for.'

CHAPTER 19

Jackson's neck was stiff from sitting at the wheel of his car most of the night. He'd slept on the plane for a few hours, but he was starting to feel it now. A few minutes here and there overnight hadn't helped matters.

His cell phone was ringing on the dashboard. He wiped his mouth, snatching it up and answering.

'Any movement?'

'It's early.'

He spoke and felt calm. Instantly. Locked his feelings away in their box again.

'Did I wake you?'

'No, I mean, he'll be getting over his flight or something. Probably slept the whole night through. Don't worry, I'll catch him as he leaves.'

'Follow him, but don't do anything yet. I want to see where he goes. And make sure you keep your eyes on him.'

'I will . . .'

'I mean it. I don't want any more screw-ups, you hear me? He should never have got on that plane in the first place. You have to deal with him, okay?'

Jackson gritted his teeth, but murmured an okay, and then ended the call, dropping the cell in the passenger seat. He wanted a drink. Something that would take the edge off.

He knew it wouldn't help.

There was only one thing that would help him.

And it wouldn't be too long until he got the chance.

He saw Sam Cooper exit the motel a half hour later. Followed him into the diner and sat at the counter drinking coffee, keeping an eye on him. When he left, he took a few seconds, dropped a few bills down, and followed him outside.

He expected him to go back to the motel, but instead he walked out onto the main street. Jackson followed in his car, circling the streets here and there, trying to keep himself out of Sam's line of vision.

Eventually, Sam knocked on a house and spoke to someone inside. Jackson couldn't get close enough to hear what was being said. He got out of the car and did a walk by, but it didn't help.

Sam walked away and Jackson was already behind the wheel. His cell phone buzzed on the seat next to him and he reached for it, still keeping his eyes on Sam.

'He's knocked on a house. Here's the address.'

Jackson waited for an answer.

'He's looking for her.'

'Right. What do you want me to do?'

There was silence for a few seconds, then finally an answer.

'It's time.'

Jackson breathed in slowly and nodded to himself. 'Understood.'

He pocketed his phone and checked the Glock.

Waited for his opportunity.

CHAPTER 20

I had another Uber drop me off at an Enterprise Rent-A-Car place. After rejecting the chance to upgrade a variety of different things – offsetting my gas emissions, a GPS for the dash, and Sirius XM, whatever that was – I walked out with the keys to a Volkswagen Jetta – a model I'd never heard of before then. It sounded exotic, but was just a standard sedan. No bells and whistles, but it would do the job. The fact it was an automatic took a little getting used to. I had never driven abroad before, so driving on the wrong side of the road took a little more effort.

After speaking to the woman who had bought my grandparents' home, there was only one other place I could think to go. Thanks to a little more googling, I found the place I needed to be.

My mother's hometown. Where her father had been buried.

Middletown was an hour's drive north from Mystic. A small town, on the banks of the Connecticut River that dissected the state, flowing to the Atlantic. I was beginning to get used to the immensity of the country, but everywhere I looked was a reminder of it. The motorways – highways – were wider, larger, longer. The sheer amount of traffic never seemed to ease. It was all a welcome distraction to where I was heading.

Ten minutes before I reached my destination, the traffic intensified. It seemed as if everyone was driving tanks – no minis, smart cars; it was an SUV and pick-up truck city. A sign ahead announced we were half a mile from Middletown and on my right the river came into view.

Another town on another river. White buildings, encroaching onto countryside that looked cold and uninviting. I passed by the centre of town and was in the fields again. The road thinned and became one lane. Finally I slowed down.

At the edge of the town, tucked away on a small road, seemingly in the middle of nowhere. On the grass verge a small sign: black letters stark against the white background, two potted plants, lovingly tended to, lying at its feet.

Green Grove Cemetery – Est 1884

Short, faded stone pillars that looked like they were original features stood at an unremarkable, understated entrance.

I parked up and got out of the car. Closed the door and it echoed into the silence. Only one other car was parked near mine.

My legs felt like they belonged to someone else. A flutter of anxiety in my chest, closing my throat.

The sound of passing cars on the road behind me quietened the further I walked. The peace and serenity seeming to place the cemetery in a sort of stasis, creating a bubble far away from normal life.

I passed a couple holding hands, heads bowed. Fresh grief, I thought. It was written plainly on their faces.

Mine wasn't all that fresh, but still, when I found what I was looking for ten minutes later, it hit just as hard.

There was a break in the headstones. The grey blocks of stone, proudly displaying long-forgotten names and dates, gave way to a short path and then, a sea of smaller plots.

I kept walking, studying each in turn. I stopped as I reached an almost bleached-white piece of granite or marble. Stared at the words etched into it, reading them over and over, as if I could change what it said.

Rogers
John – 1930–1995
Born and Died a Middletown Son.
Missed by wife Eleanor and children Parker and Laurie

Next to it was another headstone. Another grave.

In Loving Memory of
Laurie – 1964–1995
Reunited eternally, missed forever
Michael
David
Sam

I stepped forwards onto the manicured lawn and reached out to the gravestone. It was cold, smooth to the touch. I traced a finger across the letters of my mother's name. My brother's. My own.

I staggered back on the path, almost losing my footing, and struggled to keep my legs underneath me, before I finally dropped to my knees. I swiped a hand across my brow and it came back slick with sweat. I looked at the words again and they screamed back at me.

It was as if the world stopped. All I could hear was the slow beat of my heart. The words blurred on the stone and I heard a sound escape from my throat.

I had believed there was still hope.

Seeing it in black and white for the first time made it real again. Seeing my name on a gravestone wasn't something I wanted to dwell on too long.

Michael was listed first. Because they both died in that crash. Me and my father had survived.

Now, they were all gone. I was the only one left.

I didn't know when the headstone had been made, but the lack of surname disturbed me. The fact that Michael had been reduced to just a first name on a stone hit hardest. His life was worth more than this. My hand curled into a fist and I pounded the ground a few times, holding back as much of the anger I was feeling as possible.

I reached into my pocket and took out my phone. Dialled the number and waited for it to be picked up.

There was no greeting. Laboured breathing, as he waited for me to speak.

'I'm at the grave.'

I squinted as the sun appeared above me. I turned my back on it.

'Look, kid . . .'

'You don't understand,' I said, sounding calmer than I felt inside. The anger that was threatening to spill out dampened by the distance between us. 'I'm here, looking at my mother's name and date of death. The rest of us are listed as well.'

'I can explain . . .'

'Did you organise this? My dad wouldn't have wanted this here. Why are we even listed on there, with no frame of reference? We were her sons. Her husband. There isn't even a date for Michael. Is he down there with her?'

He didn't reply.

'You need to start talking to me,' I said, my voice echoing around me. I glanced to my left and saw someone in the distance. Too far away to see if they had heard me shout. I lowered my voice. 'She's gone, Tom. Always has been. Almost twenty-five years. But someone out there thinks she's still alive. You and I both know that isn't the case.'

'No, listen to me, it isn't what you think. It's just a phony. It's not real.'

I shook my head. 'I'm the only one left now. So, you tell them to come and see me. I don't know what happened back then, but this needs to end.'

'Sam, she's alive. You've got to believe me. Just stay there and don't do anything rash.'

'Goodbye, Tom.'

'Wait . . .'

I was already pulling the phone away from my ear and ending the call. I took one last look at my mother's grave and felt the final sliver of hope that I'd been holding onto slip away.

Jackson had never been to Green Grove Cemetery, but he knew what lay there.

He watched him for a few minutes, as he reached out to touch the gravestone. Take out his phone and speak to someone. Become irate the longer he talked. Place his cell back in his pocket and stand at the grave for a few more moments. Say a silent goodbye and turn away.

In that moment, he made a decision.

Jackson moved quickly. He began striding towards him, making up the ground in seconds, until he was only a few yards away from Sam.

Up close, he could see him properly for the first time. Even on the plane, he hadn't got this close to him. It gave him pause, as he took him in fully and identified what he suspected would be his weak points. How he carried himself, how he stacked up against him. They might have looked around the same weight to an untrained eye, but Jackson had several pounds more in muscle than him.

These calculations ran through Jackson's head in a flash. Almost second nature. Creating a full picture and figuring out potential problems. The faster you could do that, the better these situations went.

He was close enough to Sam now that he could hear his breathing. He could see the hairs on the back of his neck rise as he followed him. Aware of a threat, but not quite believing it.

They were almost at the exit to the cemetery, the road up ahead. He didn't have much time, but that only made things easier. A little pressure to make him focus.

As they reached the path that would lead them back out onto the road, Jackson moved quickly. He dived and grabbed Sam by the arms, twisting one behind his back and then jabbing the Glock under his ribs.

'Don't move,' Jackson said, his voice barely above a whisper in Sam's ear. 'Don't fight. I'll have pulled the trigger before you've even thought about making a break for it. If you're calm, you'll live.'

He felt Sam tense in his arms and began walking him back to his car at the side of the road.

1995

For almost ten years, Laurie had managed to live her life.

It hadn't been easy. The move had come with its own challenges. It wasn't like home in the slightest. She hadn't been used to the laid-back life of a tiny village. Small town America was different in so many ways to its UK counterpart.

They had settled in the north of England, near to where David had grown up.

He didn't have any close family nearby. It was just the four of them.

That was all the family they had needed.

She felt safe, as if no harm could come to her or her children. Or David. She had only spoken to her parents sporadically in the years since she'd left. Her brother, Parker, once. Tom more than a few times.

She was living her life. It may have been different than it had once been, but that didn't mean it was worse.

Anything had to be better than the feeling she had before they got on that flight there.

Still, when she closed her eyes at night, the nightmares would remind her of what she had escaped.

Laurie was dreaming now. The faces of her past, staring back at her in the darkness. Anger and hate. A presence in the shadows, watching her. Waiting for her.

She could feel the heat exuding from him. The betrayal, the disloyalty.

This was another time she was in that state of half-awakeness. Knowing she was dreaming, but powerless to stop it. She could feel the tears dripping down her face. The sound of a silent scream being caught in the black. And as the presence came closer to her, she began to see its face take form. Take shape. Become what she knew it was.

Him.

Coming for her.

She was aware of a hand coming from the real world. Caressing her back. A voice, trying to soothe her. Telling her everything was going to be okay. She slowly emerged from the dream and blinked sleep from her eyes. Felt reality slowly come back.

The dream faded away and David's voice became stronger. Then, a sound that made her heart stop.

The phone. She looked at the clock and saw it was a little after five in the morning.

No good phone call came at that time.

'I'll go,' David said, slipping out of bed and leaving a cold mark where his hand had been on her back. She lay still for a second, then followed him out of the room. Down the hallway, where her eldest son's door was ajar. She peeked in, saw him fast asleep and for a moment, only the two of them existed in the world. Looking down at his face, relaxed and unbothered by anything going on around him.

Nine years old. Time slipped by so quickly.

She heard David's voice answering the phone and it snapped her out of the perfect world she could create in her mind when she was looking at her son's face. She moved out of the room and closed the door gently. Walked down to where David was standing, holding the phone. The hunch of his shoulders – tension bearing down on them – stopped her in her tracks.

He glanced over his shoulder and his expression made her

stop moving entirely. Frozen in place. He pulled the phone away from his ear and stretched his arm her way.

She couldn't go to him. Couldn't reach for the phone that he was holding out to her. It was as if she knew what was waiting on the other end of that line. Somewhere, deep down, some part of her had some terrible knowledge of what was to come.

Laurie breathed in deeply and found her feet. Crossed the short space between them. Took the receiver from his outstretched hand and placed it to her ear.

'Hey.'

'Tom?' Laurie said, still not sure. 'Is that you?'

'Course it is. Remember when we rode our bikes out on Charles Mary Drive, then Field Park? You hit Mr Nelson's old station wagon and he chased us almost all the way past the river? We got in some scrapes, Sappy.'

That was their code, devised ten years ago, so Laurie knew that Anthony wasn't listening. There was something inside her that was unlocked by the sound of his voice.

She smiled, then felt it slowly slip away as she remembered. Tom knew what time it was for her.

'Why are you calling, Tom?' Laurie said, her voice shaking.

'I'm sorry . . .' Tom said. 'It's your dad. He's at the hospital.'

Laurie could feel her body tense, a low moan escape from her throat. 'What happened?'

'He was fixing a loose tile on the roof. Took a fall, but they think it was his heart that brought it on. Your mom was right there, but it's . . . I'm sorry, but I don't think he's going to make it.'

Laurie put her free hand to her mouth and she felt David's hand on her shoulder. 'What am I supposed to do?'

'I can keep you safe,' Tom said, the static on the line muffling his voice a little. It was crossing the Atlantic, thousands of miles, but Laurie could close her eyes and imagine him in the room.

'It's been almost ten years. It's time you came back to see your family. To let your mom meet her grandchildren.'

'But what about . . .'

'I haven't seen him,' Tom said, knowing who she meant. 'I heard from a friend of his a long time ago, but I sent him back with bupkis. He's still out in Greenwich, with a new woman on his arm every week. I think he's moved on, Sappy. It'll be okay.'

'I don't know,' Laurie said, looking over at the other man in her life. He looked worried for a second, then straightened up.

She couldn't forget the look in Anthony's eyes when he had told her she was his. That didn't mean that had lingered this long. Ten years almost.

He couldn't still be looking for her. He couldn't still think she belonged to him.

'You'll meet me at the airport?'

'Of course.'

'Okay. Thanks, Tom.'

'Listen, if you let me just take care of the guy, maybe we could straighten this out for good, you know?'

Laurie felt the fear crawl over her bare skin again. Not for herself this time, but for Tom. 'You can't do that.'

'It would be easier,' Tom said, a small chuckle escaping and making Laurie feel more homesick than ever. 'It doesn't matter anyway. I promise you, he's moved on. You're gonna be fine.'

'I'll let you know my flight details. Thanks for calling, Tom.'

She placed the phone down before he had a chance to say any more.

David was already moving towards her.

'I'm sorry,' Laurie said into his shoulder, as his arms wrapped around her body and pulled her in close. 'I knew this would happen one day, but I didn't think it would be this soon. I'm just so far away from them. I don't know if I'll make it back in time.'

'It's okay. We'll book a flight now.'

Laurie began to shake her head, but he pulled her closer.

'We're in this together,' he said, his voice low and unyielding. 'Nothing can happen to us as long as we stick with each other, right? Look what we've managed to do since we left – we've created a family. And nothing can bring that down.'

'Tom says it's safe,' Laurie replied, nestling into David's embrace. 'He wouldn't say that if he didn't believe it.'

'Well, that's good enough for me.'

'Mum?'

Laurie peeled herself away from David's arms and looked down at the young boy walking sleepily into the room. His arms outstretched up to her. Turned five years old a week before, but still, he wanted to be cuddled. Wanted to be carried around, as if he were still a baby.

She lifted him into her arms and felt the warmth from his body. She felt the weight of him and thought about never letting go. Of embracing him forever. The love that she felt was like no other. 'Did we wake you?'

'It's still night.'

'Yes, it is, Michael,' Laurie said, stroking her son's back. 'Come on, let's get you back into bed.'

She carried him back to his room, laying him back in his bed and stroking his face. He battled to keep his eyes open, a small smile crossing his face.

'Tell me the story.'

Laurie smiled and began to recite the poem. His eyes closed fully and his breathing became slower, as sleep took him.

That love is life,

And life hath immortality.

As she whispered words of comfort, for him, for her.

She was safe. She would be with her family.

Nothing was going to happen to her.

CHAPTER 21

The sun crept over the harbour as Carson waited. February sun, low in the sky, but still burning brightly. A windchill that made him rub his hands together, his breath hanging in the air around him. The Atlantic Ocean was calm here, gently lapping against the shoreline.

Behind him, he heard the sound of a car approaching, but he didn't turn around. Instead, he continued looking out towards the horizon, spotting a ship or a ferry in the distance. He couldn't be sure which it was from this far. If he stayed there, he wouldn't have to wait too long to find out. He knew he probably didn't have that luxury.

The car came to a stop on the gravel beside him. The driver got out and closed the door with a loud thunk.

Carson finally looked his way and gave Hunter a nod. Took the proffered cup of coffee gladly in his hands. He could feel the heat of it even through the gloves he was wearing.

'Where'd you go for it?'

'Place up on Main Street.'

'Marson's. Good. Got to support the smaller places, you know.'

Hunter murmured what he hoped was an agreement.

'I'm from round here,' Carson said, taking the lid from the polystyrene cup, and sipped the coffee. Felt it warm his insides and hoped it wouldn't take long for the caffeine to hit him as well. 'Used to go to church right round the corner there.'

'I didn't know.'

'Lot of ex-military around here,' Carson said, looking back over his shoulder. It was a quiet town, small houses, church, the harbour. 'Do their service and retire to a nice place like this. Raise a family, have grandchildren, go to church on Sunday. Nice life. If we could all be as lucky, hey?'

'I always took you for a travelling type,' Hunter replied, scratching a fingernail against the side of his cup. 'Not really from any one place.'

'I guess that just about sums me up now,' Carson said, thinking of the hours spent on the road. Moving state to state. He had seen the whole country in his younger days. One day in Salem, Oregon. The next Franklin, Tennessee.

Now, Noank, Connecticut. A place he knew better than the others.

'Is that how you came to work with Mr Sullivan?'

'Something like that,' Carson replied, thinking about his dad. Taking up the family business.

It was supposed to be a father and son team, that would last years. It had lasted barely a few months. Carson knew his old man had always dreamed of retiring with his old army buddies in the area.

He never got that chance.

'You ask a lot of questions, but never about the actual work. Why is that?'

Hunter shrugged. 'I guess I don't need to know too much about what we do. People are more interesting. Not the marks – people like us, I mean.'

'We're not all that interesting. We follow orders. We're tools. The people giving the orders – they're the interesting ones.'

They sat in silence, drinking coffee, watching the boat move towards them. He recognised the livery now – it was the ferry heading towards New London. Soon, it would slip past Groton and he wouldn't be able to see it any more. A white speck on the horizon to the west that would disappear.

'You been here before?'

'No, first time,' Hunter replied, looking around him as if he'd realised that minute where he was. 'Quiet place.'

'It's like this most of the year now,' Carson said, taking another sip of coffee. Black and hot, just as it was supposed to be. From the sweet smell emanating from the younger man's cup, he guessed his was filled with a boatload of that syrup that had been introduced in the past few years. Chain coffee shops, shovelling more sugar than a man was supposed to take in, ruining what was a simple drink. 'Few more tourists up the way, to the main towns and then Hartford, course. This place don't see that kind of thing.'

'Small-town America.'

'Not many of them left.'

'Give me a city any day of the week.'

Carson sniffed and scuffed at the gravel with his foot. 'I guess we're best getting on the road.'

'Do you think this is nearly over?'

Carson stopped at the question, looking back at Hunter. He looked younger than ever. He wondered if this was starting to become a little too much for the inexperienced man. Whether those deaths were ticking up a little too quickly.

'Maybe, maybe not. Mr Sullivan has been waiting a long time to get to this point. You should know that. And we're closer than ever.'

'You think?'

'I can feel it,' Carson said, draining the last of his coffee and placing the empty cup between his knees. 'Closer than he has been for a long time.'

'How long has he been looking for her?'

'Going on thirty years,' Carson said with a long sigh. 'She left the States in 1986. Almost a decade later, she was back here, where she belonged, but it all went south. I always thought she was already dead, but seems I was wrong.'

'There's nothing to say he's right.'

'He's paying us to prove he is.'

And that was all that needed to be said.

'It's too quiet round here,' Hunter said, emptying his coffee cup and chucking it towards the shoreline. 'Can we go?'

Carson stared at him until he moved to go and retrieve it with a sigh. Chucked it in the trash can that was near his car.

'We good?' Hunter asked, getting into the driver's side.

Carson shook his head and wondered what had happened to the generation that came after his.

'Not yet.'

But they would be soon.

Tom Miller would be dead by the end of the day, if everything went to plan. That thought made Carson smile. A closing of a chapter he needed to make personally.

He knew Anthony would be pleased for him to finally get justice for what Tom had done to him.

And that would be the beginning of the end.

CHAPTER 22

It was almost as if I'd been waiting for a gun to be held on me from the second I'd stepped off the plane. Especially when I made the decision to run towards the danger.

At first, my body shut down. I heard a voice say something in my ear, but I couldn't process what it was. My mind was racing. Trying to make sense of a situation it couldn't understand.

My pulse was racing. Too fast. I could feel sweat prickle on my forehead and reproduce. A droplet slid down and into my eye.

I was going to die.

The thought came through the fog and refused to disappear, rolling over and over, like a breaking news banner. *This is it, you're going to die here.*

I wasn't going to give up.

'I think you've got the wrong person,' I said, finally finding my voice. 'Please.'

'Keep moving, Sam,' the voice said. 'As long as you do as I tell you, it'll be fine.'

I knew he was lying. I had poked a hornet's nest and now a loaded gun was going to sting me. 'How do you know my name?'

'Stop talking.'

I was going to die. Only, there wasn't going to be any soft slide into darkness. No showreel of my life flashing before my eyes.

Fight or flight?

The same question again.

'Just tell me what you want?' I said, risking another sentence. He wasn't going to shoot me here, out in the daylight. 'She's dead. You're going to kill me for no reason.'

He didn't respond. This wasn't one of the men who had been in my father's house, I had seen enough to know that much. Still, I could sense the strength in him, his presence overbearing.

I could see a car up ahead, parked fifty yards or so from my rental car. It looked familiar, but I couldn't place where I had seen it before.

He was so close to me that I could smell his breath – mint and coffee.

I had to do something.

As if he could read my thoughts, the gun was pressed into my ribs a little harder.

'Don't do anything stupid, Sam,' he said, his voice coarse. Dry. 'It doesn't have to end here, at the side of this road. You hear me?'

Time was slipping away. If I didn't do something, he was going to put me in that car and I wouldn't see daylight again.

'Just a little further.'

A few cars passed us on the road, but they wouldn't have known what was happening. As we got to the car, he let go of me and reached forwards to open the back door.

'Get inside. Lie down on the seat.'

'No.'

He hesitated for a split second and that was enough. I turned and grabbed the wrist of the hand that was holding the gun, forcing it up to the sky, driving my fist into his stomach as I did so.

My hand disappeared into his jacket, but stopped as if it had hit a brick wall. He raised his fist to hit me back, but I moved my head at the last moment and took the blow on my shoulder. I kicked out, hoping to repeat the trick I'd inflicted on his friend back in England.

He shifted out of the way and stepped back. I still had hold of his wrist, but he pulled it away from me. I didn't think – I drew my fist back and threw it as hard as I could towards his jaw. He raised his free hand and blocked it, but I was already throwing again, hitting any part of his body I could. Kicking out and finding mostly air, as he moved swiftly and confidently, slipping punches I threw, or catching them on his arms.

Then, I overcommitted. I missed him by some distance and by the time I'd regained my balance, he had me by the throat and the gun at my temple.

I didn't move. Couldn't. The man deposited me on the back seat of the car. I crashed down with a thump and the air was sucked out of me in an instant. I fell halfway off, my head sliding down into the footwell.

Then, a sound shook the air around us and the hand let go of my body. A loud pop echoed for less than a second, followed by a grunt, a growl of anger.

I tried to turn around to see what had happened, but I was suddenly struck from behind. I thought it was someone hitting me, but the weight didn't shift, and I realised it was the man's body hitting mine.

Hands grabbed the back of my jacket. I winced with pain, as they dug into my skin. I kicked out, landing my foot on something that felt like a leg. I tried to squirm free, but I had no space to move. I was stuck there, becoming more tangled up the more I tried to escape.

'Hey, you got to move.'

It took a moment to realise that there was another voice nearby. I heard another pop and the body on mine tensed. I felt something jolt through me – an aftershock that made me jump up and regain my senses.

'Sam, move!'

It took another second before I realised it was a woman's voice, screaming into the car.

'Who are you?'

'We've got to go now,' she said, standing at the car door, something black in her hand.

I scrambled from underneath the man, who was lying prostrate on the back seat. I tried to stand, banged my head on the roof of the car and felt dizzy for a second.

His face was out of view, but I could see the back of his head. What he was wearing. I fell out of the car, landing on my knees on the ground. It was soft, taking the brunt of the fall.

I felt the woman's hand on my shoulder, soft at first, then grabbing my jacket.

I looked up at her and saw the taser in her hand. I flinched at the sight of it, expecting it to crackle into life, but she shook her head and pulled me away from the car.

'I'm a friend,' she said, breathing hard as she looked past me and towards the man she had incapacitated. 'I'm working with Tom. He sent me to look after you.'

'Get away from me . . .'

'Sam, you have to trust me. Tom said that he made your mom a promise. That he wouldn't let anything bad happen to you. So, you have to follow me. Get to your own car and follow me in mine. We'll talk when we're away from here.'

I didn't ask any more questions. I ran towards my car, grabbing the keys from my pocket and unlocking it as I reached it.

Once inside, I looked out the windscreen and saw the woman still standing next to the open car door, the taser in her hand. Another pop and then she was running back towards me. I looked in the rear-view mirror and saw another car parked behind mine.

I shifted into drive and began pulling away. A few seconds later, I saw her in my rear-view mirror pull onto the road, then

Luca Veste

speed up and overtake me. As we passed the car I'd been trapped inside only seconds earlier, I could see the man bent over in the back seat, pulling himself up. I slowed a little, trying to see him properly.

We locked eyes, but his weren't focused. He was staring back at me groggily, slowly rising up. I turned away and saw the woman's car further ahead in the road. Put my foot down and closed the gap.

I was looking for a turn off the road, thinking I could disappear, when my phone started ringing and I answered it.

'Keep following me,' the woman said, her voice surrounding me. 'We'll put some distance between us and him and then we can work out what the hell just happened.'

'How did you get my number?'

'I'm with Tom. Don't worry, I'll tell you everything as soon as we're off the road.'

'Why should I trust you? I have no idea who you are.'

There was a long sigh. 'You need friends here, Sam. I can help you. I just need you to follow me, okay? I promise I'm not with them.'

'Who was he? Can you tell me that at least?'

'No idea,' she said and it seemed to anger her. As if it was a personal insult that she didn't know the answer. 'We'll talk properly when we get somewhere safe.'

The call ended and the radio kicked back in. It took a few seconds, but then the adrenaline that had been rushing through my body began to overtake. My hands were shaking on the steering wheel. I gripped it harder, but it made little difference. I couldn't catch my breath, my vision spotting as I tried to keep focus on the road ahead.

I kept looking in my rear-view mirror, expecting to see a car chasing us down, but nothing was there.

There was a brief moment when my brain seemed to switch

on and want to make my body shut down. I fought against it. Only cats had nine lives. I'd used up two of mine in the past week and I didn't think I'd get a third.

I was as close as I'd ever been to dying and there was only one thought in my mind, playing over and over.

Never again. I wouldn't survive next time.

CHAPTER 23

The woman signalled right and I did the same. Pulled onto a dirt track that seemed to lead into woods and the middle of nowhere. Until the trees parted, and buildings came into view. I realised we were close to the centre of town – I could see the highway in the distance that skirted around Middletown. Here, there was only a single shack of a building that looked deserted. Run-down and left to the elements.

I pulled up behind her car, shut the engine off and opened the car door slowly. I left the key in the ignition and only stepped out with one leg – perched on the driver's seat ready to move quickly.

The woman got out of her car and made her way towards me. She was around my age, I guessed, but I couldn't be sure. Her eyes were a deep blue that reminded me of impossible ocean photographs in travel brochures. Her hair was tied back in a tight ponytail, a faded blonde colour. She was looking right back at me, unblinking, as if she were sizing me up.

'You good?'

I chuckled quietly. 'I've been better. I'll probably stop shaking in a day or two.'

'Quinn,' she said, but didn't hold a hand out for me to shake. 'And you're Sam.'

'Everyone seems to know me before I know them.'

'That was a close one,' Quinn said, looking past my shoulder, as if she were waiting for him to suddenly pull in behind us. 'Do you know who he was?'

I shook my head. 'I was hoping you had some idea. I've never seen him before in my life. But he knew me. He said my name.'

Quinn nodded, as if this was what she'd expected. 'I imagine he did know you. Usually people try and kidnap people for a reason round here.'

'Thanks,' I said, realising I hadn't said it yet. 'I mean, that's not enough, but you probably just saved my life. I . . . I appreciate it.'

'Don't mention it.'

'How did you even know . . .'

'I followed you there,' Quinn said, cutting me off. 'Good job I did. Had a gut feeling that you'd end up in some trouble.'

'Quinn. Who are you?'

'Like I said, I'm working with Tom Miller. We had a discussion about what to do about you and this is the result. I followed you to the cemetery and saw that guy pull a gun on you. I thought you could do with the help.'

'Are you his . . .' I said, letting the question hang there, so as not to insult. Wife or partner, daughter or even granddaughter, I couldn't be sure.

She shook her head. 'No relation. If that's what you're asking. I'm helping him out.'

'Oh, right. Like a carer, or something?'

'Not quite,' Quinn replied, turning back to me now. 'My line of work is in private investigations. Usually, it's proving a husband is cheating on his wife, or vice versa. Sometimes insurance claims and medical stuff. Few pictures and that's enough. My dad was in the military – did a tour in the first Iraq war with Tom. When Tom came back, he needed help. My dad, he's had a bad time of it. He was injured in a car accident around ten years ago, and my mom died a few years later. Now, there's medical bills like you wouldn't believe. The little I can pick up helps here and there, but it's a struggle. When Tom said he'd pay me, I couldn't say no. Only, it's for something different than I normally deal with.'

'My mum.'

'In a way, I guess. He's trying to help her. There's this guy who has been trying to find her for a long time. Tom thinks he's protecting her by being here.'

'So, she is alive?' I said, trying to keep my voice level. Trying to keep my composure. I wasn't sure I was succeeding. 'You know that for a fact?'

'Tom says she is, but she's like a ghost. I did some digging around behind his back and can find nothing other than the grave back there. For all intents and purposes, she died back in 1995.'

'What else have you found out?'

'Not much,' Quinn said, looking away again. She was constantly assessing the surrounding area. 'He told me she had been in hiding, along with the rest of her family, then that changed to another story. Apparently, her brother was over in Idaho, but he was killed a couple of weeks ago by this guy who is looking for her, and then your father, in England, I guess?'

'That's right,' I replied, trying to keep up with her. She spoke fast, her words peppered at me. 'Two guys. Both American. They cornered me in my father's house. I only just got away. They were asking about my mother.'

'And you didn't know anything about her?'

I shook my head. 'As far as I was concerned, she died in an accident, along with my brother, twenty-five years ago. My dad and I barely survived.'

'Where did it happen?'

'Mystic River. Groton side, I think? I looked it up on Google Maps and I think it happened on River Road, but I was only nine. I don't really remember.'

'I can find that out for you.'

Her feet shifted on the dirt and kicked up a little dust. It swirled around her lower legs and then settled again. I got out of the car and placed a hand on my car door. 'I don't know why they think she's still alive. Even Tom. All I have is his word and some guys trying to kill me.'

'Well, when you put it like that.'

I leaned against the car and folded my arms across my chest. 'You tasered him.'

She smiled sheepishly. 'Well, I thought it would be better than shooting him. Less messy.'

'You know, I've been waiting for a gun to be pulled on me since I landed. I assumed they were everywhere.'

'Well, they are, but I think you're unlucky to see one up close.'

Cars continued to pass us by, heading to the centre of town. I wished I was closer. Comfort in large crowds.

'So, someone wants to kill me.'

I said it with a smile, but the thought weighed heavily on my shoulders.

Quinn hesitated. 'If they wanted you dead, he would have shot you in the graveyard. He was going to take you somewhere.'

'Was it the guy who's looking for my mum?'

Quinn shook her head. 'Too young for that. It wasn't anyone I've seen before. Listen, Tom wants you to go back home. To England. It'd be safer.'

That wasn't going to happen. 'I should speak to Tom before I make any decisions.'

'That'll be tricky. He's paranoid right now. Thinks every shadow is someone come to kill him. He's probably right, to be fair. He wants to keep you safe, so he doesn't think you should be together.'

'He's the only one who can give me the answers I came here for.'

'This guy he's after . . . he has the money, power, and influence to make sure he gets what he wants.'

'What's his name?'

Something flashed across Quinn's features for a second. It looked like fear.

'Anthony Sullivan,' she said finally. 'He's . . . he's a bad guy. He made his money from construction, real estate, but there's plenty of rumours out there about him that don't make for good reading.'

'And why does he want to find my mum?'

Quinn shrugged her shoulders. 'I don't know. If he's sending guys over to England, killing your father, trying to kill you . . . well, there has to be a compelling reason for that, I would think.'

I tried to think of one, but came up empty. My dad had never told me anything about why they had left the States, but I was starting to wonder if there was a reason for that.

And the first time she came back, we ended up in the river.

'There has to be some kind of proof that she's out there,' I said, moving off the car and gripping the car keys in my hand. 'I tried looking for my grandmother, but she wasn't in the same house. I don't suppose you know where she might be?'

CHAPTER 24

Tom Miller was parked up in the same spot as the night before. Twenty-five years ago, he'd been in the same place. Back then, he had only been out of the military six months and hadn't let himself get out of shape. Now, he was starting to feel all of his fifty-six years.

Quinn had left him a few hours earlier – after he sent her to protect Sam, making sure he didn't get himself into trouble.

He had no doubts that he eventually would.

Back when Tom had served in the military, he had known a hundred Sam Coopers. Young kids, who didn't know when to stay out of the line of sight. To 'keep their heads down', as David Cooper would say.

A long time ago.

If Sam had simply done as he'd been told, Tom could have managed the situation without worrying about him. Now, he was an added headache.

A different car, but the same place. He was waiting for Anthony Sullivan to leave that morning, but there was no sign of him. He lifted his cell phone and scrolled to the number. Tried calling, but there was no answer. He didn't leave a message. There had been enough of those.

Tom got out of the car, clicked the safety off his gun, and stuck to the trees. They surrounded the property, but he knew there was a fence only a few yards into the tree line.

Anthony had increased his security in the past twenty-five years.

He needed to get closer. To see the house, to see something. Anything that would tell him he could pull this off without getting himself killed before it was over.

He kept an eye out for cameras. For all he knew, they could be the size of a pin and he was being tracked the whole way.

The tree line became thicker. He could feel the damp ground under his boots, the mud sticking and pulling at him. He pushed another branch away and there was nothing but black in front of him.

Not just a fence guarding the property now. It was a wall of black stone, that seemed to reach up past the trees and darken the skies above him.

It wouldn't be at the house where he would finally get his hands on Anthony Sullivan.

He backed up, moving quickly now, until he was out of the trees and back on the road. It was still quiet, but he dropped to the ground as he heard the sound of a car approaching. Crouched and hid himself away. A few yards away, on the other side of the asphalt, the hire car was hidden.

It felt like a hundred miles at this point.

He removed the gun and prepared himself for the worst.

As the car came closer, he gripped the gun tighter and slipped his finger around the trigger.

The vibration from the cell phone in his pocket almost shocked him into firing a shot. His heart was barely beating before that, but it kicked in now. The sweat dripped from his forehead, as a car sped past him on the road and went past Anthony Sullivan's house without slowing. He relaxed, flicked the safety back on, and holstered the gun.

He was across the road in a second or three, and behind the wheel in less than that. He put the car in drive and pulled away from its hiding place. He decided to drive around again, keep himself moving.

Tom called Quinn back once he was a few hundred yards down the road.

'He wants to see her.'

'I don't know where she is . . .'

'Not his mom,' Quinn said. 'The grandmother. Listen, I don't think he's going into hiding any time soon, if you see what I mean. He's pretty determined.'

'You spoke to him?'

'Briefly. Told him who I was. Who I was working for. And that you wanted him to go home.'

Tom let go of the steering wheel for a second and massaged the back of his neck. 'He didn't listen.'

'No. He's just found out that his mom might be alive. Do you blame him?'

'I guess not,' Tom said, trying to figure out a way in which he could extricate himself from the situation that was unfolding. Came up with naught. 'If he's out of state, at least that's something, I suppose.'

'I should give him the address then?'

Tom sighed, tried to think of another way, and failed. 'Go for it.'

I left Quinn at the side of the dirt road and drove back to the motel. Every car was now suspicious. Every person I saw deserved a second glance.

I pulled up in the motel car park and turned off the engine. Pulled out my phone and messaged Rachel. I didn't tell her what had happened, but I needed the comfort of knowing that someone out there knew where I was.

Then, I typed the name Anthony Sullivan into the search bar and added 'Connecticut'. There were far more results than I needed. I began reading. His picture came up instantly and I scrolled past it for now. Instead, I read as much as I could about the man.

Numerous newspaper articles, declaring him the state's premier real estate magnate. Construction sites with the Sullivan name emblazoned across them. All across Connecticut, dipping across state lines in more recent times.

His net worth was into nine figures easily, one site said. Although, there was talk he *could* be worth even more than that. All the pictures seemed to be with politicians, celebrities, people of influence.

Born in 1961, which made him fifty-nine years old. The most recent picture made him look at least a decade younger. Standing there, with a smile that didn't seem to reach his eyes.

I scanned through a number of articles, but it was what was left unsaid that made me wonder about the kind of man he was.

Rumours of purported 'strong-arm' tactics have never been any more than that – rumours. However, Anthony Sullivan is a man who doesn't take no for an answer. When he decides to build, he builds. If there's a deal to be done, he'll find a way to make it happen.

If I had dug deeper, I imagined I'd find all kinds of dark practices at work.

He must have a good lawyer, was all I could think. Given his wealth, I wasn't exactly Sherlocking my way through it. He probably had an army of people willing to go to any extreme to make sure he never paid for any crimes.

His story reached back even further than the results of a cursory internet search. For now, it was enough to know that he was rich, powerful, and had many friends.

I decided to take a walk from the motel. I checked the other cars around me before getting out, walked out onto the main road and made my way right. There was a narrow pavement separating me from the traffic, sparse as it was. I realised how far I was from where people lived, shopped, socialised in Mystic. I was staying on the outskirts, it seemed.

Broken brown leaves took up much of the space to walk in. The sun had broken through the clouds, giving a hint of what would come later in the year. I unzipped my jacket and let it hang loose.

A sign up ahead welcomed me to Historic Mystic. Blue and gold. It seemed randomly placed, as if it had been an afterthought.

The main road was quiet, a few cars passing me by as I hugged the pavement and the low wall that ran alongside it. Cars from the centre of town making their way to the highway behind me.

To my side, the view opened up and I realised if I'd had a different room in the motel, I would have been looking over a mass of graves.

A few more yards down the road, I came to the entrance to the cemetery. A stone arch, grand in stature. Light stone. On the top of the arch an inscription read:

I am the resurrection and the life

Two symbols bordered the inscription. The letter A and the Greek symbol for Alpha.

I thought about the idea of walking into another cemetery, but decided I was probably safe for now. Even so, I kept looking over my shoulder, and had my phone in my hand.

I didn't want to chance the idea that Quinn could come save me again.

I moved through the arch and was confronted by a sea of American flags. All sticking out of the ground, marking the graves.

I looked at the names. So many of them were inscribed with service histories – veterans of wars long gone. Some may only have served for a couple of years, then died many decades later. Still, that was the most important thing to be marked on their grave.

The path wound its way around the cemetery – vast in size, just like everything else in this country. Until I reached the far end and was suddenly looking out across the river.

It wasn't a great distance across to the other side, but I knew the river stretched all the way to the Atlantic. This was a river that flowed from and to the sea, but it was calm here.

I stared out past the riverbanks, across to the trees covering the highway that lay beyond them.

There was a reason I had come here.

On the other side of the river, twenty-five years ago, I had been dragged to safety. I couldn't be sure exactly whereabouts we entered the water, but this was the place.

This is the place where I had lost everything.

I heard the scream from the passenger seat. My mum, grabbing hold of my dad's arm as he lost control of the car. The tree that would have slowed us down if we'd ploughed straight into it.

Instead, we hit the water and went under.

I could picture them disappearing beneath the surface. My own hand outstretched and grasping thin air.

The cold of the water. The iciness of its touch. Pulling at my seat belt, as Michael cried next to me.

I screwed my eyes shut so I couldn't remember any more.

The wind picked up, sweeping in from the ocean a mile or so away. Still, I could feel it. The trace of salt in the air. The smell of it on the edges.

I walked away quickly. Before my head started pounding and my body began shaking. Before the sweat appeared on my forehead and my chest began to tighten.

Before it became a struggle to breathe.

I made my way back to the motel and when I reached the car park, my phone trilled in my pocket. I pulled it out, saw the number and braced myself.

Quinn's voice came through, straight, efficient.

'You got a pen?'

A couple of hours' drive east, back towards where I'd landed a day earlier. Rhode Island, the small state that was sandwiched between Massachusetts and Connecticut. I crossed the state line, following the directions on my phone to the address Quinn had given me.

Sunset Road, Narragansett. A picturesque street of small houses built in the middle of a tiny forest. In the small clearings amongst the trees, there were separate homes, with land all around them. The trees were overbearing, reaching high and wide. I wondered if the residents were worried during times of high wind – one could crash into your home at any point and I wasn't sure much would be left of any occupants underneath.

I was still on the southern edge of the state, the ocean still following me.

I got out of the car, then walked the short distance up a driveway, past an old beaten-up blue Ford with a tear in the soft-top. Probably a classic car in this country. I thought it would have been scrapped decades earlier back in England.

The house was yellow, matching the name of the road. It was in better shape than the car. Large black numbers were affixed to the side of a screen across the actual door itself. To the other side of the numbers, there was the silhouette of a bird in mid-flight.

I rapped on the door and waited. I heard a shuffling inside, then the door opened up slowly, a walking frame appearing first, followed by a woman bent over it, looking over my shoulder.

'Who are you?'

I swallowed and then smiled. 'Are you Eleanor? Eleanor Rogers?'

I wasn't sure if I had been sent to the right place. She was much older than I'd been expecting. My memory of her wasn't the strongest – it had been twenty-five years, after all. We had spent a few days in her home, but it was a struggle to put a face to the blur I remembered.

'No one's called me Eleanor in a long time,' she said, narrowing her eyes at me. 'I'm Nell.'

There was something so familiar about her. She had short silver hair, that curled at the bottom. Her skin was tanned, almost Mediterranean-looking. Her eyes found mine finally. 'Anyway, who are you? Who wants to know who I am?'

'I'm Sam Cooper, I . . .'

'Sam?'

She looked at me with something approaching recognition, but it faded quickly.

'Do you remember me?' I said. I didn't know if I wanted her to say yes.

'Cooper, you say?' she replied, whatever was firing in her memory doing so slowly. 'I knew that name once.'

'I'm Sam,' I tried again. 'I guess . . . I guess I'm your grandson.'

1995

Laurie's dad died on a cold February morning. She had stepped outside for just a second – getting a cup of coffee from the machine down the hall – when she heard her mom scream her name.

She had held her mom tight, as sobs had racked through her body, making it jerk like a marionette. The helplessness exuded from her in waves.

He was sixty-four years old.

Now, she was sitting in the spare bedroom of her parents' new place. The home where they were supposed to live well into their older years. A town called Mystic, closer to the ocean.

'Dad wanted to fish out on the river,' she said, as David held her. 'He had it all planned out, Mom told me. They bought this place last year because it came up on the market and was perfect.'

'It'll be okay,' David said, with more certainty than he felt. 'We'll get through this together.'

'I'm going to check on Mom,' Laurie said, pulling away from David. She went down the hallway, looking in on Sam and Michael who were asleep in the den. Her mom was sitting at the kitchen table downstairs, leafing through photo albums.

'Hey, Mom,' Laurie said, leaning on the back of the chair her mom was sitting on. 'Are these old photographs?'

'I like to look through them,' Nell replied, laying a hand on

Laurie's and patting it gently. 'Reminds me of memories I forget sometimes.'

'Parker said he'd be back in the morning. I think he's catching up with some old friends in town.'

'Out drinking, more like,' Nell said, a trace of disdain in her tone. 'He works hard, has his own place back in Middletown, but all I hear from people back there is how many times he's thrown out of bars. I hope he settles down some day. Like you did. I know this is bad, but seeing the two boys and you and David has made it so much easier.'

'I'm real glad you finally got to meet them. Photographs aren't enough.'

Nell nodded, looking back at the albums in front of her. 'And you're happy?'

'I am, yeah. We've built a life together over there now. We have our own little place in a quiet neighbourhood. The people on our street are lovely. I love being a mother.'

'And a wife.'

'I'm sorry you weren't there,' Laurie said, tensing at the sound of her mom's voice. She had known that was the worst thing about leaving for England and not coming back.

And now, with her father gone, it just brought home how much she missed not having him walk her down the aisle.

'I'm sorry for the trouble I caused you and Dad.'

'He only came to the old house a few times looking for you,' Nell said. 'Your dad told him straight that we had no idea where you were and he believed us. Eventually. Tom looked in on us all the time too. It all worked out okay.'

'Still . . .' Laurie began, then decided the apology was enough. 'I'm going to step outside for a while.'

Her mom patted her hand once more, then went back to leafing through the photo albums. Laurie opened the back door and slipped outside soundlessly. Lit up a cigarette and waited for the calmness to wash over her. She hadn't smoked in years, but as soon as they had landed back there, she had bought three packs.

She couldn't see to the end of the yard in the moonlight. The air was still and silent. The sky overhead was dark but for pinpoints of light from the stars that blanketed her view.

She took a drag and blew smoke around her in a cloud. Once she was back in England, she would give up again. She had given David so much grief about his smoking habit that it wouldn't be right if she kept on.

It was peaceful outside. The smell of the sea nearby drifting in. It may not have been the home she had grown up in, but she could see herself being quite happy to visit her mom there. She thought that maybe she could convince her to come out to England at some point too. Maybe with Tom.

Laurie wanted to share her life with them more now. Her dad passing had only proven that life was too short. Her mom was facing a life alone. She couldn't let that happen.

There was a shift of weight in the black and her heart skipped a beat or three. There was a spark of flame in the darkness and a cigarette was lit.

Anxiety crawled up from her stomach and into her chest.

She could feel her hand shaking, the cigarette falling from her fingers.

'Hello, beautiful,' Anthony said, as he stepped out of the shadows like something conjured from her nightmares. 'I've been looking for you.'

She couldn't respond. Any words she could say were lost before they made their way to her mouth.

He cocked his head, a dark smile on his face. 'Aren't you going to say hello?'

Laurie couldn't move. Her feet were stuck in place. There was electricity sparking around them, as if they were in the eye of a storm.

And even though she had to have known she would see him, it was as if she had managed to convince herself it wouldn't happen.

'You should have told me you were home,' Anthony said, his tone that of a parent ticking off a child. 'I would have made sure you were looked after.'

He stepped towards her and her stomach lurched. She thought about David inside. Her boys.

What this man would do to them.

'I am sorry about your dad,' he said, close enough that she could smell the heat drifting off his skin. 'You shouldn't be out here alone at a time like this.'

'I'm not alone,' Laurie said, finally finding her voice, however small it was. The words were lost in the space between them. Gone on the breeze.

Anthony shook his head and looked at her with a pity that made her throat close up.

'I know it must have been hard for you,' he said. 'But don't worry, I'm here for you now. It's going to be okay. I'm going to take care of you. I've never stopped thinking about you, Laurie. I always knew you'd come back to me.'

He reached out to her and she flinched back at his touch. She saw his expression change – the smile falter and his eyes narrow.

'I'm so happy to see you, Laurie. Aren't you happy to see me?'

'Anthony . . .' she said, taking a step back to increase the space between them. He quickly closed up again.

'I've been worried about you. You've been gone a long time, but I knew you'd come to your senses. Come on – let's go home.'

She slowly shook her head. 'No.'

Two shadows broke free. A tall man, his bald head glistening in the moonlight. And another, shorter, stockier. His hand was on her arm in an instant. The other behind her head, holding the back of her neck in a vice-like grip.

'Now, I asked nicely, Laurie,' Anthony said, his voice hissing at her – a snake in the black of night, as she struggled with the man holding onto her. 'Don't make things harder than they have to be, okay?'

David was only a scream away, but Laurie's throat was closed.

Anthony leaned in and the whisper in her ear was all that was needed to stop her doing anything to save herself.

'You need to come with me now, before I lose my temper and ask Carson here to do something neither of us wants to happen. You *know* what happens when I lose my temper.'

She was shaking, as she felt Carson's hand reach her jaw and begin to squeeze.

'I don't want to hurt anyone, Laurie,' he said, motioning to Carson to release the grip on her face. He placed his hands on her shoulders and she almost lost her balance. 'I just want to get things back to how they're supposed to be.'

Laurie thought about David – upstairs, waiting for her to come back to bed. About Sam and Michael – fast asleep.

She thought about what she had to protect. What she had to stop from happening.

'Please,' she said, wishing there was a better, more forceful word she could use. 'My kids.'

She'd known it wouldn't work, but desperation makes you try anything.

'Then you have even more reason not to make a *scene*.'

Laurie bowed her head and allowed herself to be guided down the side of the house.

'Good, that's what I thought,' he said, his hand at the small of her back. She spied a car at the curb, waiting for them. He turned to the taller man. 'Zoran, start the car. Carson, make sure she's nice and comfortable.'

She felt numb, as they approached the car. She hoped for a shout from behind them. For David to see what was happening.

Only, she knew that would be the end for him. Anthony would kill him if he came anywhere near them.

'You'll always be mine, Laurie.'

Then, she was in the back of the car, watching her life fade into black behind her.

CHAPTER 25

For a second, we stared at each other. Grandmother and grandson. No history shared, no stories that could be remembered. Just blood.

'Come on in,' the woman said, before I had a chance to explain any further. Her accent was softer than Quinn's had been. She was older than anyone I'd seen before – a face so crinkled, it looked like tin foil that had been scrunched up and then opened again. Short, almost translucent hair, thinned to the point I could see her scalp in places.

Still, in her eyes, I could see the familiar spark of my mother.

The smell of pine hit me as I stepped into the doorway and almost made me gag.

'That's it, just follow me, we'll get you in here.'

I waited for her to move a little more before stepping into the house proper, taking short breaths to get used to the smell. For every few steps she could take, I took half of one. Then, I closed the door behind me.

'Here we are,' the woman said, finally turning and letting go of her walker and lowering herself into a fancy chair that was on some sort of incline for ease of getting into. She leaned back and then slowly brought it down until she was in a normal sitting position. 'Please, come in, sit down and take a load off.'

On the television in the corner, some sort of talk show blared out. I watched as the woman lifted a delicate hand slowly to shut it off. I was staring at her, trying to feel something that would unlock a memory or two, but it wasn't there. Still, I realised that I wasn't alone after all – that there was a relative out here, even after my dad was gone. The thought was more calming than I'd expected it to be.

'I'd offer to get you something, but by the time I made my way into the kitchen, it'd be time for dinner. And the woman only brings one meal, so I can't offer too much.'

I hovered next to a chair opposite hers, wondering what on earth I'd walked into here. 'That's okay,' I said, watching the woman's face carefully. She blinked back, expressionless. 'You know who I am, right?'

'Of course, Sam,' Nell replied, as if it were a stupid question. Perhaps it was. 'You think I'd invite a stranger into my home?'

'I guess not,' I said, finding it impossible not to smile. 'I'm sorry for just showing up here.'

She looked back at me again; this time her face dropped a little. Serious. 'You're the eldest boy.'

I swallowed, giving myself a second to answer. 'That's right. Your daughter, Laurie, she was my mum.'

She smiled again. 'I just love the way you people speak. Yes, dear, she was your *mom*.'

'I don't know what to say,' I said, moving around the chair and sitting down finally. I leaned back and tried to clear my head. 'I haven't been over here in twenty-five years. I didn't even know you were still . . . you know, alive.'

'Twenty-five years is a long time. John has been gone that long.'

'I was up at Green Grove today,' I said, choosing my words carefully. 'I saw where he was buried. My mum was buried next to him? Michael too?'

'Tom is a good boy,' Nell said, as if she couldn't hear me. 'He calls me, checking in on me. He found me this place. He served his country. Do you support the troops? I hope you understand the sacrifice our boys make.'

'Tom brought you here?' I said, trying to get the old woman on some sort of track. 'Why would he do that?'

'Years, he served his country. Like a good boy. I always thought he should have been a part of this family, but things don't always work out the way you think.'

'Did Tom talk to you recently? Did he tell you what he's been doing?'

'Yes, he called me an hour ago. He said Laurie's boy was coming. And that's you, isn't it? It is good to see you. I didn't think I'd ever see you again.'

'Why did you move out here?'

'I think I had to,' Nell said, waving away my question as if it were an annoyance. 'It's a long time ago now. I couldn't even tell my neighbours who I was. Now, they wouldn't even believe me if I told them, but I know right enough. I know who I am.'

'You moved here right around the time my . . . that the accident happened?'

'Accident?'

'We crashed. Into the river. Mum and Michael, they didn't get out. Me and my dad, David, we did. We went back to the UK afterwards. Do you remember?'

Nell stared back at me, as if I hadn't just spoken. I wanted to say more, but the words wouldn't come.

'That must have been a long time ago. I forget things. I told her, I said, you can't run away from your problems. Got to face them head on. Same thing I told that woman across the street . . .'

Nell Rogers continued talking, her thoughts running away from her, it seemed. 'Nell . . . Mrs Rogers,' I said, trying to get her back in the room. In the current time period, the current conversation. 'I need to ask about Laurie. Can I do that?'

'Of course you can,' Nell replied, placing a hand over the other, as it shook beneath it. 'I like to remember her as a child, you know? She was such a pretty girl. The loveliest blonde curls, she had. She was always going to be a heart-breaker, that one. She should have been homecoming queen, but there was another girl. She stole the crown from her. I remember, she was so beautiful. Then *he* came along.'

'Who? My father?'

Nell's expression changed suddenly. Her lips pursed, as if she had tasted something sour. 'Took up with that man, didn't she? I didn't like him.'

'David?' I said, leaning forwards, linking my hands loosely. 'David Cooper? Was that his name?'

'Oh, I don't remember his name now, but I remember saying he was no good for her. Tom would have been better for her. He served his country, like a good boy should . . .'

'Mrs Rogers,' I cut in, trying to stop her from telling me the same story again. 'What happened with the man?'

'Oh, well, he took her away from us. He would treat her so bad. I saw her with a bruise one time. Right under her eye. Black and blue, it was. I asked her what had happened, but she lied to me. First time she ever did that, I would say. Said she banged it on a door or something like that.'

I tried to think about my dad, doing something like hitting my mum. It wouldn't come easily. Even after she and Michael had died, he had never raised a hand to me. He would get drunk, almost constantly, it felt, but he never turned violent towards me. I would get a few sharp words, but for the most part he wanted to pretend I didn't exist. I had to fend for myself. 'Are you sure this was David?'

'Could be his name. That, or John, or Paul, or maybe George.'

Or Ringo, I thought. 'This was in Connecticut, where you used to live?'

'Oh yes, long time ago now. Tom set me up in this lovely house after she was gone and I grew old here. Paul calls every now and again, but I haven't seen him in so long. She's gone now, just like my John. He died such a long time ago now, I'm sure. He was a good man. They're not easy to find these days.'

'Tom Miller moved you out here. You still haven't told me why?'

'Lot of problems back then. That man. Barely a man, I'll tell you that. He was always causing trouble. Tom said it would be easier if we all moved. Parker had to go too. Other side of the country, he said. I think he's a mechanic or something, out west. I always ask if he's settled down and found himself a nice woman, but he never tells me anything.'

I thought about telling her about Parker. That he was dead too. I thought it likely that Tom would have told her, but I didn't think she remembered. I decided against telling her again.

'What about Tom? Where did he go?'

She smiled back at me. 'He looked after Laurie, like always.'

CHAPTER 26

I was trying to keep track of Nell Rogers's wandering narrative but was struggling. 'When did you move out here? After the accident?'

'Long time ago now. Clinton was president, I think. The man, not the wife. I didn't like that one. Something about her you couldn't trust. Not that the other one we ended up with was any better.'

I had eight years to play with then. 1993 to 2001, if I remembered my US politics right. Inauguration to inauguration. It had to have been just after my mother had died, I thought. 'So, you've been here over twenty years?'

'Oh, doesn't the time fly. Feels like yesterday I was moving out of the old place. That was a lovely home. John and me, we were going to grow old together there, but life happens, doesn't it? What was the name of the place . . . the town, what was it called?'

'Mystic, right? That's where we came in 1995.'

'Yes, that's the place,' Nell said, clapping her hands together. 'After John died, I couldn't stay. I didn't want to anyway, really, but I couldn't either way.'

'The man that Laurie was with, do you remember his name?' I tried again, hoping something had shaken loose in Nell's mind. 'Was it David? Someone else?'

'Could be. I'm not sure now. Horrible man. I don't think he had a good bone in his body.'

I didn't think I was going to get much further than I had with a name, so I moved on. 'She moved to England. She married David and had two boys. Sam and Michael. Then, she came back in 1995 when John died. There was an accident a few days after he passed – Laurie and Michael died; they were buried with your husband. Does that sound right?'

'They went to England,' she replied, looking around the room slowly, her eyes finally settling on something on a bureau at the far side of the room. 'When she came back, they brought me back a little model, look.'

She slowly raised a finger and I followed it. On the sideboard, there was a miniature model of Big Ben, the gold colouring faded and peeling away. I looked back and smiled at Nell. 'Very nice.'

'They brought lots of things,' she said, remembering with a thin smile. 'British cookies, they were good. I had a lovely clock on the mantel, but the last woman broke it while dusting. I had to let her go after that. The new one is much better. African, I think. Or Mexican. Lovely, she is. Takes care of my things.'

'You never saw her again after the accident? No other time?'

'Oh, not as much any more, no. It has been a while since I saw her.'

I bet, I thought. 'She's been gone a long time. I'm the only one left.'

'Oh, there's always more people around than you think.'

Another pointed finger, that started waggling in mid-air. I lifted myself from the chair and moved over to the sideboard.

'Inside there, you can have a look. The whole family is in there.'

I opened the door to the cupboard underneath and sure enough, there were a number of photo albums. I lifted the top two and took them out.

I began leafing through them, recognising Nell as a younger woman. More family members, I guessed. There were several photographs, black and white, then colour.

Then, there was my mother as I remembered her.

She was young, smiling, and instantly recognisable.

My breath caught in my throat, as I continued to flick through the pages. There were dates underneath each photograph.

They stopped in the early 1980s.

Then, there were a few more later in the album. I continued to turn the pages, until I was suddenly looking at myself.

Nine years old, I guessed. Standing next to my mother, as she looked down at me. Then, a few more. Me and Dad. Me and Michael.

The four of us together.

'I wish I remembered this . . .' I said quietly to myself. I tried to recall this happening, but there was nothing but a blank. Everything about the trip centred around the accident. I couldn't remember the plane journey. The excitement that would have been inside me. Meeting this hidden part of my family – the new faces, the new voices. The exoticness of it all.

I placed the album back down and opened the other. A younger Nell, standing with a burly man, with forearms that would make Popeye envious. Shirt sleeves rolled up and a cigarette dangling out of the corner of his mouth. No smiles, just emotionless stares at the camera.

I flicked through the remaining pages until something fell to the floor at my feet. I bent down to pick it up and saw it was a loose postcard. I was about to place it back in the album when I saw the handwriting. I turned it over in my hand.

There was a beach – Californian, I guessed. Only as I turned it over to see the handwriting again, the postmark was in an entirely different state. Kansas. I didn't know my US geography perfectly, but I was fairly sure it wasn't on the coast.

That I did always love . . .

It was the poem. Emily Dickinson's words, scratched onto the back of a cheery beach scene.

I checked the postmark again and saw the date.

17th August 1997.

I'm okay. Immortality.

'Mrs Rogers . . .'

I was struggling to tear my eyes away from the writing. Even when I did, they landed on the date.

Two years after the accident that had torn my family apart. There was my mother's handwriting. Her words.

'Can you get that for me?'

I managed to look over at Nell Rogers, who was pointing at the floor. Where the postcard had landed, there was something else.

A small photograph. I picked it up, turned it over in my hands. It was no bigger than a passport photo, yellowed at the edges with age.

It was my mother.

Only, this time, she looked a little older. Different hair colour than I remembered.

My hands began to shake when I realised what it was.

A lump formed at the back of my throat and I couldn't breathe.

I was looking at the impossible.

It was my mother.

She was alive.

CHAPTER 27

Carson waited in the car, leaving Hunter to go inside the Enterprise Rent-A-Car place. It was the third one they'd visited already that morning and he was starting to think his hunch wasn't going to play out.

They now knew he had taken the Amtrak from Boston, but there were a number of places on the Connecticut route Sam Cooper could have got off at.

Anthony was convinced he was in Mystic, or close by.

He looked up as Hunter came jogging back over. His face was reddening by the second, which made Carson sniff and shake his head.

He wasn't really built for cardio, Carson thought. It looked painful.

'He hired a car early this morning,' Hunter said, as he got in the passenger seat. 'Didn't say where he was going. The guy said he turned up on foot, so he must've come from somewhere nearby.'

'How many motels are close by?'

Hunter pulled out his phone and began searching. Carson waited, tapping a finger on the steering wheel in time to the low music coming through the speakers. It was something new, but not as bad as the usual soulless garbage that seemed to count for popular these days.

'There's a few,' Hunter said finally, pulling them up on his phone screen. The cell looked tiny in his hand. 'We should hit every one of them. He's going to stick out round here. Someone will remember him.'

'The accent is always a giveaway for out-of-towners.'

Carson shifted into drive and listened as Hunter gave him directions. It felt good to be doing something that approached normal work.

That didn't involve him sticking a gun in someone's face. There was a time for that, but sometimes it was nice to pretend his job wasn't so out of the norm.

The Whaler's Inn and Hyatt Place were both a bust. Rodeway and the Hilton the same.

'Howard Johnson next,' Hunter said, pointing to the other side of the road. 'Diner right next to it, so we can get a coffee at least.'

Carson grunted a response, but drove into the parking lot anyway. He was already thinking about giving up. It wasn't like the old days. Now, people were more suspicious than ever.

They parked up and got out. Walked into reception and were greeted by a woman who couldn't take her eyes off Hunter from the moment he entered.

'Hey, we're looking for our friend, Sam. We think he might have got a bit lost coming back. He was supposed to meet us out front, but there's no sign of him.'

The reception girl bit the corner of her lip and looked behind her. 'I'm not sure I should be talking about a guest.'

Carson patted Hunter on the shoulder, who took the hint and moved forwards. He leaned on the desk separating them and smiled down at the woman.

'Any help would be appreciated,' he said, his voice smooth. 'He's a long way from home and we don't want anything happening to him.'

The woman smiled back at Hunter. Carson pulled out his cell and showed her a picture of Sam Cooper.

She leaned over to look and then nodded. 'The Brit, right?'

'That's him.'

'He left a couple of hours ago,' she said. 'Sorry you missed him. He wasn't waiting outside. He seemed to know where he was going. I'm sure if you wait, you'll catch him. He's not going anywhere for a few days yet.'

The glass shattered against the wall, splintering into pieces on the floor. Jackson grimaced, as he launched another at the motel room wall and watched it crash to the ground.

He needed the release. After what had happened hours earlier, his usual ability to keep his anger in check had disappeared.

He had failed. It really was as simple as that.

Standing in the small area between the bed and the window, he waited for someone to knock on the door and investigate what he was doing.

No one came and he considered throwing the TV out the window. Just to see how far he could push things.

He resisted the urge. Besides, he was already feeling a little calmer. Already beginning to feel his head clear a little.

He sat on the edge of the bed and gripped the side of the mattress, until his knuckles turned white and the palms of his hands began to burn.

On the nightstand, his cell phone vibrated against the wood and echoed around the room. He glanced across at it and closed his eyes briefly. Breathed in deeply and tried to control his heart rate.

Then, he reached across, snatched it up, and answered. 'Yeah?'

'It's me.'

The voice was enough to calm him down.

'Where are you?'

'I'm at a motel. *His* motel.'

'Where is it?'

'Howard Johnson, Mystic. Next to the diner. I've just got a room.'

'Is he there?'

Jackson could hear the strain in his voice. He guessed he hadn't slept well for the past few days either. 'Not right now. I don't know where he is.'

There was silence on the other end of the line, so quiet Jackson thought he'd hung up at first.

'Where'd you lose him?'

Jackson considered telling him of his failure. Of how some woman had got the jump on him and thrust who knows how many volts through his body. He thought about telling him how he'd jumped the gun and tried to take Sam Cooper from the cemetery.

He thought about confessing how badly he had messed things up and then quickly decided against it.

'He slipped away at some point,' Jackson said finally. 'I lost him behind some traffic and he was gone. He'll be back here before too long, I'm sure of it. Just got to be patient.'

Jackson held his breath, as he waited for him to use his disappointed voice. Instead, when he finally spoke, there was a note of acceptance about how this whole thing was starting to play out.

Badly, in a word.

'He's looking over his shoulder now. Anything could drive him away. Tell me when he gets back.'

The line went dead and Jackson stared at his cell phone for a few seconds, before placing it back down again. All he wanted to do was go back home. Away from all of this.

He wanted no part of what it had become.

He stood up and walked over to the balcony and looked out through the glass pane that separated him from the outside world. Stared at the parking lot and got himself ready.

Sam Cooper was going to die. He couldn't escape that inevitability.

CHAPTER 28

I shook my head and looked at the photograph again.

It couldn't be real. And yet, there it was, a tiny weight in my hand, that suddenly felt heavier than it should have.

'Mrs Rogers,' I said, turning back to the woman. She was staring out of the window, above the television. Her mouth slightly agape, lost in her own world. 'Can I ask you about this photo?'

She frowned at me for a second, as if she didn't know who I was. Then, something seemed to snap back into focus and she shook her head. 'You're going to have to bring it here. I can't see a thing that small from all the way over here.'

I moved closer to her, but stopped a few feet away. I didn't want to hand the picture over to her. Didn't want to let go of it.

'I don't know,' Nell said, slow and drawn out. Her head tilted to one side, as if she could see something more in the photograph that way. It didn't seem to help. 'Where is it from?'

'It's Laurie, Mrs Rogers,' I tried, but I could already see the lights were beginning to go out behind Nell's eyes. 'Your daughter.'

I tried to control the shaking in my hands, as I held out the photo closer to her. I could see it wavering in the air between us, but I couldn't stop.

'I'm sorry, I don't know . . .'

'Please, just tell me when this picture was taken? How did you get it?'

Nell shied away from me, as my voice echoed around the small room. I thought she was about to start crying and had a pang of guilt wash over me. I breathed in deeply and lowered my voice. 'Mrs Rogers, it's really important you tell me if you've seen this photograph before.'

'I need to watch my programmes,' Nell said, her voice quiet and a hint of fear within. 'You can show yourself out, can't you? Yes, I'm sure you can. My legs are tired now. I can't get around as well as I used to. I have a woman who comes in and helps me. She's from Mexico, or Brazil. One of those countries.'

'Is Laurie dead?' I asked, desperate now. 'Is this a real photo?'

Nell Rogers looked me in the eye and I could see only a little life left there. 'Dead? Don't say such things to an old woman. Tom put that on John's grave. I told him not to, but he said it was important. She's alive and well. And she's coming to see me. She hasn't forgot about her old mother, that I can tell you.'

'What are you saying? Is she coming here?'

Nell shook her head. 'I don't know if I'll have to meet her. I should find that out, thank you.'

I lifted my head to the ceiling. 'Mrs Rogers, have you spoken to Laurie? Recently?'

'I speak to her all the time. It gets lonely on your own, that I can tell you. You have conversations to keep your mind active. I speak to Laurie, to Parker, to John, to all of them.'

I pocketed the photo and the postcard. Set the photograph albums back in place and then turned back to Nell Rogers.

'You just sit tight,' I said, dropping to my haunches and trying to make eye contact with her. She was transfixed on the television now. 'I'll come back to see you.'

'That would be nice,' Nell murmured. 'I don't get many visitors. You can see your way out. I'm tired now.'

I reached out and touched her hand. She didn't respond for

a moment, then she placed her other hand on mine. 'It's so good to see you, Sam. Your mum would be so proud of you coming all this way to see me.'

I drove back to Connecticut, becoming more used to the roads now. The highway was busier, as the time ticked past five p.m. and approached what I assumed was rush hour.

I tried to concentrate on driving, but my mind – and my gaze – kept drifting back to the impossible.

Proof that she was alive.

The thought gave me some relief. I hadn't travelled all this way for nothing. I was in the right place. I was going to find out for sure. All I had to do was keep going. No matter what.

And there was nothing that would stop me now. I wasn't going to give up on her.

But if she had been alive all these years, why had she abandoned me? Why hadn't my father said anything before?

Years I spent under his roof. Years of him watching me slowly disappear into myself. Scared of saying the wrong thing, scared of doing something I shouldn't.

Scared of simply being there.

I couldn't think about my mother's reasons for abandoning me.

I pulled into the car park outside the motel and checked around me before walking to the diner and going in. It was busier now – the booths filling up and occupied by an interesting mix of people. Young families, with loud children. Older couples, sitting in the silence that accompanies longevity. Harried-looking single parents, locals smiling at the waitresses and calling them by their first names.

I waited to be seated, following the waitress to the back of the restaurant and being handed the same meal bible as earlier that day.

I picked a burger and a bottle of Budweiser to take the edge off. The waitress appeared quickly and took my order, her brightness a nice distraction from the day so far.

It was just before seven p.m. and the sky was black outside. I pulled out my phone and tried calling Rachel, but got no answer.

I scrolled to Tom Miller's name in my saved contact list and hesitated. Then, I pressed dial. It rang a few times, then went to voicemail. I didn't leave a message.

I set my phone down on the table and tried to work out what to do next.

She could be alive. Out there now. Waiting for me to find her.

I thought about what she would look like now. Whether she still had a smile that made me feel safe. Whether she could still wrap me in a warm embrace and never let go.

Whether she even still thought about me.

I needed to speak to Tom, properly. I had to book another few nights at the motel, I thought. And change my flight home. Four days wasn't going to be enough. I wondered how this whole excursion had hit my savings. How long it would take me to replace the money. Wondered what I was saving for anyway. A rainy day? Well, it was pouring down right now, without a cloud in the sky.

My mum is alive.

It wasn't like I could ever put enough away to buy my own place in London – not anywhere close, I thought. I didn't have anything to spend my money on.

I need to find her.

I jumped as my phone began trilling in my hand. Rachel's number flashed up on screen.

'Hey,' I said, feeling an instant of calm. 'You didn't need to call back this late.'

'That's okay, I've been waiting for you to call anyway. How are you getting on?'

I could hear the whoosh of something in the background, then a door close. I guessed she had been outside in her backyard.

'I found something and I don't really know what to do about it.'

I told her about everything that had happened in the last twenty-four hours.

She interrupted when I told her about what happened at the cemetery. 'Did you call the police? Sam, this is dangerous . . .'

'I know, I know,' I said, wondering exactly what I would tell the local police force. It *was* some story to tell. 'Things have happened so fast, I don't know what I would say to them. Can you imagine them believing me? Some tourist?'

'Does it matter? They're there for this reason.'

'Wait, because there's more.'

When I was finished, Rachel didn't say anything. I waited, wanting her to give me a reason to keep going. It didn't seem like she could think of one easily.

'It was definitely your mum? And her writing?'

'I think so,' I said. 'I just can't know for certain. Nell, my grandmother, she was very confused. And alone. She talks to her dead husband, so I've got no idea if she's really spoken to my mum or not. At this point, if she is alive—'

'And that picture seems to be the best proof you have that she is.'

'*If* she is alive, then what has she been doing for the past twenty-something years? Maybe she's been hiding for a good reason and me being here is just making things worse.'

'Maybe, but you could also finally get closure and be able to move on with your life.'

I thought about that. Closure. Something I'd thought I already had.

'If she's alive, she probably knows you're there,' Rachel said, her voice soft as silk in my ear. 'That's a reason to stay.'

'I know, you're right.'

'I'm glad you're already realising that, this early on,' she teased.

Silence grew between us, until I wondered if she'd fallen asleep on the other end of the phone. I opened my mouth to speak, but she managed to get there first.

'Just be careful, but you're not the type to just give up.'

'You can tell that about me?'

'Well, no, not really, but I couldn't think of anything else to say, so I've just started regurgitating those horrible Instagram quote-of-the-day posts, haven't I?'

I laughed genuinely at that, a few seconds passing before Rachel joined in.

'I feel better just for talking to you,' I said, as the laughter subsided. 'Maybe it's not as bad as I think.'

The waitress came back over, plonking down a plate, the size of which I'd never seen, on the Formica table. The burger was as big as my head and there were enough fries joining it that I imagined a vast field of potatoes had been stripped bare just for me. I smiled a thanks to the waitress.

'My dinner has just arrived,' I said, trying to work out how the hell I was going to pick the burger up. 'I'll let you go and get some sleep.'

'Well, stay safe.'

I promised I would try and looked down at the plate once I'd pocketed my phone. My appetite had come back. I tried to clear the plate, but I think even if I'd had three friends with me, we'd have still struggled. I drained my beer and then another. Left a number of bills on the table, hoping they were either enough or not too much, and left the diner. Walked back to the motel and scanned the car park. No suspicious cars. No eyes on me.

I don't know who I was kidding. I had no idea what I was even looking for really.

I stood in reception for a few seconds, trying to decide what to do. I thought about the man back at the cemetery – someone had been watching me when I arrived. It wasn't out of the question that they could know I was in this motel.

There were a few around the area, so I thought I could get another room easily enough.

I made a decision. Early the next day, I would book in somewhere else. Just to be safe. Back in my room, I lay on the bed, staring at the TV, and drifted slowly into sleep. Some bad reality show about house improvements, that was interrupted every five minutes by adverts, finally did it for me.

And I didn't wake until I heard someone trying to break into the room from the balcony.

1995

There was something worse than dying.

Laurie knew that now. Sitting in the back of the car, Anthony opposite her.

She knew he was going to win.

And that was worse than eternal darkness to Laurie. That was worse than being stuck six foot underground, slowly turning into worm food.

She ran over numerous options on the journey. How she could get herself out of the situation. Each one came back to the same end result.

He would kill her, then her family.

'Maria is at the house,' Anthony said, as if they were enjoying a simple car ride together. As if this was totally normal. 'She'll fix you something to eat.'

Laurie stared back at him.

'You're a psychopath,' Laurie said, spitting the words towards him. Venom and violence dripping from them. She may have been afraid, may have been trapped, but she couldn't stay quiet. Not now.

If her words had hurt, he didn't show it. He simply looked back at her, unblinking. Then, he shook his head and leaned forwards. She saw a familiar flicker in his eyes and she braced herself for what was to come.

'This will be much easier if you stay in control. You know what will happen if you don't.'

She wanted to say more. To scream at him.

'Everything is going to be fine now,' Anthony said, sitting back on the plush leather seat and stretching his arms out. 'It's all as it's supposed to be.'

Laurie opened her mouth to respond, but didn't get a word out.

The car was moving in the wrong way.

Instead of forwards, suddenly they were going sideways.

Laurie had a split second to wonder why she couldn't hear anything, before she realised the side of the car was indented and coming towards her. Then, she was on the floor, landing on her shoulder. There was a ringing in her ears, before she felt the impact from the other side of the car where she was lying, bringing it to a stop.

She glanced over her shoulder, grimacing at the pain, seeing the twisted metal of the side of the car, something embedded inside it.

Anthony was lying on the back seat, blood coming from his head, reaching into his pocket.

Laurie tried to get up, but her head spun with the effort. The door behind her suddenly gave way and she was being lifted from the car. Two strong hands, under her arms, pulling her outside.

She shook and began to struggle. Began to fight.

'Laurie, it's okay,' she heard a voice say and at first she thought it was Anthony. That he had somehow transported himself outside and was taking her away.

Only, there was life in the voice. There was good.

'Tom?'

He smiled down at her, then his expression changed and he dropped her to the floor. He was on the ground next to her in a breath, cursing.

Something flew past them and the echo of a gunshot rang out. She turned to see Carson emerge from the car, a gun drawn and pointing towards them.

'We've got to move *now*,' Tom said, taking hold of her hand and then shielding her behind him.

He shot quickly, accurately, into the side of the car. Six shots, spaced together, where Anthony had been sitting.

Nothing came back.

'Let's go,' Tom said, taking her by the arm and breaking into a run. 'Robert, cover me.'

There was another car idling nearby, a man in a crouched position holding a rifle towards the place they had left. He shouted towards them, but his words were lost on Laurie.

She had a moment to realise that she was being saved, before she understood that this was just another beginning.

CHAPTER 29

I was on my feet in seconds. Staring at the balcony window, covered by the curtains I had pulled closed only a few hours before.

It was as if I was still dreaming. Standing at the edge of a river, watching the water stream past me. What lay beneath its soft blue surface. The darkness unseen.

Light from the television cast an unearthly glow on the room. There was another sound outside – a scrape of metal – and I was already moving. I grabbed my bag, pulling it over my shoulder and slipping my feet into the trainers I'd left at the side of the bed. I heard a louder noise from behind me, but I was pulling the door open and exiting the room.

I jogged down the corridor, heading for the back entrance to the motel. I flew down the steps, before pausing at the door. I fumbled for my room key, as I scanned the car park outside, looking for anything that didn't fit.

There was nothing but the dim glow of the streetlights.

I scanned my keycard and pulled the door open, a blast of cold air engulfing me as I stepped out. The rental car was a few feet away and I ran towards it, my key out and unlocking the doors.

As I reached for the handle, I felt as if a truck hit me, slamming me to the ground. One second, I was standing and facing the car, the next, I was looking up at the night sky.

'Don't move.'

The voice could have been from a nightmare. As if the world had morphed into something while I slept and now what haunted me was in physical form.

A dark shape blotted out the sky.

'Sit up and keep your hands on your knees.'

I slowly did as I was told.

The dark shape moved and came into focus – an angry giant, who had found me sleeping somewhere I shouldn't have been.

I knew instantly who he was.

'We meet again,' said Carson. 'Only, this time, I have my friend here that will stop you making any quick movements, right?'

I saw the glint of a gun in his hand. Pointing towards my chest. My heart fell into my stomach. I glanced around me, trying to work out an escape plan. Carson reached down and grabbed me by the jaw.

'Hunter, get the car.'

He brought me up to my feet and after a few seconds, a car pulled up alongside us. I tried to struggle away, but he forced the gun under my ribs.

'Get inside, or you'll die here.'

I relented finally and was deposited in the back seat. Hunter was behind the wheel and he turned the car around and parked up on the other side of the motel. Carson was sitting next to me, his gun still aimed at me.

'Take us to her.'

I must have looked confused or unwilling to agree, because before I had a chance to answer, I was smacked into the side of the car. An explosion of pain thudding into my jaw. At first, I thought he had shot me, but as I reached up to my face, I realised he had struck me across the face with the gun.

'I'll ask again,' the man said, more calmly than I thought possible. 'You're out of options here. Either take us to her, or we kill you. Here and now.'

'I don't know what you mean,' I mumbled, holding onto my jaw tentatively. I could move it, so I didn't think it was broken. 'She's dead.'

This time, the explosion happened in my ribs. I saw his arm come down quickly and directly into the side of my body. The air was sucked out of me, leaving me gasping for breath. My brain didn't seem to know what pain to process first – the jaw or the ribs.

'Don't make me do this, kid.'

I caught my breath finally and felt saliva spill from my mouth. It tasted bitter. 'I . . . I've got nothing to tell you.'

'We both know that's not true. Where is she?'

'I swear, I don't know.'

Carson tilted his head, studying me. Nodded once to himself. I saw Hunter rifling through my bag on the front seat; I tried to move, but waves of pain shot through my body.

'Now, it's very simple,' Carson said, not a trace of pity in his words. 'I'm going to ask you some questions and you're going to answer them. Every time you tell me a lie, I'm going to hurt you.'

I had no doubt that he was telling the truth. I also knew there was nothing I could tell him that would stop this.

I reached around, trying to find the door handle, kicking out as I did so. Carson crawled over me, pinning me down with his full weight so I couldn't move. He pressed his forearm against my chest, so I couldn't move.

'If you don't know where she is, how about how to contact her? Can you call her?'

I swallowed back the bile rising in my throat. Squirmed until I had freed one arm. 'How can I? She's dead.'

He drove his fist into my face. I raised my hand just in time, partially blocking the blow, but it still sent my head spinning. He kept one hand gripped on my shirt, but moved so his weight wasn't on me.

'I'll ask again . . .'

'Wait, wait,' I said, holding my hands up, trying to make myself as small as possible in the confined space of the back of the car. 'I don't know. Really. I haven't found her.'

'Right, good, we're starting to get somewhere. Where have you been today? Who have you seen, spoken to?'

I hesitated and felt a crack against my shoulder and then a hand grabbing a fistful of hair on my head. I shouted out in pain, but a gloved hand came across my face.

'Who did you see?'

They didn't know. They must have been following me, but they didn't know about Nell Rogers. I mumbled against his hand and he released it a little. 'I was trying to find my family, but I couldn't. That's all. To see if they knew anything. I was going to try again tomorrow. I just wanted to tell them about my dad. My mum is gone, I don't know why you're looking for her.'

I waited for another hit. Another burst of pain. None came. It seemed he bought the lie. At least for now.

'Why come all this way if you didn't think she was alive? That's what the old man told you, right? You're looking for her, right?'

I shook my head, as much as I was able to anyway, and my eyes felt like they were going to fall out. I felt a wave of nausea and tried to swallow it back. The man grabbed me by the jaw, making me cry out.

'I don't want to repeat myself.'

'I never believed it,' I whispered, the effort to talk becoming almost too much. 'I was there when she died. I know she's gone. Yeah, I want it to be true, but I know it can't be. But if there's a chance . . .'

'You travelled all the way here because you thought there was a *chance*? I don't buy it.'

He let go of my jaw and I slumped on the seat. I shook my head, trying to think straight. To work a way out of this situation.

'Now, I'm going to ask you again. Where is she?'

'I . . . I don't know.'

He shifted and dug his hand into my knee. It suddenly felt locked in a vice. I could feel him squeezing it more and more.

'You know, we've waited a long time to get close to your mom,' he said. His words came through a fog of agony and despair. My mind couldn't seem to make sense of them.

'He's been looking for her for a long, long time. And he's going to find her. She stole something from him, and I'm going to help him find it. You're going to help me get that.'

'I . . . I can't . . .'

'Look at this, Carson,' Hunter said, but I was barely listening. I was trying to shut out the pain, as he gripped my knee in his hand. It felt as if he was twisting the bone, gnarling it. 'That's her, right?'

'Yeah, what about it?' Carson replied, letting go of me finally.

'It says 1997,' the younger man said to Carson. 'That means she got out alive.'

I sat up and saw Hunter pass Carson the photograph I had taken from Nell's house earlier that day.

'Give that back to me,' I spat towards them. 'Now.'

Carson snapped his attention back to me. 'Where did you get this? Was this from Tom Miller?'

I managed to move, so my back was against the car door. There was inches between us.

'Tell me who gave you this.'

I shook my head. I wasn't going to answer.

Carson sighed and shook his head. 'I admire your balls, kid. I do. But it's done. Tell me. Or I'll make sure your mom sees your body before the end.'

'No. I . . . I can't.'

Carson stared down at me for a few seconds, then his shoulders slumped. 'I guess you've made your choice. She'll know you tried your best, but that wasn't enough.'

Out of the corner of my eye, I saw Hunter shift forwards and lean over the front seat. I saw him lift something in the air between us and knew what it was.

I was staring down the barrel of a gun and I had no way out.

CHAPTER 30

It was taking too long.

It was supposed to be quick. Over and done with. Get the answers they were supposed to and then call him with the good news.

Anthony poured another measure of whiskey and stared at his cell phone. They had been at the motel for almost thirty minutes and there hadn't been another word.

Sometimes, he wasn't a patient man. He tapped his fingers against the desk and stared across at Zoran who was sitting opposite.

'I should have sent you,' Anthony said, taking a glug of whiskey and enjoying the burn down his throat. 'You know to keep in contact.'

'Carson will do good.'

Anthony raised his eyebrows towards Zoran, but didn't disagree. 'This is the problem with making plans. God laughs for a reason.'

Zoran sniffed, which Anthony took as all the response he was going to get from him.

'Look up stoic in the dictionary and there's a picture of you, right?'

Zoran stared back at him. 'When it is time to talk, I'll talk.'

Quick and painless. That's what Carson had said it would be.

Only, this wasn't quick and probably not painless.

There was nothing to do but wait.

It shouldn't have been like this.

If she had just done as she was told, there wouldn't have been any need for this violence. Now, she had brought her own son into it.

Such a shame.

'You ever hear of Newton's third law, Zoran?'

Zoran looked back at him as if he hadn't said a word. Anthony was used to it.

'For every action, there's an opposite and equal reaction,' Anthony said, as if Zoran was a captive audience. 'So, the way I see things has always been based on that simple fact. If someone is in my way, I have to show force in response. I'm reacting to their presence, correct?'

Zoran pursed his lips, but didn't respond.

'If a guy comes all the way from the UK, looking for his dead mom, and he's going to cause a problem for me, then I need to react in an equal manner. Or, if some woman, for example, does something to me, I have to respond in kind, yes?'

'It must be so.'

Anthony was standing now, his hand hovering over the glass decanter. He could already feel the effects of the whiskey taking hold. The room dimming a little. Blurring.

'You don't agree?'

Zoran opened his mouth to reply, then closed it. Shook his head.

'No, go on, I'm interested in hearing what you think? I'm right, aren't I?'

'Second law of thermodynamics.'

Anthony cocked his head. 'Yeah?'

'Well, energy in an isolated system cannot be sustained. All this energy on one thing, it is being wasted. Energy, it is flowing on and on, all for one cause. It is becoming useless. There is a fixed limit advancing and soon it will all be done. Useless. It is unsustainable.'

Anthony stood over Zoran for a few seconds, then turned away. 'I prefer when you don't speak.'

'So do I,' Zoran replied.

Anthony checked his watch again. Thirty-five minutes.

Another five and he would call Carson.

Jackson woke from a broken sleep, his neck stiff from sitting upright on the motel bed.

He rubbed the back of his neck and grabbed a bottle of water from beside him, looked over at the clock on the dresser and saw it was now close to four in the morning. He got up off the bed and peered into the darkness of the parking lot.

There was a new car in the lot. It must have been a noise from out there that had woken him.

He looked down at it, and could just make out the make and model.

The engine on. Idling. Red lights glowing in the darkness.

And his senses were on fire again.

He didn't believe in coincidences.

Someone had come for Sam Cooper while he slept.

He saw something being thrown out of the window, then the car sped off.

Jackson was on his feet and grabbing his cell phone.

He would be damned if he didn't get to Sam Cooper first.

CHAPTER 31

I started pounding against the window and shouting for help. I felt Carson's arms move across me, but I was flailing like a fish on dry land.

'Listen to me,' Carson said, his voice close enough to my ear that it sent a shudder through my body. 'You're going to do as we say. If you so much as squeak, I'll put one in your head. If anyone comes out to see what is going on, you'll get a bullet in the leg, they'll get two in the head. Understand?'

I balled my hands into fists and fought against the urge to drive them into Carson's body. Hunter got out of the car. The door opened behind me and I fell out onto the ground. The ground felt as cold as ice and I winced.

Carson took a firm hold of me, as Hunter propped open the boot and stood to one side.

'No, I'm not going in there.'

'You don't really have a choice in the matter.'

I tried to pull away, but Carson was stronger. He lifted me, as if I weighed nothing, and in no time at all, I was being dropped onto the soft interior of the boot. Then, an echo of noise, followed by silence.

Car doors slammed shut and I heard the engine rev. I screamed into the darkness. A squeal of tyres and I was thrown backwards in the small space, hitting my head against the inside of the boot. I felt around, trying to find something, anything, I could use to defend myself.

There was nothing.

I cried out again, but I don't think it travelled far from the confines of the small space I was lying in. The car went over something and I bumped against the top of the boot. I tried to shift my body, find a comfortable position, but it was pointless. I was in a foetal position, barely able to move my arms or legs out.

I closed my eyes and tried to control the panic I was feeling, every bump in the road sending shock waves of pain through my body.

The more I thought about my situation, the angrier I got.

I ignored the pain, the hurt, and kicked out with all my force, but the boot held. I must have put some dints in it at least, but it stayed firmly closed. I turned and concentrated on the shelf that separated me from the back seat, feeling for any sort of catch or release. I turned around on my side and tried to think.

A release. On the inside, it wouldn't be by the seats. It would be at the lock that closed the boot itself.

I felt around the edge of the boot lid and my fingers settled on something. I got closer to it and realised it was glowing a little in the dark.

My hands began to shake, as I saw a way out.

I pulled on the release and it came away in my hand. The boot stayed closed.

'You bastards . . .'

I was going to kill them. Whoever they were. I didn't care any more.

I found the taillights and used the heel of my foot, slamming it against the brake lights as hard as I could manage. I could feel the energy spilling out of me in every action I took. I kept going, until I could barely feel my feet, the numbness running through every single one of my muscles.

I stopped after a while, as my mind began to set itself right again. I could feel sweat cascading down from my forehead. My throat was dry; every swallow felt like I was choking on sand. The heat inside the boot of the car was stifling.

There was a jolt, as the car pulled up at what I assumed was a light. I listened carefully, trying to hear the two men talking within the car. There was only silence.

Then, an explosion of sound. It took me a few seconds, but then I realised what it was.

A gunshot.

Tom Miller had been here before. Chasing down a car, in the middle of the night, hoping that he wasn't too late.

Another day, another Cooper to save.

Only this time, he felt responsible. It was because of him that Sam had got himself into this situation.

The car was a pair of brake lights in the distance. A blur of darkness, without any real form.

'Where do you think they're taking him?'

Tom glanced across at Quinn in the passenger seat. She was holding onto the dash as the car lurched forwards, speeding down an empty road.

'If they take him to that house in Greenwich, he won't stand a chance. By the time I get in there, he'll be dead.'

He didn't wait for her reply.

Up ahead, he could see the lights growing brighter – he was gaining on them by the second.

Then, they glared fully and he almost careened into the back of the car. It had stopped at an intersection. Tom banged his foot down on the brake and heard a whoosh of breath escape from Quinn.

He didn't think twice. He shook off his seat belt and was out

of the car in an instant. Gun drawn, he saw past the trunk where
Sam was being held and stepped to the side. Levelled his weapon
and shot out the front tire.

When the bullet flew past his head, he realised his mistake.
He should have aimed for the driver. Not the car.

CHAPTER 32

Carson was already firing back, even as Hunter was throwing the car into drive and barrelling through the intersection.

'Who the hell was that?'

Carson wasn't listening. He was trying to see into the darkness behind them. The blown-out tire caused the rear of the car to skid, rubber being shredded on the asphalt.

He fired again, the smell of saltwater in the cold, night air. From the little he could see in the side mirror, he thought he'd hit something. The wind rippled through the open window and blew through the car.

The road twisted ahead and Carson felt the vehicle battle against them.

'Drive,' he said, redundant as it was, as Hunter was speeding on an empty road. His rough, huge hands encompassing the wheel and almost swallowing it whole. The car felt as if it was struggling to stick to the asphalt. Gliding along as if they were sliding on ice.

Carson looked behind him, hearing shouts coming from the trunk. He allowed himself a quick smile at the thought of Sam Cooper thrashing around back there, before he tried to concentrate on the road.

Sure enough, two lights came out of the shadows. He could hear the screech of the wheel underneath them and didn't think it would be long before the rubber detached itself entirely.

Carson aimed towards the lights – straight down the middle –

and fired two shots into the distance. He heard an echo and then a thud, but the lights kept coming towards them. Streetlights had long since disappeared behind them and now all he could see was the few yards illuminated by the headlights.

Sweat flicked down from his brow and hit his free hand. Beside him, he heard Hunter swearing under his breath. The bigger man was still struggling to keep the car on the road, but Carson couldn't allow that into his thinking.

There was a much bigger problem coming up in the rear-view mirror. Carson crawled over the console and onto the back seat. The banging from the trunk was louder now, thudding against the seat as he tried to get himself situated.

'Shut up back there, or I'll start firing your way,' he shouted, his voice losing its power as the car shook one way and then another. Carson leaned back a little, shielded his face, and then shot out the back window.

Glass shattered around him, but it gave him an uninterrupted view to the car behind them.

At first, all he saw was the girl in the passenger seat. Even as he shielded his eyes from the headlights, he still couldn't see the driver properly. He levelled the gun in his hand and aimed for the space he thought should be occupied by whoever it was. He squeezed the trigger and a flash of light burned through the night sky. He almost saw the bullet ping off the hood of the car.

The girl disappeared.

He fired two, maybe three shots more, but his aim was off.

'Keep her straight,' Carson said, ducking down and turning to Hunter driving.

He moved slowly, peering over the back seat, gun drawn.

They were closer now. He could see the driver better, but Hunter was still struggling and he couldn't get a clear shot. He tried anyway and missed.

Carson ducked down again, just as the car clipped them from behind.

He smiled to himself as the headlights on their car shifted to his right. Slid across the road, until all he could see was shadow.

They had lost control.

'Stop the—'

Then, he was thrown across the back seat with a thud. His body hit the side of the car, taking the wind out of him.

They were falling.

It wasn't the car that had been following them that was sliding off the road.

It was his.

I heard the first gunshot like a dull thud. An echo of report, then a thump somewhere close by. Someone was firing on the car and I was a sitting duck.

I heard another shot hit the car, but it was almost as if it were happening elsewhere. I was concentrating solely on getting the hell out of the car.

The car moved and I was thrown into the side of the boot, my shoulder bearing the brunt of the impact. I turned back gingerly, trying to create space where there was none to be found. I heard my own shouts, my own screams, as I felt the car slide around.

I tried to raise my legs again, but it was too cramped back there. I imagined kicking out and raising the lid of the boot, but I couldn't get enough leverage behind it. I took to pounding against the lock, hoping I could shift something at least. Get a little sliver of hope.

There was none to be found.

It was quiet for a second, then a shot rang out that seemed to explode directly above me.

I screamed again, louder, then heard a voice slicing through the darkness.

'*Shut up back there . . .*'

I lost whatever else he said, as the car jerked to the side violently, but I didn't think the sentence ended well.

There was a beat of almost silence, then more gunshots above me. I flinched at each one, holding my head in my hands, as if that could save me.

Another shout from within the car, but I couldn't make out what was being said.

I hear another shot, then Carson's voice came through clear.

'*Stop the . . .*'

Then, a thump into the side of the car, an unearthly screeching sound which seemed to start some way away. It vibrated along the side of the car.

I felt the car turning and was powerless to do anything about it. A feeling of weightlessness, then a crashing sound.

The sound of water.

When the passenger in the car smashed out the back window, Tom turned to Quinn instantly.

'Get down and stay down.'

Seconds later, a bullet came through the windshield and embedded itself into the headrest above where Quinn was now crouched down. Tom could barely see over the steering wheel, as he hunkered down.

He wasn't looking to the side of the road, so he didn't see the river. He was concentrating too hard on not losing the car in front.

They couldn't make it far on three wheels. All he had to do was outlast them.

From the little he could see of the tire he had blown out, it wouldn't be long before it disintegrated. Still, he wasn't about to leave things to chance.

'Hold on,' Tom said, gripping the wheel tighter and pushing his foot further to the floor.

The moment the impact came, he knew they would leave the road.

Tom stamped on the brake pedal, as the car in front spun out of sight. He opened the door as it left the road, and was walking fast towards them as he heard the crash of water.

That was when he realised there was a river off the side of the road.

Until then, he thought the worst that could happen would have been a head-on impact into a tree or something, but this was worse.

Head on, Sam would have been okay. He was in the trunk. Probably a few bruises, but he would walk away fine.

Sam was locked in the trunk of a car that was going to be submerged.

Tom started sprinting towards the rapidly dimming lights in the distance.

1995

You don't always get to choose your final words.

Sometimes, you don't know it's the end. When it's all over and there's no chance for a final goodbye.

It was almost one a.m. by the time Tom had driven Laurie back to Mystic. He pulled to a stop outside the house and jumped out of the car. Ran around to her side and ushered her towards the house.

'Get David and the kids,' he said, breathing heavily. 'I'll wait here.'

Laurie ran to the house, just as David opened the door.

'What's going on?' he said, looking past her and towards Tom on the street. 'What happened?'

She told him quickly – about Anthony taking her from the backyard, of the men he had with him, and Tom saving her life. She could see the fire in his eyes, but reached out and took hold of his arm.

'I'll kill him . . .'

'No,' Laurie said, grasping him by the shoulders. 'We have to go. Now. There's no time.'

'But—'

'Get the passports and anything else we need. I'll get the boys.'

He hesitated for a moment and then relented. Ran into the house ahead of her. She heard the television playing softly in the living room as she followed. Her mom asleep in front of it, making soft noises as she dreamed restlessly. She thought about waking her, but couldn't face it.

She crept down to where her two boys were asleep on the pull-out beds in the den. Sam stirred first. He opened his mouth to shout, but Laurie leaned forwards and placed a finger across his lips.

'Shush,' she whispered, her eyes brimming with tears. 'We need to be very, very quiet.'

He looked back at her, a frown on his face. 'But . . .'

'We're going on an adventure,' she said, reaching out and handing him his coat. He slipped it over himself, half asleep. She bent down and took Michael from where he was sleeping. He didn't wake, snuggling into her chest, as she lifted him up and carried him out of the room.

They moved to the door, careful not to make any noise.

David came down a minute later – a small bag in his hand. They stole out of the house and down the path.

Tom was waiting, looking up and down the street, shifting from one foot to the other. He came towards her as she reached the end of the drive.

'You and David get in the rental,' Tom said, glancing at David. 'I'll follow behind you.'

'My mom . . .'

Tom was about to answer, when headlights lit up the night sky. A car pulled onto the street behind them, still a hundred yards away.

'Go,' Tom said, lifting Michael from her arms and depositing him in the back seat. David already had the door open for Sam, who sleepily lifted himself into the car. He then rushed around to the driver's side and got in.

'Just keep driving,' Tom said, then he was gone. Laurie was already moving around to the passenger side and getting in.

'Where are we going, Mum?' Sam said, still whispering, even as David put the car in drive and sped away from the curb.

'You'll see,' Laurie replied, wondering how far she would get, before that answer wouldn't be good enough. 'Try and sleep, like your brother is.'

She knew by just one glance in the rear-view mirror that he wouldn't. He was wide awake now, eyes wide with excitement.

'Keep going,' Laurie said, laying a hand on David's arm. He was staring into the rear-view mirror, as the car behind approached the house. 'Don't look back.'

Laurie looked over her shoulder, as she saw Tom come into view. Saw his arm extend and then two gunshots explode into the darkness.

She screwed her eyes shut, as the car jerked violently. David swore under his breath, turning off the street and putting his foot down.

'Mum?' a small voice said from the back seat, more curious than frightened. 'Dad? What's happening?'

'It's okay,' David said from the driver's seat, before she had a chance to answer. Calm, cool. Collected. No hint of the fear that she knew would be coursing through him. 'Everything will be fine.'

As they sped down roads and made turns at random, Sam's cries became more scared. Each one was a knife in her heart.

A few minutes down the road, she saw David look behind him and then turn to her.

'I think we lost them.'

Laurie looked back, seeing an empty road. She felt relief, then dread, as she thought about what she had left behind. 'Tom . . .'

'He'll be okay,' David said, reaching out to her with his free hand. 'He can look after himself.'

She murmured an agreement, but that didn't stop her thinking about him. What might have happened. Not just to him, but her mom too.

'I don't know where we are,' David said, peering out onto the road ahead. 'Have you seen any signs?'

Laurie looked out and could see the river alongside them. 'I think if you keep going straight we'll hit the highway.'

They fell into silence, punctuated by more questions from Sam in the back seat. Laurie was giving him one-word answers, still thinking about what she had left behind for Tom to deal with, until it became too much.

'We have to go back,' Laurie said quietly. 'We can't leave them back there alone.'

David shaped to answer before the car lit up inside and they were thrown forwards into the dash.

The car was behind them. Trying to force them off the road. She could see nothing but headlights behind her, but imagined Anthony behind the wheel. His dead eyes focused on her.

David put his foot down again, as Sam started sobbing behind her. Michael took his brother's lead and soon the car was filled with noise.

'Hold on,' David shouted, gripping the wheel with both hands. Laurie looked back to the road ahead and saw the bend too late. They were going too fast, the car struggling to stay on the asphalt.

The headlights disappeared from behind, the car looming up beside them. Laurie could see shadows inside the other car. Then she screamed as they slammed into the side of their car. David desperately tried to keep it on the road, but the car shook from side to side, before finally losing control.

Then, they were falling into the black of the night.

They hit the water and the force knocked Laurie forwards and into the dashboard. Her head spun, as water began pooling around her feet instantly. She looked over to the driver's side and saw David was out cold. Blood dripping down his face.

She tried to open the door, but it wouldn't move. The window was open, the river rushing in. Her vision blurred. She turned around slowly but couldn't see a thing. Only darkness. Shadows. Ghosts.

She couldn't see her children. Her two boys, sitting in the back. She wanted to see them. One last time.

Her last thoughts, as unconsciousness took her, were of her family.

At least they were all together.

She couldn't even say sorry.

And as the water filled her lungs and she couldn't breathe any longer, she thought of nothing but the fact she had failed them all.

Anthony was up there somewhere, she knew. Watching them die.

He had won.

She had always been his.

CHAPTER 33

Tom dived into the water, the cold hitting him like a train. It shocked the breath out of him and he swallowed water as he tried to fight his way back to the surface. He thrashed his arms around, until they hit the air and then his head followed. He spat water out and gasped in a lungful of air.

In the distance, he could hear the car's engine silencing. The pull of the river further in. He heard shouts coming from all directions – Quinn behind him, a male voice ahead.

He tried to ignore them.

'It's okay, Sam,' Tom said, quietly to himself, as he struggled against the current. 'I'm coming for you. I'm coming . . .'

All he could see was Laurie's face in the water below. The past coming back to him – that moment he hadn't been able to save her, twenty-five years earlier.

He blinked back the memories, as he tried to forget. To concentrate. Only, there was David Cooper, emerging from the depths, grasping hold of his arm. He saw Sam, stuck in the car, trying to get out. Michael, struggling with his seat belt.

That had been the last time he'd been in water. Once you'd been to those depths, you didn't want to return.

'Tom!'

It was Quinn's voice, but it may as well have been a stranger's. He wasn't listening. He was trying to gain purchase on the riverbed below, but he wasn't finding anything underneath his feet and the more he moved, the more the water tried to claim him.

The water was moving faster than he'd been expecting. The riverbank disappeared behind him, as he struggled for a few moments against the current. It rose and crashed against him, as he forced himself to take a longer breath and calm.

Tom fixed his eyes on the car a few yards in the distance, and went under again.

I'd smacked into the boot lid, throwing my hands around my head as we tumbled down. Falling into nothingness, before we'd crashed into the water.

That was the sound I'd heard. I had a few seconds to wonder if it was my own paranoia, but that was quickly dispatched when drips of water began hitting my face.

I lifted a leg slowly, testing my ability to move. That worked, so I tried the other.

Then, I brought both together and used all my strength to kick out against the lid of the boot. I could feel air coming through a gap – some kind of damage that had happened in the crash.

Finally it gave way and for a split second, I was free.

Then water rushed in and my body was submerged.

I pushed hard with my feet and rose to the surface. I was out of the car, at least, but straight into another bad situation. The current was strong, pulling me away. I grasped onto the edge of the car, trying to hold on.

I couldn't swim. Had never learned. Had avoided the water at all costs. I could barely tolerate a bath – making sure every place I lived in had a shower.

I went under again. Came up and was facing the other way. The darkness, only slightly illuminated by the lights slowly dimming beneath the surface of the water. I heard a splash behind me and I felt my hands torn away from the car.

I was fighting against the water instantly. Doggy-paddling my way against the strong current of the river, trying to find my way back to the riverbank I thought was only a few feet away.

'Sam!'

The shout cut through the night, but it made barely a dint in my mind. I was too busy trying not to give in to the panic and adrenaline coursing through my body. I had to get to dry land.

It was a losing battle.

My body was still in shock from the cold, moving slowly against what was becoming a more forceful current the further I went. And that wasn't far. I was furiously thrashing my arms against the water, but seemed to be stuck in place.

I caught sight of something ahead of me and it gave me a renewed purpose. It was the tree line at the side of the road where we'd flown into the water. I doubled my effort. I was desperately pushing through the water, which felt like moving my arms through quick-drying concrete. My head was going under and under, swallowing more of the water, but I kept going. Kept moving. Unwilling to allow myself to be beaten.

Something slapped across my face, but I couldn't see what it was in the dark. It scraped against the skin and I could feel the sharp, biting pain that sprung from it.

I continued to move my arms, kick my legs, as the growing tide tried to steal me away from my goal.

I could feel the energy draining from me, being sucked into the dark water and disappearing.

If it wasn't for the iciness of the water, I could have been anywhere. The black was an embrace – trying to keep me from seeing what was really happening.

Underneath, it was darker still. Nothing but black, all around me. I couldn't breathe – every time I kicked my legs to return to fresh air, the river pulled me closer. I kicked my legs, already burning from the effort. I was losing the fight.

The nightmare I'd had for twenty-five years was coming true. I was living it.

I heard myself cry out and my throat felt hoarse. It was almost a croak of effort, but it was all I could manage before the water began to drag me down again.

There was a moment when I thought I saw Michael under the surface. It became real – the memory of leaving him inside the car, watching him cry out to me. His last moments, watching me leave him behind. The fear in his eyes.

In that second, I lost control. I was trying to keep my face above water, but it was too late. I was being dragged under and there was nothing I could do about it.

CHAPTER 34

I spread my arms and stopped moving, the weight of the water dragging me down to the bottom of the river.

I barely felt the hand around my wrist. Dismissed it as my mind giving me a moment of relief before my body gave in. It didn't matter that I could feel the pressure on my skin. Then, a heavier grip around my arm.

I was still in the water, but I could feel the ground beneath my feet. Someone's arm was around me, almost dragging me along the surface of the river. I could hear someone shouting in the near distance, but I couldn't make out the words. There was a low voice in my ear, telling me everything was going to be okay.

I grasped hold of something in front of me – branches, a bush, something – and pulled myself onto dry land.

I had somehow made it out.

I crawled out of the water and lay on the ground for a few seconds, trying desperately to get my breath back. Someone was leaning over me, holding my head up and talking softly.

'It's going to be okay,' she said, pulling me to my knees.

I recognised Quinn's voice. 'What . . .'

'We need to move.'

I looked up slowly to see Quinn next to me. A man over to my other side.

'Can you stand?' he said, and I understood that it was Tom.

'Yeah,' I tried to say, but my voice was cracked and it came out as a whisper. I nodded numbly.

I began to shiver, as the cold air hit my wet body. My clothes clung too tight, making it difficult to move. I crawled on my knees, before managing to lift myself up onto my feet. I was drenched through and moved my arms to hug them around my body.

I felt Quinn's arm around my shoulder and followed her as she pulled me away.

I allowed myself to be bundled into the back of a car. Tom ran around to the front seat and got behind the wheel. He screeched off at speed, as I stared blankly out of the window at disappearing scenery.

'This is Groton.'

It was the first time Tom had spoken on the short journey. I recognised his voice from speaking to him on the phone – the deep timbre of his tone filling the small space in the car.

I looked at the passing buildings in the low morning light. Another small town, across the river from Mystic, only this looked more like the suburbia I knew from TV. Low-level homes lined the street outside, wooden pylons separating them from each other. No white picket fences, but plenty of green patches of land.

I turned back to Tom driving. He looked older than the faded memory I had of him. I guessed he would be the same age as my mum, if she was . . . well, I couldn't think of that again.

Fifty-six years old. That sounded about right. Only a couple of years younger than my dad, but the difference was startling. His chest was like a barrel and what hair he had left was clipped short. He had a few days' stubble on his face, grey and spiky. He looked like he could chop logs with his hands alone.

We turned off a long street and down what looked like a dirt track. The tree line grew thicker around us, until an empty driveway outside a small home appeared. Single level, it seemed, small and grey in colour, offset by a bright white door with cream-coloured concrete steps leading up to it. The early morning light was beginning to sneak through the night, as we reached the door.

We left the car and approached the house. Close up, I could see towards the back that the building was bigger and thought I may have been mistaken about it only being a single-level home.

'Whose house is this?'

Tom turned back, one hand on the door. Quinn answered for him. 'It's a safe place. No one knows about it. Tom needed somewhere to crash and this was the best option.'

I didn't move.

Tom stepped back towards me. 'Come inside. We'll talk. I'll answer any questions you have.'

I relented, trusting that he hadn't saved my life for no reason.

We walked into the house and down a small hallway until I found myself in a kitchen-dining room that smelled faintly of bleach and grease.

'Take a seat,' Tom said, his back to me. He finally found what he had been rooting around for and threw a towel in my direction. I caught it and absent-mindedly ran it over my face and hair. There wouldn't be much to be done about my clothes.

'I've got spares for you to change into, but I'm not sure they'll fit right. You want a drink first? Coffee, juice? Something stronger would probably be best, but I don't have anything.'

When I looked at him, I had that feeling you have when you run into someone at a supermarket or out on the street. A moment of recognition that you can't quite place. Someone you think you know, but then, in the next moment, can't think of how or when at all.

I knew him. That was enough.

'Now, you gotta make a choice,' Tom said, talking to me as if I were a child he was trying to placate. 'You want to get changed first, or ask me your questions?'

I thought for a second, as my feet squelched on the floor and my T-shirt and jeans epoxied to my body. It sent another shiver of ice through my body.

'Some dry clothes would help.'

He nodded and a few minutes later I was dressed in clothes that almost fit me. I had found my phone in my pocket. It still had a few percent of battery left and seemed to be working. My wallet was in my back pocket and I took that out too. Inspected it and found my cards still in the slots, but the dollars were wet through. I transferred it all into the new clothes.

I thought about my bag – my passport was inside. It would be at the bottom of the river now, I guessed.

I was stuck in the country until I could get a replacement. It was something I couldn't think about yet.

'Coffee or juice?'

'Coffee is fine,' I replied, sliding onto a chair around a small table. There was another seat opposite, but no others.

'Quinn, do you mind?' Tom said, looking past me and over my shoulder. I turned to her, as she gave him a nod and moved towards the kitchen. She came back with a juice and set it down on the table in front of Tom. She went back and began fiddling with a coffee maker.

'Right then,' Tom said, and I saw his face in the light properly for the first time. He looked down at me for a few seconds, then sat carefully opposite me, still studying me. 'You feeling okay?'

I laughed hollowly. 'What do you think?'

'I understand,' Tom said, fiddling with his glass of juice, setting it at the correct angle in front of him. 'I told you not to come here. That it would be too dangerous. You should have listened to me.'

'I . . . I had to,' I replied, still snatching glances at him and trying to grasp hold of the memories I had of him. 'How was I supposed to just stay in London when there was a chance she was alive? You could have just told me the truth over the phone.'

'I hoped I had more time,' Tom said, his jaw tensing. He struggled to get all that close to the table in front of him. He cleared his throat and the chair creaked underneath his weight as he shifted. 'Still, it's a long way to come when you're not sure what you're going to find.'

'How did you find me tonight?'

'We were keeping an eye on you,' he said, picking up his glass and taking a drink. He returned it to the coaster in front of him and then fiddled with the way it was placed again. 'Good job too. If we hadn't got there in time, you'd be dead already.'

'Did you know they were coming for me?'

Tom shook his head. 'I didn't think he would come after you directly. I got that wrong.'

'And by "he", you mean . . .'

'Tell me,' Tom said, leaning back slightly, the chair creaking in protest. 'What do you remember about your mom? You remember what happened?'

I frowned, wondering why he wouldn't answer my question, and hesitated before responding. I didn't know how much to give away. 'I was nine. We came over because her dad – my grandfather – died. She came into the room we were sleeping in. We had to leave really quickly. Then . . .'

'You got in a car.'

I nodded, staring off into the distance. 'I was scared. I remember that much. Mum and Dad, they were both trying to pretend nothing was wrong, but I could sense it. It was clear we were in danger.'

'Do you remember the crash?'

I shifted uncomfortably and didn't answer. I heard him exhale and glanced back his way. He was staring at me intently, as if he were testing my memory.

'Of course I remember it. We went into the river. I was screaming, my dad was knocked out cold. I couldn't help Michael get out and then my mum was gone. The car went under and the last thing I saw was Michael still stuck in his seat.'

He looked me over, sensing there was more, I guessed, but seemed to accept that much for now. 'You were just a kid.'

'I was back then,' I said, growing tired of the conversation and all that was being left unsaid. Unanswered. 'Now, I want to know what happened. All of it. The truth.'

He pointed to his head and smiled sadly. 'There's someone who would kill to know what I have up here.'

'I think I have a right to know.'

There was a moment when he simply stared back at me – his eyes dark and unyielding. I held them with my own and didn't look away.

Soft sunlight, peeking through the thick blinds covering the windows, glinted off the glass in front of him. He let out a long exhale of breath and finally looked away.

'I've worried about this moment for so long, that now it's here, I realise I never thought about what I would say to you.'

'Well, I'm here now, so start talking.'

'I was there that whole weekend. I was the one who pulled you and your dad from the river. But, that wasn't the end.'

CHAPTER 35

Quinn brought me in a cup of coffee and then stood off to the side by the door. She was listening, but I didn't take notice. I was concentrating too hard on Tom in front of me.

'When I called you last week, you said that you promised my mum that you'd keep me safe. You were her friend?'

'Yeah. I've known her all my life. We grew up together.'

'Just a friend?'

He hesitated and I knew instantly that there was a lie coming.

'It was never like that,' he said, the lie on the table between us. 'I joined the army straight out of high school. I never married, never had my own kids. I was there for Laurie through all the highs and all the lows. Helped her when no one else could. And finally, helped her escape.'

'But who was she trying to escape?' I said, waiting for the same name Quinn gave me.

'This Sullivan guy?' He hesitated and then leaned back in the chair. 'Anthony Sullivan. Your mom and him were childhood sweethearts, but there was nothing sweet about him. He treated her like crap for years. By the end, she wasn't allowed to make a move without his say-so. In the end, she met your dad and I helped her get away. They ran to England and that should have been it. Only, Anthony wouldn't let her go. He tried for a long time to track her down. Then, in 1995, she came back here and he sought her out.'

'He's the reason Michael died.'

A small nod. 'I couldn't save him,' Tom said, his voice smaller.

A little of the life had gone from it now. 'I thought it was safe for her to come back. I was wrong.'

'How did that night happen?'

'I couldn't get to the crash in time. He came out of nowhere. I slowed him down, while your mom and dad got you all out of the house, but not long enough. By the time I'd caught up, he'd already forced the car off the road.'

'Michael.'

Tom nodded slowly, sadly. 'The car ended up in the river. They took her, but left the rest of you for dead. No one knew your mom survived for a long time, but I found her and helped her escape some months after the accident. Your dad had no idea. That was for the best. I helped Parker move west and Nell moved out of state too. I couldn't take any chances. At that point, he was willing to do harm to find her. Only, Parker stupidly got picked up on a DUI and his real identity came out. Anthony found out.'

I shook my head. 'And Parker was . . . ?'

'Your uncle. Your mom's brother. He was killed a couple of weeks ago. Anthony Sullivan found him. I came back here after your dad followed him into the grave. That's when I knew he was on the trail again. Twenty-five years and he finally got a lead. Can you believe that?'

'I can't believe any of this.'

'I've been out west so long, that I almost began to believe that maybe he was dead. No such luck on that front, kid.'

'I found a photograph in my grandmother's house. Of my mum. Apparently from a few years after she died. So, I'm going to ask you again and I want the truth. Is she alive?'

'Yes.'

'So you're telling me that she watched her son die and still ran from her family. Left me behind. Made me think she's dead. Made my dad really believe she was dead?'

He opened his mouth to answer and then looked down. 'Yes.'

I gritted my teeth, as I gripped the edge of the table.

'We had to be careful,' Tom said, smoothing back his hair with a careful touch. 'To keep you safe. If Anthony knew you were around, he would stop at nothing to find you and hurt you, to bring her out.'

'Well, if that's true, if she's alive, then tell me where she is.'

Tom shook his head. 'I can't do that right now. But she *is* alive, Sam.'

'Prove it.'

Tom smirked, as if he were impressed with me. 'I will.'

It seemed impossible. I struggled to believe a word he said.

'Right now, we have to get you far away from here. He'll find out soon enough that you're here and then things will really go south.'

'I'm not going anywhere with you until you tell me what I need to know. Tell me, if she's alive, where she is right now. Right this second, where is she?'

He sniffed, but wouldn't look at me. 'I . . . I don't know right now. But it's okay, I'll fix this.'

'You don't know anything,' I shouted, sensing Quinn pull away from the wall. I was on my feet, pacing around.

My mum was still gone.

My brother and dad the same.

I shook my head and looked up towards the ceiling. The wood panelling was faded and there was black mould in the corners. 'She's gone, isn't she? She's not alive. You only wish she was. You're running around – like the rest of them – trying to pretend she's out there. Truth is, you have no idea what happened and more than anything, you can't accept the truth.'

'Listen to me, that's not the case. I swear to you—'

'I'm leaving,' I said, standing up and walking towards the door. I turned as I reached it and looked back at him. 'I can't do this any more.'

'Sam, Anthony Sullivan is out there looking for her and he won't stop until he's found her. He's evil. He'll find you again and do the same. And I won't be there to save you. He'll stop at nothing—'

'I almost believed it,' I said, cutting him off before he could go any further. 'That's the only reason I came. Hope. That's what kills you, you know? It looks like it's doing a fine job on you.'

I pulled open the front door and left before I had a chance to change my mind.

CHAPTER 36

I left Tom Miller's house, my hands sweating as I flexed them open and shut. I looked around the street – everything strange and out of place. I had no idea of where I was, what I was going to do. Everything within me screamed to run and keep running until I hit Boston. Get on the next flight home and forget everything I had learned in the past week or so.

I thought about the photograph of my mother, now gone from my possession. Supposedly showing her alive. I couldn't make sense of it. Nothing felt right about any of the story that had been told to me.

The silence on the street was stifling – surrounding me like fog and making it hard to think straight.

The echo of the front door slamming shut behind me made me jump in surprise.

'That went well,' Quinn said, coming out and leaning against the car in the driveway. 'Come on, I'll get you a cup of coffee up the street.'

I looked behind her towards the house and saw Tom in the window. He was staring out at us, not moving.

'I should be leaving. I should be getting the hell out of this place.'

'Why aren't you then?'

I didn't respond.

'Come on,' Quinn said, standing up. 'You can't leave in this state.'

*   *   *

The coffee shop was a few minutes' drive away and was pretty empty by the time we sat down at a table. It was an independent store, rather than one of the identical chain shops that seemed to exist everywhere else. The décor was almost luminous green – bright enough to offend. It looked like so many places I'd only seen on television or cinema screens and now I was sitting there looking like I belonged. Although, I doubted that anyone local would agree with that.

I ordered coffee, but wasn't sure I would drink it. Quinn was sitting across from me, studying me closely.

'I feel like I'm in an aquarium,' I said, trying to avoid the eye contact. 'You don't have to look so hard.'

'Sorry,' Quinn replied, a blush almost coming to her cheeks. 'It's just I'm trying to figure you out. You came all this way, yet you don't seem to know anything.'

'I guess so,' I said, unable to come up with a better answer. It had been a big decision to make, but I'd barely considered it. It had felt right at the time. 'I guess I've been putting this off for so long – you know, coming back here.'

'Do you remember much of being here?'

I shook my head. 'Not really. Bits and pieces are coming back to me, since I got here.'

Apart from the river. The look on my brother's face as we hit the water. The sound of the water.

I closed my eyes and tried to block it out.

'Do you remember her? Your mom, I mean.'

I took a breath and saw her in my mind. Every day, the image had become a little more faded. Now, it was as if there was fog around her, that I needed to concentrate hard on to clear. Mental snapshots, that didn't capture life.

'A little,' I said, clearing my throat and lowering my voice. 'I was nine years old when she . . . died, I guess. I wish I had more memories, but the few I have are enough to get through life.'

Quinn tilted her head to one side, studying me again. 'It must have been hard.'

'Well, it wasn't easy. It destroyed my dad. He was a shadow of himself for the rest of his life. Before I went back last week, I hadn't spoken to him in years. I think I was too much of a reminder of everything he lost.'

She nodded in response and I found myself wanting to open up more to her.

The waitress delivered the coffees and I made an effort to make mine somewhat drinkable by pouring in milk and emptying a couple of sugar packets into it.

'And you've never suspected that she was alive over the years?'

'No. It was just me and my dad. He was a shell of who he had been, so until he told me she was alive right before he died, I never questioned it.'

'You really don't know for sure,' she said. She stared back at me, before something shifted inside her. It was as if she were having an internal discussion with herself and a decision had been made. 'Look, I'm going to be straight with you. I don't think your mom is really out there.'

I raised my eyebrows. 'I found a photograph at my grandmother's house . . .'

She looked at me with something approaching pity that made my stomach churn. 'It's not like those things can't be doctored.'

'I guess, but why?'

'Sometimes,' Quinn continued, taking a sip of coffee. Her nails tapped against the cup, manicured and pristine. 'Sometimes, it's easier to live with an idea than the truth. I think you're in danger if you stick around. Maybe it's best if you get out of

Dodge. Your mom isn't going to suddenly turn up and make all this go away. I don't know what all of these men think they're going to find, but she's gone. Long gone. They're looking for a ghost and killing to find it. If you don't want to be next, I'd suggest getting on the first plane out of Boston and going back home.'

It wasn't the worst idea I'd heard. 'You think so?'

'What else is here for you?' she said, and leaned back in the booth. 'You came here for answers and I think you've got them. Your mom is gone and some people can't accept that.'

'But why are people looking for her? Why are people prepared to *kill* to find her?'

Quinn placed her hands in her jacket for warmth and shrugged her shoulders finally. 'Obviously, she was mixed up in something she couldn't handle. I think she died back in '95. I can't answer how, or what happened, but you ever hear of Occam's Razor?'

'The most likely answer is the obvious one?'

'Bingo. People these days see conspiracies everywhere they look. Sometimes, it's quite simple. She died twenty-five years ago, and because some people can't accept that, they keep looking for another answer. Another reason or explanation. Tom has convinced himself she's out there, but he has zero evidence. Then, there's Anthony Sullivan, who has all the money in the world, but that's not enough.'

'She left him for my dad.'

'Yeah. And maybe that's enough to kill people over – someone stole his woman and he wants her back – but that's thin. I'm sure he has other reasons. But, he's been looking for her for twenty-five years, has all the money to do so, and hasn't been able to track her down. Doesn't make any sense. No. She's gone, I'm sorry. And before you get yourself even further into this, you need to get out of here and somewhere safe.'

I couldn't find a way to disagree with her. I'd had one photograph that pointed to the possibility my mum was still alive, and the last words from my dying father. Someone who was confused and desperate.

It wasn't concrete enough.

'I need to go home.'

Quinn slowly nodded her head. 'Before you get yourself killed.'

CHAPTER 37

Carson felt his knee bobbing up and down and let it happen. It was better that than him start showing his anger in any other way. Especially given where they were.

Anthony was pacing behind his desk, as Carson and Hunter sat on the other side, like two naughty schoolchildren summoned to the principal's office. It had been over twelve hours since they'd pulled themselves out of the river.

'What do I pay you for?'

Hunter began to answer, before Carson held a hand up to shush him. The last thing they needed was for someone's mouth to get them in even more trouble.

'Explain to me why Sam Cooper isn't in front of me now.'

Carson thought about it and shook his head. 'He's got friends over here.'

'That may be,' Anthony said, stopping for a moment and leaning forwards on his desk. 'But that just brings me back to my first point. I mean, that shouldn't matter in the slightest. You're supposed to be the best, Carson, but when it comes to this situation, you keep letting me down. What do I pay you for?'

'I know . . .'

'Thirty-some years ago, you and your sadly departed father were supposed to be watching her. And what happened? You let her get away. Your dad pays for that with his life. Ten years later, she escapes again. You're always the one I'm relying on, but I'm starting to doubt your loyalty to the cause. Too many mistakes being made. Is there something you want to tell me?'

Carson closed his mouth, clamping it shut, because his initial thought of what he wanted to say would get him killed. He took his time. 'I've always been loyal to you.'

'Don't make me question it, Carson. We've done good work with each other and you've been rewarded well, haven't you?'

'It won't happen again.'

'I know it won't,' Anthony said, as his phone rang on the desk. He put it to his ear and listened.

Carson waited, his knee beginning to calm down a little with its jitters now. Getting out of the river hadn't seemed too difficult. He'd realised the extent of his problem a few minutes later, when he saw Tom Miller driving away with Sam in the back seat.

Anthony ended the call and smirked at the two of them.

'You have another shot. Tom Miller is at an address in Groton. Alone. You think you can handle him?'

Carson grinned. 'It would be my pleasure.'

'Good. I know you've been waiting a long time for this. Go deal with him.'

Tom Miller slugged back a warm beer and took another can from the six-pack. He'd turned the radio on – some classic rock station played.

The reunion with Sam hadn't gone as he'd planned. That was easy to figure out. The poor kid had no idea what had happened twenty-five years ago and what had happened since.

And it was Tom's fault.

Selfish wasn't a word he liked to use to describe himself, but that's what he had been for all this time. He had pretended that he was thinking of everyone else, but really, when it came down to it, he had wanted something to be true and had made the world around him fit to his own vision.

Now, it was all coming crashing down around him and he wasn't sure what he could do to stop it.

He tapped the top of the can in time with the song playing on the radio and thought about Laurie.

About everything that had been lost.

It was never going to be over.

Tom pulled the tab, lifted the beer to his lips. As he felt the liquid touch the back of his throat, he heard a noise outside.

He dropped the can and pulled out his gun, swinging it towards the noise.

Behind the house was a small backyard, then a thick line of trees that reached out as far as you could see.

Tom moved to the back door, listening for a second, before he pulled it open. Icy air rushed in, but he was already moving, ducking out onto the back porch in one movement. He looked out onto the yard and didn't see any movement. No one out there.

The hairs on the back of his neck disagreed with his assessment.

He moved forwards silently, his eyes scanning from left to right. He had his gun drawn low, his finger hovering above the trigger.

Wind brushed through the trees and he looked in that direction. Narrowed his eyes and waited.

Something silently hit him in the thigh and he fell to the ground.

Tom got on his side and fired off two shots, wood splintering from the trees ahead. He swore, feeling the blood escaping from his leg. He panted short, slow breaths, getting himself upright as much as he could. His throat cut off any breathing, as pain snapped into focus, his leg sending the signal all over his body.

He'd been shot just above his knee. He didn't have time to consider that, though. He fired another shot towards the trees and then shifted himself back, sitting against the wall on the back porch.

There was a moment of silence, when all he could hear was his own heart beating. His hand was steady, targeted at the tree line.

Another explosion above his head, over to his right-hand side. He fired back two shots blindly, hearing a whispered expletive escape.

'Tom, you're done.'

His head dropped as he recognised the voice. It had been a long time since he'd heard it.

'I'm here to talk,' Carson said, his voice travelling through the backyard, hidden from view. 'I know you're already hit. Let's make that the last one, yeah?'

Tom breathed out. The last time he had seen Carson, he had been holding onto his father, as blood dripped from his chest.

He had one shot left and he didn't think he'd make it back inside to reload.

There was a moment where he had a sense of what he *should* do. He should lift the gun to his head and squeeze the trigger. Fade to black. It'd be over for him, but they wouldn't get a single word in return.

Tom licked dry lips. Swallowed down something that burned his throat and lifted his gun to his head.

Counted to five and hoped he'd make up his mind by then.

CHAPTER 38

Quinn parked up outside my motel and I saw my bag in one of the flower-beds that lined the car parking slots.

I had my passport back. And the keys to the rental car.

'Things are looking up,' I said, as I moved back to the open window, where Quinn was sitting at the wheel. 'Listen . . .'

'It's okay,' she replied, waving away my thanks before I could give it. 'Just look after yourself.'

After that awkward goodbye with Quinn, I rushed in and checked the balcony window for damage. It looked okay from a quick glance, so I left without checking out and found my car outside.

I drove to another motel across town and booked another room. I picked up some food and then tried to sleep. Only, every time I felt myself letting go, I was underwater again.

I looked up flights home that were leaving that evening, but there were still so many questions left unanswered. The photograph of Mum could have been doctored, but I didn't know why someone would do that, only to hide it at Nell's house. My grandmother may have been confused, but it felt like she had spoken to my mother at some point.

I couldn't ignore that photograph.

Then, there was the fact that Anthony Sullivan was so convinced she was alive. Willing to do anything to find her.

Tom held the key, I was sure. I remembered that he said he was going to try and find her, but if he really knew she was alive, why would she be lost now?

Too many questions. And he was the only one who could answer them. I made a quick, considered decision.

I wasn't going home.

I couldn't.

I couldn't live without knowing the truth.

Tom Miller may have been many things, but at that moment, he was the only person that could help me. I searched through Google Street View and found the diner where Quinn had taken me. From there, I retraced our steps and found the house.

The drive wasn't long. Only a couple of towns over from Mystic. The sky was growing darker by the time I parked up down the street and walked towards the house, slowing as I got closer. The hairs on the back of my neck stood on end, as I got closer.

The front door was slightly ajar. The screen door moved slowly, as the wind picked up and blew it open and closed. Music was creeping from within. An old song. Classic rock.

'Tom?' I called inside, unwilling to go in. I didn't want to move any closer. I pushed open the door and forced myself forwards. The blinds were shut inside and I couldn't see anything in the darkness. The floorboard underneath my feet creaked loudly and my heart sped up its beat.

'Tom?' I called again, only this time I lowered my voice and it came out as a plaintive whisper, lost in the music swirling around the hallway. I moved further into the house. The back door banged against the wall, cold air rushing through, and I heard someone shout from the backyard.

'Tom, you're done.'

I moved forwards, hitting the back door as it banged back into place. I jumped and my heart threatened to crash out of my chest and onto the ground. I turned around, expecting to find someone standing there holding a gun to my head. Telling me to get on my knees, and then a finger tightening on the trigger.

No one was there.

I couldn't see a thing.

I looked outside and saw something on the porch. A trail of red, that stopped over to the left.

'Tom?'

Then, I felt a shift in the air. A weight lifted, a creak on the wood.

And then something crashed into my side and I was falling to the ground.

I hit the deck and saw someone holding onto a gun with one hand, his leg with the other. I made as if to shout out, but was smacked across the head, sending me sprawling back.

It went dark for a moment. When I came to, I searched for Tom quickly.

He was almost unrecognisable.

His face was a dark mass, blood drying on his skin. Swollen and misshapen.

I released a moan, from somewhere deep inside me.

I swallowed, but my mouth was dry. I felt nauseated, my insides churning and the lack of food that day threatening to bring up nothing but bile.

Wind chimes clanged from above us, sounding like bells ringing in a long-forgotten church. They snapped me out of the fugue state I had been sliding into. I blinked a few times and tried to think clearly. Carson was blocking my view in an instant.

I tried to look over to my side.

Above Tom, Carson's partner was grunting with effort as he brought his foot down.

Again. And again.

I looked away.

'Sam, you need to be smart here,' Carson said, not a trace of emotion in his voice snapping my attention back. 'You've got away from us a couple of times, but this is your last chance.

Level with us. You can still make it out of this. You just got to come clean with us. Where is she?'

The larger man was inflicting more violence on Tom. I couldn't watch, but I heard enough to know he had to have been unconscious.

I shook my head, heard myself moan again as Carson pushed a gun against my temple. 'I swear, I don't know,' I said, hearing the fear in my voice. The alienness of it. 'I wish I did.'

'Here's the thing. I want to believe you. I really do. But you've been lying to me from the start. You know she's alive. So, let's skip the part where you're screaming for mercy and help me out here.'

I wanted to. If I'd known anything, I probably would have told him. Only, there was nothing to say.

'I . . . I can't. She's dead.'

'Hunter, if he moves, put one in his other leg.'

I looked towards the younger man. Hunter. He was pressing his gun against Tom's left knee. Waiting.

'She's alive,' Carson said, turning back to me. 'And she's close. That's all we need to know.'

'You don't know anything,' I managed to say, the slightest movement of the gun making me swallow bile in anticipation. 'We're chasing a ghost. A picture can be manipulated, you know. Just because it looks like her, doesn't mean it is.'

'That is true,' Hunter said, but was waved away by Carson. 'I'm just saying . . .'

'It's real,' Carson said, snapping back, booming over the music that was still coming through from the other room. 'Now, tell me where I can find her.'

'See, *Hunter* knows it,' I said, spitting out what felt like my last words. My head swam every time I moved. 'If she were still alive, don't you think she would have found a way to let me know?'

'Not if she didn't want to,' Carson replied, but I sensed doubt in his tone now.

'You obviously don't know many mothers,' I said, not sure if I was convincing Carson, or myself. 'I knew mine. She would never have left me thinking she was dead for twenty-five years. She would have found me and let me know she was okay. Don't you understand? Just because we have hope, it doesn't make it real.'

'Quiet,' Carson said, but I was barely listening. I was trying to move another inch without him noticing. I could see Tom Miller behind him, stirring a little.

'You're just saying this because you can't bear the idea that she abandoned you, kid.'

'Maybe, but I think I knew her better than that,' I said, praying Tom was regaining consciousness. 'I think I know *people* better than that. She wouldn't be able to live without knowing I knew the truth. No matter what happened.'

'She had good reason to hide.'

'Not forever.'

'This doesn't matter, Carson,' Hunter said, but was immediately shut down.

'That's enough,' Carson said, unsure of himself, and not enjoying the feeling, it seemed. As if he couldn't trust his own decisions. 'Last chance, Sam.'

I managed to move a little, so my weight wasn't on my ribs. Not broken, I thought. Just bruised. I don't know why I suddenly felt that was important. I didn't think it was going to matter too much in a few seconds. I lifted myself up, my back to the opening into the house. I could feel the wood floor inside, as I slowly backed away from Carson.

Carson lifted the gun away from my head and stepped back a little. 'Look at me.'

He had said those words before but this time it felt like they meant more.

'That's enough, kid,' Carson said, stopping me from going any further. 'I'll tell her you tried your best. It just wasn't enough.'

I could still hear the music playing from the other room. My heart smashed against my battered chest.

Tom made a noise, making both of their heads snap his way. I didn't hesitate.

A picture that had been hanging on the wall by the back door had crashed to the ground at some point. The glass had broken free of the frame and a nice, hefty slice of it was lying there, just in my line of sight. Not chunky enough to kill, I imagined, but it would be better than nothing.

I grasped hold of it, feeling the sharpness of it dig into my hand. Swung it round and plunged it into the leg of the nearest person to me.

CHAPTER 39

There was a pause, then a scream. I saw Hunter fall backwards, down the steps, and crash into the backyard. I was already moving, scrambling back into the house.

I heard Tom's voice, through a fog of confusion. I heard them crashing into each other – one still screaming in pain, the other swearing and trying to get back to his feet.

I fell to the floor and my hand passed over something sharp and I realised it was another glass fragment from the picture. I picked it up and managed to get to my feet, just as someone rushed into the house and hit me square in the chest. I staggered back, into the living room space and clattered into the coffee table, smashing through it.

There was a thud against my face and I raised my hands to protect myself. I was still holding onto the glass, and the next fist that came flying towards me met an edge of it.

'Motherfu—'

I didn't hear the rest, as a fist flailed at the side of my head and my ears started ringing. I saw a much bigger shadow loom up and roar.

Tom.

I could see them both now, as the blinds had fallen to the ground and the outside light – what there was of it at this time of evening – cast them in a new glow. I saw the younger man coming in slowly, clasping hold of his calf. Tom standing over him.

Carson turned away from me – seeming to sense the shift of

power he'd once had. I moved slowly, trying to get myself upright, my head swimming with effort.

I could feel myself slipping away again. I tried to hold onto the adrenaline high, but I was struggling. The room spun around me.

Then, I saw a shape on the floor and made a grab for it.

Carson's gun.

Something smashed on the other side of the room and I swung the gun round in that direction. Gripped it firmly in my hands.

I heard shouts, as the men swore and screamed into the near darkness.

I closed my eyes, my hands shaking in front of me.

'Do it, Sam.'

Tom's voice rose above the other sounds, stark and clear.

I tried to steady my hands, but the shaking had become uncontrollable.

They killed my father.

An eye for an eye makes the whole world blind.

I didn't need to see any more.

I squeezed the trigger. Heard a pop. Two more. Then something else through the fog of horror. A ringing in my ears.

I could hear the rush of water in my ears. A river in the distance, getting closer. Ready to swallow me whole. Envelop me and take me away, down into its hidden depths.

Glass shattered, over and over, the sound piercing my mind, echoing in my ears.

I was lying on my back. Staring at the ceiling. Someone was near me, a voice, speaking to me. A hand caressing my arm and whispering.

'It's okay, Sam. It's going to be okay.'

At first, I thought it was my mother. She had finally found me in the afterlife. I turned my head to the side, a wave of sharp pain bursting free.

'They've gone,' I heard another voice say.

'Who are you?' I said, my voice scratchy and hoarse. 'Where am I going?'

I sat up, the hand on my arm slipping away. Tried to blink reality back into my sight, but nothing I saw made sense.

'It wasn't you,' I heard Tom say from across the room and then I realised what I was looking at. 'Carson got me on his way out.'

Tom was holding something against his chest. Breathing slow, hard. Every one an effort.

On the floor next to him, a body not moving.

'What happened?' I said, my voice sounding alien in my own head. I coughed and felt something rise up in my throat. 'I . . . Did I?'

I felt a hand on my shoulder, as I tried to get to my feet. Quinn.

'You missed,' she said, trying to pull me to my feet. 'We need to go.'

'Take him and get out of here. I'll be gone before you even get me to my feet.'

Tom was struggling to speak. I crawled across the floor towards him, shrugging off Quinn's hand as I did so. Whatever he was holding against his chest was soaked with blood. His hands were black with it.

He coughed, and something spilled from his mouth.

'She's out there, Sam,' he said, his voice rasping and almost nonexistent. 'Find her.'

'Come on, we have to go.'

'Where is she? I don't know where to find her.'

Quinn was dragging me to my feet and I couldn't stop her.

'There's no time,' she said, out of breath now. 'They could be here any second.'

I looked back at Tom, but his eyes were closed and I couldn't see his chest moving.

She led me out of the room, up the hallway, and outside. She shoved me into the driver's seat of my rental car and paused at the open door.

'Can you drive?'

I nodded numbly, finding the keys and turning the engine over.

'We just need to switch cars. Follow me up the road and we can ditch this one. They'll know what you're driving.'

'Okay.'

We pulled out of the driveway and ten minutes later, she signalled to the side of a random street. It looked much like what we'd left behind, anonymous and hidden.

She waited as I jogged back to her car and got into the passenger seat.

'Let's go.'

'We're already out of here.'

She pulled away, gathering speed quickly, until we were away from the street, the town, in seconds. I kept looking back, waiting for a car to appear behind us, following us into the night.

No one appeared.

I turned back to the front, trying to make sense of what had happened. I realised I was still holding onto the gun. I didn't know what to do with it. I slipped it into my jacket pocket.

'I think I shot him.'

'Tom told you . . .'

'How could he know?' I said, running my hands over my head, wanting to pull on my hair. 'I think it was me.'

'You did what you had to,' Quinn replied, firmly. I looked across at her in the driver's seat, hands gripped on the wheel. She looked drained of life, but she turned to me and gave me a reassuring smile.

'It's going to be okay,' she said, reaching out and resting her hand on my arm. The warmth her touch left on my skin instantly soothing. 'Don't worry. Nothing's going to happen to you now.'

For a moment, I believed her. Then, the dread and anxiety filled me again.

'How did you know to come?'

'I knew something was up when I couldn't get hold of Tom,' she said, peering ahead at the road, seemingly trying to decide which way to go. I didn't care what direction she chose. 'I decided to drive by and see what was going on. I saw your car parked outside and then another. I was outside when I heard the shots.'

'What happened to the other guy in the house? Carson?'

She gripped the wheel tighter. 'I saw him escape out the back. He was too quick for me.'

'I think the younger one was the one I . . . the one who was dead. He called him Hunter.'

'Same two who took you from the motel?'

'Yeah,' I said, my breathing beginning to return to normal. 'The same two.'

'I thought you were going to drop this whole thing. That you were going to get the next flight out the country?'

'I wish I had.'

I took a breath and then told her why. That annoying voice in the back of my head, that wouldn't let up. That while there was still the slightest possibility that my mum was out there, I couldn't just run away.

'I understand, but this is serious, Sam. You have to get out of this.'

'If I give up now—'

'You don't know where she is.'

'I can find her,' I said, trying to keep the edge I was feeling out of my tone. I frowned as I watched her wince, a fleeting touch to her neck. 'Are you okay? Has something happened?'

'I'm fine. Just wrenched it when I got into the house,' she replied, shaking it off. 'How can you find her?'

I sighed and felt the adrenaline flowing out of me. I was tired.

My head heavy on my shoulders. 'I still have my grandmother. I could maybe get some sense out of her.'

I checked over my shoulder again, seeing nothing but empty road.

'Don't worry,' Quinn said, picking up a little more speed as we turned onto a highway. 'We just need to get somewhere safe. You have a few more hours before they can track you down, at least. Relax.'

I wanted to believe her.

CHAPTER 40

Carson had barely got out of the house alive.

He lit another cigarette, snapping closed the lighter and throwing it back onto the passenger seat. Inhaled and instantly started coughing. Hard enough that his vision blurred, as his eyes watered. He inhaled again and it subsided a little.

The car rumbled quietly, as it sat idling in the parking lot. Carson took another drag on the cigarette and then he opened the window. Threw the half-smoked cigarette outside and then closed it again.

He stared out of the windshield, then felt the anger rise inside of him.

Carson balled his hands into fists and pounded them against the wheel. Expletives showered the space, gushing from his mouth and filling the car. He didn't stop until his hands ached and throbbed and his throat was too hoarse to continue.

Hunter was dead.

A young kid, who had his whole life ahead of him. A good worker. Took orders and did as he was told. Didn't argue, listened, and learned.

He would have gone far.

And now, he was lying dead. Soon to be moved to some anonymous Connecticut morgue.

Neither of them had seen it coming. Heard it coming. The first Carson had been aware there was someone in the room was when his ears were ringing and blood was splattered across his face. He wiped it again now, still feeling the stickiness of it on his skin. He had scrubbed it raw already, but it was still there, as if it had seeped into his skin and could never be taken away.

He didn't have the energy to pound the wheel again.

He didn't know who had followed them there. Distracted them long enough for Sam to get off a shot first.

Carson knew one thing though – whoever it was wouldn't be long for the world. He'd make sure of that.

The box of cigarettes beckoned to him from the dash and he snatched it up again. Removed one and let it hang limply from his lips. This time, he didn't light it.

A black car pulled up beside his in the parking lot and he took the cigarette from his lips and threw it on the passenger seat. Got out the car and let himself into the other.

'Well?'

Carson told Anthony what had happened.

'You screwed up. Again.'

Carson wanted to disagree, but he knew he was right.

'Is there anything that can link Hunter to me?'

'No,' Carson said, Hunter's face flashing through his mind. He shut it down quickly and let himself forget. 'He was paid in cash and his cell was a burner. I only ever called him from my own and that's already at the bottom of the river.'

'Did he have family?'

'No clue,' Carson said. He'd never asked. Wouldn't get the chance to now. 'I can find out if you need me to?'

Anthony shook his head. 'No need. It's done with.'

And just like that, Hunter was forgotten.

'Tom Miller?'

'Dead. As good as, anyway.'

'And the kid got away?'

Carson swallowed, then nodded slowly.

'Tell me why I shouldn't ask Zoran here to make you disappear?'

Carson glanced at the bald head behind the wheel. Tensed his jaw and placed his hand closer to his waistband. 'Because I can fix this. I've been loyal for a long time. You need a third?'

He waited as Anthony took out his cell phone and lifted it to his ear. 'Get me everyone you've got,' Anthony said.

Carson could hear the barely constrained anger in his voice. It dripped from every syllable. It took everything he had in him to keep from taking his gun out and getting the hell out of there.

He had to be calm.

'I want an army.'

Anthony ended the call and stared back at Carson.

'Look, boss, why don't . . .' Carson began to say, but Anthony raised a hand to stop him in his tracks.

'Tell me you got something out of the pair of them. That's all I need to know. Make yourself at least a little useful to me.'

There was a moment of doubt then. A creeping certainty that things weren't going to work out in the end. That this was one job too far.

He dismissed the idea instantly. He hadn't come this far to let it all fall apart.

He would find Laurie Rogers.

He would kill Sam Cooper.

'I have his cell,' Carson said, holding it in his hand. 'It's locked.'

'Let me take a look.'

Carson handed it over. It may as well have been a brick for all the use it would be for now. He had no doubt Anthony Sullivan would have the contacts to go through it, but that could take hours.

He didn't think they had the luxury of time any longer.

'Good, I'll get this broken into. I have someone looking for her mom and . . .' Anthony stopped mid-sentence as his cell phone rang. He looked at the number and answered it instantly.

'You got him?'

Carson could only wait, wondering who was talking on the other end of the phone.

'You know where he is? Good.'

Carson tensed, feeling his blood pressure rise at the thought of someone else getting to the kid first.

'No, stay there. Wait for us to arrive. Give me the address to the motel.'

Anthony noted down the address on the reverse of the paper Carson had handed over. Then, he ended the call.

'He's in a motel up in Moosup. That's an hour away. With Tom Miller dead, he's the only thing that can get us to her.'

Anthony leaned forwards and passed the address to Zoran behind the wheel. He took one look at it, nodded, then put the car into drive.

'Who was that?' Carson said, placing his hand on the side of the car, as it turned around in the parking lot.

'Someone else who has been working for me,' Anthony replied, settling back into the leather seat and closing his eyes.

Carson waited for him to say more, but there was only silence. He settled back into his own seat and wished he could close his eyes. He was feeling every single one of his fifty-some years on the planet. The bones aching, the skin stretched and taut. The muscles screaming for rest.

He didn't have long left in this type of work.

He just hoped to go out on his own terms.

Jackson ended the call and watched Sam Cooper and the woman emerge from the car. They were back at a motel, somewhere in north Connecticut. He checked his GPS and found the name of the town. Moosup.

He wasn't sure how far they had driven, but it didn't feel like far enough. An hour was barely a dint in this size state.

He knew it wasn't.

There was nothing to suggest the motel had been picked at anything but random. Some anonymous run-down place, that probably wouldn't ask many questions. The problem with that is it worked both ways. Both for those trying to hide and those trying to find them. It was an imperfect place to be when you were being hunted down.

Still, he couldn't help but be impressed that Sam had got this far. With everything against him, the fact he was still alive said something about the man.

There was no escape from inevitability for him though. With who he was up against, it wouldn't matter in the end. There could be only one outcome.

If Jackson was right – and he usually was – then Sam Cooper wasn't long for the world.

The events of earlier that evening had only made that clearer. Too many obstacles to overcome. Too many to avoid.

Once someone like Anthony Sullivan wanted you dead, the odds were against you surviving.

It didn't matter to him. It couldn't. Sam Cooper wasn't a real person to him any more. None of them were. They were simply pieces on a chessboard, being moved around by an unseen hand.

Still, there was something that shifted inside him when he saw Sam Cooper emerge from the car, stooped over with the effort of staying upright. The adrenaline would have left him by now. He wasn't used to this type of thing.

But Jackson had a job to do.

And he didn't have to wait long.

A black limo pulled to a stop and disappeared into the darkness a couple of hours later. He leaned forwards. A man who looked as if he bench-pressed small villages got out of the passenger side. Dressed in black. He was quickly joined by the driver – smaller, but no less intimidating.

The driver of the limo got out and opened the rear door. Anthony Sullivan stepped out. He walked slowly, but with purpose, towards the motel.

Two more cars pulled in. More men got out.

Jackson was already out of the car. He breathed in deeply, trying to clear his mind. He had to focus, but it was proving difficult.

He knew his role, but there was something inside him screaming to be heard.

He took out the Glock resting in his waistband and clicked the safety off.

CHAPTER 41

We had driven north for an hour before we found a motel in a small town that seemed to be in the middle of nowhere. We had barely passed a house after we arrived, before the lights from the motel sign appeared and Quinn pulled in.

She got out first, while I took my time, scanning the other cars parked up and looking for anything that didn't fit in. Outside of the motel was in darkness – the light from the rooms not finding its way out and down onto the scant few vehicles parked there. Beat up old cars, that had long ago seen better days. The air was thick with secrets and clandestine meetings. A car pulled up on the other side of the parking lot, facing away from us. I waited for someone to get out and a few seconds later, someone did. He was too far away to see, but he was walking away from us anyway. Someone with somewhere to be.

I followed Quinn into the motel, checking over my shoulder one last time before pushing my way inside. The reception area was quiet, as we waited to be checked in. A fish tank bubbled away, the glass green and grimy. The refreshments stand next to it was empty.

We made our way up to the room and I busied myself making sure the door was locked. I looked for something to prop up against the door for extra security, but apart from the small refrigerator, I couldn't see a thing.

'We'll be okay,' Quinn said, watching me, lying on one of the twin beds in the room. 'No one knows we're here.'

'Okay, okay, I'm just thinking things through. I know it's fine.'

Only, I knew it wasn't going to be, no matter how hard I tried to convince myself otherwise. There was something evil following me, trying to cut off every avenue in finding my mother. It had been in Firwood before I had arrived there.

It had started with my dad's last words.

'You need some rest.'

I knew Quinn was right, but my mind refused to shut off. Trying to make sense of everything that was happening and resistant to the idea that there was no explanation.

I lay on the bed next to Quinn's, as she switched on the TV to some reality show, somehow following it despite the constant interruptions of businesses selling stuff. I stared past the screen for a while, both of us in silence.

'Why now?' I said, my voice barely above a whisper. Vocalising a thought that was rolling around me over and over. 'Why after all this time?'

'I don't know what you mean . . .'

'It was twenty-five years ago. Then, nothing until now. It really took them twenty-five years to find her brother? Could this be my fault?'

'You said you hadn't spoken to your dad, right? He was attacked before you were back in Firwood, so how could you be at fault?'

That made a little sense, but it didn't begin to answer every question I had. What had begun back home in England seemed to have followed me to this anonymous place in north-east America. That meant I was part of it.

No, I thought. Parker Rogers had been killed before my dad was attacked. I thought about the place it had happened.

'Did you find anything about Idaho when you were looking into my mother?'

'No, just about Parker's death,' Quinn said, staring back at me unblinkingly. 'He was picked up on a DUI. He was living under a different name, but they found his real ID in the car. That's how they ran the story in the news – it was a local report – I can send you a link. Some guy who had lived there for over twenty years had a different name. Not a big story, but enough on a slow day. I guess Sullivan had some kind of alert set up with his name. No one in the town knew who he really was.'

My uncle.

He was the beginning.

Why?

What had he known?

'He told them,' I said, quietly, working things out so I could make sense of it. 'Parker told them where they could find my father.'

'That makes sense.'

'So, twenty-five years go by and everyone has managed to stay underground. Then, Parker is found and sets this whole thing in motion.'

'It doesn't explain how you and your dad didn't know she was alive. If she is.'

'We didn't,' I said, looking across at Quinn, who lifted her hands up. 'I wish I did know before now. Then, maybe, I'd know where to look for her.'

'You can tell me,' she said, her voice soft and understanding. 'Do you think you know where she might be? Your mom?'

I frowned in response. 'No. I'm not even convinced she's alive.'

Quinn studied me for a moment, then seemed to accept it. 'Well, if she is alive, and knows about Tom, she'll do one of two things. Either go deeper underground or come out fighting.'

My head found my hands and I leaned forwards against my knees. I wanted to pound against the bed in frustration, until my hands turned red raw. Until I couldn't lift my arms any more. Instead, I composed myself enough to think straight. I needed to keep a clear head. 'I'm going to take a shower.'

I lifted myself up off the bed and made my way to the small bathroom. Leaned against the closed door, and the full weight of where I was hit me. At the same time, Michael's face appeared in my mind and wouldn't go.

Forever five years old.

He had only turned that age a week before the accident. Before him and Mum died. Or disappeared. It didn't much matter, I guessed.

Mum saves her smiles for you.

That was what I had told him one night, leaning down from the top bunk.

Michael had been special.

Mum's special boy.

I was a few years older and was no longer a boy apparently, special or otherwise.

I turned on the shower, but didn't get in. Instead, I slid down to the floor and held as if to stop myself from running away.

I sat on that damn motel bathroom floor, in a place I didn't know, in a country nothing but foreign to me, and I wept.

I cried for my mum. For my dad, for Tom Miller.

I cried for them all.

But especially for Michael.

The boy I tried so hard to forget.

I didn't know what I was doing there. Tom Miller had been my only coherent connection to the past and he was dead.

'Sam, are you okay?' I heard Quinn shout through the closed door. She banged a couple more times, before I stood up and opened it.

'I'll be a few more minutes,' I said, making to close the door, before she put a hand on it to stop me from doing so.

'I'm here,' Quinn replied, catching my eye and not letting go. It seemed she could see right through me. Into my thoughts, reading me easily. 'You're not on your own. Just talk to me.'

I hesitated, letting her open the door more fully. She brushed past me, switching off the shower. Then, she turned to me and folded her arms across her chest.

I didn't know what to say. What to do. She was a stranger, really. I'd known her less than twenty-four hours. Yet, there was something about her, about the situation, that made me want to tell her what I was feeling.

'What is it?'

'It's all of this,' I said, gesturing around the bathroom, the motel room, out the window. 'I shouldn't be here. I don't know what I'm doing, where I'm going. What I'm supposed to do next. I'm looking for answers to questions I don't even know. What's the plan? Where do I go from here? I need to do something, but I have no idea what that *something* is. I shouldn't be here. People are getting hurt. Killed. Because of me being in this country. All looking for a ghost. And I know I can't stop.'

I took a breath, looked away from her, as she stared back at me.

'I'm scared of what might happen,' I said finally, voicing my worst fear. 'Either she's alive and left me alone all these years, or she's dead, and I'll get killed looking for someone who can't be found. There's no outcome here that won't hurt.'

'There's more, isn't there?'

I breathed in and out slowly. I *wanted* to talk about it. To someone from this place. I needed to. It had been weighing on me for so long, that it almost felt like a part of me. Only, it shifted and begged for attention constantly.

I told her everything.

I told her about my brother Michael. About us in a car, at the bottom of the river. About watching him drown in front of me and how I didn't, *couldn't* save him.

How, afterwards, my father could barely look at me. As if it were my fault.

And it was, because I was the older brother and I should have kept him safe.

Quinn didn't say anything. Instead, she looked at me for a few seconds and then crossed the space between us quickly and held onto me.

I felt her body against mine and at first I tensed up. Then, I wrapped my arms around her.

And began to feel everything easing inside me.

CHAPTER 42

I ached all over, my muscles pulling and tightening with each movement. My body felt bruised, as if I'd just been twenty seconds with a heavyweight boxer holding a grudge.

'We should go to someone,' I said, breaking the embrace finally. 'If we just explain what's been going on, maybe the police could help.'

'We can't do that,' Quinn replied, unable to hold my gaze. She held herself, shivering against an imperceptible breeze. 'They would wonder why we ran from the scene. We need to find out if your mom is really out there or they'll just blame you for everything.'

'You can't do this,' I said, turning back to face Quinn. She was staring back at me now, surer of herself, a steely gaze on her face. '*I* can't do this. Not to you. This isn't fair. You were just trying to help Tom. There's no reason to put yourself in any more danger.'

'Let me decide what's fair or not. I'm here of my own free will. You think this is the first time I've got involved in something that has got out of hand? I know what I get myself into.'

I looked around the room, seeing how small it was, how anonymous-looking. The thin carpet, the scuffed dresser and old television propped up on top. I let out a soft chuckle. 'I can't believe we're here.'

'Neither can I,' Quinn replied, a smile creeping across her face. 'I should have just made sure you went to the airport. You'd probably still have all your faculties intact.'

'Hey, I think I'm doing okay for someone who was almost killed. Three times now?'

'You've survived somehow. Despite being a terrible aim.'

I shook my head. 'I've never shot a gun before, okay? Anyway, they seemed too professional for one of them to end up dead accidentally.'

'What are you thinking happened, then?'

I blew out a sigh. 'I don't know. I think someone came into that house before you.'

'You think?'

'Yeah,' I said, rubbing my forehead and wishing I had some painkillers. 'I remember there being a noise before I heard gunshots. It distracted them just long enough for me to get my shot off first.'

Quinn frowned. 'Who would that be though?'

I shook my head. 'I have no idea. It's not like I've been here long enough to make any friends.'

'Long enough to make enemies.'

'I guess so. It doesn't make sense. And I can't imagine he'll be happy. The one left alive, I mean. They're sure I know where my mum is – whoever this Anthony Sullivan is. And I don't think he's going to give up that easily.'

'And you don't.'

'I don't. I'm still not sure she's even alive. Even after all this, what evidence do I have really? A photograph – the only solid piece. Then, I have the word of a stranger, who was quite plainly in love with my mum years ago and wouldn't easily accept her being dead. I don't know how truthful he was being. My grand-mother, who was confused about what decade she was in, never mind about seeing a daughter she knew died twenty-five years ago. And my dad's dying words, when he was so out of it he probably didn't even know what he was saying. It doesn't amount to much.'

I took a few steps and dropped onto the edge of one of the beds. The television was still playing – another advert for some drug or other. There seemed to be a lot of those. I shifted around, trying to find a comfortable way to sit that didn't hurt, but gave up before continuing to talk. 'It's all just a mess.'

I let silence fall over us again. My eyelids began to droop the longer I sat there. I wondered if someone had already called the police after hearing gunshots. Finding Tom's body. Whether they were already out searching for me. Whether the further we travelled, the longer we were on the road, the easier it would be to track us down.

And then what?

'We need to make a decision.'

'I've come too far, I guess,' I said, the ghost of a smile playing across my lips. She didn't return it. I thought of my little brother and that was enough. If it wasn't for me, then it would be for him.

I couldn't let his death be the thing that haunted me any longer.

If my mum was out there, still, then she could share the burden.

Quinn tucked a strand of hair behind her ear, returning her hand to her side, then smacking her hip. 'Well, then it's settled. First thing in the morning, we get back out there and find her. Get cleaned up and then make a proper plan.'

She looked away from me and scanned the room. 'I need a drink, don't you? And some snacks. I saw a vending machine on the way in, I'll go get us something.'

I murmured an agreement, but my eyes were closed. I felt her hand on my shoulder briefly, as she picked up something from behind me. Her purse, I thought, but I only opened my eyes a little to see her leave the room.

I should have gone with her. Or instead of her, really. But something told me she could look after herself okay.

Better than I was taking care of myself, I thought, as I let my eyes close and the dull ache of pain rock within me.

Quinn paused at the door and looked back at Sam lying on the bed. She could see he was already dozing off, and given the events of earlier, she didn't blame him for doing so.

Seeing him there, so peaceful at first sight. So damned at the next. It shifted something inside her that was becoming more difficult to push away. When she had reached past him as he lay on the bed, she had wanted him to pull her towards him. To disappear into his embrace and never come back up again.

Only, she knew that wasn't going to happen. That life could never be hers. Once he learned about what she did – what she had done in her life – he would turn his back just like all the rest.

That was her lot in life.

She held onto the door for another second, then walked out.

She felt the weight of the gun at her side and wondered if she would have to use it again soon.

It was glued to her now. She had almost made a fatal mistake the day before, but thankfully a taser had been enough to save Sam from whoever that man had been at the cemetery.

It made her teeth grind together as she thought of that stranger. Who he was and how he was involved. A loose end she didn't like.

She made her way down the hallway, towards the end of the corridor. With every step that she got further away from Sam, she felt both more anxious and more calm, in some weird sort of dichotomy of emotion. The sheer weight of being around him and him being out of sight weighing against any normality.

There were double doors separating the corridor from the vestibule at the end, where the vending machines radiated their welcoming glow. As she pushed them open, she felt a gust of cold air flow up the stairs and breeze past her, riffling her hair across her shoulders.

The sound of a door closing below, softly in the neon light that lay in front of her.

Quinn approached the machines and began feeding dollar bills into the slot.

Her senses began firing, as she heard footsteps coming up the stairs behind her.

She didn't want to turn around. Didn't want to see who they belonged to. Instead, she continued to feed dollar bills into the machine, as if by ignoring what was approaching her, it would cease to exist.

Only, life didn't work like that.

One hand reached towards the gun in her waistband. She could feel her fingers shaking, as fear crawled out of her stomach and up her throat.

She knew what was coming.

The footsteps grew louder, but Quinn refused to turn around. Refused to see what was coming. If she could just live in glorious denial for a few more seconds, she would. If she could live in a world where she and Sam were the only ones in existence, that would be okay.

She felt a breath on her neck and gripped the gun tighter. As the vending machine clunked and dropped yet another product down, she moved. Finally.

The gun was in her hand, finger on the trigger, pointing upwards against the chin of the man behind her.

She stared into the dead blue eyes of the man who had approached her, his face impossibly unlined and unaffected by age. He stared back at her, his expression flat and unreadable.

'Quinn,' Anthony Sullivan said, making her skin crawl with fear and regret. 'You've done impeccable work. Now, where is he?'

CHAPTER 43

I was dozing when I heard the motel room door open softly. I was instantly awake, my heart threatening to crash through my chest, before I saw Quinn standing in the doorway.

I smiled towards her, but she didn't return it. The door was still open behind her, as the welcome fell from my face.

Quinn stepped forwards, levelling a gun at my chest.

'I'm sorry,' she said, her expression one of pain and regret. 'It's just business.'

Behind her, the door filled and I cowered against the bed frame instinctively.

'Quinn, what's going on?'

I didn't recognise the voice that escaped from my mouth. It didn't sound like me. Quinn hesitated, wiped her cheek, and then returned her hand to the gun again.

'I tried to tell you to leave.'

'What are you doing?' I asked, but I knew the answer. The only one that made any sense. 'You're working for him.'

'You need to just do what they say,' Quinn replied, staring back at me. Her hand was steady. Not a flicker. It didn't move.

'It's time to go,' the man standing behind Quinn said.

Carson.

Then, I caught sight of a man I'd only seen on Google before that night.

The man who was looking for my mother.

The same man who had killed so many to get to this point.

Anthony Sullivan.

'Quinn, you can't let this happen.'

Anthony stepped forwards and laid a hand on her shoulder.

'Quinn,' he said, his voice a growl now. 'I hate to break up the start of this little heart-to-heart, but I think it's time we left.'

I sniffed, biting the inside of my bottom lip. 'He's going to kill me, you know that, right?'

She shook her head again, more vigorously this time, but I could see she knew it was the truth.

'Why are you doing this?' My voice echoed around the room. Anthony didn't flinch. 'Why are you trying to find her? What could she possibly have that is worth this?'

He didn't answer me, but I remembered what I'd heard once. That there were only a few things people killed for – money, power, love, and for the thrill of it.

I guessed it was a mixture of all of them for him.

I turned to Anthony Sullivan. Standing there, impeccably dressed in a suit I guessed cost more than my monthly rent. Not a hair out of place. A chunky watch on his wrist, that glistened in the motel room light.

'You know, I've waited a long time to get close to your mom,' he said, leaning against a wall. He smoothed out a crinkle in his suit jacket. 'A long, long time. She stole something from me and I've given everything trying to find it. Well, the time has come to pay me back.'

'Is it money?' I said, hearing the desperation in my tone, as Carson stood in the doorway, blocking escape. I could feel the hate coming from him in droves. 'I can pay you whatever it is. Please. I can settle the debt. Killing me won't help. She's dead.'

'You can't afford what she owes.'

'We have to go now,' Quinn said, and this time she seemed more composed. 'Just come quietly and it'll be okay.'

'I'm not going anywhere,' I said, sounding more confident than I felt. 'You're going to have to drag me out of here.'

Anthony stepped to one side and two of the largest men I'd ever seen came into view from the hallway outside the room.

I was hopelessly outnumbered.

I braced myself, knowing it wouldn't last long, but I didn't care.

I had to fight.

Jackson followed at a distance – watching the men enter the motel ahead of him, as he stuck to the shadows. He didn't want to give away his presence too quickly, but he could already see that time was running out.

It wasn't until he was at the bottom of the stairwell and heard the conversation between Anthony Sullivan and the woman who had been working for Tom Miller that he realised the situation was worse than he'd first thought.

Anthony's voice was like a knife slicing through him. He had spent years trying to run from him; being this close made him feel as if it was all over.

'*You can't kill him.*'

'*Let me decide the best way to handle this . . .*'

'*I'm serious. If you kill him, you'll never find her. She'll disappear again. You need him alive.*'

Of course, he'd had his suspicions about Quinn – anyone who was involved in this situation needed to be looked at – but he hadn't known she was working for Anthony Sullivan. Now, he wondered what else he had missed throughout all of this.

This mess.

If people had just left well enough alone, then none of this would be happening. Instead, people would die. On and on, with seemingly no end.

He took the stairs two at a time, checking the area for cameras, but not seeing any. The motel struck him as one still stuck a few decades in the past – able to keep its secrets, unlike others closer to the cities.

He heard them move down the corridor, towards what he guessed was Sam's room. Quinn had been told to go first, but it didn't seem like Anthony Sullivan and his goons had waited too long to follow. He could hear a raised voice as he made his way to the closed doors separating the vestibule from the corridor. He risked a glance through the glass square in the middle of the door and could see the two bigger men waiting either side of a room halfway down.

Distance was an issue, Jackson quickly realised. By the time he had made it through the doors and into the corridor, they would already be turning to see his approach. Even if they considered him to be just a guest of the motel, he didn't think they'd have any problem dealing with an unintended interruption.

A loud crash echoed from the room and breached the thin doors he was standing behind, making the decision for him. Jackson didn't think twice.

He burst through them, gun pointed in front of him, just as the two men entered the room.

Jackson was sprinting behind them, hoping with each step that he wasn't too late.

CHAPTER 44

I took a step back, my foot striking the other bed in the room, and in one movement I was on the other side of it. On the floor, crouched down and waiting. I reached behind me, trying to find my jacket.

My only chance to get out of that room alive.

I finally got my jacket in my hand and frantically searched the pockets, hoping it was still there.

They were empty.

My heart fell a few hundred feet, as I realised Quinn must have taken the gun.

I grabbed the only thing I could see. Stood up, holding onto a drawer I had managed to pull out from the bedside table behind me. Quinn was closest, Anthony Sullivan was behind her, a look of wild amusement at my appearance.

'That's not going to help you, Sam,' Anthony said, shaking his head. 'Hasn't anyone ever told you not to bring a drawer to a gunfight?'

I didn't answer, locking eyes with Quinn and waiting for her to make her move.

When she did, I swung the drawer back into the balcony, smashing through the glass.

The sound echoed around us.

I was already jumping.

I dived onto the balcony, landing on the concrete with a thud. The cold air hit me instantly – as if I had jumped into a river in the dead of winter. The adrenaline was quickly replaced by the agony of hitting cold concrete with an already injured body. Only, there was no time to think about that. I had to keep moving. I had bought myself a few seconds, but they would count for nothing if I didn't keep moving.

I was up on my feet, wishing I knew exactly what lay beneath the balcony.

There was a metal railing separating it from the drop below and I moved to crawl over it. It was higher than I'd been expecting, but I got one leg over it quickly and was about to lift myself over when I felt a hand on the leg still on the other side.

The grip was firm, as I tried to struggle away from its hold. I kicked out, but it only served to put me off balance. I turned and saw Quinn still in the room.

Carson was red-faced, breathing heavily, one hand on my leg, the other disappearing behind him and then, empty, reaching for my shoulder.

I kicked out again, but didn't connect. Then, he was on me, grabbing hold of me with both hands and pulling me back from the railing. I could smell the sweat and cigarettes on him, his breath hot on my skin.

I felt the hand on my shoulder squeeze. His fingers dug into me, pain spearing down my left-hand side, and I fell back onto the balcony with a crash. He didn't waste time, throwing his weight on top of me, trying to lock my limbs into position so I couldn't move. I could feel his strength, despite his age – or perhaps because of it – bearing down on me and could feel my own sapping away. I turned my head, trying to squirm away, as an empty feeling slowly dissipated inside me.

He was going to beat me to death. That's how it felt. I caught his eyes again and in them was red and fire. Anger, exploding over me, and there was nothing I could do to stop it. I couldn't lift my arms to shield myself. I couldn't get away.

'Okay, that's enough, let's get him out of here.'

Anthony Sullivan's voice came through the fog and I had never wanted to be anywhere else in the world more than in that moment. I continued to struggle under the older man's grip, his weight, but I could barely move. My body was moving of its own accord, jerking in movements that I couldn't control.

Then, my ears were ringing.

My mind shifted and I felt like I was underwater suddenly. The darkness in my vision swarming over me and the weight of water surrounding my body. It was as if I were drowning and all I could hear was the flow of a river in my ears.

I wanted to let it take me down.

There was another thud of noise. I heard a muffled scream and then the weight on top of me shifted a little.

I felt something whizz past my head and then an echo of something striking metal. Then, Quinn flashed across my vision and the weight was gone entirely.

I managed to get onto my side. Ahead of me, in the room, I saw two large men, lifeless and broken. One sprawled out on one of the beds, the other on the floor, propped up against the wall. Sitting there, his head lolling into his unmoving chest.

Carson was slumped over on the balcony to my left. A rapidly forming pool of blood spilling around him.

I saw two people fly past me, taking hold of the balcony railing, before disappearing from view.

And the blurred outline of a man moving towards me, a gun in his hand, pointing in my direction. I couldn't see his face clearly, but I could feel his presence.

It was as if the night had taken form.

I shrank away slowly, my shoulder hitting the metal railing behind me, a dull flash of pain travelling down my arm and into my fingertips.

The man continued to move towards me.

There was nowhere else for me to go.

I heard crunching glass, saw black boots coming to a stop next to me. Then, an exhalation of breath and a curse word or three.

A hand shot out and I flinched, scrunching my eyes closed and waiting for it to be over. Waiting for the white light. The tunnel.

The end.

Only, the hand gripped me under my armpit and brought me back into an upright sitting position.

'Sam, it's okay,' he said, as my head swam with agony and confusion. 'You're safe now.'

I opened my eyes slowly and saw the man squatting down in front of me. Felt every muscle and bone tense up in response.

It was the man from the cemetery.

I had gone from one nightmare to another.

I wanted to scream. To cry out in pain until my throat was hoarse from the effort, but I couldn't make a sound.

I shook those feelings away and got ready to fight again.

Quinn managed to get Anthony to his feet, somehow. He had taken the brunt of the fall from the balcony and was being slow to recover.

'Move,' she said, grabbing hold of his upper arm, but feeling nothing but resistance as she tried to drag him away. 'We've got to get out of here.'

'We're not going anywhere . . .'

'It's too late,' Quinn hissed at him, glancing above her and hearing something on the balcony. A bullet scratched against the asphalt beside them. In the distance, the limo screeched around the parking lot and she saw Zoran at the wheel. 'We're dead if we stay.'

That seemed to be enough and she managed to drag him to the waiting car. Stuffed themselves in the back seat, as another shot rang out above them.

It wasn't until they were a couple of miles down the road that she started to breathe a little easier.

'That was too close,' she said.

'Any idea who he was?'

'I think it was the same guy who tried to take him from the graveyard.'

'You got a name? Who he's working for?'

Quinn shook her head. 'Sam didn't know.'

Anthony reached into his jacket and took out his cell phone. Dialled a number and waited. 'Have you got into it yet? . . . I need what's in that cell, now . . . you don't need to concern yourself with that . . . listen to me, stop talking now, or I'll take a screwdriver to each member of your family and make you watch, understand?'

He ended the call and threw his cell down on the car floor. He was breathing hard, his hands shaking. Quinn shrank back in her seat.

She waited, as he took some deep breaths in and out and then picked up his cell, as it dinged with a notification.

'Zoran,' Anthony said, still reading whatever was on his cell phone screen. 'Take us to the office down in New London. We'll regroup there.'

He sat back in his seat and grinned at Quinn. The sight of it sent a shiver down her spine.

'Look,' she said, trying to sound calm. It didn't quite work. 'Maybe you could drop me off somewhere. You don't need me any more.'

'If you want to get paid, then you'll stay exactly where you are. Given recent events, I'm going to need every spare pair of hands I can get.'

Quinn swallowed something bitter down and wished she'd never got involved with this man in the first place.

But then, she thought of the money that would be coming to her, and that made her feel much better.

CHAPTER 45

I felt his hands on my arms and tried to move away from them. 'I'm here to help you.'

I didn't believe him. I didn't believe anything.

'We have to go. Now.'

I shook my head in response to the stranger. 'I'm not going anywhere.'

'You don't have a choice,' he said, lifting me up as if I were nothing. 'We have to get out of here.'

I let myself be led past the chaos of the motel room, stepping over a body I tried not to look at on the floor. There was another on the other side of the room.

Three dead men. I guess this stranger liked his odds better than I had.

'Who are you?'

'Come on,' he said, ignoring the question and pushing me down the corridor. 'Down the hall, out the doors, then a flight of stairs. My car is just outside.'

We made it down the flight of steps and out into the cold air of the night. I could feel myself shaking and tried to stop.

I spied Quinn's car still in its spot. I didn't have her keys. Behind it, woods. Enough places to hide.

'This way—' the stranger said and I didn't wait for him to finish the thought. I took off running in that direction.

I thought I was sprinting. Running faster than I'd ever done in my life. With each step, freedom beckoned. The woods were thick and I could last the night hidden there. Emerge in the daylight and work out my next step from there. My legs burned with effort, but I was going to make it.

I made it a hundred yards before being tackled to the ground.

'Hey, stop,' he said, pulling me up and gripping me by the wrists, pushing my arms up my back until I grimaced in pain. I felt the barrel of a gun in my back. 'I'm trying to help you survive the night.'

I allowed myself to be led to his car and got into the passenger seat. The stranger made his way around to the other side of the car. He stuck the car in drive and pulled away.

'Where are we going?'

He ignored the question, as I almost tumbled to the footwell as he screeched out of the parking lot and onto the road.

I pulled my seat belt on and glanced across at him. I looked at the wheel and thought about wrenching it to the side. Crashing the car, so I could escape. Only, he was holding the wheel with one hand, the other lazily in his lap, a gun in it. Pointed towards me.

I gave up on the idea. At least for a moment or two. 'You didn't answer my question. Who are you and why did you help me?'

'I'm not the person who can answer your questions,' he said, looking straight ahead at the road. He was younger than me – solidly built, his chest threatening to burst through his tight jacket. His head was shaved and a few white marks were visible through the buzz cut. A small scar cut into his eyebrow.

He was young, solid-looking. Week-long stubble and a sharp jawline. His skin was a darker shade of pale, the result of living in sunnier climes, I guessed. It ran deep. His knuckles had white flashes of scars, as they rested on top of the steering wheel.

Whoever he was, he didn't look like he had run away from anything in his life.

'Let me go.'

The stranger sighed, as if I was an irritant. 'No, Sam.'

'Then, what? Where are you taking me?'

'Somewhere safe.'

I assessed my options and realised they were limited. My passport and all my money were still in the motel room back in Mystic. I had no idea where I was, no way of getting back there.

The reality of the situation hit me.

'Please, just let me go,' I said, holding my head in my hands. 'I won't tell them about you.'

'You want to go to the police and explain everything? They've got nothing on you right now.'

'Maybe they'll believe me if I just tell them the truth. About the other men and what they did.'

'We can't do that,' the stranger replied, swerving around a slow-moving car in front and onto the highway. 'Look, just sit back, relax, it's all going to come right. If we go back now, after you've run, they'll just blame you for everything. And I won't be around to see the fallout.'

'We can't do this,' I said, turning back to face him. He was staring at the road ahead, a steely gaze on his face. 'I can't do this. It's not right. I don't even know who you are and you say you're helping me escape. All while holding a gun on me.'

He looked down and seemed to notice what he was holding for the first time. It disappeared into his jacket. 'There, happy? Now I'm not holding you at gunpoint. I'm a friend.'

'You tried to kidnap me last time we met. Forgive me for thinking you might not be a *friend*.'

'I'm trying to help.'

'You're a stranger with a gun. I've not had the best experiences with those lately.'

'You can call me Jackson,' he said, glancing my way before going back to looking at the road ahead of him. 'And you're Sam, so now we're not strangers any more.'

'I guess it's good to meet you,' I replied, still checking over my shoulder to see if we were being followed. 'How long have you been following me?'

He shook his head. 'I've been along for the ride since you got back to Firwood. You've had a crazy week. If I'd been able to, I would have made myself known earlier.'

'You're involved then. With who? Anthony Sullivan?'

'Not in this life.'

'Who then? Tom?'

A beat, then he shook his head. 'Just wait. It'll all make sense soon.'

I left it for a few moments, but I had too much to say. 'It was you. In Tom's house. Earlier?'

'You're a bad shot.'

'Or good, if you're the dead guy. If you hadn't been there, he'd have survived.'

'It was you or him,' he said, checking his mirror for the road behind him. 'That's just how things go.'

'So people keep telling me.'

He let the silence grow a little, as he sped the car up and overtook a few other slow drivers on the highway. He glanced up at the rear-view mirror again and seemed happy with what he saw. 'All you need to know for now is that I'm not going to let that man hurt you. Or anyone else. If I can help it.'

'He's not going to quit. He thinks I can help him find my mother. Only I haven't got the first clue where she is.'

'You don't.'

'I don't,' I shifted in my seat, trying to find a comfortable way to sit, but gave up before continuing to talk. 'It would make things easier if I did.'

'I bet.'

Five or ten minutes passed and Jackson exited the highway

and onto quieter roads. He was peering out of the windscreen, looking around for something.

Finally, we parked up outside a bar, a winding road leading round it. We sat there for a few seconds; a car went past us on the road but didn't slow down. The gravel on the drive seemed not to have been disturbed in a long time. I could see a harbour beside the old building, an oasis of calm in the early morning light. As we got out of the car, I could smell the sea, and boats were rigged up in the water surrounding us.

'Where are we?'

'Noank,' Jackson said, walking ahead and towards the building. 'It's the town over from Mystic, where you were staying.'

I looked at the sign on the roof of the building. Seahorse. The pale green paint was peeling in places and I couldn't see into the small windows. The doors looked solid and dark.

Above, the clouds were black, the light fading in around us. I felt a chill in the air and wrapped my arms around me. I felt the first few spots of rain and wished I had a proper jacket. It was only going to get worse.

'Follow me,' Jackson said, walking off around the side of the building. I looked back towards the bar and realised that we hadn't come there for this.

As we made our way around it, I noticed a break in the boats. A wide gravelled drive and brown fences. Jackson was looking in every direction every few seconds.

I walked behind him, watching his back, as it tensed beneath his coat and his shoulders came up. In front of me was a building with dirty brown wood cladding, which was broken in places. It seemed to have been a boathouse at some time in the past. Now, it looked like a strong wind would take it at any point.

Behind it, I could hear the sea, rushing against the shore.

'What are we doing here?'

'Not much further now.'

I moved slowly across the gravel. An old beaten-down car was idling on the pathway. It was dusty, dirty, looking as bad as the building behind it.

I imagined a gun being trained on me. My head, I guessed. At any moment, I would hear a pop and that would be it. Lights out.

Maybe I wouldn't even know it was over. I'd seen that on some American TV drama years before – you wouldn't even hear it when it happens.

You would just cut to black.

I shuffled forwards, my body bruised but still working. I heard birds lifting from the trees and into the air and I tried to follow their flight. I couldn't see them.

I heard the water, splashing against an unseen dock behind the house.

Then, I saw someone moving out of it and coming towards me.

There, on the driveway, a woman standing, looking back at me. I thought she was a mirage at first. Something my tired brain was tricking me into seeing.

Only, I could smell her. I could see her. She was real. She looked different. Older, hair shorter, wrong colour. Her face wouldn't match the one I had held in my mind for almost twenty-five years.

'It can't be . . .'

'Sam,' the woman said and that's all I needed.

It was her.

It was my mother.

She was alive.

Three Days Ago

She knew something was wrong when Tom left home.

He couldn't lie to her this time.

The small town in Arizona where they had spent the past twenty-five years was emptier without Tom by her side. They had struggled for the first few years, but lately it had been good.

Good enough, anyway.

And then, a couple of weeks earlier, he had left quickly and without warning. She had called her mom, hiding up north in Rhode Island. Hiding from *him*.

It was becoming more difficult to have a normal conversation with her. Laurie had spoken to Tom about moving her down to Arizona. He was making plans to do so.

'Parker hasn't called me,' her mom had said. 'He always calls me, every other day.'

That was the first indication that things were going wrong. Then, Jackson had left in the middle of the night, the day after Tom, and suddenly she had been alone.

Tom would call her, but he wasn't telling her the truth. Then, he stopped calling altogether. Wouldn't answer the phone. She left so many messages, but they all went without a response.

She didn't know until Jackson called her a week ago.

'It's me,' Jackson said, his voice coming down the phone from so far away. 'You didn't tell me . . .'

Tom had lied to her. For twenty-five years, she had shared her life with someone who had kept something from her.

'David was here,' Jackson had said, ripping her heart in two.

'What . . . how?'

Jackson had told her where he was. What had happened.

Who was there.

'I'm sorry, Mom. I thought you knew and hadn't told me.'

David had died. Michael was gone too. She grieved for them all over again.

Only one of her boys had died in that river. Once she was over the shock, she grieved for them all over again.

Tom had helped her escape to a small town, where they pretended to be together. A normal family. Only, Tom trained Jackson to kill out in the backyard, in case he couldn't protect her if Anthony Sullivan came back. She couldn't tell anyone her real name. And she lived every single day with the fear that she would be found.

She had lived that long, with this shadow hanging over her.

And all the time, her family had still been there.

She lifted the phone away from her ear and screamed into the empty house. Thought about Tom and what she wanted to do to him.

Twenty-five years, she had lived under the same roof as someone who had lied to her.

They had been close – she knew many people in the small town thought they were married. They had been their own messed-up version of a family.

It had never been anything but platonic. A marriage of convenience. He had never pushed her into turning it into something more. And she had never wanted it to be. She still thought of David. Of her two boys. That heartbreak was something she could never get over, even if she'd wanted to.

Twenty-five goddamn years he had been there for her. And he had been lying the whole time.

'Come home,' she had said, her words stilted by anger. 'It's not safe.'

'Someone has to watch Sam,' Jackson had replied, his voice steady, determined. 'I can help him.'

Now, her phone was ringing again. She had spent days thinking about Sam. About David. About everything that had been taken from her.

She blamed Anthony.

She blamed herself.

She blamed Tom, most of all.

'He's coming back,' Jackson said, as she answered the phone. 'He's bought a ticket to Boston.'

'I have to go back there.'

There had been silence on the cell phone. Jackson absorbing what she was saying.

'If you go back, you're signing your own death warrant,' Jackson said, finally able to find words.

Only, they weren't enough.

'He's my son,' she said, looking outside of the small house they had shared all that time. Where Jackson would chop logs for the fire. Growing bigger, stronger, every single day. She thought about Sam, all those miles away. Dealing with her past, without her knowledge. And somewhere, deep inside, she wanted to kill Tom for all the lies he had told. For everything that had been taken from her.

'I have to see him.'

'I understand, Mom.'

He didn't. He couldn't. He would never know the ache of guilt that had festered and thrived inside her for all that time. The grief for the family she had lost, that followed her, a black cloud that she couldn't shift. The years working a dead-end job in a diner in the small town. Making small talk with the same patrons who came in day after day. The way her heart skipped a beat every time the chime above the door jingled and she looked up expecting to see Anthony walking through the door.

He couldn't know how she wished for an end, but couldn't even have that release with Jackson in her life.

How she had to live for him.

'He's lived all these years thinking I was dead,' Laurie said, feeling a tear form and drip slowly down her cheek. 'Thinking I wasn't there for him.'

'I'll keep him safe, Mom,' Jackson replied. 'Until you get here.'

'Tom sent you there.'

'He thought it was for the best,' he said, his voice low and barely there. 'He knew what you would do if you knew Parker had been killed. That David was still alive. You might do something that would put yourself in danger.'

He was right, but that didn't mean he had the authority to make that call.

And he sure as hell didn't have any right to put Jackson in that danger either.

'I'll be there in a couple of days.'

She had ended the call and put together a bag quickly. Took the money she had been saving for a rainy day out of the jar and stuffed it in her purse. Then, started up the car and set off across country. Left Arizona behind and began crossing the states. A journey that would take a couple of days, but she couldn't buy a plane ticket.

She was supposed to be dead. Paid under the table as a waitress, no social security number. If she needed medical treatment, it was provided by someone Tom could pay off.

Her life had been taken from her.

And now, she was running again.

Only this time, it was *towards* the danger.

CHAPTER 46

I couldn't move.

What I was seeing was so divorced from reality, that it was almost as if my body had shut down in response. The wind died around me, the aroma of seafood and lavender settling over us. I stared at the woman, trying to convince myself that what I was seeing was real.

'Sam . . .'

Her voice broke the spell. I forgot about Jackson. I forgot about the dead men I'd left behind me in my wake.

I forgot about Quinn, about Anthony Sullivan. About Tom Miller. About my father, my brother.

I only had eyes for my mum.

I ran to her.

'Mum?' I managed to whisper, a croak of a word that fell from my chapped and dry lips. It wasn't enough of a word.

She didn't say anything, simply reached out a tentative hand to my shoulder, before I fell into her arms.

She smelled the same. She felt the same. It was as if I were twenty-five years younger in an instant. I was a small boy again. I buried my head into her and held on tight.

'You've grown so much,' she said into my shoulder. The words being lost in my skin.

I didn't want to let go. Ever. I wanted to stay in that embrace for the rest of my life and forget the world.

I heard a voice behind me and the world shifted again.

'We need to get going.' I found myself snapping back to reality. I jumped and turned around, placing my mum behind me. Jackson stood a few yards away, still as the ground.

'They're going to find us,' I said, spitting out the words in a panic. 'They always know where I am.'

I felt a hand on my shoulder again and the soothing words I had waited so long to hear.

'It's okay, son,' my mum said, pulling me back around to face her. 'You're safe with us. We're going to pick up my mom and then we'll be out of here in no time.'

'They're looking for you. We have to keep you out of sight.'

'It's fine,' Mum said, nodding towards Jackson and leading me back towards his car. 'They don't know I'm here. Tom took care of your grandmother – they won't be able to find her.'

I could hear her voice, but it was as if it were through a bad satellite signal. Nothing made sense any more.

All I could do was follow them.

I got into the back seat with my mum. She held onto my hands, as Jackson pulled away and stared straight ahead.

Mum studied me, looking me over. 'Are you real?'

I felt as if I were locked in a dream state. 'Yes. Same question to you?'

'I think I am,' she said, then held onto me. I felt her body moving, the cry of relief. Her tears were wet against my neck.

'I can't believe you're alive,' she said, pulling away from me and stroking the side of my face. 'I wished every night to see you again.'

My smile grew wider, then it began to dissemble. Falling from my face to the bottom of the car like leaves in autumn. I swallowed, wanting to ignore the feeling that was rising inside me. Opened my mouth to so many questions, but nothing came out.

'Every night, I went to bed, praying I could see you again,' Mum continued, shifting back in the seat and blocking the view out of the side window, as the scenery changed around us. The burgeoning sunlight disappeared and the car was colder. Darker. 'I'm sure you have questions . . .'

I couldn't hold back the tide any longer. It had built within me and couldn't be quelled. 'Questions? Yeah, you could say that.'

'Sam . . .' she said, wincing from the sound of my voice. She held up a hand to Jackson in the front as he tensed in response.

'Hold on,' I said, stopping her in her tracks. 'I need to figure this out.'

Her expression changed, becoming more neutral in an instant, but I ignored it. I looked away and down at our hands, interlocked together. I took mine away.

'First, tell me who he is?' I said, pointing at the back of Jackson's head.

'That's Jackson. He's been helping you.'

'I don't think you understand what I've seen this past week. So many people trying to find a ghost. Well, now you're here, sitting beside me, as if it's the most normal thing to happen. As if we're not in danger. As if everything is going to be okay.'

She shook her head. 'There's things you need to know. To understand.'

I laughed at that. Barked out, forced out. It echoed around the car and I thought I saw my mum wince again at the sound.

'You think? How about we start at the beginning.' I tried to stay calm, but I knew what had been building inside me for the previous few days.

It wasn't desperation to find someone lost.

It was anger at her possibly being alive and letting me live my life not knowing.

'We can do that,' she said, moving her hands towards mine again. I recoiled from her touch. 'Wait.'

A look of hurt flashed across her face. I ignored it.

'I need to know why. Why did you do this to me?'

She hesitated, then closed her mouth. I could see her mind working overtime, trying to find the right words to say. I didn't give her time to come up with anything.

'Twenty-five years I've believed my mother was dead,' I said, and I could hear the anger in my tone. I didn't care any more. 'I *grieved* for you. For all that time. I watched Michael die and I was left on my own with a man who was broken by it all. And now you're here and there doesn't seem to be a reason why I had to.'

'I didn't know . . .'

'How could you not know?' I continued, spitting her words back at her. 'I was the one you left in that river. I was the one who travelled back to the other side of the ocean and grew up thinking you were dead. Do you know how that feels? No, of course not. You have no idea.'

'I do—'

'No, you have to listen to this. You've been alive all this time. You were gone and Dad wouldn't talk to me. So, I was left to try and work out what had happened, and you know what I did? You know who I blamed?'

She didn't answer, but I could see her shoulders tense, her body rigid.

'I thought it was my fault,' I said, my voice hitching on the last word. I swallowed it back. 'I thought it was something I'd done and that's why no one would tell me what happened. And now, I find out that you've been alive all this time. That you could have told me where you were at any point, but instead kept this lie going. I've lived my life on pause for twenty-five years based on a lie.'

'I'm sorry,' she said, but it wasn't enough and she knew it. I could hear it in her voice. 'If you'll let me explain, I can tell you everything.'

'You have let me be attacked, almost killed, and done nothing.

Dad is dead. Your brother, Parker, gone. Plus Tom, probably your oldest friend. All of them gone. Because of you. Why would you do this to me? How could you do this?'

'Because I thought *you* were dead,' she said, turning back to me now. I could see the hurt in her eyes, the redness in her cheeks. 'I thought I was the only one who survived the crash.'

I was out of breath, my throat raw with the effort, but I had so much more to say. Only, I didn't think I had any more words. Only anger.

And now, I didn't know what to feel.

'How . . . ?'

'Look, I know you're hurt and I'm sorry,' Mum said, her voice wavering, as she battled to stay calm. 'Believe me, I'm feeling it too. As soon as Jackson told me you were coming here, I got in that car and started driving. I wanted to get on the first plane to London, after Jackson told me you were alive. Only, I can't leave the country. I can't get a passport, because then he'll know where I am. I've been hiding from *him* for the past twenty-five years. I thought I had lost you all and I wasn't going to let anything happen to Jackson. If I'd known, I would have done anything to get back to you.'

'Where have you been?'

'I had to disappear quickly. There was no time to second-guess things. Tom told me you were all gone. Anthony wasn't going to stop searching for me, so I've been hiding ever since. A small town in Arizona. No one knew I was alive, other than Tom. He said it was easier that way.'

'Easier for who? Not me.'

'If I'd known you were alive, you would have been with me. Only, that danger would have still been there.'

'Well, guess what, it turns out nothing could stop that danger in the end. Look at me. Look at what's happened.'

'I know, I know,' she said, her voice cracking. 'I've made a lot of mistakes in my life. But I promise, if I'd known, I would have come for you.'

'Michael's still dead.'

She turned back to me now. 'Sam . . .'

'He was just a little boy, Mum,' I said, stumbling over the words as tears sprang to my eyes. I felt a tear roll down my cheek and I wiped it away. 'He was five years old and he really is gone. He's dead and it's my fault I didn't save him.'

This was the real reason I was angry.

Michael was dead and it was because of me.

'Sam, look at me.'

I lifted my head, as my mum laid a hand on mine. I tried to pull away, but she only held onto it tighter.

'It wasn't your fault,' she said, as I lifted my head and looked at her. 'I'm sorry you've lived with this. I didn't know. I thought I'd lost all of you.'

'Tell me everything.'

And for the rest of the journey, she told me her story.

1996

She had stopped counting the days since she had been pulled from the river. Stopped counting the hours since she had woken in the trunk of a car.

Stopped counting the minutes since Anthony had imprisoned her in his home and told her that her husband and children were dead.

At first, she hadn't believed him. If she had survived, then surely, they had. Eventually, she had stopped asking.

She had stopped believing.

Stopped hoping.

Anthony came into the room. Locked it behind him and approached her where she was lying on the bed.

He sat down next to her and she flinched as he reached a hand out towards her. He didn't seem to notice.

'How are we both today?' he said, laying his hand on her stomach.

She turned her face away from him, trying to keep what little food was left inside her from coming up.

'You need to eat more,' he continued, as if he couldn't see how she was responding to his touch. How she was responding to his presence. 'You have to keep your strength up.'

He patted her stomach softly and then stood up. 'I have to go away for a couple of days, but Maria will be here. And others, to make sure you don't get into any trouble.'

He leaned forwards and placed a kiss on her head. He smelled of cologne and cigarettes.

Then, he was out of the room, the lock snapping shut as soon as the door was closed.

Like every night, she cried herself to sleep, wondering if there was ever going to be an escape from life.

She was asleep when she heard the first knock on the window. At first, she didn't know what it was. Only that something had woken her.

By the second and third, she was on the floor at the side of the bed, her whole body shaking.

When she finally realised the sound was knocking on the window, she whispered a silent prayer and hoped it was someone on her side.

'Let me in.'

She slowly rose from the floor, seeing a blurred outline behind the shades. She drew them back, inch by inch, until she saw who was standing on the balcony outside.

Tom.

Laurie felt a tear fall down her cheek, her breath becoming shallow, as she felt a wave of relief wash over her. She blinked back more tears.

It didn't feel real. As if she were dreaming him. She shook her head and looked again.

He was still there.

She tried to find a way to open the window, despite knowing it was locked.

'Use something to smash it,' Tom said, his voice muffled through the glass.

Laurie looked around and saw nothing heavy enough to break the window. Her eyes landed on the pillow on her bed. She crossed the room and picked it up quickly and almost sprinted back to the window. Lifted it in her hand and formed a fist behind the cushion.

'Stand back,' she said, her voice barely above a whisper.

She used all the force she could and pounded her fist into the glass. At first, it held, but after a few more hits, her fist crashed through.

Tom moved the broken bits of glass out of the way and came into the room. She collapsed into his arms.

'I never stopped believing,' he said into her shoulder. 'I knew you were alive. I wasn't about to give up. Not when they hadn't found your body. The police told me to stop looking, but I never listened. They didn't know you. They didn't know *him*.'

She couldn't speak. It was a dream. It had to be.

Tom pulled her away and held her outstretched and looked down at her. Winced as he saw her protruding stomach and then held her again.

'David . . . the boys . . . ?' Laurie's voice was a whisper. A plea.

Her heart broke as he looked down at her and hesitated. Then, shook his head, looking away from her.

'I'm going to take care of you now. He'll never find you again.'

'How do we get out of here?'

Tom looked back towards the balcony and shook his head. 'Through the house.'

'He locked me in.'

She could see him tense at that, but he shook it away quickly. He moved towards the door and had the lock open in less than a minute.

Tom looked back towards Laurie and gave her a wink. 'There's stuff I've learned over the years.'

He led the way, Laurie following close behind. The house was silent – one man sitting in a chair by the front entrance. Tom turned to her and placed a finger against his lips. They crept past him, without making a sound. Made it into the kitchen and then out the back door, where a key had been left in the lock.

Outside, the wind and rain battered down around them. When they reached halfway down the winding driveway, he stopped. They were off the drive itself, hidden within the treeline that bordered it, but if they moved any further, they would be exposed quickly.

'Wait here,' he said, looking around him. 'Plan A – we go out this way. Through the gates. I know there are people at the gate. I managed to slip past them, but I'm not sure I fancy my chances of that happening twice. I need to check the route out. Plan B, we escape through the woods instead.'

'I'll come with you,' Laurie began, but he shook his head.

'If they see me, I might have to do something you don't want to see. If I'm not back in five minutes, run to the woods. Don't look back.'

Then, he disappeared. Her mind went numb, as she shivered in the cold and rain. She heard footsteps behind her, but she didn't look.

She didn't want to. She tried to keep herself as still as possible, but she knew her heartbeat was echoing around her. That the thoughts in her head could be heard from a mile away.

A figure stepped out of the shadows and for a brief moment, Laurie thought it was Tom. That he had found her again and everything was going to be okay.

Then, she saw who it was.

'Laurie,' Maria said, stepping towards her. 'What are you doing out here?'

Laurie opened her mouth to speak, but no words came out.

'Were you thinking that you could just leave?' she asked, a smirk on her face. 'You think you could get away with that?'

'Look . . .' Laurie tried to say, but Maria closed the distance between them in an instant. She had her hand around her jaw before Laurie could react. Squeezing.

'You'll keep your mouth shut,' Maria said, her teeth bared. 'Tell me, were you just going to leave him again?'

Laurie tried to shake her head, but Maria's grip was too strong. Her jaw was locked in place and all she could feel was the force in it. It was as if her head had been stuck in a vice.

'Don't lie to me. Is it true? After everything he's done for you?'

Laurie felt the enemy of a tear escape from her eye. She could see the black of Maria's eyes, staring into her own, and knew there was no way out.

'I'm sorry,' Laurie managed to say, before her head was thrown backwards. She hit the tree behind her and slumped to the floor. 'I promise, I'll go back . . .'

'I don't want to hear it,' Maria said, standing over her. She looked down and spat on Laurie's face, then took out a gun and pointed it towards her. 'It wasn't enough that you ran once before. That you broke his heart. You come back here and make him think everything is going to be okay. Pretend that you love him, as much as he loves you. I won't have you do that to my brother. He deserves better than you. You're not going to steal his child. The world will be better off without you. When I tell Anthony, he'll agree. Once that baby is born, you're gone.'

'No, please.'

'You think I care what you want?'

Laurie felt a sense of calm wash over her.

'You have to let me go . . .'

'No chance.' Maria leaned forwards and grabbed hold of Laurie's shoulder. 'You're coming with me. Anthony will be back soon and you'll be a good little girl until then. You'll do as you're told, you'll have this child, then I'll make sure personally that you never see him grow a single day.'

Laurie shook her head, her hand moving towards Maria's.

Tom had shown her something when they were younger. Something his father had taught him.

She used it now. She squeezed Maria's wrist, then with her other hand, placed her fingers in just the right position. The gun fell from her hand and clattered to the ground.

Laurie didn't hesitate this time.

The sound of the gunshot was loud in the darkness. But no less deadly.

Tom found her again.

'They're distracted enough that we can go around them . . .'

He stopped as he reached her and looked down at the ground. Saw Maria's body at her feet.

'We've got to get out of here,' Tom said, a look in his eyes she had never seen.

Fear.

Laurie had killed the one person that Anthony truly loved.

'We have to disappear. He'll come looking for you with everything he's got.'

'What about her?' Laurie said, trying not to look at Maria's body. The blood pooling around her head. 'They'll know it was me. What do we do? We can't leave her here. DNA, they have . . .'

Laurie was breathing rapidly, unable to get her words out. She looked to Tom, pleading with him to help her.

Tom ran a sweaty hand through his hair and thought. Finally, he stared back at her and it wasn't a question. It wasn't a suggestion.

'Your dad's grave.'

* * *

Moving a body was more difficult than they tell you. Tom had carried her most of the way, but Laurie had to help here and there. Mainly by moving branches and clearing a path for Tom to walk through.

He had to kill two people at the gate. She hadn't seen him do it, but it had been too easy to get past there with Maria in their arms.

Finally, they had made it to his car and dumped her in the trunk.

Laurie was already trying to forget what came after that.

'What happened? After he got me out of the river, what happened?'

They were sitting in Tom's car. The sun was slowly rising, casting a hazy glow over the fields surrounding them. It reminded Laurie of something David would say.

'Red sky at night, shepherd's delight. Red sky in the morning . . .'

'I'm sorry,' Tom was saying, as Laurie shook off the memory of David's voice. 'I tried to save them, but I was too late.'

'So, they're all dead? Really?'

'I'm sorry,' Tom repeated, as if it were his fault. As if he had been the one who was responsible for their deaths. 'Listen . . .'

'We need to go back,' Laurie said suddenly, pulling on her seat belt and pointing to the road ahead of them. 'We need to wait for him to come home. I'm going to kill him too.'

'Laurie . . .'

'No, Tom,' she said, her voice echoing around the car. She grasped hold of his arm and fixed him with a glare. 'He killed my family. He deserves to die.'

'It's too late,' Tom said, placing his hand on hers. 'They're already gone and if we go back now, there'll be no escape. And after what has happened to Maria, he's not going to want to listen to you. You'll be dead before you even see him. He'll have an army out looking for you right now.'

'But . . . my kids, Tom. He killed my kids.'

'I know. I know.'

Laurie lifted a hand to her face and thought about Sam and Michael. How scared they must have been. How frightened the dark made Michael and how Sam had never learned to swim.

She felt hollow. As if someone had come along and stolen a part of her. And maybe they had.

'We have to leave. Tonight.'

Laurie wasn't really listening. She was trying to keep her mind from tearing itself apart.

'We'll drive south,' Tom continued, holding onto her hand, as she stared out onto the empty road. 'I'll make sure Parker and your mom get somewhere safe and then we can work out what to do later.'

Only, there would be no later. There was no future. Just Laurie and the child she was carrying inside her. The child she had no love for, no desire to meet. She saw it as evil, growing there.

She put her head in her hands and screamed.

'It's going to be okay,' Tom said, wrapping his arms around her and holding her close. 'I'm going to take care of you. Of all of you. You don't have to worry any more. He'll never find any of us.'

It took a long time, but she finally believed him.

CHAPTER 47

For a moment, there was only the sound of the car on the road. No one breathed, no one spoke.

I couldn't stand the silence any more.

'This can't be happening,' I managed to say, my throat closing up. I tried to swallow the emotion down. 'This is too much.'

'Sam . . .'

I stopped her talking, waving her words away. A thought entered my mind and wouldn't leave. 'I died, didn't I? In that motel room. Or Tom's house, maybe? I died and this is hell, isn't it?'

Jackson stared back at me in the rear-view mirror. Mum patted my hand. 'It's okay . . .'

'It's not okay,' I said, too loud. She flinched as I shouted back at her. I heard an echo of the smack on the side of the car from my fist banging down on it. 'Tom took something from me. From you. Once you were safe, you could have come back for me. For Dad. He stole you from us. How could he do something like this? Dad was broken after we left in 1995. We didn't talk, we didn't have a normal life. I never got the chance to tell him it was true. That you are alive. Because of one man's lies.'

I was breathing heavily, slumping back in the seat in exasperation, as the sky lightened around us. I stared out the window, at the foreign land I found myself in, and wished I had never gone back to Firwood.

'I don't know why Tom did what he did,' Mum said, her voice flat, calm. Yet, underneath, there was a sense of the anger she was holding back. 'I know what he would say. That he was just trying to keep me safe. People thought I was dead. Tom knew if I came back, Anthony would just find me again. I think he told your dad to get out of the country fast. Like, that night of the accident. That's why he didn't stick around. That's why Anthony didn't know you both survived.'

'Well, turns out it was all for nothing, because he managed to track your brother down, who revealed where Dad was. So, Parker is dead, Tom is dead, I'm over here in the eye of the storm, and Anthony Sullivan now knows we're all involved.'

'It's going to be fine,' Mum said, placing an arm around me and shushing me as if I were a small child with a scraped knee. 'We're going to work it all out.'

I shrugged her away. 'You can't work this out. They're killers.'

I turned to Jackson now. 'And, I'm guessing you're the son?'

His eyes found mine in the rear-view mirror, then my mum's.

'Tom never told me until last week. Even then, it was only about David.'

I felt something course through me. A red, dirty anger, that I couldn't handle.

I forced myself to breathe slowly, but it did little to dissipate the feeling inside me. I could see Jackson tense at the wheel, as if he could sense what I was trying to hide within me. I searched his face for anything that looked recognisable. Something that would connect the two of us.

'Tom wasn't your father then.'

Jackson eyed me in the mirror for a second or two, then shook his head. I turned back to my mum. 'Tom helped you escape from Anthony. Convinced you we were all dead and that if you didn't follow him across the country, you'd end up the same.'

'I feel the same anger . . .'

'Pull the car over.'

Jackson hesitated, so I made as if to open the door, despite us doing way faster than the speed limit.

'Okay, okay,' he said, slowing down and then pulling over to the side of the road.

I pushed the door open and walked away from the car. I could see the water in the distance and wanted to walk until I met the shore. Submerge myself in the sea and never come out again.

I screamed until my voice gave out. Bent over and placed my hands on my knees and tried not to retch.

There was a hand on my back, but I shook it off. I heard my mother's breath hitch and a weak sob escape her throat.

'I need to leave,' I whispered, my head in my hands. I tried to think of a way this day would end well. This week. This life. I couldn't think of a single thing. 'I can't do this.'

Then, I heard Jackson's voice.

'Hey. Listen, you're okay. We can get through this.'

He moved around so he was standing in front of me. I straightened up and stared at the man in front of me and there was nothing there. He may have had my mother's eyes, but that was the only similarity. He was a different build to us all. A different look – darker. His gait more easy, his bone structure more prominent.

He looked more like his father than anyone else.

'I wish we could have met in different circumstances,' he said, and for some reason it was the first thing I really believed since I'd entered the house. 'I didn't know why Tom sent me over at first. When I found out who you were, I wanted to tell you. Back at the cemetery, I was planning on doing just that.'

'You could have spoken to me back in Firwood?'

He nodded. 'I know. I've got to take some of the blame. But it's true. All of it.' He handed me a bottle of water. It was warm to the touch.

'I've been with you every step of the way. I was too late to save your father. Too late to stop you finding out the way you did. Too late for Tom. But I never let anything happen to you.'

'So, you're my brother then. How have you been?'

He smiled back at me, but it seemed painful. 'Marginally better than you.'

I sighed and something clicked in my head. 'You killed those men in the motel room. Just shot them down, like they were nothing.'

'It had to be done,' he said, and there wasn't a trace of emotion in his voice. He admitted killing someone as if he had picked up milk on the way home. 'Tom trained me from when I was a kid. I had to be ready, in case something like this happened, I guess.'

I thought about the life Jackson had lived. Taught from an early age to look over his shoulder constantly. Told that he had to be ready at a moment's notice to kill someone.

I wondered what that kind of upbringing could do to a person.

And when I compared it to my own, I suddenly felt guilty.

'I should say thank you. You saved my life.'

He said nothing, but his shoulders tensed and I felt the sheer size of him even with the distance between us.

'What happened? What was it like?' I said and he understood what I meant.

He sat down with a sigh and looked at me with a blank expression.

'I can't really remember things from back then. Nothing but half-formed blurs before the age of eight or nine. I remember flashes, if that makes sense?'

It did, but I didn't say so. I wondered how much of our memory from being young was real.

'Mom was quiet when I was growing up. Tom taught me things. He took me hunting. Showed me how to shoot straight and not be seen. She didn't tell me anything until I was much older. She would read all the time. Shutting herself off from the world, I guess.'

He was like steel, but I could see the humanity within him.

'I watched him drown, you know,' I said, wanting him to hear it. 'If you're trying to work out where the anger comes from. Even now, I can still remember how cold the water was. Freezing. I don't know how I managed to get out.'

I paused, took another sip of water, easing the pain in the back of my throat. The more I talked, the harder it became to ignore.

'He was in the back seat. He couldn't get his seat belt off,' I said, my voice quieter. I didn't care if Jackson wanted to hear it. I wanted him to know. 'I always helped him, but I panicked. I got my own off first and was out the car before I remembered he couldn't do his own. I could see his face. How scared he was. The river . . . it was too strong for me. I couldn't go back.'

'Mom only got out because she was dragged out of the river unconscious. She told me that she was trying to get to you both when Anthony Sullivan got her first. *He* let your brother drown. Not anyone else.'

'It was still my fault,' I said, shrugging my shoulders, as if it was settled. 'I was the big brother. He was relying on me and I failed him. I was a stupid kid, who killed his younger brother.'

'You didn't. Anthony Sullivan is to blame.'

'And then, I lost everything,' I said, feeling the anger brewing up inside me again. 'I grew up on the other side of the Atlantic, while you got her. Tom let me believe she was dead. How could anyone do that? What could possibly be a good enough reason for it?'

'The reason was us,' he replied, unfurling his arms and scanning the road around us. His biceps strained against the T-shirt he was wearing. 'I'm the reason she had to run in the first place. She was pregnant and knew she couldn't let him be a father. And if you knew she was alive, they would have killed you to get to her. That's what Tom told me.'

I felt the anger swell inside me again. Jackson sensed it too.

Then, I realised I was missing something.

'My phone . . .'

Jackson raised an eyebrow. 'We can get a new one.'

'No,' I said, my eyes darting back to the car. 'It has Nell's address in it. If Anthony can get into it, then he'll . . .'

I stopped and remembered Quinn.

'She told me where she lived. She game the address.'

'We have to go,' he said, pulling me up and jogging back to the car. Once inside, he reached into his jacket and pulled out something black. 'Take this.'

He handed it over and I felt the weight of the gun in my hand.

'Just point and shoot, right?' I said, shaking my head. 'As easy as that.'

'Only use it if you have to.'

My mum was looking between the two of us. 'What's going on?'

Jackson was already shifting into drive, screeching away from the side of the road. 'He knows where your mom is.'

I heard a low moan escape from my mum.

'He'll find her.'

Ten minutes felt like a week, as we finally wound our way through familiar streets. Sunset Road came up, empty and devoid of life.

Jackson slowed down as he turned into the road, managing a few yards before the first gunshot rang out.

CHAPTER 48

I didn't hear the windscreen shatter. I only felt the glass hit me in the face and my ears ringing with sound.

The door opened to my left and I saw Jackson in front of it, crouched down, lifting his own gun and firing into the distance.

I looked back over my shoulder and took hold of my mum's hand, pulled her out of the car. I realised I'd dropped the gun Jackson had given me as we'd left the car, but it was too late to go back for it. I held onto my mother, pushing forwards as fast as I could in my bent-over stance. I heard another gunshot – this time closer – and risked a look over my shoulder.

'We have to get to her,' Mum said, her eyes finding mine. 'He'll kill her.'

Jackson had his back to me, before stepping to the side of the door and firing again.

On the driveway of the little house on Sunset Road, where an old woman lived, I saw Anthony Sullivan walking slowly towards us. I saw him smile and it was as if Satan himself had taken human form and come up to play.

I shouted Jackson's name, just as he stepped out again.

Time seemed to slow. I saw Anthony Sullivan crouch, as Jackson fired into the space he vacated. I was sure I could see the bullet leave the gun and cleave the air above him.

Then, Anthony's gun levelled in slow motion. I saw him shoot, before I heard the echo of its retort.

I heard the gun pop, glass shatter, and then Jackson hit the floor. Mum screamed beside me, a horrible, nasty sound against the serene backdrop of the leafy street. I pulled her back as she tried to rush towards him, but she was stronger.

I couldn't see Jackson, but he had hit the ground next to the car hard. I wasn't sure I wanted to see. I glanced over. I couldn't see blood, but I didn't think it would be long.

'Hands on your head, kid,' Anthony Sullivan said, his deep voice booming across the distance between us. 'On your knees. Or you'll get one like him.'

I couldn't move even if I wanted to.

I could see my mum reaching where Jackson had fallen. Still screaming and shouting, but I could barely process it. Nothing seemed to be permeating my mind.

I was staring at Anthony Sullivan. The way he had shot Jackson as if he were nothing to him. The way he looked at me, as if I was a minor annoyance.

The way he looked at my mother.

I saw the man raise his gun and something inside me snapped.

I ran forwards, covering the distance in a split second and placing myself between my mum and the gun he was pointing towards her.

'Please, don't,' I said, my voice shaking and barely even audible. 'Please. What do you want? Anything. What do you need?'

My mother was breathing hard behind me, an angry bull getting ready for a fight. I reached out with a hand and it landed on her arm. I kept my eyes on the man.

'You can't give me what I need,' he said, still holding the gun towards me. 'Move out of the way.'

'No. I can't do that.'

He fixed me with a glassy stare and I thought I saw his finger twitch. I braced myself, waiting to be hit, but nothing happened. He continued to stare me down.

'Move.'

'No.'

'He's dying,' I heard my mum scream out, desperately, to no one and everyone at the same time. It seemed to snap something in the older man's stare. 'Someone call 911.'

Anthony turned and shouted towards the black car in the middle of the street. 'Zoran, make sure you get her.'

That was all I needed.

I ran towards him, moving quicker than I thought possible. I threw myself at him in the last moment, as he turned the gun towards me. I expected to hear a shot, a ringing in my ears, but instead I collided with him and fell to the ground. He was underneath me, my weight taking us both over. I heard something skitter to the ground.

He was fighting as soon as we landed. He had his hands on my arms, then I felt a smack in my jaw. I cried out, felt a punch to my solar plexus and the breath completely disappeared.

The weight of him was on me now, as he turned over and I was on my back. I raised my hands slowly, as he pummelled fists into my face. I deflected some of the blows, but it was a useless exercise. He was stronger, much stronger, than he looked. I felt his blows raining down on me and struggled underneath him.

There was a shout from my mother, but my eyes were locked on his, trying to dodge his fists, as they kept coming. I felt spittle fly from his mouth, dropping onto my face, and it was as if I was being mauled by a large dog.

I dropped my hands for a second, caught one in the temple, but threw my own. It didn't have the same weight as his, but the blow still landed forcefully in his side and I felt his weight shift on me. I managed to turn on my side, feeling his hands on my head, trying to smash it into the ground. I squirmed away, and was suddenly free of him.

As he came back at me, I aimed a kick towards him, connecting with his shoulder and pushing him back down. I raised myself to my knees, but he kept coming. I reached back and grabbed a bunch of stones. Grasped hold of them and as he came closer, I smashed them into the side of his head. Saw blood spurt from my hand, as the stones cut into my flesh with the force.

He was knocked back, landing awkwardly on the gravel with a loud thunk. I managed to get to my feet and didn't stop. I stepped forwards and raised my foot, smashing it down onto his ankle.

He roared in pain, as the bones in the lower half of his leg groaned in response.

I made as if to stamp again, but he shifted and came towards me. He tackled me to the ground and I toppled over, landing on my side with all my weight. I shouted out and felt him fall on me again.

I thought about what giving up would be like. Just lying back and letting this thing end. For it to all be over.

Something inside me wouldn't let it.

I could feel him crawling off me, moving away. I felt his weight lift from me and I was free again. I gasped in air and got back to my feet.

He was moving away, trying to raise himself to his knees, but failing. He crawled instead, pulling his body along with his hands.

I stepped forwards and stamped on his smashed ankle again. I heard him scream and grasp his leg.

Then, I heard my mother's shout.

'The gun, Sam, get the gun.'

I scanned around the ground and saw the black weapon where it had skittered across the gravel. That's what Anthony Sullivan had been going for, I realised, before I rushed towards it and picked it up. Turned around and held it in my hands.

I didn't know how to use it, other than what I'd seen others do. I held it in front of me; my finger slipped in and found the trigger.

I pointed it at Anthony Sullivan and hesitated.

It wasn't like back in Tom's house. In the darkness, I hadn't seen who I was shooting at.

I had only fired into the blackness of space.

Anthony stared back at me, watery eyes finding mine as his cries of pain stopped. He turned his head to the side and spat blood onto the ground.

Turned back to me and chuckled. 'Go on, do it,' he said.

I could see my hands shaking. My arms ached. I felt as if a thousand needles were sticking into my body. 'Just . . . just stay down.'

'Shoot him,' Mum screamed, cradling my half-brother's head in her lap.

I turned back to Anthony Sullivan and tried to keep my hand steady.

I wanted to do it. I wanted to squeeze that trigger and end his life. I was in control of his fate. Of my own fate, for the first time in the past week.

He smiled at me, then looked past where I was standing and over my shoulder.

'Quinn,' he said, his voice a growl now. 'I know you told me I shouldn't kill him. But it turns out you might have to.'

I looked quickly to my right and saw Quinn pointing a gun at me.

'Go on, kill me,' Anthony said, that sick grin on his face again. 'But you'll be dead a second later.'

I hesitated. It was stalemate and he knew it.

I couldn't do it.

I let the gun fall from my hand.

Quinn stepped forwards, levelling the gun at my chest. 'I'm sorry, Sam,' she said. Again. As if it would fix everything. 'It's going to be okay.'

I looked back towards my mother and she was being dragged

to her feet by a tall, bald man. I couldn't see Jackson from where I was standing.

I heard her shout, 'Sam, I'm sorry.'

'I've got what I need,' Anthony said, stepping back and away from me. He turned and looked over at the car he'd arrived in. There was a giant by the door, pointing his gun towards us. Tall, bald head glistening in the morning light. He had hold of my mum with his free hand, as she struggled against him.

'Zoran,' he shouted. 'Put her in the trunk.'

I was helpless, watching as my mother was led around the car. Quinn backed away slowly, following Anthony as he made his way back to the car too.

'Kill him,' Anthony shouted back to Quinn. 'You'll get nothing unless you do it now.'

We locked eyes. I held my hands up, as I shifted towards where I had seen Jackson fall to the ground.

She stared back at me. Lifted the gun towards me.

And then fired.

CHAPTER 49

I went down instinctively. Even as I knew she had meant to miss me. I heard the car screech away, the engine sound disappearing in a matter of seconds.

My ribs began throbbing in agony again, as the impact from throwing myself to the ground won its battle with the adrenaline coursing through my veins. I held onto my side, as if I could somehow hold the pain back.

It didn't work.

I felt anger then.

It was good.

I forgot about the pain, the agony, the hurt.

I forgot about it all.

I lifted myself up and gritted my teeth against the aches and pain my body was feeling. I thought about pointing that gun at Anthony. How close I had come to squeezing that trigger and ending his life.

I had wanted to do it.

Now, it felt like my chance had gone.

Next time, I wouldn't hesitate. I was going to kill him.

I thought about how he had taken my family from me. Of how he had made my mum run for so long and finally had her in his grasp.

He hadn't killed her on that street, which meant there was still a chance to save her. He wanted something from her and I had an idea of what that might be.

I wasn't going to settle for anything less than that man at my feet, no longer breathing.

I could feel the energy spilling out of me in every action I took. I kept going, until I could barely feel my arms. The numbness running through every single one of my muscles.

I was struggling to catch my breath. I could still feel the anger, but it had been joined by guilt and grief. I half walked, half crawled to where Jackson was lying, just as he shifted onto his side.

'Jackson?'

He turned to me, a grimace on his face. The road beneath him was stained red.

'Where is she?'

I shook my head. 'I couldn't stop him.'

A growl emanated from him, as he got himself more upright. He shifted back until he was sitting against the car behind him. 'We have to go after him.'

'You need to go to the hospital.'

He spat out something that looked like blood. 'I'll be okay. Just help me get to my feet.'

I peeled back his shirt and saw an angry entry wound, just above his heart. I was no doctor, but it looked like he had been a couple of inches away from being killed instantly.

'She told me to stay down,' Jackson said, as I balled up his jacket and began pressing it against the wound. 'Said it was better if he thought I was dead.'

'Brace yourself,' I replied, putting even more pressure against his chest. Another growl, but he didn't scream out in pain. 'We need to do something about this.'

In the distance, I heard sirens getting closer. Curtains twitching from the surrounding houses.

'We have to get out of here first,' Jackson said, lifting himself up slowly. 'Can you drive?'

I nodded. 'We're not going to get very far in this car though. The windscreen will give us away.'

I helped him up and he grimaced again.

I knew neither of us was going to give up any time soon.

We had a common goal now.

Find our mother. He pointed towards the driveway over to our left and I saw the car outside Nell Rogers's house.

'Is she . . . ?'

'Only one way to find out.'

There was something worse than dying.

Laurie knew that better than most people.

Laurie had held her son's head in her hands, watching his chest hitch and rise.

He had looked peaceful almost. Serene. The blood from his chest slowly drained from his wound, turning the left side of his body reddish brown.

She was losing another son. It was happening again.

There was nothing she could do to stop it. She had never felt more powerless in her life. Yet, she had known it had all been leading to this point. Every moment, every action, every inaction. It had led to her lying on the ground, holding her son as he slowly bled to death in her arms.

'Stay down, let me do this.'

Those could be the last words she ever said to Jackson.

Sam. Her last words to him hurt more. They weren't enough. She still couldn't believe he was alive.

Anthony had stolen so much from her, she didn't care that the anger was becoming everything. That she was allowing it to take over and guide her.

One of them was going to have to die to end this nightmare. And she was going to make sure it wasn't her.

The car moved and she bumped up against the inside of the

trunk. She had been lifted inside and dropped as if she were nothing. The trunk lid closing and plunging her into darkness. She was panting for breath, the heat increasing by every second.

Her instincts, honed over years in the hot Arizona sun, began to kick in.

She knew where he was taking her.

She began to visualise the house in Greenwich. The layout, where everything was. Anthony didn't like change – she knew that above everything about him – so she didn't think much would be different now. Even all these years later.

The journey was long and stifling. By the time the car came to a stop, her anger had been overcome by guilt, grief, exhaustion.

Of wanting this to all be over.

There was a jolt, as the car pulled up and stopped entirely. At first, Laurie thought it was another red light, but then she heard a car door open and shut.

She breathed in deeply. There was still anxiety running through her body, that fear of what was to come, but she had to think as clearly as possible.

She couldn't wait until she was taken into the house. She was going to fight from the first moment she could.

There was the sound of boots crunching on gravel, coming around the side of the car, before they stopped at the back.

She was ready.

This was going to work. It had to. There was nothing else she could do.

It wasn't for her any more. Not just for her life. It was for her sons too.

The trunk was opened and Laurie blinked at the light that suddenly flooded in. Once, twice.

Then she sprang up and out.

CHAPTER 50

I was driving way over whatever speed limit existed on those roads. I didn't know. Couldn't focus enough to check.

I was only thinking about one thing.

Getting to Greenwich, Connecticut.

We were at least half an hour behind Anthony Sullivan's car, which I was trying to make up by pushing the piece of crap we were driving beyond its probable limits.

We had taken my grandmother's car – it started up on the third try, which was something at least. At first, I didn't think it was going to work at all. Jackson had spent the first twenty minutes of the journey patching himself up with medical supplies he had taken from her house.

'You ever met her before?'

Jackson snorted. 'Not in person. I've spoken to her on the phone.'

'She's not got much left going on in her head,' I replied, pulling into the middle lane and undertaking a slower car in front. Its headlights disappeared quickly behind me. 'She probably won't remember us being there.'

'That might be a good thing.'

We had left as the police were talking to a neighbour. Two cop cars had arrived on scene, but I knew more would be coming. We probably missed the cavalry arriving by seconds. Instead, we had turned out the driveway and driven out the other way, without a single stop.

We had been lucky.

Now, we were headed west, along the south coast of Connecticut. The car was juddering underneath us, as I tested it to its capacity. According to Jackson's phone, it should have been more than a two-hour journey.

My plan was to break that comfortably.

The highway was quiet, thankfully, but it still required concentration, given I was unused to driving on the wrong side of the road.

My heart started beating hard the closer we got.

'I don't know anything about the place,' Jackson said, his voice gravelly and pained. I couldn't begin to imagine the agony he was feeling, but he seemed as focused as I was. 'A mansion, that's how Tom described it.'

The mention of Tom's name made me grit my teeth. I didn't say anything. Then, I thought about Jackson. About the position he had been placed in. Not only was the man who had raised him turning out to be someone I could barely think about, but his actual father was worse.

'He's your—'

'I know,' Jackson said, shifting in his seat. 'You don't have to remind me.'

'I'm just saying, doesn't that complicate matters for you?'

Jackson sighed and turned to me. 'You think I might have divided loyalties?'

'It's not that.'

'I get it, I do. But I know what kind of man he is. And I know where he deserves to be. He might be my father, but he isn't my dad. He's no one. He has hurt our mom for the last time. She doesn't deserve this.'

I nodded, believing him.

He was trying to focus.

'I imagine he'll have a fair few people guarding the place,'

Jackson continued, pulling out his gun and checking how many rounds were left. He reached down and pulled two more from various places on his body. 'You still have the gun I gave you?'

I shook my head.

'Don't worry. Take this one. Don't just point and shoot. We don't have the ammo for that.'

'I'm not sure I can do this,' I said, my voice quiet. Shaky. 'I'm not cut out for this . . .'

'We have to,' Jackson cut in, quieting me in an instant. 'There's no other way out of this. We can't just leave her to die.'

'I don't even know why he's doing this.'

'You do.'

I opened my mouth to disagree, but I thought about the story my mum had told me. How she had managed to escape. What she had to do to survive.

'He wants to know where his sister's body is.'

'That'd be my guess.'

I gripped the steering wheel tighter, as the roads became narrower and the surroundings leafier. The weather turned and the sky turned black. It felt as if the night had come hours earlier than it was supposed to. We may as well have been driving into the middle of nowhere and I imagined that was exactly what we were doing.

'She won't tell him,' Jackson said. 'It's what will keep her alive until we get there.'

He pointed off to the side and I turned into a smaller, somewhat country lane. It led onto a two-lane road, black and uninviting.

'It's only a little further. Pull in up there.'

I followed his directions and pulled the car over. Turned the engine off and let the headlights disappear. It was completely dark outside now and I could barely see my hand in front of my face.

'Look,' Jackson said, turning to me. 'I'm going out there and trying. She would do the same for me, the same for you. I know that. I was the one who told her you were alive and if you would have heard how she reacted to that, you wouldn't question her feelings in any way. Are you with me?'

I breathed in deeply, closed my eyes and felt a million thoughts crash around my head.

'Of course I am,' I said finally, as if it were an easy decision to make. Instead, I knew I was giving up. On life, on a future.

Because I knew we had no chance.

'Let's do this.'

The trunk opened and Laurie sprang up and out.

She was screaming, trying to hit anything in her path. She knocked one person to the ground in a blur, before spinning to one side and starting to run.

She didn't see him coming.

Zoran appeared as if from the shadows, catching her by the throat and throwing her across the drive. Stones dug into her skin. She felt the ground with her hands, trying to pull herself up.

As she looked up she realised she was already surrounded.

That plan was always going to fail, she thought, then started laughing. Coughing, endless laughter. She could hear the maniacal nature of it, echoing around the desolate courtyard.

She didn't think she would ever stop. As tears sprang from her eyes and wet her cheeks, as her stomach cramped and pins and needles stung her legs.

She felt a hand on her shoulder, that instantly quieted her. Cold and hard.

'Come on, get up,' Anthony said, pulling her to her feet. 'Stop acting like a fool.'

He turned her around to face him. She looked back defiantly, staring into his cool blue eyes that had once held so much sway over her.

'Move. I won't ask twice.'

She stared back at him for a second, then felt something press into her ribs. He spun her around again and pushed her forwards. Laurie almost stumbled back down to the ground, but Anthony's hand was under her armpit in a second and pulling her along.

The sky was black above them. Dirty clouds that would soon open. A calm breeze swirled around them, as Anthony led her from the car and across the courtyard.

In front of her was a building that she had tried so hard to forget. It loomed over her, its white walls grey and uninviting in the darkness.

She was silent. Concentrating on what had changed. What was still the same. Taking in every inch of her surroundings.

He took her inside, pulling her all the way as she resisted as much as possible. Dragged her up the staircase she had once felt was her own. Past the art that she had picked out to hang on the walls. The vase she had chosen to sit on a table.

It was all still there.

Down the corridor that led to his office. Zoran was ahead of them and he opened the door dutifully.

Anthony threw her to the floor once they were inside and Laurie felt the burn on her knees as she landed.

He strode across the office, pouring himself a drink as Laurie pulled herself up and leaned back against the wall closest to the door. It closed with a quiet click, leaving only the two of them in the room.

Anthony drained the first drink, then poured himself another.

'I never stopped looking for you,' Anthony said, walking around the desk and resting against it. 'Even when they told me you were most probably dead by now, I knew I'd get you back.'

'You never had me,' Laurie spat at him. She laid her palms against the floor and raised herself up the wall.

'You're alive for one reason. I could have killed you back on that street. Or dumped your body in the sea on the way here. I didn't do that and you know why.'

Laurie began to shake her head, before he held up a hand to stop her.

'You're going to tell me what you did with Maria.'

Laurie stared back across the room at him. 'I'm not telling you anything.'

The glass smashed against the wall, inches from her head, in a split second. She hadn't even seen him throw it.

She was on her feet now, her hands placed against the wall.

She didn't move. Even as he crossed the room and came towards her.

He paused as he reached her, then wrapped a hand around her throat.

'I'll kill you in the next ten seconds unless you start talking.'

Laurie could feel the air leaving her body, as his hand constricted around her throat. She pulled away from him, but he grabbed at her shirt, tearing away the fabric. She continued to fight, until he used all his weight to pin her against the wall.

'It's over,' Anthony said, his voice echoing around them. 'Give in to me.'

She screamed, trying to fight back, but he was too powerful. Too strong.

There was a knock at the door and for a moment Anthony squeezed harder. Then, he let go of her and she dropped to her knees, coughing breath into her lungs.

'What is it?' Anthony shouted, pulling the door open. Zoran stood outside, staring back at him.

'Two men are outside. Security cameras picked them up.'

Anthony glanced back at Laurie, who felt her stomach fall several stories. He turned back to Zoran.

'Make sure they're dead this time.'

CHAPTER 51

As we reached the gate to the house, the heavens opened above us, making it even more difficult to see.

The rain beat down on us. I paused with the gun in my hand. My whole body was threatening to shut down in protest at what I had put it through in the past twenty-four hours.

It was as if I were in the throes of a fever dream. I screwed my eyes tightly shut, trying to block out the sounds and sights that existed around me, and calmed instantly.

'You ready?'

I opened my eyes and murmured an agreement towards Jackson that was lost in the rain and wind that swirled around us.

'Let's do this.'

I breathed in and out once, then fell into step behind Jackson.

I was going to die there. In that driving rain in a foreign land, with nothing but a gun I didn't know how to use and a feeling of despair in the pit of my stomach.

'We can do this,' he said, something approaching belief in his voice. 'We're going to save her.'

I nodded, flicking spots of rain towards him. He stared back at me for a second and then turned towards to the gate.

I kept expecting to look up and see the red and blue lights of police cars. The shouts of men and women in uniform, telling us to get down. To stop what we were doing. Perhaps even a civilian – passing by, wondering what two men with guns drawn in front of them were doing at this hour.

The gate looked sturdy enough, but Jackson moved past it quickly. He scanned the wall in front of us, which looked impenetrable at first glance.

At the second, it looked worse.

'How do we get in?'

Jackson began to answer, when metallic whirring came from the gate and we both turned to see it open.

'Get down!' Jackson screamed at me, pushing me to the ground as he spoke. I dived down, just as the first shot flew past my head. I turned quickly, fumbling with the gun in my hand, trying to find the trigger.

Jackson was already firing back. Two shots and then there was a thump, as a body hit the ground. Two more shots rang out and two more bodies fell to the ground. I looked to where he was crouched, staring intently into the rain, towards the gate.

'Let's move.'

I followed him in a half crouch, as we made our way slowly towards the open gate. He came to a stop and I almost crashed into the back of him.

There were three men on the ground. I couldn't see them clearly enough, but they weren't moving. I got close enough to one to see a perfect hole in the middle of his forehead.

'We need to keep moving,' I said, looking ahead for any other movement. 'The longer we stay in one place, the bigger the target we are.'

'Stay close by,' Jackson said, seemingly sensing my thoughts. 'Shoot anything that moves and doesn't look like our mom. Trust me – they'll think twice about breaking cover if they know we're firing back.'

I nodded a response. Jackson ducked around the gate and we kept moving forwards – Jackson ahead of me.

I could see something in the distance, but I realised quickly that there was still some way to go before we reached the house.

The driveway was stone for a few feet, before turning back to earth. It was becoming muddier as the rain fell, but at least the weather was giving us some cover. Jackson motioned to his side and we moved off the driveway.

Trees lined the track leading up to the house and we went from one to another, moving forwards slowly.

'Wait.'

Jackson had his hand raised. He moved his head round the tree we were behind and suddenly bark was flying into my face. I was on the ground in an instant – Jackson landing on top of me. He was up in a millisecond, firing back in the direction the shot had come from.

For a few seconds, all I could hear was the echo of gunshots and my own heartbeat. I looked down at my own hand and saw the gun still in my hand, hanging limply to the side.

I grit my teeth and found the trigger.

I wasn't going to be caught out again.

I lay flat on the ground and saw something glint in the distance and cleared my head of thought.

As I looked around the tree, I saw someone emerge from the darkness. The clouds broke a little and I could see how close we were to the house.

Only it wasn't just a house. It was a great monolithic building, jutting from the earth and blocking out the sky.

It didn't look like a home. It looked like a prison.

Jackson was still firing into the shadows, but I knew in an instant that he couldn't see the man firing back at us.

'Jackson!'

As Jackson stepped out of cover, he hesitated as he heard me shout.

I was still raising the gun in my hand and trying to find a target.

Jackson went down just as I squeezed. My ears rang, my

shoulder jerked back and I had to steady myself. I couldn't see where Jackson had fallen.

I saw the man coming closer. He looked like a giant in the darkness. The man Anthony Sullivan had called Zoran, back in Rhode Island.

I had a second to make a decision. I levelled the gun and hoped my aim was true. Then, I shot.

'It won't bring her back,' Laurie said, her words almost lost in the fog of anger that was radiating from Anthony. 'Killing me, my sons, my brother, David . . . none of it will help.'

'It helps me,' Anthony growled through gritted teeth.

'Jackson is your son,' she said, seeing the resemblance between them that she always tried to ignore. 'You know that, right? And you shot him without a second thought.'

'I don't know what you're talking about.'

He had killed his own son. It was written clear across his face. Only, Laurie could see it wasn't pain he was feeling. It was pure, unbridled anger.

Directed at her. Outside the rain crashed against the glass panes of the door that led out onto the balcony. The sound of gunshots dulled by the windows. She tried not to think about what was happening out there.

'You lost me in 1986,' Laurie said, having to raise her voice over the sounds that sneaked inside. 'Only, it was before that I knew I didn't love you. That I didn't want to be with you. It took meeting David for me to know what love really was. He treated me differently. Equally. I was happy for the first time in years. The only problem was you wouldn't let me go.'

Anthony stared back at her, close-lipped, but even in the low light of the office she knew she was hitting a nerve.

'My dad died,' Laurie continued, inching across the wall, slowly. Buying as much time as possible. Anthony turned his back to her and poured himself another drink. He picked up a lighter and sparked it into life and Laurie moved another few inches. 'I had to come back. It had been almost ten years. I thought you would have moved on by then. Tom told me it was safe, only it wasn't.'

'We had something that should have been enough for you. We had history. We had everything.'

Anthony stared coldly back at Laurie and she could feel the hate emanating from him.

'I was yours, right?' Laurie said, her weight on her right foot. She stared past him. If he had noticed that she was now a good few feet closer to him, he made no sign. 'Your property? You weren't about to let me leave you. You had ten years to get over me. Why not move on and let me live my life?'

'You were *mine*.'

'Thirty-five years. That's how long you've made me run for.'

'You should never have left me.'

Laurie shook her head and took another step. 'You killed them all.'

'You killed Maria.'

Laurie tried to ignore the feeling of guilt that welled inside of her. Instead, she concentrated on the fear that was dissipating with each passing moment in his presence.

He became more human, less monster.

'When she was young, I bought this for her,' Anthony said, reaching into his shirt and snapping something away from his neck. 'One each. She wasn't just a sister to me, Laurie. She was the one person I had left in the world. And you took her away from me.'

'If this goes on,' Laurie said quickly, feeling the moment slip away from her; feeling her presence in the world go with it, 'it'll never end. Not until we're all in the grave.'

'You'll be there soon anyway,' Anthony replied, trying to

inject his tone with the same growl it had before. Only, she could hear the barely constrained emotion there. His pain, his loss.

'Why did you have to do it?' Anthony said, pounding a fist against the desk. His voice echoed around the room. 'She was innocent.'

'So was I!' Laurie screamed back. She swallowed and tried to grasp control back. Focus. When she continued, her voice was lower, steadied. 'It didn't stop you. I don't want you. I don't belong to you. We can still both walk away from this.'

For a moment, Laurie thought that it might happen. That he would let her go. That he would walk away and never look back. She could feel her hands shaking, but Laurie knew what was coming.

'An eye for an eye,' Anthony said, his voice firm and final.

Laurie thrust her hand in her pocket and pulled out the necklace she'd been carrying for twenty-five years.

'Here,' she said, throwing it to the floor, over to the other side of the room. She waited for Anthony to see the glint of metal and then scramble across towards where it landed.

He was on his hands and knees, picking it up carefully and lifting it towards the light.

Laurie was already moving. She reached the desk, just as Anthony was rising up. Knocked over the decanter of brandy, spilling it across the desk as she tried to open the drawer.

Anthony roared from ten yards away and she jumped back, pulling the drawer out alongside her. She swept a hand across the desk, spilling more alcohol, filling the air with sickly sweetness.

She smashed more bottles against the desk, liquid pouring everywhere. The silver lighter landed next to her hand and she flicked it on in an instant. The alcohol caught light quickly, but that wasn't enough. Anthony jumped back away from the burning, but Laurie was already moving – she tore away a large piece of her shirt where Anthony had torn it earlier and shoved it into the last bottle standing. Then, she flicked the lighter again.

It caught in an instant and she threw the burning bottle towards him. There was an explosion that she only heard, as she dived to the floor.

As the flames grew higher around her, she could see his form coming through them. A black shadow that would soon be upon her.

The fire burned brightly, strong, smoke billowing in seconds. It was consuming the room as if it had been waiting to satisfy its hunger for years. The drawer was next to her and she put her hand inside it.

She found the gun she had known would be in there and lifted it just as Anthony came through the flames.

CHAPTER 52

S he didn't hear the gunshot.

She only felt the recoil and then the look on Anthony's face as he went down.

There was a black hole in the middle of his forehead.

Laurie looked at it, transfixed, staring at his face. His sunken features, his greying face.

For a second, she thought that he would rise up, one last hand around her throat, one last smack across the face. One last chance to hurt her and everyone she loved.

She moved slowly towards him, gripping hold of his shoulders and shaking his body. She wrapped her hands around his throat and squeezed.

It was too late. He was gone and it had been too quick. He deserved so much more.

There was nothing around her but black.

She collapsed to the floor, choking on the smoke that was now filling the air around her.

Everything had been leading to this point. When she would finally be free of him.

Yet, now it seemed that she was destined to die alongside him. In the house that had been her prison for so long. Next to the man who had taken everything away from her.

She wasn't going to let that happen.

She was going to fight until her last breath.

As the fire took hold, she saw Anthony Sullivan's lifeless eyes staring back at her.

I fired, just as Zoran levelled his gun in my direction. I watched him go to the ground on one knee, but it still seemed as if he were as tall as me. He lifted his arm in the air and the tree behind me lost half the bark on its trunk as I dived to the floor.

I wasn't hit.

I looked around, trying to see Jackson, but he had disappeared in the darkness. I heard a crash from the direction of the house and looked up just as the giant fired another shot that whistled past my head.

Flames were coming out of the windows, a series of explosions occurring throughout the house. The fire was taking hold quickly and I had only one thought in my mind.

My mum was in there and I wasn't going to let her go. Not now. Not ever.

I pointed the gun in front of me as I moved, seeing the man a few yards over to my right, scanning the area for where I'd gone.

I fired a shot his way. He ducked, but was already firing back. I threw myself to the ground, my stomach hitting the mud. The rain battered down, the wind picking up and throwing smoke our way.

I fired again into the rain and heard someone cry out. I risked a look and couldn't see him any more. I carefully rose to my feet, holding the gun out in front of me, my finger slipping off the trigger as the rain came down harder.

I didn't hear the shot ring out. I just felt it hit me. It was like an animal bite, sinking its teeth into my chest and sucking the air from my throat.

I went down to one knee, then two. Lifted a hand to my chest and pulled it away. I tried to see if it was blood, but I couldn't blink away the black. I felt a shadow cross over me and I looked up and saw him standing there.

The gun was still in my hand. I lifted it up shakily and then it was gone. Swept from my hand in a single movement.

I felt the metal against my forehead. Pushed back against it.

There was no way I was going to close my eyes this time. I was going to look into his.

They weren't going to win.

'Well played,' Zoran said, looking down at me, then smirked.

I stared back at him.

Waited for the cut to black. To nothingness

Instead, I saw his head explode before me. I went down instinctively, thinking I'd been hit again. Only, I was still breathing. I was still living.

I felt a hand on my shoulder and I moved back quickly. That sent a ricochet of agony through me.

'You've been hit.'

I blinked into the rain and saw Quinn come into focus.

'Here,' she said, trying to press something against my shoulder. 'Let me help you.'

I looked to where Zoran had fallen and then back to Quinn. 'Get away from me.'

She flinched at my voice, then tried to come back towards me. I scrambled on the ground and found the gun Zoran had been holding. I picked it up and pointed it towards her. 'I mean it,' I said, finding the trigger and wrapping a finger steadily around it. 'Leave now, or I'll kill you.'

'Sam . . .'

I lifted the gun in the air and shot. It echoed around us and I saw Quinn jump back in surprise. I brought it back down towards her and felt calm.

'I'm . . . I'm sorry,' she said, then she disappeared into the night. I watched her go, until she was nothing but a memory in the rain as it fell.

'Jackson!' I shouted, turning in a circle, trying to find him. 'The house . . . we have to get to her.'

There was no answer. I got to my feet gingerly, felt the fabric that Quinn had tried to hold to my shoulder fall to the ground. I reached down slowly and picked it up. Held it against me, as if it was going to help.

My breaths were coming in shorter rasps. I could almost feel the blood seeping out of me. My eyes blurred a little, but I wasn't going to stop.

I made my way towards the house. The front door was open and within a minute I was stepping out of the rain and into the dry.

Only, there was nothing but smoke in my line of vision.

I shouted out. 'Mum! Mum, where are you?'

There was no answer. I kept moving, trying to keep my legs underneath me. 'Mum, tell me where you are?'

My vision swam, black spots appearing at the periphery of my sight.

Still, I kept moving forwards. A staircase was in front of me and I knew the fire was coming from up there – that's where I'd seen the flames. At the far left of the house.

I don't know how I reached the top, but by the time I left the last step behind me, it was as if all the energy had left my body. I collapsed to the floor, started crawling along instead. I took the fabric away from my shoulder and held it over my mouth to stop inhaling the smoke.

I could see a closed door ahead of me and concentrated on that. The smoke was black, the flames getting closer. I could feel the heat swirling around me, my skin resisting each movement.

Nothing was going to stop me.

I hit the floor. Screamed into the void, as my body tried to give in.

I roared and lifted myself up. Fell down again. My eyes were closing. The fire burned above me and I could only feel the heat and the pain.

There was a moment when I couldn't go on any more. When the past week had finally won over and I was lost.

Then someone was supporting me. An arm under my armpit. I opened my eyes and saw nothing but the black smoke and flames around us.

'I've got you.'

There were no more words.

Just a mother and her son, escaping from a burning house. From hell.

AFTER

For twenty-five years, Anthony had been tracking down a ghost. It had taken Parker Rogers being arrested for him to finally get a lead for the first time. Parker led to my father, which led to Tom travelling across the country. It had opened the floodgates.

He had tried to kill his only son just so he could get to her. I didn't want to think about what could drive a man to do that.

I called Rachel as soon as I was able to. She was the only one I told the entire story to. I needed her to know upfront.

She was on the next plane she could catch.

Sometimes, you just know.

Being able to be that honest with someone – for the first time in my life – was like a release. I didn't care that it had taken me a while to find someone to share my life with, I only cared that I had found her.

I met her in Boston. Took her down to Mystic and showed her the place where I had lost Michael. We laid flowers at the side of the road and she held me until the fading evening light meant I couldn't see the river any more.

After that, back at the motel on the other side of the river, I felt something leave me. Whether it was guilt, or overwhelming grief, I wasn't sure. Living through what had happened in the past week had changed me, but that didn't mean I had to carry it like a weight.

I chose to focus on the good.

To focus on what had been given back to me.

I found them after the funeral. I knew they wouldn't miss Tom's last journey.

I stopped at the line of gravestones, flowers fluttering in the breeze.

Green Grove Cemetery.

Rogers
John – 1930–1995
Born and Died a Middletown Son.
Missed by wife Eleanor and children Parker and Laurie

I knew there was someone buried underneath the dirt with my grandfather. Only, it wasn't my mother.

It was Anthony's sister, Maria.

Michael was buried next to them.

Headlines about Anthony Sullivan and his various business practices had dominated the press for a few days, before they went back to their favourite subject – an upcoming presidential election.

I found out about Quinn from the local news station. A small afterthought, the last piece that may have linked me to the crime scenes across the state.

Police were looking for her in connection with the motel room shooting in Moosup. A grainy still from a CCTV camera was all they could show of her at the scene. The guy working reception mentioned a man being with her, but couldn't give a description.

If they found Quinn, then it would be my word against hers.

I was free. Clear.

'Have you been to see your mum?' I said, as we fell into step, after the service. I had hung at the back, trying to remain unseen.

Mum nodded. 'She's not the same person I left behind. We spoke on the phone over the years, but it wasn't until I saw her in the flesh that I realised how far gone she was.'

'She needs help.'

'I know,' she replied and there was pain in her voice. 'I missed having her in my life and now it's too late.'

'If there's one thing we can take from this, is that it's never too late.'

My mum took hold of my arm and brought me close.

'Where are we going then?' I said, pulling away from her after a few moments. 'We need some time together.'

'Somewhere far from here,' my mother said, walking between her sons, her arms locked in ours. Thankfully, the burns had been superficial.

I'd almost lost her again. Instead, we were both saved.

They found Anthony's body in the wreckage of the house. The fire had taken hold, destroying the building quicker than I thought possible.

Jackson was still unconscious when we got outside. We managed to get him back to the car and away, just as the first fire crews arrived.

It's amazing what money can buy you in the States, I found out. A doctor willing to ask no questions was the first thing. Another old friend of Tom's, Mum had told us. Someone from their home state who would help out at a moment's notice.

Tom seemed to have a few people like that. Which made me wonder why he never used them in twenty-five years. Why he spirited himself and my mother away to Arizona and told her my dad and myself and Michael were all dead.

He knew that wasn't true.

I would ask her one day, I was sure of it. How she felt about what had been taken from her. About the man who had done that.

It could wait.

★ ★ ★

I didn't really remember the journey to the States as a child. I remembered the night of the crash and going home. I had no memory of holidays abroad or anything of the type before that.

I wondered if any of my family would remember better. If their memories would be the same as mine.

It was simmering for all that time. Pressure building up daily. The balloon expanding and expanding, until there was nothing else it could do but pop.

Now, I watched as strangers let go of the side of the boat and entered the water.

An older woman pulled herself up the ladder and back onto the boat. Smiling.

It's great in there. You should definitely do it.

I had my doubts about that, but I knew I had to. The water looked dark, uninviting.

'Come on,' Rachel said, an encouraging stroke on my shoulder. 'You're going to be fine. You can do this.'

I grimaced towards her. She had come with us to the Florida coast, deciding it was better to be in the sun than the dreary March weather back in the UK. She had been wary at first, wanting me to spend some time alone with my family. I had convinced her quickly that I wanted her to be with me.

It was just right.

Above me, the sun beat down and felt like a warm embrace. I lifted a hand to shield my eyes and watched for clouds that were never going to appear.

I lowered myself down, a pang of fear with each step on the ladder. Imagining sinking to the bottom of the sea, never to be found.

My swimming skills were nonexistent.

I let go of the ladder and entered the sea. I had to kick my legs to and fro, but found it surprising how buoyant the water made me. I kept calm and lay on my back, still moving my legs.

The impossibly blue sky overhead was beautiful. The warmth

of the sun counteracted the coolness of the sea water.

I was smiling.

Jackson entered the water, pointed at my chest, and then his own.

Matching scars. Healing a little more every day.

I thought of my dad. The broken man who had failed me, but more so himself.

I thought of my mother, a stranger I could finally get to know. To understand.

I thought of Michael.

It wasn't my fault.

And, I think that the feeling I had in that water is what I'd been searching my whole life for.

I accepted what happened. My role in it. Everything I couldn't change, but could now live with.

I let go and drifted away, looking up at the sky. I closed my eyes and felt at peace.

For the first time in forever, I didn't have to think about anything.

It was me and the water.

I was safe and, finally, so were my family.

Before he died. Before the funeral. Before the trip down to Florida.

Before she allowed herself to believe she had Sam back, Laurie went to see him one last time.

She had Jackson drop her off at the hospital in New London. He didn't ask questions, although she knew he had a lot of them. She hoped they would come in time and that she would have the answers that would help him.

'Do you want to see him?'

Jackson didn't turn his head. 'No.'

Laurie nodded, knowing that she wasn't going to change his mind. Got out of the car and headed inside. Waited for her opportunity and found Tom's room.

The board told her he was a John Doe. They would find out

his name the next day, when Laurie would call and let them know. Anonymously.

He would be buried with his service intact. A veteran of the first Iraq war deserved that, at least. They didn't have to know what he'd been doing for the past twenty-five years.

Laurie opened the door slowly and entered the hospital room.

It was late at night, quiet and almost still. He'd crawled from the house and had been found in the middle of the street, unconscious and bleeding, by a neighbour. They had called 911 and he had ended up in this hospital.

Laurie only knew because it was on the local news. A story buried beneath everything else.

Tom was lying there, looking bruised, beaten, but peaceful.

Laurie closed the door behind her and made her way across the room. She didn't sit down. She looked down at Tom's hand, heard the rhythmic beep of the machine that would keep him alive for a few more hours, perhaps.

She took hold of his hand and held it in hers.

'I know why you did it,' she whispered, watching his face. There was no reaction. It was as if he could wake up at any moment, but she knew that wouldn't happen.

'It wasn't your decision to make. It never was. Not yours, or Anthony's or David's. I didn't belong to any of you.'

She let go of his hand and backed away. She thought she saw a flicker of something in his face, but decided it was the light playing tricks on her.

'I'm going to live my life now. Finally.'

When she reached the door, she turned back one last time. Looked back at the man who had saved her life, but also stolen it.

'Goodbye.'

Then, she walked away.

To live her life.

Finally.

ACKNOWLEDGEMENTS

This book exists thanks to the work and support of many, many people. My deepest appreciation to the following . . .

The town of Mystic, Connecticut, for being so welcoming and answering all my ridiculous questions. Special thanks to the staff at Bank Square Books for pointing me in the right direction a few times. I loved visiting and can't wait to return. For Val and Jo, who gave me, and my family, more than they'll ever know. I love you both. The Quiz C's – Mark B, Craig, Cally, Susi, and Mark E – for getting me through the past year by the power of quizzes. Jo Dickinson, for continuing the journey. Thank you so much for all the brilliant notes, for pushing me to get better with every book, and believing in me. I'm so glad to have you in my corner. You're the best. For Carolyn Mays, Sorcha Rose, and the rest of the Hodder team, I'm so excited to be with you all. Thanks so much for making me feel at home instantly and I can't wait to get this thing started. For all the readers who continue to enjoy and support the books. I couldn't appreciate you more. You're the reason I get to do my dream job. The Royal Literary Fund for all their support. All my friends in publishing – I've missed seeing you in the flesh, rather than as heads on my computer screen. Here's to more real-life festivals in the future. To my fellow Fun Lovin' Crime Writers – can't wait for regular gigs again! The Veste, Woodland, Hale, Kirkham, Brisk, and Smith clan. Mi Familia.

And the best for last, as always, Emma, Abigail, and Megan. My everything.